A NOVEL

SO CLOSE

PAULETTE KINCAID

WinePressPublishing
Your Book, Defined. Since 1991.

ISBN 13: 978-1-4141-1675-4
ISBN 10: 1-4141-1675-6
Library of Congress Catalog Card Number: 2009914233

"You can live in and around the truth…but still be so very far away from it."

—Tim Ferguson

With deep appreciation to John and Rachel for their patience, love, and support while this book was birthed. Thanks to Terri, Dad, Ginny, and Phillip for their encouragement, invaluable support, and insight.

CHAPTER ONE

Sunday, ten fifty-eight a.m.

I BARELY REMEMBER now what life was like before it happened. And it's only been a few hours. What I do remember are the most inane things. Like waking up a little before eleven, my head pounding, wondering if the bottle of aspirin was still in my nightstand drawer. My very next thought was to wish for a Caramel Frappuccino while, in the back recesses of my mind, making a note to call the bank and protest the overdraft charge on my daughter's account.

But if I could go back in time I would gladly give up my coffee habit for life and never again complain about a mere headache. And I sure wouldn't waste a precious moment calling our bank about anything as mundane as a $30 charge that was probably Holly's mistake anyway. But the days of making simple choices have been taken away, and there's no going back.

It all happened on Mother's Day, of all days. Not that it would have mattered, but that was another reason it seemed to catch me off guard. I could still hear Mom giggling almost girlishly when she called to ask me to sit by her in church, and I had promised I would. She said she had everything she needed and it was the only gift she wanted, and I remembered smiling as I shook my head, knowing it meant I would have to sit in the second row. I wasn't especially surprised at her request though, for she was easily pleased and extremely sentimental. She could laugh loudly with no inhibitions or break out in tears a moment later, either one at the drop of a hat. It had been a bit embarrassing growing up. Then why, all of a sudden, did her tears seem precious? Perhaps because I inherently knew a good number of them were shed on my behalf. Regret started welling up again, just like an emotional tidal wave about to knock me off my feet.

Knowing all the plans we'd made, I really was disappointed a migraine had chosen this day to attack. But if I would have bothered to analyze it, I would have also admitted that Mother's Day wasn't one of my favorite Sundays. The problem was that living in the Bible Belt meant that every good boy and girl, no matter his or her age, was expected to attend church on Mother's Day. But I had heard every proverbial sermon that could be preached on the subject, and I always fell short. My own mother seemed pretty wonderful—especially now in retrospect—but as for myself? I felt inferior in that department. Never absolutely *sure* the sermon wasn't being preached to me directly, and since I spent enough time criticizing myself, it just hurt too much to have a sermon permanently nail the guilt to my heart. I just felt tired.

I had come up with a plan, though. It had worked once before, and I was hoping it would again. I would show up as church was letting out, apologize profusely to Mom, explain how my headache made me late and I didn't want to interrupt the service by walking down front. We would go to lunch and no one would be the wiser. And best of all, I wouldn't have to hear one word of the sermon.

If I close my eyes, I can almost place myself back in those early morning hours. Faintly hearing my husband, Mark, and daughter, Holly, getting ready for church. Some shuffling, some rustling. When Mark got out of bed, I whispered, "Bad headache, I'll meet you at church later," and turned over, placing the pillow over my eyes without waiting for a reply or seeing the disappointment on his face. So grateful when he slipped me an ice pack a moment later. I dozed back off, knowing it was mandatory if I wanted a slim chance of functioning later. But my slumbering was restless as I tried to block out their movement, clinching my eyes tighter, willing myself to stay asleep.

One of my deeper regrets now is not opening my eyes to tell them goodbye, to blow a kiss or give a wink. If I'd looked up, my twenty-one-year-old baby girl might even have whispered "Happy Mother's Day." Now all I remember was trying to ignore them so I could go back to sleep. But I've gotten ahead of myself. My lamenting didn't begin until much later.

After hitting the snooze button a couple times, I finally forced myself to jump out of bed when the clock said 10:58. I hit the shower running, knowing I would have to rush to get dressed in time. While the hot water washed away my last vestiges of sleepiness, I was thankful to realize the ice pack and extra couple hours of sleep had done their magic. I only barely felt a bit of tenderness around my temples. I was glad I'd already planned what I was going to wear, so with a little less attention to detail than I normally would have taken, I managed to run out the door convinced I was still timing it perfectly and would arrive as church was letting out.

Sprinting down the sidewalk toward the car, there was a particular moment when I realized something wasn't quite right. My favorite season was in full bloom, and it was odd that the first thing I noticed was a faint smell of smoke. After a split second I rationalized someone was throwing their mom a 'first of the season' barbecue. Knowing how much my parents enjoyed grilling, I almost regretted our lunch choice, except for the fact that we had made reservations at an elegant restaurant I knew they couldn't afford, and I was looking forward to pampering them both. But it wasn't the only thing I was excited about. We had splurged and bought tickets for them to go on a ten-day cruise of the Bahamas. Mom had talked about going on one for years, and Mark and I had worked overtime for months so we could surprise them. I couldn't wait to see the look on her face.

But after a couple of whiffs, I knew the smell wafting through the air wasn't an aroma of barbecue. With the car door half open, I looked around, trying to find the source. Sure enough, a couple of streets away, I saw a fierce spiral of smoke and was surprised I hadn't heard any fire trucks, figuring they must have driven by while I was drying my hair. If I wasn't trying to time my arrival to church, curiosity would have made me drive by, but after looking at my watch again, I decided it would have to wait until after lunch.

But turning back to get in my car, I saw another fire in my peripheral vision maybe a couple of miles farther to the west, and this one made the fire in my neighborhood seem minor. There were multiple, billowing plumes of black, tar-like smoke and a helicopter hovering. I tried to calculate the distance and figured it might be the sprawling shopping center that recently opened. For some reason I hadn't even focused on the sounds in the air until I saw the helicopter. Then I heard an echo and spun around in time to see two helicopters speeding away in the opposite direction toward another couple of scattered smoke clouds several miles north.

I frowned, muttering, "What is going on?" The fact that our church was in the general direction of one of the larger plumes gave me another reason to get there quickly. So without another thought, I jumped in the car, backing up, barely taking the time to glance in the rearview mirror.

My mind already with my family, I was probably a tad careless backing down our long, winding, obscured driveway. When I was barely a couple of feet from the street, I heard the strangest shrieking sound, so frighteningly close that I slammed on my brakes, the seatbelt yanking me back and burning my shoulder. Unfazed, I jerked around, squinting and bobbing my head to look between the headrests in an attempt to see what, or who, was making the noise.

My eyes finally found and focused on Daniel, our older neighbor who lives across the street and down two houses. A very sedate, well-to-do gentleman who works at a bank near my downtown office, Daniel was a quiet, sweet, hardworking man. He'd even given me a lift once a couple of years ago when my alternator went out while Mark was out of town.

But this was a different person running down the middle of our quiet street, his hands over his ears, a terrifying wail coming from deep inside. It almost sounded like he was howling a long, drawn-out "Noooo!" over and over and over. I rubbed my eyes as I watched the peculiar spectacle for a few seconds. He had to have lost his mind or something. I felt disturbed and sorry and embarrassed for him, but at the same time, didn't think I should go after him alone and had no idea what else to do.

CHAPTER ONE

The sight left me uneasy, and I wondered what had pushed him over the edge. That would be another thing for me to do after lunch. Check in with his wife, and see if she needed help. If my judgment of his mental capacity was correct, she was going to need a good neighbor, but I would have to drop it for the time being.

As I finished backing out of the driveway, a little more cautiously this time, I felt anxious with a somewhat unfamiliar impression of not quite being in control. There was a chance I might be late now, but at this point I just didn't want my tardiness to bring attention to me or mess up the special day we had planned. And I sure didn't want to see Mom's disappointment or hear a different kind of sermon about missing church or broken promises. Amazing how, even as an adult, I could be sent back thirty years with one parental look.

Although our neighborhood was usually a lazy, mostly "sleep-in neighborhood" on Sunday mornings, it seemed like there was an inordinate amount of traffic winding slowly through the streets. I attributed it to proverbial "Sunday drivers" and was irritated at myself for sleeping those few extra minutes. I heard sirens in the distance and, combined with the whirring helicopters, it was creating a unique concoction of sounds that didn't quite belong with a pretty spring morning.

Several long minutes later, I finally reached the intersection leading out of the neighborhood, and once the car in front of me moved, I saw the reason for the delay. Two cars had crashed headfirst into each other, almost totally blocking the entrance to our subdivision. Over the years so many people had run this particular stop sign, I'd always known it was inevitable that there would be an accident here one day.

I felt time slipping away as one by one cars carefully crept around the wreckage, having to drive over a part of the curb just to get by. When it was finally my turn, I joined the inquisitive drivers slowing more than necessary, trying to get a closer look, but the angle of the accident kept me from seeing much. My stomach was growling and my watch was ticking louder and louder, so I tucked my curiosity away, with my next thought being, "Get me out of this traffic and to the restaurant!"

I never did get to eat a bite of food.

CHAPTER TWO

Sunday, twelve thirty-three p.m.

IT SEEMS LIKE yesterday we moved into this neighborhood. Holly was barely a year old, but the main reason we chose the location was because it was near the church. It had proven to be a good decision over the years, quite often because I was always running late, not unlike today. I remembered our choice being influenced because Mark sang in the choir, played in church ball leagues, and there were always children's programs or activities, so we figured we might as well save time and gas. Some really good times and good friendships had formed over the years.

I was mere minutes away from them, so despite the odd start to my morning, I still had hopes we would enjoy a leisurely lunch while we celebrated. *About time*, I thought with a wry smile. My daughter was finally old enough to make a big deal about Mother's Day, and even spend some of her own money. Then I remembered my impatient outburst the evening before, and hoped she wasn't upset with me. That could make for an awkward lunch if she was holding a grudge.

After passing the fender bender, I fully planned to speed just a tiny bit to make up for lost time. But what was normally a lazy side street with the occasional car, was now a bumper-to-bumper mess. Directly in front of me was an over-sized dump truck so I couldn't even see what the new delay was. The out-of-control feeling I experienced earlier was returning with a vengeance, and then I looked in my rearview mirror and saw people getting out of their cars and leaving them in the middle of the street, walking past my car.

I'll admit that over the years I've occasionally talked back to other drivers, and today it seemed so appropriate. I incredulously whispered, "People! Have you *never* seen an accident before?" But my curiosity was piqued, my unnoticed irritation wasn't fazing a soul, and an ever expanding crowd was walking past. I wondered if there was any possible escape route, but saw I had blocked myself in by pulling up too close to the truck in front of me.

I sighed and got out my cell phone, texting Mark and Holly the sad truth. "Sorry. Headache got worse. Didn't make it to church in time. Trying to get there now but bad traffic. Be there ASAP."

After not moving another full minute, I nervously checked my gauges since my car had overheated recently. I always had that nagging fear of car trouble and hated being stranded, so I felt edgy. It didn't help that the very second I looked at the gauge the car hiccupped and the heat gauge began to rise. When a puff of smoke slipped out from under the hood, I shook my head in disbelief, looking off into the distance, and sighed. Finding it hard to hide my irritation, I murmured, "What else can happen?" I shut off the car, closing my eyes tightly, wishing someone were here to help. When a tear slipped out from under my eyelids I knew the frustrations of the day were getting to me.

The remnants of my Mother's Day spirit was slipping away, and I felt a tiny throb hit my temples again. I was afraid I was going to have to force myself to be civil during lunch. I determined to do my best and fake it, although my perceptive daughter and husband could usually tell when something was wrong. This was becoming one of those days when you wished you could get back in bed and start over. I looked in my rearview mirror and by now maybe thirty cars were lined up behind me, with a steady stream of people walking past. I figured I might as well join the thrill seekers, since I couldn't keep my car running, and see what kind of trouble had convinced everyone to create this impromptu parking lot.

One bizarre thing about the parade I was joining was that it wasn't a talkative crowd. Here we were on a beautiful Sunday, one of the most important holidays to boot, I thought with a wry smile, yet everyone had such strange, somber looks on their faces. Like everyone was on a special mission, or walking to a funeral. Everyone seemed to have a sense of where they were going, except me. It made me slightly curious, and after slamming my door shut, I anxiously rounded the dump truck blocking my view, and in a moment all my witty responses dried up. I gasped out loud and my hands began shaking.

On the overpass directly ahead of me was an eighteen wheeler that had partially slid off the edge of the bridge with most of its cab dangling over the side of the overpass. From this far away I thought I could see a slight teetering, and it was frighteningly obvious that the entire truck could topple at any second. Now that I saw what the big deal was, my irritation disappeared and I quickened my pace to match those of my fellow empathizers, even passing some of the slower ones.

But what I saw next made me forget the now inconsequential slowdowns I'd been experiencing. I couldn't control the "No!" I yelped, when I saw the rest of the accident. Apparently the eighteen wheeler had previously collided with a Sunday School bus and it had already toppled off the overpass.

I continued my awkward half run, half walk toward the crash, and when I was finally close to the invisible line people had drawn around the accident, I scanned both sides of the highway, disturbed that there were no police to be found. Had no one thought to call 911? I had to wonder if the cops were around the bend down the highway, in their favorite hiding spot they used to catch speeders.

As I stared in a daze at the partially crumpled bus, I was vaguely aware of the continually growing crowd, and when I couldn't see what was happening up ahead, I began maneuvering my way between those distracted by chatter, little kids unaware of the real danger, and grandmothers afraid to get closer.

The front of the crowd had stopped within about fifty feet of the bus, and by this time I had inched myself to the front of the line. Everyone was relieved when we finally heard a siren, but it was almost an insult when one of those smaller fire trucks pulled up. Shaking my head, I muttered, "You've *got* to be kidding!"

It didn't take a rocket scientist to figure out one small truck would never be able to keep the eighteen wheeler on the overpass much less prevent, or even delay, the inevitable. They needed cranes and multiple fire trucks! But as I watched them dodge debris scattered on the highway, I could tell they were more interested in the Sunday School bus, which sadly meant they had already given up on the truck and it was going to eventually fall. My eyes felt like they were bugging out of my head and my hand covered my mouth in horror as my heart began beating faster.

There were so many things happening at once and everyone seemed to be watching a different detail of the scene being played out before our eyes. Some of the people began yelling out to the firemen to see if they could help, yet others made stupid suggestions any idiot could see wouldn't work. An old guy with a cane stumbled up giving no one in particular second by second reports on the status of the teetering truck, as if we needed his reminder to imagine impending death. But a moment later I was transfixed with a new dread when I thought I saw a slight movement inside the cab of the truck.

For some reason I had assumed the driver had been able to crawl out the other side of his cab since there was no sign of him. Someone else obviously saw the same thing and yelled, "Look in the cab!" and our heads jerked up as we realized the situation was even more appalling now. A gloom settled over the crowd as each of us realized that unless something miraculous happened the driver was doomed because the truck was moments from crashing over the edge. I felt like we were living inside a horror movie that was distasteful and distressing at the same time. I couldn't bear to look.

Then a teenage girl near me yelled "No! Look!" and pointed to the cab. At the same instant I heard deep, guttural screams and moans comprised of a bizarre mixture of agonizing pain and fear. I sucked in my breath when I saw the tiny wisps of flames licking between the hinges of the cab's door. Within two seconds the tiny flicker had matured into full blown flames and engulfed his cab.

The powerlessness I felt sickened me and the previous quiet sighs bled into empathetic groans, spreading throughout the crowd. I heard a lady beg her husband, "Can't you do something?" I saw mothers grabbing kids, hiding their faces so they couldn't see the predictable end. I wished someone was hiding my face. I wondered where his family was, hoping they never heard about his final moments. The sight of his excruciating suffering was unbearable. But as terrible as it was to hear his screams, a hush descended as we wondered how long it would take before the silence came, knowing exactly what that would mean.

I will never forget the next moment. For a brief, interminably long second, the man writhing in agony opened his eyes, looking down toward us and, inexplicably, it felt like my eyes met his. I've never felt so helpless. Tears not cried for months or years inadvertently began spurting. I had to break my gaze first, with no options but to look toward the ground. I couldn't bear to see his pain and unspoken pleading. I prayed it would end soon for his sake.

I stood silently, side by side fellow uncomfortable observers as we collectively cringed, agonizing over the fact that we could only helplessly stand by as the man died screaming. Almost in unison we realized the next emergency was directly beneath the cab of the truck, where the bus was already partially smashed, smoke pouring from its engine. With the truck driver writhing so viciously, the cab was visibly shaking and I knew it wouldn't be long. Internally I was screaming at them to hurry, to break into the bus and rescue the children before the truck fell.

Moving to the left of a young man so I could get a closer look, I saw that only two firemen had come in the fire truck. Others must have just noticed it as well because I heard a lady say, "Dear God! Why on earth wouldn't they send more firemen to such a dreadful accident?" Her comment seemed to spur some of the braver men in the crowd, so, despite the danger, they ran toward the bus, frantically trying to help pry the rear emergency door open. The rest of us stood by helplessly, watching and hoping we weren't about to see an entire group of children and rescuers killed right in front of us. I kept hearing occasional sobs and others breathing loudly and unevenly, trying to control their emotions just like I was. A man behind me began stupidly stammering something about how he would have gone to help the firemen, but figured if the truck fell we might need his help. Even in the midst of the dire situation, I saw a lady near him turn back, looking him straight in the face, giving him a look of utter disgust. I could read her thoughts as if she was screaming them, that she knew he was just as scared as the rest of us and how his excuse sounded cold and lame.

Since catching the eye of the driver, I was consciously refusing to look toward the truck cab, until I heard a new kind of groaning and a loud creak. Despite my intentions, my gaze was drawn back to the truck just as a flaming ball of fire erupted, high into the sky. There was a loud pop and I jerked instinctively, then heard a higher-pitched, guttural shriek, eventually dwindling down to nothing as the driver slumped over into the flames and out of our sight. The relief I felt was not only because I knew his pain was finally over, but because his hellish screaming was no longer resonating. He was the first person I'd seen die, and for a split second I wondered which side of eternity he had just joined.

We all froze for a fraction of a second and no one spoke. A solemnity descended as if we were giving the man his moment of silence. But the moment ended as quickly as it began when the screeching sounds of scraping metal woke us up as the firemen used their jaws of life to bend open the door of the bus. My mom-sense belatedly kicked in, realizing we were missing the most important sound of all. Although the front cab of the bus had been definitely smashed in as it tumbled off the freeway, the rear portion where the children would have been sitting didn't look quite as damaged. And even though there was a good chance most of them were severely injured, I knew we should at least be hearing children screaming or crying.

Then, with no warning, the second front wheel on the truck slipped off the overpass, upsetting its balance enough so that its entire load of metal pipes began falling off the truck, bouncing all over the highway, most of them falling off the overpass directly onto the bus below. The unbelievably loud clanging and rolling of the pipes caused most of us to scream and the rest began yelling for the firemen and bystanders to get out before the truck fell on them. From my angle I could barely see through a couple of the bus windows, but as soon as the first pipe hit the roof, one of the firemen and all the other guys dashed out the back door they had just bent open.

Then I saw a movement and glimpsed the other fireman, deep inside the bus, leaning intently over a seat as if completely unaware of the imminent danger. The screaming escalated to a new intensity, almost in unison, hoping the earsplitting tone would convince him to leave in order to save himself. Even his buddy stood just a few feet away, not even out of harm's way himself, screaming and frantically motioning him to leave.

Slowly but surely several of us realized we weren't helping anyone and if we didn't move back there was a good chance we would be hurt. A couple people took charge and began pushing people back, when almost on cue, there was a different sound, one we had dreaded, sounds of wrenching, groaning metal as the bottom of the truck began scraping the concrete, sliding in the only possible direction, down off the overpass. Helpless, for a moment we froze, watching in silence as the eighteen wheeler teetered almost vertically, then, in a surreal slow motion, crashed into a massive fire ball directly on top of the Sunday School bus below.

As soon as the first bumper of the truck hit, everyone instinctively shielded their heads with jackets or newspapers or anything else we could find as we turned to run. Simultaneously with the first sounds of smashing metal, pieces of flying debris, burning rubber, and metal slivers like ice picks went flying hundreds of feet in every direction. I now knew why police never let anyone near accident scenes. Every person in the first few rows were either cut or burned or both. People were moaning and crying out in pain, and then I heard a man begin screaming.

Turning in the direction of the rasping sound, I was horrified to see a young man covered in flames from the top of his head to his feet. Those around him were slapping at him and pushing him to the ground trying to put the fire out. Momentarily mesmerized and wincing empathetically, my attention was jolted back to reality when I had to slap my own arms from flying sparks. I watched as several men gingerly wrapped the young man in someone's coat, running off to a nearby car to find help. His screams turned into agonizing moans that were finally silenced when the doors shut and, as if choreographed, we turned back to the horrifying scene that had started it.

After he was out of sight, the horror of what we'd just seen created a palpable heaviness. Words would never be able to explain how awful it was. Our mouths were open and dismay evident on every face. The heat from the fire was intense and the surrounding air was sticky, making it feel like we were in the middle of a hot summer day. The experience was made even worse by imagining what was beneath the wreckage.

There was only one unspoken question. How many children had been trapped inside the inferno? Now that there was absolutely no chance of saving anyone, we had nothing else to do but watch the fire burn like a bonfire gone haywire and a pensive silence engulfed us again.

Almost to a person we had jumped back as the truck plummeted off the overpass. Once the truck settled, I could see the cab had hit the bus then fallen backward, ending up almost upside down while entirely smashing the rear portion of the bus, exactly where the fireman had been crouched a moment before. Numbness overtook me for the next several minutes as I watched simultaneous explosions as multiple gas tanks took turns exploding one by one, like a finale of a Fourth of July fireworks show.

By this time there was no counting how many people were gathered and gaping from every possible direction. There were even gawkers on top of the overpass, standing right where the truck had dangled just moments earlier. It was obvious the tanks had been full because the blaze was growing rather than dwindling. The crackling of the fire would almost have been hypnotizing, if it weren't for the intense heat and the occasional spitting of metal pieces. No one was chatting. Voices were conspicuously absent. We were all lost in our private thoughts.

Then, from somewhere near the back of the crowd, we heard a yelp, and we all turned to look. I could see a little grandma with stringy gray hair in a messy bun wearing a long multi-colored dress pointing farther down the highway. I was about to ignore her, when a couple of guys started sprinting in the direction she pointed, and after a few seconds, word trickled back and I heard someone mumble something about the surviving fireman. I had temporarily forgotten about the one not inside the bus, assuming he'd been too close to the explosion and hadn't made it. The crowd began rearranging itself so we could all get a better look. Apparently the explosion had saved the fireman's life by throwing him maybe a hundred feet down the highway. He'd been knocked out and was just now stirring. As the word traveled, three or four more guys ran to help.

He'd gone unnoticed for several minutes as we watched the exploding fuel tanks, but by now, several people were surrounding him and I saw someone had pulled a tarp from their car to carry him with. Even from my vantage point, I could see one side of his head was singed, and one of his arms looked raw, bloody, and scorched. Part of his shirt had burned off and I saw a gash on his cheek.

Someone ran and gave him a bottle of water and one of the guys yelled out the proverbial "Give him room to breathe" as if we were sucking his last bit of oxygen. I was hoping we could hear his side of the story before they took him away, and since no one was backing up, I had to assume others wanted to as well. Not that we *needed* more gruesome details, but we were thirsty for any possible glimmer of hope.

It seemed to take him an eternity to drink the bottle of water, especially since he had to stop and cough a couple of times. I was sure he needed medical attention, but I, for one, wasn't about to let him get away without telling us something! After getting a closer glimpse and deciding that his injuries didn't look life threatening, I decided if no one else was going to speak up, I would force the issue, so as they were hoisting the tarp up on their shoulders to carry him away, I yelled out, "What about the kids? How many were in the bus? Were they...?"

I'm sure my audacity shocked those around me, because a few people looked back to see who was interrupting his medical care, and only then did I feel a bit guilty. At first I didn't think the fireman had heard me, because he didn't flinch or change his expression or even look in the direction of my voice. When I saw no reaction, I felt a bit deflated and embarrassed, and decided I wouldn't bother asking again. But then, slowly, he raised his head, looking in my general direction. I grimaced when I saw drops of blood oozing from another cut on his forehead that I hadn't noticed before, and I felt guilty again.

With great exertion he belched out the words "There *were* no kids on the bus" before falling backward with a wince.

After we received that piece of juicy information, only a millisecond of silence passed before the crowd began clamoring and took over for me. Everyone surged even closer, while someone yelled out, "No kids on the bus? You're saying no one died except your buddy and the truck driver?"

The fireman gave an exaggerated sigh, perhaps thinking, *Two wasn't enough?* but instead he said, "Well I sure didn't *see* anyone else in the bus."

Only a fraction of a second later, an elderly man asked, "What about the bus driver?"

Abruptly the fireman seemed to recognize he was the center of attention and back on the job, realizing it was his duty to share what he knew. He rose up a bit higher on his elbow, shaking his head, and said, "I didn't see any bus driver either..."

Once again, for perhaps the two seconds it took for that bit of information to sink in, we all looked at each other to see if anyone else was making sense of it all. Finally a brash teenager asked, "Not even a dead body?"

The fireman looked out into the distance at no one in particular for a long while, and I felt, in a strange way, he was measuring his words. Finally, he said, "I'm thinking there'd been bus trouble or something and everyone was already out before the truck crashed into it. It must have been empty, thank God."

We all paused to digest, when a frumpy, middle-aged motherly type asked in a loud, grating voice, "Well then, *what on earth* were you two rummagin' around on the bus for, endangering your lives, if there wasn't a human being to save?" The utter brilliance of the question amazed me, and, like the rest of the crowd, I turned back to look in his face, especially waiting for this answer.

I sensed that it was the last question he would answer, so I hushed a mumbling neighbor so I could hear his explanation for his friend's tragic death. After a pregnant pause, he finally said unconvincingly, "Well, there was a huge mess on the bus. Lots of books and papers and clothes and stuff everywhere, I mean, we had to be sure there weren't any kids hidden anywhere, you know..."

The same insistent lady asked in her grammar-free slang, "Yeah, but once ya seen there weren't no kiddos in there—why did your buddy keep digging around when you was already high tailed outa there?"

By this time I had maneuvered my way closer to the front of the crowd, so I was almost staring straight down into his face, and saw a slight, imperceptible change in his demeanor I couldn't quite place. When he finally answered, it seemed like he set his jaw and hardened his voice to keep it from cracking, and finally, matter-of-factly said, "Jimmy's little boy went to that church and rode that bus every Sunday. He yelled out that he'd found his kid's Bible and one of his new shoes. He was trying to find the other stupid shoe." His voice cracked and his

eyes blinked rapidly. "I would've bought his kid another pair of shoes…
I just couldn't make him leave."

You could tell he was finished. He clinched his eyes shut, as if
trying to stop the visualization of those last seconds and how futile his
screaming had been to save his friend. But at that moment every one
of us was picturing a sad father looking for a second shoe. It wasn't a
pretty vision.

We had crowded around the fireman so close we could almost
feel each other's breath until, one by one, we retreated into our own
private thoughts and then physically began backing away, as if afraid to
catch anyone else's eyes. We were all thinking the same thing, though.
How someone's two-second decision, a foolish hesitation over a pair of
unimportant shoes, had changed a family's life forever. He probably died
clutching his kid's Bible. I tried to imagine how his son would feel…
when he realized his Dad had died for him.

CHAPTER THREE

Sunday, one forty-four p.m.

WITH THE FIRE continuing behind us and no one attempting to put it out, I could tell we were at a loss as to what should be done next. Inexplicably bonded together in a matter of fifteen minutes by the worst tragedy most of us would ever witness, we were uncomfortable to find ourselves standing so close to strangers now that the trauma had passed.

Those who had run to help the lone survivor were carrying him down the street now that our inquisition had ended, obviously on a mission to get him some medical attention. The shrapnel-damaged fire truck had taken away their obvious choice of transportation, and it looked like they were carrying him somewhere. From my vantage point, it looked like the back tires of the fire truck had exploded, and something had flown into the windshield exploding it into a million pieces.

By now cars were parked in every direction, making side streets and access roads virtual parking lots, so rather than wait for a car to become untangled, the guys were walking at a brisk pace down the access road. In no time at all they were a couple of blocks away, weaving in and out of the maze of cars. I remembered a 24-hour walk-in medical clinic about three blocks away and figured they were headed there. I saw the guys stumble as one of them tripped, and in a sad way it reminded me of pallbearers carrying a casket. Once my mind went down *that* path, I began fretting, wondering who would end up notifying their next of kin and would they ever get a proper burial? I felt sad imagining two families waiting at home, wondering why their husbands or fathers hadn't returned.

Despite the fact that the excitement was over, no one seemed in a hurry to leave and people were now creating impromptu clumps of individuals dissecting what we had just experienced. But that meant that those who wanted to leave, like myself, were inevitably parked between cars with no owners in sight. I finally shook myself from my daydream as little by little most of my fellow gawkers moved on, and then I was standing alone. My first thought was to realize my family had to be distraught by now! I looked at my watch, realizing church should have dismissed almost forty-five minutes ago. Despite my earlier text to Mark and Holly warning them about the accident, they had to be wondering where I was. Maybe in all the commotion they had called and I just hadn't heard my phone.

As I began walking back to my car, I pulled out my cell phone, squinting in the bright sunlight to be sure I was seeing correctly. No texts, no messages, and no missed calls. Was my phone not working? Or had church gone longer and they hadn't even missed me yet? That was strange. I knew Holly was never far from her phone and checked it every few minutes. Maybe our cell service was down.

Although the bulk of the crowd had moved away from the immediate scene, a good number were still loitering in the general area. Everyone had stunned looks on their faces, a little bit unsure if they should leave yet. I saw people stopped, whispering, and some just standing, staring, pointing. And of course there were those oblivious to the fact that they were in the way of the rest of us ready to leave. Walking past the final group blocking the way to my car, I heard the dump truck driver talking on his cell phone about the missing children on the bus, telling someone he knew where they were, and although I'd never seen him before, overhearing his words gave me comfort.

Once my hand touched the car door, I remembered it overheating and my apprehension returned. Maybe with plenty of people still around I could beg someone to give me a jump, or borrow some coolant, but hopefully I wouldn't need either. Meanwhile, I would give up on texting and just call Mark. They were *never* going to believe the kind of morning I'd had or what I'd just experienced. For the first time in my life, I had the best excuse for being late!

Thankful when the car started without a hiccup, I relaxed a bit and took a deep breath while I dialed Mark's number and turned the air conditioner on. My mind was whirling in so many different directions. My car radio had been on the fritz for months, so I chose a CD, turning it up a little louder, and grabbed a piece of gum. By that time, Mark's phone had rung at least ten times. I wondered if it was on vibrate, or if he was just ignoring it because he was talking to someone. I was even ready to leave him a message, but it kept ringing and didn't go to voicemail. I muttered, "I'll try Holly. I *know* she'll pick up." Pressing 3 on my speed dial, I heard it start to ring and closed my eyes. My head was hurting a bit again. But nothing a good, ice-cold raspberry tea and a grilled chicken salad couldn't fix. I had already decided what I would order, and it was sounding better and better.

I looked down at my phone to be sure I had dialed the right number thinking, "Why isn't *she* picking up either? And why are their phones not going to voicemail?" Frustrated, I threw the phone in the seat, deciding to just forget it and drive straight there. Maybe they had heard about the accident and were driving to find me, or perhaps there were street closures keeping them from getting to me. It was frustrating to think I was barely a couple of miles from them and our phones couldn't connect us.

Thankfully, the car behind me had worked his way out of his tight spot, so I was able to do the same, and I backed out carefully. The dump truck was still not moving, and, in fact, a larger cluster of people were surrounding him now and the group was growing. Personally, I was talked out and crowded out. I wanted to get away, and I wasn't sure what else there was to discuss.

I gently honked, trying not to be rude but just enough to get their attention so I could squeak by. I expected looks of irritation or even a rude hand signal, but although everyone moved out of the way, not even one person looked in my direction. I had even rolled down my window ready to explain how I was anxiously trying to find my family, but no one even appeared to be aware I was there.

Rolling my window back up, I heard a young man say, "My grandmother always said this would happen..." and I tried imagining what on earth his grandmother could have said to make people seem riveted to his words, but by then my window was closed and I didn't have time to hear the rest of his story. My morning had been so exhausting, I was tempted to drive back home and climb into bed. And if Mark or Holly would have answered their phones, I might have convinced them my headache was back with a vengeance, and asked if we could reschedule. But as it was, no one was answering, so I had no choice but to keep going.

As I waited for traffic to move, I wondered if the accident would be on the news later, and decided I would watch even though I rarely bothered anymore. It was always so negative, just plain tiresome. Fifteen minutes later, having barely gone a block past the accident, I reached an intersection with a four way stop and saw another accident where vehicles coming from three different directions had run head into each other. From the looks of things, I could only guess all three cars were totaled. I wasn't surprised there were no police since they hadn't shown up to the last accident. It was obvious these people had gotten tired of waiting for the wreckers too. I *knew* rush hour was going to be terrible tomorrow morning if these accidents weren't cleared up by then.

I slowly inched my way around the accident, trying to see if I recognized any of the cars, since it was fairly close to home and church, and I felt a sense of relief when I didn't recognize any of them, except... Driving around the last car, I glanced back and saw a bumper sticker with our church's name on it! I slammed on my brakes and parked right off the edge of the road. I got out of the car, looking around, hoping no one would think I was trying to steal anything. I just wanted to see if I knew whose car it was.

The car doors were unlocked, so I opened the passenger door and looked in. I wasn't surprised to see a Bible on the seat, but what on earth was the lady's purse still doing there? And with the doors unlocked! Why would anyone leave their purse, even if they *were* tired of waiting on a wrecker? The neighborhood wasn't *that* safe. As I glanced around the car, I realized the lady was no neater than I was. When I noticed a sweater and other clothes on her seat as well as a pair of pretty sandals on the floorboard, I smiled, knowing exactly what had happened. I had done the same thing myself many times. Whoever this was, had figured they would have to walk a ways to get help, and their "church" shoes weren't made for walking. She probably kept an extra pair of shoes in her car, and changed into them before she took off. In fact, if I got back into my car and drove toward the church, I might run into her, since there was a good chance her first instinct had been to walk back to the church and ask someone for help.

After just a moment's hesitation, I picked up her purse so it wouldn't be stolen, then figured I might as well see whose it was. I opened her wallet and saw that it belonged to Alexa, a young lady from our church. We didn't hang out together but I knew her, and the first thing that popped into my mind was when she had given her life story at one of our women's meetings a while back. Unaware of her past, I had been surprised to hear her admit to having three abortions, two before and even one after she had started going to our church. It was hard not to remember her story every time I saw her. I was always a bit in awe of people like her who shared the most intimate details of their shame-filled past, apparently without continuing to feel the guilt and remorse. The kind I was prone to feel.

I knew I personally still felt guilty over things I had done over the span of my life, and I sure wasn't about to advertise them to anyone. I wondered if I had just never fully understood forgiveness. I was afraid if I ever shared my sins, past or present, the list would make it around the entire church that same afternoon and I would never live it down. Because of that fear, I had never been much into sharing weaknesses. Not with family, or youth pastors, and rarely even friends. I shook my head, realizing my mind was wandering again. I needed to get back on the road, but the strangest emotions and thoughts kept surging through me.

I locked Alexa's car doors and tucked her purse under my arm. No reason for her to return and find someone had stolen her car *and* her cute sandals! Walking back to my car, I felt a familiar worry tickle me when I saw I had left my car running. Opening my door, I quickly checked the gauge, hoping the idling motor hadn't caused it to overheat again. Indeed, the car was beginning to heat up ever so slightly, so I knew I needed to get going fast. At the very least, I needed to meet Mark so I could ride home with him and not end up stranded.

Pulling back onto the road, I could only hope for no more distractions until I got to church. I visualized our lunch as I told them everything I'd seen that morning—all in one short drive! The day had worn me out, so I was already figuring I deserved a good Mother's Day nap after lunch before I went on any more excursions.

As I turned the corner, I saw another long line of cars ahead that looked as if it were growing instead of diminishing. My sigh was louder than normal, and I felt a bead of sweat on my forehead. I had turned the air conditioner off in the hopes of delaying the overheating, but this traffic jam wasn't going to help matters. I strained to see what this problem might be since there were at least twenty cars ahead of me, and when I squinted I could see the traffic light flashing. I rehearsed in my mind any short cuts that might bypass this mess, couldn't think of any close enough to make a difference, so I stayed where I was, barely inching along, in full worry-mode by now.

After maybe four or five minutes, I was second in line to cross the intersection and now saw a policeman in the middle of the street, pointing cars in the opposite direction from where I needed to go. As the car in front of me turned right, I pulled forward ready to use my most sympathetic voice while giving reasons why I had to go straight.

The cop's eyes looked right through me as he muttered in a monotone voice, "Ya gotta turn left or right—no one goes straight; that street's closed."

I wasn't dense and could tell he wasn't in the mood for excuses, but I had already wasted an hour trying to navigate a five minute drive, so I assertively told him, "Officer, I'm so sorry but my entire family is at the church up ahead and I've lost contact with them so I really need to go straight."

I was relieved and a bit surprised when his hardened eyes turned back and actually focused on mine. But with a semi-sneer on his face, like he thought I was joking, he said, "Lady! We've *all* lost contact with people, but you *still* can't go down that street! Until the authorities tell me differently, no one goes down that road. Either drive to the nearest hospital and see if your family is there, or go home and wait for them to call."

CHAPTER THREE

It was my turn to look at him like *he* was crazy. "What are you talking about, Officer?" From the moment I'd stepped out of my house this morning I seemed stuck in a surreal world where nothing made sense, and it obviously wasn't over. It felt like I was wearing snow boots running through a river of honey. After he'd begrudgingly muttered his half-bit of information, he started to walk to the next car, so I leaned out my window, and with an even more urgent ring to my voice, called him back, "Officer, *please!* What's going on? I haven't the faintest idea what you're talking about. Why would I check to see if my family was at the hospital? Has something happened at the church?"

His unkindness seemed unnecessary and especially cruel as he said, "Ma'am, I don't know if you just landed here from another planet, but don't tell me you haven't seen accidents all over the place today. It looks like a battle zone around here! I don't know if anything happened at your church or why I was told to close down this street, but until I get word that it's safe, I'll keep everyone out. No one knows yet if this was terrorism or not. I'm just trying to do my job. So turn around, go home, and call every hospital in the state if you feel like it. But you're not going down this street as long as I'm standing here."

I can only attempt to poorly explain what happened the split second he finished talking. Every lucid thought, every tiny bit of mental acuity I prided myself in, every normal thought process terminated. My mind was empty. Blank. After a moment, I focused again on his face, and even in my confusion, I recognized a look of utter impatience bordering on anger. My ability to comprehend had vanished. Was this what it felt like to lose one's mind? It took everything in my power to form the words and then find the strength to say, "Seriously, do you think I should check the hospitals?"

Any shred of previous tolerance was completely gone from his voice, and his brutality had increased. "Lady," he screamed. "Go home! Watch the news! There's a long line of cars waiting for *you* to get out of the way so they can get home too! I don't have time to catch you up on the day's events. Get your head out of the sand and wake up! But don't do it on *my* street. It's been a horrible day for all of us. Now *move!*" By this time his face seemed contorted in an evil way, as he pointed in the direction he expected me to go.

25

Without warning, tears stung my eyes. Partially because I felt I'd been the recipient of undeserved anger, but more so because a deep abiding fear had settled on me as soon as his words penetrated the fog in my mind. I had no alternative but to turn the corner. So I did. My mind was spiraling out-of-control, and I had trouble thinking clearly. I pulled into the parking lot of a grocery store I was passing, put the car in park, and stared straight ahead.

I prided myself on being a clear thinker, so I figured I just needed to sit and think this through. Was the policeman trying to say he *thought* terrorists were responsible for some of these accidents? Was that the explanation for the fires today? But he didn't really seem to know himself why the street was closed; he was just trying to get me out of his hair. There were other streets that led to our church. I would just have to find one that avoided any other angry policemen that might attempt to block me.

By this time I had a funny feeling I wasn't getting a Mother's Day lunch, or if I got a meal at all today, it would be this evening. My hunger had dissipated momentarily, but I was desperately thirsty, so before heading to the church, I decided to run into the store and get several bottles of water. As I turned the car off, I glanced down at the gauge and saw that it was almost at the peak of overheating. Now, more than for my own thirst, I needed the water to calm my car down. I wondered if I would be able to figure out where to pour the water.

As I got out of the car, I grabbed my wallet, immediately smelling a new odor of fuel mixed with burning rubber and a nastier, acrid scent. I could now see the exact location of the larger fire I'd seen from home this morning. At the other end of the shopping center, it looked like a fuel truck had jumped the curb plowing through an intersection, headlong into the last few stores and restaurants in the strip center. I had been inside every one of those businesses many, many times, and knew some of the owners personally. Flames were still lapping at several of the roofs, coming through broken windows, creating spirals of smoke with thick potent plumes. The helicopters were long gone, but the fuel truck was still lodged halfway through a Chinese restaurant, and I couldn't bear to think of the massacre that happened as the truck barreled through the brick walls. It gave me chills looking at it, and the thought of terrorism crept back in.

CHAPTER THREE

Shaking myself, I hurriedly walked toward the store wondering whether I should take extra water to the church in case there was an even bigger emergency there. I went directly to the drink aisle, quickly grabbed two cases of water and stuck them in my cart, heading back to the check-out lane. While I passed all the kiosks that sell things you don't need, I grabbed a few packages of crackers and cookies, figuring they might come in handy.

Once again, I found myself in an interminably long line. Impatiently waiting my turn, I looked in the cart in front of me and saw five cases of water and three gallons of milk. I watched as they checked out and saw the customer suddenly leave, crying, without taking the stuff in her cart and I felt sorry for her. I had been in her shoes a few times when my card wouldn't work. It was finally my turn to check out, and as the young man scanned my items, I took out my debit card, slipping it through the machine. But when the cashier noticed what I was doing, he said dryly, "Ma'am, the machines aren't working. I can only take cash until we're told differently."

So my bizarre day wasn't over. You know how you can go from being in a foul mood one minute, to hearing good news and your emotional state instantly changes? Well, it works in the opposite direction as well. I had temporarily felt keyed up at the thought of finding a way to outwit the pushy cop and help my family, when the cashier had to ruin it. My mood tanked immediately. Louder than necessary, I answered sternly, "You've *got* to be kidding me! *No one* carries cash anymore! There's no way I can use my card? You can't run it through manually?"

Surprisingly the teenager didn't chew me out but sympathetically explained, "No ma'am; I know, it's a hassle. I wish I could. I don't have anything to do with it—I'm just following the rules."

Fighting back the tears, I lowered my voice and whispered desperately, "Can you keep my things here until I find a place to get cash and come back?"

Then it was his turn to be impatient. "Lady, all ATM machines have been emptied. Your card won't work anywhere—it's not just our store. Haven't you heard? No one can use credit cards, debit cards, or ATMs right now. All banking computers everywhere are down! So if you don't have cash, you're not buying anything anywhere today."

I looked back at the growing line of people behind me, expecting to see sympathetic shoppers as upset as I was, but instead I saw a line full of scary, angry, impatient people, apparently not surprised by his announcement. Then I heard a voice far back in the line yell, "Move on, lady!" and I lowered my head so no one could see my tears.

I felt the blank cloud return, keeping me from fully comprehending the words the cashier was speaking. In an out of body experience, I looked inside my wallet and saw what I had feared. Not one dollar bill, not one penny. Not even enough change for *one* bottle of water. With nothing left to do, I left the water and snacks in my basket and shuffled numbly out the door. I wouldn't have been surprised to discover a hidden camera with someone jumping out yelling "You're on candid camera!" it felt so surreal. Except it wasn't funny, and there was no camera.

Opening my car door, I slumped into the seat, exhaustion seeping into every part of my body. Any benefits gained by sleeping in that morning had long disappeared. Like a robot, I mechanically put my key in the ignition, barely having the oomph physically or emotionally to turn the key. It ended up not mattering anyway, because as soon as I turned the key, I heard the clicking sound I often feared, especially when Mark wasn't around. Once I heard that noise, I knew the car wasn't going to start. I gently leaned my forehead on my steering wheel in a slow, deliberate motion and cried. All the emotional control I prided myself in had disappeared, and tears came whether I wanted them to or not. The worry, uncertainty, frustration, and shock, on top of the overpowering, out-of-control feeling that was accelerating hit me all at once.

I longed for the days years ago when someone else was in charge, when I would have been hugged and told not to worry about it, that it would be taken care of. But those days were long gone. In my mind I heard my Mom's answer to everything, "Annie," she would say, "just cast your cares."[1] I wasn't sure how to do that with my situation at the moment. Wiping the remains of my tears away, I almost felt embarrassed for losing it, but decided I deserved a break. It had been a rough day.

I had no idea.

CHAPTER FOUR

Sunday, two twenty-nine p.m.

I SAT THERE composing myself for a few moments. "Deep breaths," I kept telling myself. I thought back over my odd morning and felt uncharacteristically emotional. From the faint smell of smoke as I left the house, to the strange sight of my neighbor going berserk, culminating with all the accidents, watching people die mere feet from me, then hearing a policeman suggest that I check the hospitals for my family, ending with my car breaking down, it had not been a normal Sunday morning. Without warning, I recalled the truck driver's eyes as they bore into mine and was afraid I would revisit that scene in my nightmares. But then with the bombshell the policeman had dropped, perhaps I hadn't even seen the worst of it yet. I wasn't sure how to react at this point. All I could feel was a muddled confusion and a wish not to be alone.

In the pit of my stomach I was still feeling that occasional uneasiness because I'd had no contact with Mark or Holly or my parents. The only thought that brought comfort was knowing that if one of them had been seriously injured, *someone* from the church would have found me. The only explanation I could come up with was that perhaps another one of these strange accidents had happened near the church, and knowing my family, I could picture them right in the throes of the emergency. My daughter was training for a medical career, so I could see her trying to help those who were hurt, and Mark was a strong guy, so he would be helping move wreckage or pulling people free from rubble, and my parents would be doing what they did best, comforting or praying.

For not the first time that morning, I wished I would have bit the bullet, ignored my headache, and gone with my family to church. It wouldn't have killed me. I was beginning to feel a peculiar twinge of loneliness mixed with my anxiety and just wanted to be surrounded by family.

On a lark, I tried each of their cell phones again. First Mark, then Holly, Mom, and Dad. No one answered. That was frustrating in itself, but my mind turned back to my own current problem. If I didn't have my new pair of uncomfortable high-heeled sandals on, I would have just walked straight to the church from the store. But as it was, I knew I couldn't make it, and I didn't even have money to buy a cheap pair of flip-flops. I tried to think of anyone who lived close and who could jump my car or give me a ride, but I came up blank. All my work friends lived too far away to help. Scrolling through the numbers in my phone, I got a lump in my throat seeing how few phone numbers of true "friends" I had. The kind you call when you have an emergency. Most of the numbers stored in my phone were for a *purpose*. Friends of Holly's or church people I might need to contact for one committee or another. And saddest of all, there were more store numbers, restaurants, and auto repair shops than numbers of real, genuine friends I wouldn't be ashamed to ask a huge favor from. After today, I figured I needed to get out more.

I decided to call some of my church friends in case they still had phone service, or hadn't gone to church that morning. I tried Amber, then Ellen. No answer. Then I tried Paul and Kathryn and even Sue. Nothing. Had no one turned their cell phones on after church? My heart kept being conflicted. I wanted to be irritated, yet my concern pushed back the frustration I was feeling.

I sighed loudly. With car trouble, no one around to help, and even my contact list coming up dry, I'd have to resort to begging a stranger for help. I *hated* doing that. Not only the "approaching a stranger" part, but I always hated appearing helpless or needy. I would much rather help someone else in trouble than ask for help. But without a better idea presenting itself, I tentatively got out of the car and looked around. If I didn't know better, I might have thought everyone was preparing for an ice day or that we were under a tornado warning. There were people everywhere with carts full of bottled water, canned goods, and commercial size bags of pasta and rice. I saw one guy who looked like he'd bought out the entire battery department! It felt like I was in the middle of a disaster recovery area. Was there really a chance we'd been attacked by terrorists?

For now, though, I just needed to stay focused and find a way to get to church. I didn't have the time or energy to figure out what everyone else was doing, although I was amazed and a bit jealous they had cash on hand. I was so thirsty and kept wishing I hadn't emptied the change out of my car yesterday.

Sad thing was I wasn't even sure how to raise the hood on my car so someone would know I was having car trouble and have pity on me. I looked around, hoping to catch a kind soul's eyes so I'd have the nerve to ask for help, but it was like everyone was having his or her own bad day. I thought we lived in a friendly town, but no one was interacting or looking at anyone today. In fact it was quite the opposite. It seemed eye contact was distinctly being avoided. But I needed to either get to the church or get home in case Mark or Holly were there. I imagined, just like me, they were frantic with worry. We were going to have a wild time swapping stories this afternoon, but I needed to get to them first! I finally decided to walk down the middle of the parking aisle so I couldn't be ignored.

Then I saw a battered pick-up truck headed right toward me. Wouldn't have been my first choice, but I couldn't be picky now. As they got closer, I saw with apprehension that a young punk was driving with a couple of rough looking guys with him. I half-heartedly waved as I moved out of their way, thankful he had slowed down rather than running me over. I walked over to the driver's side a bit timidly, unprepared for his silence and surly expression. He wasn't making it easy on me, forcing me to spit out what I needed. So I said, "Um, I was wondering if there would be any way you could jump my car or drop me off at my church or give me a ride home?"

I was appalled when the kid actually had the gall to look me up and down and sneer a bit before looking over at his friends and saying, "Whaddya think guys?"

Unable to avoid their faces, I saw expressions that gave me a glimpse into what evil might be hatching in their heads. I instantly regretted flagging them down and began looking around for another possibility. But the parking lot was thinning out, so despite my fear, I decided to bite the bullet, and tried once more, "Please? I really need to get to my church," I found myself begging.

I saw one of the guys whisper something to the other who smiled, nodded his head, then nudged the driver with his elbow. I swore he whispered, "That might work," before grunting, "Get in the back. But we sure ain't going to no church, and we don't have jumper cables, but we'll drop you off at your house."

My heart sank. Why couldn't I have picked a little old lady to beg for a ride rather than three punks who probably had ideas of robbing or raping me? Then he gunned his motor and, with a belligerent look, said louder than needed, "Do you wanna ride or not? We're not waiting all day for ya." My desperation exceeding my better judgment, I decided to accept the ride and hope I was just being paranoid and wouldn't regret the decision. But then there was the little fact that I was wearing a skirt! Were they *really* going to make me sit in the back of their truck? For a fraction of a second I stared at them, hoping they were teasing, but the driver glared back and the other guys looked like they were sharing a joke and enjoying the prospect of me climbing into the truck.

By now I wasn't even sure I would be able to recall all the strange things that had happened to me today. I could see Holly laughing her head off whenever I got the chance to recount the story of me climbing into their truck with my skirt on. I could almost see myself hamming it up, because she loved a good story and a good laugh. Shaking my head, since it wasn't funny yet, I walked around to the rear of the truck, not having the faintest idea how to open the back gate. But I had a funny feeling if I didn't jump in quick, they would drive away and no one else was offering a ride. Thankful my skirt was long, I hiked it up just enough not to trip over it, hoping no one in the parking lot was watching the outlandish sight. While straddling the gate getting ready to twist my other leg over, I looked in the bed of the truck and sighed.

They had been shopping as well and had bought several cases of water and sacks of groceries, but that wasn't what made me sigh. Evidently they were planning some gardening, because the only place for me to sit was on a big pile of compost. In the background I heard distinct chortling as my benefactors enjoyed my discomfort. There was no way I could keep my balance on the side of the truck, so having no other choice, I grimaced and sat down as gingerly as I could. I figured many days from now I might laugh about it. Then again, maybe not. I doubted I would ever wear the skirt again. Then I sighed, realizing I hadn't told the kid where I lived.

Before I could yell out my address though, he gunned the gas pedal like he was upset because of the extra seconds I'd taken, and I fell back sprawling, covering my blouse with compost. What a hateful kid, I thought. I glanced back into the cab in time to see them all laughing, and I closed my eyes, just wanting the ride to be over. I looked up ahead and saw a stoplight and knew I'd better get his attention. I gingerly made my way closer to the driver's window so I could yell directions. But each inch I moved covered me more and more with filth and the nasty smell was enveloping me. When he lurched to a stop, I yelled as loud as I could, hoping his window was still open.

"I live in the Sunnybrook Addition—do you know where that is?" I felt the wind steal my words.

Without a moment's hesitation he yelled back, "I know where you live," in a strange, low, monotone voice. Then, "I know Holly." As soon as he said those words, I turned and looked toward his rearview mirror, his eyes met mine, and I felt a chill go through me. I broke the uncomfortable gaze first, turning around, no longer worried about the compost engulfing me. I was sure I'd never seen him before in my life, and found it quite troublesome that he knew Holly. And if he'd recognized me, why on earth hadn't he been nicer or invited me to sit in the cab while his friends choked on manure? I knew I would question Holly about him and make sure he *never* visited our home again.

As we drove the last few blocks, the smell was so bad I kept my hand over my nose to keep from retching. I eyed their cases of water, wondering whether I could wrestle one out of the plastic casing without them noticing. After their lack of hospitality, at the very least I deserved a bottle of water. But just as I got up the nerve to edge closer, he sped up as he took a corner, and I went flying to the other side of the truck bed, smashing my head against the side in the process. I felt like I was going to black out as tears sprang to my eyes. "God! Please! Just get me home," I cried.

Wiping my eyes and rubbing my head, it seemed the normal four to five minute trip was taking at least twenty minutes. I felt myself getting car sick with all the weaving in and out he was doing to avoid accidents still scattered around. Finally closer to my neighborhood, I hunkered down inside the truck, not wanting neighbors to recognize me. Thankfully, just a few moments later we pulled onto our street. Without a bit of hesitation, or asking for my house number, he passed my house by a few feet then jerked the truck in reverse, backing into the beginning of our driveway before screeching to a halt. I was startled again because it proved he really *did* know exactly where I lived.

I knew now not to expect any help out of the truck, so with no choice but to put my hands right smack dab in the middle of the compost, I attempted to stand up. Carefully hoisting my skirt up high enough not to catch the heel of my shoe in it, yet fully aware three pairs of eyes were following me, I gingerly stepped over the tailgate in my now ruined sandals.

My second foot had barely touched the ground when the driver yelled out, "We'll see ya later!" while the other two howled with laughter. The driver hit the gas pedal barreling straight out of the driveway sending rocks flying in my direction. Even with the despicable treatment I'd just received, I'd been about to thank him, and was a little ticked he didn't even wait. *I hope I never see them again,* I thought. I wondered if I knew his parents. I would have to remember what he looked like so I could describe him to Holly and warn her.

I disgusted myself. I smelled like a pig farm, or worse. I shook as much of the compost out of my skirt and blouse as I could, finding pieces in my hair as I bent over to shake it out. If we ever *did* go out to eat today, I would have to take another shower. I started the long walk up the driveway, hoping beyond all hope I would see Mark and Holly's cars where they belonged, but as I turned the bend, I sighed, disappointed. They must still be at church and now, because those boys refused to take me to church, I was stuck at home with none of our cars. I was mad at myself and second guessing yet another one of my decisions today. Why had I not forced the issue so those punks would have just taken me to church? Were none of the decisions I'd made the right ones?

Looking again at my cell phone for the umpteenth time, I hoped again I had missed their call while I was in the compost heap, but still, nothing. I couldn't remember when we'd gone this many hours without some type of contact, so I knew their situation must be serious. I decided if it was our phone company's fault, I would change to a new one in the morning. "Mark must be *livid*," I fumed, picturing him trying to reach me, worried, but to no avail.

Still anxious, yet relieved to be home, I stepped onto the porch while reaching in my purse for my keys. A tiny sinking feeling started at the base of my stomach. Suddenly frantic, I began grasping inside my oversized purse. In desperation, I turned it upside down on the porch not thinking twice when my lip gloss and pens rolled off the porch and Tic Tacs went flying in every direction.

"*Please* don't tell me I left my keys in my car," I cried out loud. When it was obvious I had, I slowly lowered myself to the porch, sitting down on the edge, on top of papers and receipts and the scattered Tic Tacs, staring blankly, looking so far off into the distance that I saw nothing. My mind was racing, yet I wasn't thinking of one thing in particular. I could sense my mind trying to find a safer spot to land than what I was finding on planet earth. When a backfiring motorcycle drove by, it shook me back to my senses. I had no idea how long I had been sitting like a statue.

Getting up abruptly, my face hardened and resolute, I reached down into the flower bed in front of the porch. Picking up the biggest rock I could find, I stepped onto the porch with an emptiness on my face. Walking to the door as I scattered more of the items from my purse, I heard a crunch and knew I'd broken my mirror. Not pausing for one second, with one continuous motion I smashed the rock into the decorative glass right above the door knob. A bit shocked to find I'd hit it harder than intended, I was also surprised to see how fragile it was.

From the top to the bottom of what had been a beautiful specimen, the window had shattered into all sizes and shapes of jagged glass that flew inside and out in every direction. Quite unlike my normal protocol, I didn't stop to calculate how much it would cost us, but merely reached through the broken glass and unlocked the door, yelping as a piece of glass with a jagged edge caught me on the soft spot under my wrist piercing through my skin.

Undeterred, my fingers found the deadbolt and unlocked it. I was bound and determined to get inside if it was the last thing I ever did. Crunching glass every place I stepped, I opened the door, breathing a sigh of relief to be home and in one piece. Without a thought for the mess I was leaving on the porch, I stumbled into the living room and collapsed on the couch. I was slightly comforted by the familiar and the calm. The house was exactly as I'd left it just a few hours earlier. Even the newspaper scattered on the couch was soothing. But somehow a strange, different type of quietness was seeping out of the nooks and crannies, and I shivered.

Suddenly focused on how tired I was, I kicked my shoes off and even closed my eyes for a few seconds, but then the phone rang, causing me to jump. I couldn't hide my relief to hear the wonderful sound as I yelled out, "Finally!" still not believing Mark hadn't found a working phone before now. As I tried to jump up from the couch, I was surprised how stiff I'd become from my morning's excursions, and my pause made me just a second late in reaching the phone before the answering machine kicked in. I was about to grab it anyway when I looked down at the caller ID. I saw my work number and quickly jerked my hand back. I was appalled, thinking they would possibly call me to come in to work on Mother's Day!

So I stood beside the phone as a voice I didn't recognize began speaking in a monotone voice:

"This message is for all Jordan & Graham employees. Please be advised that because of current circumstances, our worldwide offices will be closed for at least the coming business week. Like the majority of corporations, our auditors need this week to analyze current financial standings after today's events. This week will be considered a temporary layoff and will be unpaid for all employees. For safety reasons, security keys in each office building have been turned off and there is no building access until further notified. It is of high importance, however, for you to immediately log onto the firm's website no later than within one hour of receiving this message. You will see an emergency login, where you will need to confirm your contact information for the coming week. No other firm programs will be accessible until notified. Clients calling our firm's phone numbers worldwide will be given the simple message that our offices are closed. As we have been instructed to do, the names of employees not logging in within one hour will be placed on the government's "Watch List" and provided to the FBI."

I heard an imperceptible click, and the phone went dead.

CHAPTER FIVE

Sunday, two fifty-nine p.m.

MY MIND ATTEMPTED to process the words I'd just heard. I hadn't moved a muscle since the voice began saying words I couldn't comprehend. By the time the message was over, the frown on my face seemed permanent. Without understanding the message, it somehow seemed to fit like a missing puzzle piece in the bizarre day.

It was so evident now that there must have been some type of terrorist attack tying the fires, accidents, and who knew what else together. I couldn't recall exactly what the message had said, and the words seemed to get dimmer and dimmer the more I tried to recall them. I pressed the listen button, glad I had let the recorder pick up. Had they said something about me getting an unplanned vacation? Wasn't that a good thing? I would welcome not having to go to work tomorrow, except I also faintly remembered hearing the words 'unpaid'…and *that* would be a problem.

I sat down next to the phone, and the voice I still couldn't place droned on repeating the odd, but matter-of-fact sounding message. The faint smile I'd allowed to settle on my face, in anticipation of a week of unexpected vacation, disappeared. My mind began racing again. I was confused. We had worldwide offices and they mentioned that, so this obviously wasn't a localized threat, otherwise they wouldn't have closed every office. But for an entire week?

It seemed so bizarre that a tiny sliver of doubt crept in and a whisper of a smile returned. My heart stopped beating quite so wildly as my sixth sense kicked in. Although I hadn't recognized the voice, the fact that it was so outlandish, gave me a clue that *someone* was playing a trick! I worked with so many practical jokers, and it sounded exactly like something they would do! Try to convince me not to show up for work, making me the brunt of their joke! And to think I almost fell for it!

But then, just in case, the "responsible" part of my personality nudged me. The message had said if I didn't do what they instructed within an hour, my name would be put on some FBI list. So in the remote case this was serious, I'd better log on. If it was a joke, I would never admit I had checked the website, that was for sure! Once I logged on, it would be obvious, and if, for some strange reason it was true, hopefully I would find a plausible explanation. And all the while, I felt this nagging urge to get to church and find Mark and Holly. As soon as I logged on, I would turn the news on and then hopefully find a ride to church.

Standing up to go into the bedroom where my computer was, I glanced down and saw that, not only was I leaving trails of compost on our new cream-colored couch, but the cut on my wrist had left droplets of blood. Funny, how priorities change. I had just yelled at Holly last week when she dropped a ball point pen on the couch, leaving a tiny dot, but after this day, I looked at the blood stain and, without a word or a sigh, I turned and walk into the bedroom. Walking toward my desk, I saw the alarm clock flashing, meaning once again, our neighborhood's faulty power system had surged since this morning. So of course it also meant our computer had involuntarily rebooted. I hoped one of Holly's school assignments hadn't been on the screen, or I knew what she would be doing this evening.

Under my breath I said, "This sure hasn't been the *best* Mother's Day." Sitting down in my desk chair, I glanced at the mess on my desk and flipped the computer back on. Waiting for it to warm up, my eyes rested on stacks of clutter I never quite seemed to master. I knew one of the stacks had bills that had to go out tomorrow. I couldn't forget, or Mark would be upset. I'd done that a couple of times, left bills on the desk for about a week after they were due, resulting in several late fees. Of course if the phone message was correct, there would be plenty of time to get them out in the morning.

Then the worrywart side of my personality kicked in, remembering her saying we didn't get paid for next week either. That would mean I needed to look at our budget before those bills went out. A new kink causing more anxiety. Then, considering another possible twist, I wondered if Mark's company would also close, because if they did, we would have to pull from our dwindling savings account to make ends meet for the short term. Surely our companies would let us exchange vacation time rather than go unpaid. As soon as I logged on, I would shoot payroll an email asking if there was any way we could do that.

My computer was programmed to go directly to my firm's homepage so I could check email from home, and my heart skipped a beat when I didn't see the normal logo when the website came up. Instead I saw something that eerily mimicked what the voicemail had described. In place of the usual login, the entire screen only had two lines of text, asking for our login name and password. I looked up at the web address at the top of the screen to be sure it hadn't malfunctioned. It didn't even look like something our normal IT Department would put together. No fancy graphics, not even a nice font. Merely large words in the middle of the screen reading "Emergency Login."

I still wasn't sure why I was obeying a strange voice with even stranger directions, but out of curiosity as much as anything, I logged in. It was disconcerting when it accepted my login and password, taking me to a second screen where it told me to click on my office location and to enter my home address and phone numbers where I could be reached. At the bottom of the screen in tiny, plain letters, was the chilling phrase.

> *"Our email system is not available at this time*
> *(along with all network programs);*
> *we are attempting to reestablish server connections."*

I felt like I was living on a stranded island. Not only was my cell phone not working, but now I couldn't contact anyone by email! How exasperating. Since there were no other options, I went ahead and clicked the "Submit" icon at the bottom of the screen and the entire screen went blank except for a small,

"Thank you.
Reminder: All offices closed until further notice."

"Until further notice!" I yelped. That is *not* what the voicemail message had said! Very few people I knew, me included, could miss even *one* week of pay without hurting, much less until further notice! I hoped they had just worded that message incorrectly.

I tried to click somewhere else on the screen to find any other information or get to our homepage, but there were no other icons, links, or further information. Then, without warning, the screen froze, and I moaned, "No!" I was sure that so many of my fellow workers were also logging in to beat an arbitrary deadline we'd been given, that it had overwhelmed the system. I could only hope it had accepted my login before it had frozen.

My hope of catching online news was temporarily delayed while waiting for the computer to reboot, so I decided to turn on the TV to figure out what had been going on this morning since all hell broke loose. Right as I got up from the desk to find the remote and get the bottle of water I'd been craving for hours, another power surge hit the house as if prearranged for that moment. I glanced back just in time to see the computer monitor flash before slowly fading to black as all the house lights went out.

Silence gradually descended. Amazing when there's no television, music, or computer motor running, no phones, fridge, or even the quiet whirr of a ceiling fan, how silent a house can get. And lonely. I felt out of the loop ever since the policeman accused me of being from another planet, so not being able to check email or finally watch the news now that I realized I needed to, was aggravating. I was pretty sure terrorism had hit, and since it must have also affected our own city, I was becoming seriously worried. I waited impatiently a few minutes, my fingers involuntarily drumming on the edge of my desk, trying to will the electricity back on by staring at the computer. I needed contact with someone, anyone! The longer I waited, the more it looked like this frustrating outage might not end soon, especially if the electric company was as backed up as the police appeared to be. I waited a long ten minutes, then shook my head tiredly and stood up. The temptation to lie down and take a nap was strong, but the urgency to get to my family was stronger, so I knew a nap wasn't in the cards.

My wrist was still stinging from my break-in, so I decided to bandage it, meanwhile picturing the scene when I finally caught up with Mark and Holly. We teased each other all the time, and after they heard about my experiences today, I *knew* they would laugh, saying I shouldn't have tried to slit my wrists over my so-called *rough* day! I got my first aid kit down, and before I could catch it, several more drops of blood splattered onto my lap, ruining my new skirt for sure, before anyone had even seen it.

Inspecting my wrist, the cut seemed deeper than I'd thought, and I saw a tiny sliver of glass still embedded. With a pair of tweezers, I gently pulled it free, sprayed my wrist with antibacterial spray, put a Band-Aid® on it, and then wrapped my wrist again with a longer bandage. I knew that what I *should* do next was go and clean up the glass in the front foyer and on the front porch and find a board to cover the door, but I didn't feel that industrious at the moment and it didn't seem as important as finding my family. I was always relieved to leave the "manly" jobs for Mark. After he shook his head at the fact that I broke the glass because of my impatience, I knew he would fix it.

Frustrated with being stuck in the house, and not wanting to wait for them to come home or the electricity to come back on, I put on my walking shoes, determined to find a way around the policeman and get on the church property. The house was getting stuffy and I was getting more and more anxious by the moment. It was cooler outside so I figured I would feel better after a walk anyway, and the couple of miles to church would do me good. I just had to remember to have Mark take me by the shopping center to pick my car up on our way home.

With my plan made, I tied my shoes, put my hair in a pony tail, and decided to take three bottles of water for us. My original idea of helping a whole crowd had blown up in my face, but at least I could take Mark and Holly a bottle. I hoped Mark hadn't grabbed the last one when he left for church. But sure enough, as I opened the fridge, not only did I see we were out of water, but knowing now that I couldn't buy anything without cash made our fridge look frighteningly empty. I hoped the debit card system was restored soon so we could stock up.

Before I allowed myself to start worrying about *that*, I grabbed my purse, closed what was left of the front door, and gingerly crunched through scattered glass as I walked off the porch, grabbing my wallet still sprawled open on the porch step. There wasn't any reason to lock the front door, so I headed down the sidewalk. I felt a strange sense of déjà vu stepping onto the driveway. Was it only a few hours ago I was a carefree mother walking this same path to meet my family for a special lunch? Why did that seem days ago? I shuddered, remembering that in one morning's time I had witnessed at least two people die in front of me, and there was no way of knowing what else I was about to discover.

Walking down the long winding driveway, I remembered the fire in my own neighborhood and decided to see whose house had been burning earlier. Perhaps my friend Tanya, who lived a couple of blocks over, would be home so *she* could drive me to the church. It would only take a few minutes detour to see if she was home. If I was lucky, my five minute walk to Tanya's would save me a forty-five minute walk to the church.

So instead of turning left, I turned right at the end of the driveway, beginning my brisk walk, actually enjoying the fresh breeze and sunshine. I glanced to the left as I passed Daniel's house. It looked totally shut up, the blinds pulled and his car in the driveway. I wondered how his morning had ended and if his wife had taken him to the hospital or if they were even inside. Although we were acquaintances, he had been so distraught, I felt I would be intruding if I knocked on their door now. I would just have to watch out for them and hopefully catch his wife outside later.

At a brisk pace, I walked the rest of the way to Tanya's house, surprised to see no one else outside or moving about. Spring usually brought people out of the woodwork, ready to embrace the beautiful weather, working on their yard or watching their kids play. Maybe everyone was still indoors celebrating, or still out at restaurants, like I should have been. But as I rounded the corner, my heart sank and I sucked in my breath.

Tanya's house was the one that had caught fire! I began mentally kicking myself for not driving by earlier when I first noticed the fire.

What had been a beautiful, lovingly decorated home was no more. They had scrimped and saved just to get their down payment and her husband had taken a second job to furnish it the way she wanted. In a deep, empathetic funk I mechanically walked toward their shell of a home. A strange sight in an otherwise beautifully groomed neighborhood, I was a bit surprised neighbors weren't out still gawking, like you would expect. I wondered where Tanya was now and hoped she still had her cell phone since that was the only number I ever used.

Since there wasn't anyone around to stop me, I decided to get closer to the house to see if I could tell anything. I gingerly walked around pieces of rubble that must have spewed around the yard as items inside the house exploded. As I walked closer, something startled me. Instead of the car already being in the garage when the fire started, it looked like the car might have *caused* the fire by crashing into the water heater, which looked punctured. Apparently the car had caused it to blow up because it had then folded itself onto the hood of the car. My eyes grew larger and my stomach began hurting.

"Oh God, please don't tell me Tanya was in the car when it exploded…" But I felt compelled to check. As gruesome as it might be, I couldn't just leave. I was glad I had changed into walking shoes now. The metal garage door was partially raised but totally singed with the paint melted off. I gingerly walked on top of burned pieces of wood and debris that had fallen from the upper floor as the house disintegrated in the heat. I could still feel residual heat and then noticed some of her daughter's items that had fallen through the ceiling from her bedroom over the garage. Looking up I could see the sky through different parts of the roof that were destroyed. It was obvious no one else had been in the garage yet and that scared me. My heart grew more and more heavy as I prepared myself for the inevitable scene I was about to uncover. I knew it could end up being imbedded in my brain for the rest of my life, but I couldn't leave my friend here.

By now I wished I'd grabbed a pair of gloves. With all the rough pieces of wood I was moving, the half-burned roof shingles, and debris from the second floor, I could tell I had more than one splinter in my hand. I refused to feel sorry for myself though, when it was obvious my friend had gone through a lot more. Then I saw a large beam resting against Tanya's car door, jamming it shut. I knew I couldn't get the leverage I needed to move it myself, so I carefully backtracked, going over to the passenger side.

With all kinds of fragments covering the car and the back window totally blackened, I still couldn't see inside. Thankfully, not as much debris was on the passenger side. I didn't want to sprain an ankle since I had a long walk ahead of me, so I made my way gingerly.

I reached the car door, touching it gently, unsure of what I would find. It was still hot. Sadness overwhelmed me. I grabbed the handle and yanked it open. A puff of smoke escaped the moment there was a crack, and I knew nothing had been able to live inside the car. I slowly bent down so I could see inside the smoky, charred car where I had spent countless hours shopping with my friend. Bracing myself for the worst, my mind had trouble concentrating on what I finally saw. The seat cushions were entirely burned away and mostly bare metal springs were left with only slivers of material here and there that had somehow escaped consumption. On the passenger seat I saw a big lump of melted, burned black leather with a small charred chain attached that I could tell had been Tanya's purse.

But there was nothing in the driver's seat. I had been afraid to imagine what her burned remains might look like, but there was nothing there. Somehow, miraculously, she must have been able to jump out of the car in time. The relief I felt brought tears to my eyes. I breathed a breath I'd been holding for a long time and whispered, "Thank God she's alive." I was surprised she hadn't come to my house or called me, but perhaps an ambulance had taken her to the hospital or I hadn't heard the phone. At least I wouldn't be attending *her* funeral this week. I would check in with her later in case she and her family needed a place to stay. Mentally I made a note of where the bags of clothes for charity were located back at home. They would go to a great cause now.

Once I realized the emergency wasn't as tragic as I had feared, I was ready and anxious to get to the church. So with barely a glance back at a house my friend would never again live in, I started hoofing it out of the neighborhood as fast as I could walk.

CHAPTER SIX

Sunday, three thirty-two p.m.

THIS WAS NO leisurely stroll. I was on a mission. I pulled my cell phone out of my purse for at least the tenth time that day and it might as well have been dead. No messages missed. Not a text saying "Don't worry, we're all right." It was as if every person I knew had fallen off the planet. Looking closer, I saw it was roaming, which made me feel a little better. If the satellite was screwed up, that issue might be the root of our communication problems.

I kept trying to figure out a plausible explanation for no one coming to get me though. Even without cell phone service, there were enough people at church who knew where we lived, and since we didn't live far from the church, I found it strange no one had come looking for me. I looked at my watch and saw it was 3:32. I'd left my house only a little over four hours ago, but it felt like I'd lived a lifetime since then. We would have been finishing our Mother's Day lunch by now. It felt a bit surreal.

After a block or two, I was winded. I could have jogged to the church and gotten there a lot quicker, but my jogging threshold would have limited me to about a block before having to stop and recover. I still tried to keep up the pace. If I just walked at a steady rate, I could be at the church in about thirty to forty minutes. I was determined to take the exact route my family drove so I wouldn't miss them in case they were driving home. My only goal was to avoid that stubborn policeman.

It hadn't taken long to walk the few blocks to the intersection leading out of our neighborhood, and I still had a glimmer of hope I might recognize a face so I could ask for a ride; but so far I hadn't. Every car had their windows up and most people looked pretty grim. It didn't make me feel any better about my own situation, realizing they knew more about what had happened this morning than I did. I didn't have the courage to tap on a stranger's window, so I did my best to stay focused and just walk.

Reaching the original two-car accident at the entrance to my neighborhood, I walked out into the street on a whim and looked down into the car closest to me. It was messy, but nothing stood out to make me more curious, so I kept walking. Rounding the bumper, though, my peripheral vision saw something that didn't belong, and I stopped short. There was a tiny pink bicycle wedged between the cars! I gave a shriek as I leaned closer. *Surely* that wasn't my neighbor's daughter's bicycle? A precious six-year-old with long blonde hair who reminded me of Holly every time I saw her. I didn't even want to imagine.

I bent down until my face was inches from where one car's bumper had hit the other's, with the bicycle linking them. My mind whirled, imagining how difficult it must have been trying to comfort her mother. Pink ribbons attached to the little handlebars were still fluttering, even though they'd been straightened out between the grills of the respective cars. The tiny seat had flipped up making it perpendicular to where it should have been. And then I saw it.

One of those little plastic license plates advertised on the back of cereal boxes. Holly had put one on her bicycle years ago too. The little plate was facing away from me, teetering between one of the grill rims. I reached between the broken spokes of the wheel, almost knocking it down into the grill where it would have been lost to me. Gingerly using my fingers like tweezers, I plucked it from its precarious position. Flipping it over, I saw the one word I didn't want to see: 'Laura.' I closed my eyes and held my breath for a moment. What were the chances there was another girl in our neighborhood named Laura with a pink bicycle? Probably not great. But if it was true, I now had at least three neighbors who were going to need help. My heart hurt thinking of the moment my neighbor was told about her precious little girl.

I stood up slowly, oblivious to the cars passing, not caring if anyone watched. I reverently placed the license plate in the inner pocket of my purse promising myself I'd find my neighbor and give it to her. More death in a few hours than I might have witnessed my entire life. And to make it worse, I didn't know whether I was ready to walk onto a scene at my own church that might be worse than all the other accidents witnessed today. If only I'd turned on the news as I was getting ready for church this morning, I could have saved myself a lot of trouble by driving directly there. I could feel my expression beginning to match the empty countenances of everyone else I was seeing. If our country was being attacked, on top of all these random accidents, no wonder everyone had a morbid look on their face. I felt a profound sadness and dread overtaking me. In a way I didn't fully understand yet, I didn't think I would ever live the same carefree life I'd been living. Only later did I realize that was the clearest thought I'd had all day.

With no desire to look inside the second car and without even glancing in that direction, I walked by with my heart still fluttering from what I'd seen. I kept thinking how cruel life was to make my friend have to plan a funeral for an innocent six-year-old. I knew better than to blame God, but nothing was feeling fair about this day. I could tell I was getting closer to the Sunday School bus accident because the fuel spill odor combined with the burning rubber and scorched leather was attacking my sinuses with a vengeance. I had hoped to see evidence of cleanup or at least that the two bodies had been recovered, but the site didn't look any different.

My fear was that the accident at church was so devastating there were no emergency vehicles left in the city to cover the other accidents. Too much thinking was sending my imagination to far off places, so instead of trying to form lucid thoughts, I thought I'd better just walk and not think.

I had to believe they were okay, that we would just have lots of things to share this afternoon. I took the first left immediately after passing the accident, along the route my family usually took, avoiding the street the policeman had blocked. With no cars coming from the direction of the church, I could only hope they weren't blocking off the route I was taking. I had a couple more turns before I would be able to see the church, so I had no choice but to keep plodding along.

Another block of walking took me past a neighborhood convenience store, and I had to weave in and out of a long line of cars waiting to get into the cramped parking lot. The stalls of cars getting gas had their own traffic jam going, with lines at each pump. I glanced into the store and could see that it was standing room only, with another twenty or so outside waiting to get in. People were carrying out cases of beer and bottled water and bags of ice. I imagined maybe some of them had experienced the same power outage I had. Then I had to laugh when I saw a guy carrying about twenty cartons of cigarettes out of the store. "Now *that* will help him survive a terrorist attack!"

I turned the corner, walking faster and faster until I was out of breath. Thinking about my unplanned week off, I got a bright idea. While I was off I would get my home office organized, get caught up on sleep, and start a solid exercise program. I could even walk back and forth to the church every day. That would be a good start, and maybe I could even pop in and see one of my friends who worked there. And if I did it every morning when it was still fairly cool it wouldn't be quite as hard as it was right now.

Finally. One more turn and I would be on the final stretch. I saw a little crowd up ahead and tried to squint through the trees to see what everyone was swarming around. As I got closer and the trees cleared out, I saw another house fire. I'd lost track of how many fires I'd seen today. Working my way through the edge of the crowd, I passed the house, glancing over just as a man moved, creating a gap so I could see the burned shell of a house. I stopped in my tracks. Another car had plowed into a garage and this one had still been shut. The wooden pieces were splintered in uneven places with barely an opening for the car and it had stopped in the middle of the driver's door. I knew this day had distracted me, and I wondered if, out of fear or worry or terror, people were turning to alcohol or drugs or what it was that was causing distractions like these that were now ruining lives.

I looked around at the people on my left and right, hoping someone would share details, but no one was offering, so I asked a stranger, "What happened?" There was silence except for the occasional splintering of wood and debris falling inside the house making muffled crashes. Finally an old guy a few feet away said with a slow drawl, "Same as everywhere, missy, same as everywhere. A car crash here or the plane crash at the church. It's the same thing everywhere."

I whipped my head around at his words, but he'd already turned his back. My heart began pounding inside my chest. Had he said something about a plane crash? Was that why the street had been closed? Suddenly I didn't need any more information from this guy; I just needed to see my family for myself after that shocking tidbit, so I pressed on with a new urgency.

Walking was no longer sufficient, so I picked up my pace and began to jog the last few hundred feet. It seemed like an eternity since I'd left home, and I felt a blister forming on my heel, but I could finally see the church in the distance so there was no stopping me. I felt a bit better because I didn't see any street closures or huge smoke spirals. If an airplane had really crashed into the church, *surely* the NTSB or FAA or one of those other government agencies would be hovering around the property, even more so emergency personnel. I wondered if we would be forced to have church in a different location for awhile. What a hassle *that* would be.

With my heart just a bit lighter knowing I would see them soon, I took my cell phone out, hoping I might finally be surprised and find a message from someone, but, again, there was nothing. I sent another text to Mark and Holly saying, "I'm two minutes away. See you in a sec." It looked like it went through. I wondered if Mark had forgotten his cell phone in his car. I was just hoping there wasn't anything wrong with my parents. But by this time my brain was exhausted from wondering, and I was tired of worrying.

I was almost there and would soon see for myself.

CHAPTER SEVEN

Sunday, four thirteen p.m.

WALKING WITH A renewed purpose, I couldn't help but continue rethinking earlier decisions I'd made. If only I'd heard about the plane crash earlier, I wouldn't have stood around watching that accident for an hour, then forced to go through all the rigmarole after that. I could have been with Mark and Holly the last several hours, instead of experiencing this long stressful day by myself. I shut my eyes a second, fighting away the images forever seared in my mind, definitely relieved to have less than a block left. I was amazed and puzzled why there was so little traffic. Church had been out a long time now, but if an accident had *really* happened, wouldn't curiosity seekers be around, or family members coming to check on people just like I was?

Out of breath, I slowed my pace as I entered the parking lot, and the sight confused me further. It looked as if church was still going strong. In fact, it looked so normal I checked my watch again. Still doing what I did best, trying to figure out the world's issues, I wondered if they were having an impromptu prayer meeting because of the accident. And, strangely enough, as I surveyed the property from a couple hundred feet away, I still couldn't tell where or if a plane had crashed. I had assumed the wreckage would immediately be obvious if the rumor was true. Perhaps it was in the back of the property. Or maybe that man had gotten confused about which church was hit. But then why was everyone still here? I was even more surprised people weren't milling about in the parking lot. Even during church services there were always the late-comers, or early-leavers, and I saw neither.

Ready for my unplanned walk to be over, I cut through the parking lot, working my way through the maze of parked cars. I saw a couple of abandoned stalled cars, and as I got closer I saw a car still running with no one in it. That made me pick up the pace, knowing they must have run into the church, worried just like me, although I thought they were a bit brave to leave it unlocked and running. Even if this *was* a church.

Keeping my eyes open and surveying the land as I reached the sidewalk, there were knots in my stomach as I reached out to open one of the glass doors that lead into the foyer. I could immediately tell something had happened. My first thought was how much of a mess it was, and then I saw broken glass all over the floor and broken pieces of metal and wood chunks. I looked around to see if one of the glass doors had broken, but they all looked intact. The large wooden doors leading into the sanctuary were closed and I didn't hear a thing, so I figured everyone was praying quietly. I didn't even hear the normal background music we usually had during prayer. I didn't want to cause a commotion, so I headed toward one of the doors I knew didn't squeak.

I felt a strange draft of air and looked around, assuming someone had just opened a door, but saw no one in the foyer or down either of the long hallways. Then I felt something cold drip on my arm, looked up, and screamed! Directly above me was a medium sized plane that could probably seat twenty people. It appeared to have almost *landed* on top of our decorative foyer cupola, smashing the top down but yet hanging seemingly from metal threads, amazingly not yet fallen to the ground. It had broken most of the panes in our foyer's glass ceiling, greatly bending the metal framing that composed the entire skylight structure. I couldn't believe no one else was in the foyer or that emergency personnel weren't swarming the place. I could almost hear the structure groaning with the weight. This was what had obviously contributed to all the junk on the floor, and as I squinted into the sunlight, I could see where part of the bottom of the plane had ripped open as it crashed.

At that moment I felt another drip and recognized the smell. It was fuel! The tank must have been punctured and was slowly leaking. This place could blow up any minute! Prayer meeting or not, everyone needed to get out of here! I whirled around to run toward the sanctuary doors, not worrying about the squeaky door any longer. Before I could reach the sanctuary, however, I hit a small puddle of fuel that had been accumulating for the last couple of hours, and my feet went out from under me as I fell soundly on my rear end. I knew it would hurt in the morning, but I couldn't hesitate. My tail bone was aching and now damp, but God forbid if a spark appeared from somewhere, this whole building would go up in flames. I *knew* the fire department's track record for the day and we couldn't hope to be saved by them.

I gingerly rolled over onto all fours, both of my hands and knees now wet as well, trying to stand up without slipping again. At that moment I heard a loud wail inside the sanctuary and although the sound bothered me, I felt better knowing that's where everyone was, although amazed they weren't aware how dangerous the situation was out here. I would have to interrupt them so they could all move to a safer spot.

I dried my fuel-drenched hands on my clothes as I walked a bit more tentatively toward the door. But just as I placed my hand on the door handle, I was almost shoved to the floor when a lady I barely recognized burst through the door with tears streaming down her face. I was taken aback as she let the door slam, stopping to stare at me like she was seeing a ghost. Her open eyes and mouth seemed cavernous, and I had to squelch a rude comment. Instead, I said, "Do you need help?"

I assumed her demeanor was wrought with fright, but it turned to derision and disdain as she wrinkled her nose saying, "You! Of all people! You can't help either one of us," as she ran out the front doors, dodging debris. I was offended and hurt. Forgetting for a moment I was in the church foyer with a prayer meeting going on inches from me, I said out of embarrassment, "Do I *know* you? How do you *know* if I can help you or not?" Trying to calm myself, I turned back again, this time determined that no one would keep me from warning them. I placed my hand firmly on the door handle and pulled, hearing the loud squeak I had previously dreaded.

After opening the door, I walked into an unusually darkened sanctuary. Something didn't seem right, and it took a moment for my eyes to adjust to the shadows. I expected to see someone up front leading prayer or worship, but I didn't see any leaders.

Did I mention my Dad is the pastor? If it wasn't so tragic, I would be the first to enjoy the irony. Amazing, though, after all these years of being on my own, married and with a grown daughter, I still thought of myself as the *preacher's kid*. I looked around, curious that I didn't see Mom or Dad or even an usher I could query. I knew as long as anything was going on at the church they would be around somewhere. But it didn't appear anyone in particular was leading the gathering. Just people scattered here and there, most of them looked like they were silently praying. A few just staring into space. The squeaky door I had worried about didn't get one person's attention. I had reminded Dad many times to have the janitors fix it. I had begun to think he didn't have it fixed on purpose to deter people from coming into church late. Perhaps me in particular…

I finally recognized a couple I knew on the far side of the sanctuary as they opened a side door and light streamed in. I began trying to figure out what to do next without bothering someone who was praying. The only thing I could figure was that after the plane crash they had moved the majority of people to the youth building. Otherwise there wouldn't be so many cars still in the parking lot. I just hoped people hadn't been hurt by the falling glass and had to set up a makeshift hospital in the choir room or something. When a tornado hit a nearby town years earlier, the Red Cross had used one of our buildings as their headquarters, so maybe that's what was happening now. It had taken me far too long to get here, but I could finally pitch in and help now. This day was teaching me many lessons. One of which was that, compared to other people hit by life and death situations today, I was very fortunate and thankful.

Since this prayer meeting didn't seem to be an organized event, and I didn't see anyone else I recognized, I decided to leave and find where the main crowd had gathered. Particularly, my own family. Just as I turned to go, I heard a familiar voice say "Annie," barely loud enough for me to hear. I turned in the direction I thought the voice had come from, and in the shadows near the front altar area I barely made out a man's form.

CHAPTER SEVEN

I squinted, not recognizing who it was, thinking it strange he didn't appear to be looking at me now. A shadow from one of the chandeliers was covering his face so I couldn't tell who it was. He was sitting on the steps of the platform with his chin between his knees, almost in a seated fetal position. Even though he wasn't very welcoming, I wasn't going to walk out now without getting some information at least, so I started the long walk down the aisle toward him. As I was walking I heard a strange noise and saw a phone underneath one of the seats vibrating wildly. Then, as if on cue, a phone began ringing unanswered on the opposite side of the auditorium, interrupting the quiet.

A slightly uncomfortable feeling developed the closer I got to him. I was pretty sure he was the one who'd called out to me, yet he wasn't looking up, wasn't saying a word. Had I imagined he was the one, or was I going to be interrupting a stranger lost in his thoughts?

Then, when I was perhaps twenty feet away, a young teenage boy's voice burst out on the far side of the sanctuary, exploding with a stream of obscenities, words damning God, damning my Dad, and damning the whole world before one long-lasting wail and then sobs. The second his tirade started, my feet stopped moving and my eyes and mouth dropped open in disbelief, not only because I had just heard the most horrible words spewed like sewer across the church, but amazed at his gall in doing it while people were praying! What on earth had my Dad done to make him that angry? I was glad my Dad wasn't in the room to hear it. His outburst lasted maybe fifteen or twenty seconds, and it made me so uncomfortable that after the first couple of seconds, I began looking around at the scattered people to see their reaction. Solidifying my feelings of being in the middle of a dream, not one single person looked up or even acted like they had heard him.

I continued walking toward the front of the church, but then the man who had presumably called my name started moaning, and my hand began trembling again. This was no *ordinary* prayer meeting, and it didn't seem to be comforting anyone. I wasn't sure if it had anything to do with the plane crash or the terrorist acts or what, but as soon as I got the information I needed I wasn't going to be hanging around in here.

Now that I was close, I hesitated to approach the suddenly distraught man, so I paused, not quite ready to leave without talking to him first.

I began slowly moving forward again, passing an older lady I hadn't noticed because she was hunkered over so low in her seat, sniffling and quietly crying. The fear inside me was growing again. Had something happened to my Dad; were these people praying for *him*?

By this time I was standing directly in front of the man with his head still entrenched between his knees. I was sweaty, filthy, and tired; otherwise I might have waited for him to look up, but instead I said quietly, "Did you say my name?"

I could tell my voice didn't startle him. He had known I was there. But he still took his time lifting his head until he was finally looking straight up at me, squinting as if it hurt to open his eyes. "Jeremy!" I said, finally recognizing our singles pastor. "I'm so sorry; I didn't realize it was you," I said sincerely and apologetically. Jeremy was the newest addition to our church staff, having been with us less than a year. We had gone out to eat with him and his wife several times recently. He had such a great sense of humor and seemed to be doing such a good job with the singles.

I wasn't very tall but began to feel uncomfortable having him look directly up at me, so I sat down beside him on the steps. He still hadn't spoken a word, so I touched his hand gently and asked, "What's going on, Jeremy; are you okay?" I said, compounding my questions clumsily. I barely caught him glance at me with an inscrutable expression, yet he didn't immediately answer, nor suppress a loud sigh. I filled the awkward silence with my most important question, "Jeremy! Please! I need to know where Mark and Holly are; and Mom and Dad. Is everyone in the youth center? I need to find them!"

He raised his head a bit more stiffly, this time tilting his head as he looked directly into my eyes. I detected an uncharacteristic hardness in his voice as he said, "You're kidding, right? Where've you been?"

A bit stung by his harshness, I quickly explained, "I woke up with a headache and stayed home! Listen, Jeremy, I've had a horrible morning and I've been trying to get here for hours. I was coming to meet everyone for Mother's Day lunch!"

I didn't realize I'd spoken so loudly until an old guy on the first row of the balcony yelled out, "They ain't taking you to lunch *today*, girl!"

I was embarrassed and bewildered and upset. This strange rudeness coming from everyone was hurtful and frightening. As I looked toward the balcony, I tried to see what kind of person would pretend to know what my family was or wasn't planning on doing today, or what I'd done to deserve his comment for that matter. Unless the guy knew something I didn't. The fear must have shown on my face when I turned back to look at Jeremy. He grabbed my attention when he said sadly, "Annie." I decided to keep my mouth shut and just stare at him. After another pause he asked gently, "Have you watched the news or listened to the radio at *all* this morning?"

I shook my head slightly before saying a quiet, "No. I mean I know something's happened because I've seen a lot of accidents and fires and I saw the plane that hit the foyer. Was it another terrorist attack? Has my family been hurt?"

Jeremy closed his eyes again and I saw him barely swaying side to side. Did I imagine the tiniest of groans escaped his lips? "I don't think I can talk to you about this, Annie," he said in a grim tone. "Just go back home. Watch the news."

It was my turn to look at him like he was crazy. "Jeremy!" I said as I grabbed his arm. "I am not going anywhere until you tell me what you know," I said a bit too loudly with an insistence I couldn't really back up. He sighed again, staring at me with the most intense look, yet his eyes seemed tired and blank and bottomless. Since I had absolutely no idea what he was going to say, I knew better than to interrupt, so I just waited quietly.

"Annie, look around; what do you see?" he said flatly. I was confused. I had been in the sanctuary about ten minutes now and there were maybe thirty people in the huge room, all acting a bit strange, I thought.

"What do you mean? I see people crying and praying! What did I miss?" I asked, getting a bit impatient with his guessing game.

"Look behind the pulpit," he said angrily, forcing his words through clenched teeth.

I figured the electricity had gone out or someone had turned off the lights. The shadows being cast through the few windows in the sanctuary were not allowing enough light in to help me follow his directions. I squinted, looking in the direction of the pulpit, but it didn't help. Slowly getting to my feet, I walked up the rest of the steps toward the pulpit and could see something was on the floor behind it. When I reached the pulpit, I bent down and knelt beside what looked like my Dad's brown suit jacket crumpled on the floor. I felt a chill course through my body and my mind began racing. I whirled around ready to yell back to Jeremy, not realizing he had followed me and was kneeling right beside me. "Jeremy! Did my Dad have a heart attack? Is he at the hospital? Is he okay?" I could barely spit the words out, my breathing was so erratic. No wonder the whole church was acting so strange! Were they mourning my father? "Oh God—Jeremy—tell me he didn't die?" My heart was breaking to think I might not have been here in his last moments of life.

Jeremy didn't answer; instead he looked at me as if he wished I were a brighter pupil and that he didn't have to spell it out. "Annie, look underneath his jacket." With question marks still in my eyes, I switched my gaze back to the jacket I distinctly remembered Mom buying him last year for his birthday.

Knowing for sure now that some kind of catastrophe had occurred, I lovingly lifted the folds of the soft fabric of his jacket, preparing to fold it. But as I lifted the jacket from its resting place, my eyes lit on what was underneath the jacket. I looked up at Jeremy, then back again, trying to interpret what I was seeing. Dad's shirt and slacks were bunched up underneath his jacket, the belt was still in the loops and connected at the latch, and, embarrassingly, his old-fashioned underwear was there as well. I had given up on hearing Jeremy talk, so I just stared while my mind began shutting down.

"Jeremy, did Dad have a stroke or a heart attack? Why did they have to undress him here? Did paramedics do this?" Jeremy viciously grabbed Dad's slacks out of my hands, revealing the final items, Dad's dress shoes, with his socks tucked accordion-style inside them. "Jeremy?" I whispered pleadingly as chills were replaced with an unwelcome heat that began to course through my body.

"Annie," he said coldly. I have never heard a voice as hollow as his was at that moment. "I was standing right behind your Dad, waiting to give the announcements," he blurted out, as he no longer tried to control his sobbing. I had to strain to understand the rest of his sentence since his words were now intermingled with a strange, sad wailing, "and your Dad disappeared right before my eyes."

CHAPTER EIGHT

Sunday, four twenty-nine p.m.

NO WORDS IN any language can describe what washed over my spirit, soul, and body the moment those words left Jeremy's mouth. I had never before experienced heart palpitations or anything of that sort, but, without any exaggerating, my heart stopped beating. I distinctly felt I was having a heart attack. My body began trembling uncontrollably. His words sent a lightning bolt of shock, fear, and dread straight into my physical and spiritual heart. I felt the blood drain from my face and the light extinguish from my eyes as my inner core died. His eyes bore a hole straight through me. He must have seen the physical change in my body because he grabbed my arm and started urgently yelling, "Breathe, Annie!" as I simultaneously felt consciousness leave and slipped from his grasp, hitting the floor.

I fondly think back on that moment now. Those brief seconds of unconsciousness were the last moments of peace I will ever again experience. I was almost angry to be awakened moments after hitting the floor when I felt air hitting me in the face as Jeremy fanned me with a church bulletin. Coming back to consciousness, I heard him yelling over and over in my ear, "Annie, Annie!" Then I felt nauseous as a wave of sick realization from what I'd heard the moment before, hit me again. It felt as if I'd been viciously slapped in the face. Even in my stupor I found myself wishing I had hit my head and died on the spot, and I felt a strange anger rise up against Jeremy for not leaving me out cold. I was deeply disappointed when my heart began beating rapidly again.

I didn't realize then how many times that same longing for death would return over and over, again and again. And if possible, each time the desire hit, it grew stronger and stronger.

As I lay on my back, not far from where I had prayed many times at the end of services, I felt like someone had drained the energy from my body. I slowly, purposefully opened my eyes just to stop Jeremy's maddening screaming in my ears. He was still kneeling over me and our eyes met with a strange, unspoken, desperate sadness. In one last attempt to return to sanity, I mustered the faintest of whispers, so quiet he had to bend closer while I slowly and deliberately said, "Did you say what I think you said?"

Jeremy looked at me with the kind of pity reserved for the most horrible situations, and whispered back, "I'm *so* sorry. For you *and* for me. But Annie," he began, without trying to hide the horror in his eyes. Hot tears bubbled out of his eyes, dropping in multiples onto his shirt as he said, "I saw it with my very own eyes. It *really* happened. Just like we were taught." Before the last word was out of his mouth, I clinched my eyes closed, silently begging him to shut up. His words were verifying the deepest, darkest fear that had first arrested me moments earlier. And as he recounted his experience, it obviously reminded him of his own fate again. I kept my eyes closed as he crumpled in the opposite direction, sobbing and wailing and then screaming, "God, No! No! No!" over and over again as he pounded the platform with his fists. Tears streamed down the sides of my face.

Inside my head I kept screaming, "He's *got* to be wrong!" If what he was hinting at really happened, *I* wouldn't be here *either*! I whipped around to stare again at the pile of Dad's clothing Jeremy had used as visual reinforcement for the words he hadn't wanted to speak. I searched for any other explanation. There had to be one. I just needed to be able to think clearly. But unbeknownst to me, a sobbing moan had already begun rising deep within me. A mournful groan erupted without warning, without time to feel embarrassed or the need to stop it. I recognized the terrible noise, because I had heard its match coming from others today.

I knew Jeremy heard me, for he paused from his own grief, and I opened my eyes just in time to see his empathetic look. Through miserable tears and a brand new, aching fear, I cried out, "Are you *positive* that's what happened?" He looked at me with a strange expression, and right then my eyes began opening to a new truth and a hurtful realization, that the rest of my life would evolve around intensely private pain and each one of us was going to experience this separately. This would not be a group effort. Those of us left here would not be banding together in small groups, commiserating with one another. There would not be twelve step meetings where one by one we stood up, telling our personal horror stories, ending with "My name is Annie, and I was left behind that day..."

Instead, there was no doubt we were all alone in our individual grieving when Jeremy impatiently responded with a half smirk, half evil shriek, "*Look around, Annie!* Walk all over the stupid platform! Look in every chair! For God's sake, go look in the nursery and see if you can find *my baby*! There's no mistake! *We screwed up!*"

When he finished his tirade, a great, palpable silence descended upon the entire auditorium like a heavy, wet blanket. I knew without looking that every person in the auditorium was looking in our direction and it was now obvious to everyone what an uninformed fool I'd been. I had experienced shame and humiliation many times and had yet to come up with an adequate antidote. But if possible, this disgrace was worse than the combination of all other disgraces ever experienced.

Now that I'd been told what had happened, I understood some of the shock from those around me and how it was multifaceted because of the simple fact that the "preacher's daughter" was still here, proving something had desperately gone wrong in my life, not just theirs. Then topping it all off, was the obvious fact I hadn't been at church this morning but living in a bubble, perhaps the only person on the planet clueless about it until two minutes ago.

I'm really not stupid. It had to have been the combination of everything. Maybe because it was Sunday, coupled with the fact that it was Mother's Day, and the additional oddity of me not turning on the television before church, or not being able to listen to the radio as I drove around. The bubble had been wrapped securely around my mind, keeping me totally in the dark. But there's no point looking back now. It doesn't fix anything, and knowing it earlier wouldn't have changed the outcome.

Should I be ashamed it never crossed my mind for one fraction of an instant that something *other worldly* had occurred? The problem is if you never consider a thing, or imagine it happening, you're unprepared when it does. It had never crossed my mind that I would experience this. And for those who were *not* surprised, even believing something is true but so far off you don't need to worry about it yet, brings its own kind of unbelief. At this moment in time I would give anything to go back and have a moment to consider the worst possibility. For a chance to be shocked by imagining this day so it could have awakened me and changed my course of action and eternal future. But I hadn't done that and it hadn't happened that way. I felt myself going into shock again.

In my defense, I'd had at least one of these moments when I was a child just learning about God. I heard the story along with everyone else—that Jesus would one day come back for His followers and how we needed to stay ready for that day. I remembered having one of those "Aha" moments when I was about ten years old. Mom was always at the house when I came home from school. Except for that one time. I had come home to an empty house. The door was locked, and there was no note saying she would be back from the store or even a hint of where she might be. And for just a few minutes I remembered wondering. I can remember the icy fear that gripped my little, impressionable, pliable heart.

That memory brings pain now. That day my mind had been immediately drawn to things I was participating in, even as a ten year old, that I knew weren't acceptable to God. My heart convicted me immediately, and right when I was thinking about getting down on my knees, Mom pulled up in the driveway. Feeling a bit foolish, my fears dried up, and I never told anyone about it. I did remember praying the next Sunday, asking God to forgive me for those things, but that tiny fear I experienced that day was not even in the realm of comparison to the grim reality I was facing now.

I tried to remember the last time my conscience had spoken to me, even in a faint whisper, but sadly, I couldn't remember. I sat there dazed while thoughts flew in and out of my brain with no control over which ones came or went. I remembered hearing sermons about having a "seared conscience."[1] I could remember a teacher explaining it. How your inner voice could become hardened, callous, and unfeeling. How if you turned off the voice enough times, it stopped speaking. In my dull state, I could only wonder if that had been my problem. Or if seared wasn't a strong enough word. At the moment my conscience felt as crisp as a piece of burnt toast.

Why did it seem more despicable to be caught in this situation since my Dad was the pastor? That little piece kept slamming into my brain every few minutes, like a prosecutor yelling at the accused. Scriptures Dad always quoted kept returning to me, ones I didn't remember learning. Of course I went to Sunday School every week, but was never great at memorizing. Amazing though how those verses had no trouble mocking me now. I could remember one about my own heart deceiving me.[2] I never had understood that concept. I knew we weren't supposed to outright lie, cheat, or deceive others. I'd been on the receiving end of that a few times, and perhaps occasionally deceived others, but why on earth would I allow my *own heart* to deceive me? But suddenly, finally, I understood the verse perfectly. Because my heart *had* deceived me, it had totally convinced me I was okay when I wasn't, and the scripture had come to pass. It had kept me from "delivering my own soul."

As soon as Jeremy's words faded into the sanctuary carpet, my eyes burned as tears spouted out like a sprinkler head gone amok. Not only because of the unkind, unfeeling way in which he had responded, but mostly because I was just beginning to comprehend the enormity of his words. I wasn't about to let my mind try to grasp how different life would be yet. Then, unaware of my own actions, I slowly got up off the floor and began almost unconsciously doing what Jeremy had bitterly suggested I do.

I walked over to where the worship team would have been standing and saw several groups of clothes and personal effects in piles here and there. I walked over to the keyboard and saw clothes haphazardly strewn where Danny always stood as he led beautiful worship music. I saw his wedding ring and glasses teetering on the edge of the keyboard, stunned to silence and tears streaming down as I realized he no longer needed them where he was now. He had just gotten married a few weeks ago in a beautiful wedding ceremony. I touched his still-shiny wedding ring and folded his glasses in a private moment of respect.

My mind kept whirling as I chastised myself and internally criticized myself, screaming inside my brain while the torment began anew. Why had I *never* anticipated this day? In all of my imagined intelligence, had I been so stupid to assume the majority of us would just live and die, and because we believed in God and went to church, everything would end okay? I felt a very real anger rising up inside of me against whoever started the flawed way of thinking that assumed everyone who acknowledged God or lived "a good life" would end up in heaven. Every funeral I'd ever attended described the deceased as "in a better place now" and "resting in peace" and I knew I wasn't the only one who had fallen for that lie. It had become a common thought process for the world, *much less* Christians who knew better.

And then I remembered another Bible verse I had heard preached over the years, and it did nothing but sting now. The verse mentioned that not very many people would get into heaven or something to that effect.[3] I had obviously not taken it literally, and for sure never imagined it would describe me. Questions and accusations continued darting back and forth into every corner of my mind, but there were no answers to be found. No sufficient rebuttals.

I walked over to where the choir stood. I had lifelong friends who sang in the choir. The men stood right in the middle with the altos on their right and sopranos on their left. I reflectively looked at each seat, almost picturing those who usually stood there, then wondering why the choir hadn't been full that morning, especially for Mother's Day. Then my eyes opened wide, realizing it could only mean one thing. Every place there was a gap—where no clothes were strewn—meant a person had walked away. The tears of remorse and shock returned.

I stepped off the platform and like a zombie began walking toward where my mom sat. Always the second row, on the aisle. I sat down beside her seat and a quiet whimper emerged as I saw the new Mother's Day suit we had just shopped for two days ago. The beautiful silky fabric, muted pinks and purples had slithered to the floor in a delicate heap on top of new white sandals. My eyes strayed to her purse, wide open on the seat to her left, a pack of gum balanced on top of it with one piece half pulled out of the wrapper, like she had just been about to pop it in her mouth. She never used the boxes of Kleenex kept at the end of each row, instead liking old fashioned hankies, and I saw hers now, the one with her initials on the corner, poking out of her Bible. Each little detail screamed out, slapping me in the face and my heart.

Numbness like a cloud seemed to be sheltering my mind, almost like a gift, but the problem was each minute that passed, from seeing Dad's clothes and now Mom's, the cloud was beginning to disappear and a deep-set panic was replacing it. I reverted back to childhood memories as I contemplated how Mom and Dad had raised me to *expect* this day, but in the end I had failed them *and* myself. And then I stood up, a wild look on my face and a new clarity. A guttural *"No!"* came out of me as if for the first time realizing that if Dad and Mom were really gone, then Mark and Holly…

I left Mom's row, looking wildly in all directions for where Mark and Holly might have been sitting. "I didn't know!" my mind was crying out. I had no idea where he sat when I wasn't with him, but I wandered over to where we normally sat together, looking up and down the rows. I chastised myself again for not even opening my eyes to greet him that morning; because of that, I didn't even know what color shirt he was wearing.

But then I spotted his well-worn Bible, and my heart sank. He was gone. He had left me. *Oh God!* How on earth…? My despair was intense. I knew my composure was leaking away and a physical depression was coming over me like a fog. I sat down on the seat where Mark had been only hours earlier, picking up his shirt and holding it to my face while I cried like a baby, eventually hyperventilating and choking several times. A palpable loneliness enveloped me, without one soul around who cared or anyone having any power to soothe me. I was eventually able to swallow and took a deep breath, deliberately breathing in the smell of cologne emanating from his shirt, realizing this was the closest I would ever be to him again.

As sad as funerals are for loved ones, I was sometimes comforted by being able to memorialize, remember, and reminisce about ones we had lost. Looking at them a final time, touching their hand, and giving them an official "good-bye." As hard as funerals were, it was better than what I had to face now. There was nothing to hold on to, say goodbye to, or touch a final time. There would not be a reason to plan funerals. There were no bodies.

I so desperately didn't want to be here anymore, on earth, but especially in church now. I didn't care to have people watching me and have to hear gasps every time someone saw me. I gently folded Mark's shirt, mentally telling myself I would never wash it. I folded his slacks, placing them on top of the shirt. Like Dad's, Marks' socks were crumpled inside his shoes. I noticed poignantly that even his cross necklace had fallen into one of his shoes. I saw a glint on top of his shoes and squinted until I saw it was his contact lenses. Of all things. Tears sprang to my eyes. With not a twinge of jealousy, I realized his eyes were perfect now because he had been changed, had literally received perfect eyesight "in the twinkling of an eye."[4] I couldn't follow where those thoughts wanted to take me, or I would literally go insane and never make it out of there. I knew later, though, there would be no way to stop them.

I finished folding Mark's things and saw his Bible on the seat beside him opened with a note pad and pen, like he was ready to take notes. He had always been a doodler, and I saw he'd written my name and his, side by side as if we were back in school. The tears returned. College sweethearts no more. Then I saw his cell phone flashing and vibrating, and I knew too well who it was who had left him messages. I opened his phone with a despondent sigh and saw he had my voicemail message and texts. Every one of them after he had already been taken from this earth. And I had been utterly oblivious.

With a new level of regret and shame, I realized they must have already been in heaven a few hours before I discovered what happened. Then my mind clouded over again without warning, like when the barriers go down right before a train crosses the tracks. In the same way, my mind must have known I was in danger of going over the edge if I analyzed it too much right now, so it just shut down. I had no power to stop the trembling though.

I could hear Jeremy, still sitting on the platform, begin crying again, and it woke me from my stupor. He sounded so pitiful that my motherly instinct wanted to go comfort him, yet I felt an equally strong need to be comforted myself. It felt strange to feel myself completely being overtaken with self-pity. How were we all going to live in a world if everyone felt like this? My urge to escape this painful place was getting stronger, so I decided to go find Holly's things and leave as soon as possible. My heart felt old, worn out, wrinkled, and hard.

I walked across the auditorium to the section where the younger generations usually congregated. I felt like I was watching myself through a tunnel, walking about in a daze. A strange, unpleasant sensation, like I was in self-preservation mode, overwhelmed me. The first five or six rows had jeans, shirts, dresses, or skirts on almost every chair. Shoes, purses, Bibles, and odd things like glasses, belts, and cell phones were strewn everywhere. There were water bottles, gum wrappers, and evidence of lots of activity just a few hours earlier.

I knew some in the college and youth group had experienced a real reawakening over the last several months and I often watched them worship freely and earnestly. Thinking back, I remembered worshipping earnestly myself sometimes, but then at other times my mind was a million miles away, a painful reminder now that outward worship alone wasn't a true indication of anything. But by the looks of all the piles of clothing, I had to guess quite a few had been sincere. After the first few rows, though, it began to be a bit more sporadic. I saw two or three chairs with things on them, then three or four empty chairs. Knowing what that meant brought profound sadness. No rhyme or reason. I kept looking. I had no idea what Holly had worn, so I looked for a purse or shoes I might recognize. Then I started feeling anxious when I couldn't find any of her things.

I walked back up to the front row, going chair by chair again, hoping I had just walked by her things in the dark. I saw Bibles with names imprinted on them, obviously graduation or baptism presents. Curious, I looked at a couple of the names. I nodded, knowing several of them and how they really had seemed like "good kids," and remembering how glad I was when Holly hung out with them instead of others I knew who seemed headed down the wrong path. I'll admit I was a bit shocked by one stack of clothes I found, because I would never have dreamed she would be gone. Proving again, that when it comes to the question of where someone spends eternity, assuming means nothing.

I saw no sign of Holly's clothes on the first, second, or third row. Rounding the end of the third row with the intention of methodically continuing my way up the fourth, I suddenly heard a muffled sob over in a corner almost totally obscured by shadows. I backed out of the row I was in, curious as to what I'd heard since I hadn't realized anyone was close to where I was standing. Squinting into the darkness, I tried to inconspicuously walk in that direction, when the back door of the church opened, shining a beam of light right into the corner. It was then I saw with horror something I hadn't yet considered.

I saw about fifteen young people huddled so close it looked like they were creating a human fortress. Their heads were lowered as though sharing deep, dark secrets; however I didn't hear a peep except for that stray sob a few seconds earlier. I saw shoulders shuddering like people do when they're trying to hide that they're crying, but their bodies weren't cooperating. I hadn't even thought of how young people would be affected, especially if their parents and siblings were gone.

I was more than likely looking at a group of kids I'd known since they were born, suddenly orphaned. How would they survive? I couldn't imagine how I was going to survive *myself* right now, and I was a self-sufficient, fully employed, adult woman. How could they finish school, or would it even matter now? Would they be able to live in their parents' homes alone or would there be hundreds of thousands of homeless young people? At the present the government didn't allow those underage to live by themselves, so would huge orphanages be necessary to accommodate them or would they roam homeless, undetected, uncared for? How could they survive without parents or grandparents? Among the ones I saw, maybe only half of them drove. But even if they could, I didn't see any way for them to be able to support themselves. My heart grew even heavier thinking about all the potential consequences.

I was just turning back to my own task at hand, when the young man closest to me suddenly turned, looking me full in the face. A multi-leveled pain washed over me in waves as Sam's wide-eyed, mournful look and quiet gasp showed his disbelief. The shame so dangerously near the pinnacle of my emotions, resurfaced instantaneously. Sam had been in our home so many times. Talking around the kitchen table about his future, about life and God, but yet here we both were. Proving that neither one of us had been experts about any of the subjects.

Our gaze ended up being a second too long until it became uncomfortable, as I realized sadly, that both of us had just been talking the talk and not walking the walk as I remembered some old-fashioned preacher saying. My next wave of pain included an overwhelming hopelessness for Sam, knowing the future he had mapped out was over. That had to also be part of his mourning now. If he hadn't realized it yet, his life would never be normal again. All his dreams dashed. I knew his parents had scrimped and saved for him to be able to go to our church's Christian school and had worked hard to qualify for a loan so he could go to a prestigious business school. I knew exactly what would happen next. Once the school discovered his parents were no longer alive, as co-signers of his loan, it would be rescinded. I had heard he was almost engaged to Angela, and with my peripheral vision I tried to see if she was in the huddled group. I had a feeling she was missing, and that had to be an additional source of pain.

With nothing to say to each other, we exchanged mutual looks of empathy before he turned back to his group. Right before turning back to continue my own search, I saw one of my daughter's best friends out of the corner of my eye. She was shaking and sobbing, lying almost prostrate across another girl, seeking relief that wouldn't be found. Carrie had been in our home more times than I could count and was one of the college leaders, along with Holly, who helped mentor the younger high school students in the youth group. I had been so relieved when Holly began hanging around her a few years ago, and I distinctly remembered pushing Holly to "be more like Carrie." As I watched Carrie sob, I desperately hoped Holly hadn't taken my advice and that I would still find her clothes somewhere. I despised the bare nakedness this day was uncovering. I had loved Carrie, in her own right, and not only as Holly's friend. But I had misjudged her. And myself.

After the shock of seeing her, I purposed not to look any closer at the cluster of young people. I didn't want to know who all was there. Didn't want to have more kids on my mind to worry or wonder about. Just as I wanted very few people to know I was still here. I didn't want to stand and stare, so despite the deep pity I felt, I continued my search with an urgent energy.

I *knew* this was where Holly usually sat, but a strange uneasiness kept creeping into my soul. *Surely* she wasn't in the group of kids sitting on the floor and I hadn't seen her? "God, No!" I screamed silently. It was bad enough thinking *I* had screwed up royally and was now stuck in this God-forsaken world, but please, please, please, not Holly. I already knew I was going to be shocked and surprised over and over as it became evident who had disappeared and who was still here. And I hadn't even begun processing my own personal shock.

I slowly finished inspecting the fourth row, rounded the end of the fifth row, and began searching with a determination to look at each chair one by one, when I saw Jeremy intently watching me out of the corner of my eye. I figured he already knew if Holly was gone, since he had been here in the aftermath. But I couldn't bear for someone else to tell me the devastating news if she hadn't disappeared…or the devastating news if she had.

Amazing how both scenarios would be distressing. But I knew both would be. Whichever one it was, it would kill me. If I had to look on every seat in the entire sanctuary, I would. She might have been in the restroom or in a classroom when it happened. I would go down every hall in the church if I had to. What on earth were people going to do if they didn't know? I had never, ever experienced hopelessness like this. It was settling in my spirit, obviously determined to stay.

I knew my face showed the fear I was feeling as I inspected each seat in the next to the last row. There was a slim chance she could have sat in another section, but not usually. I began the trek down the final row, and my eyes fell on a seat in the middle of the row. Holly loved the color turquoise. I sighed. There they were. It looked like she'd worn that cute little turquoise and white dress with her high, stiletto heels, the kind I stopped wearing years ago. Her coordinating purse was there along with matching jewelry that had fallen and scattered as she left the earth. I reached the seat where just a few hours earlier she had been worshipping God in her own quiet, sincere way. My eyes closed tightly and a sob escaped, picturing Holly with Him.

And then the most heartfelt tears I had ever shed in my life began to flow like a plug had been yanked out of my heart. I knelt tenderly, respectfully in front of her seat, burying my face in her things, absorbing as much of her presence as was left. The few years I had loved her had not been nearly enough. We had started a new phase in our lives, enjoying a mother/adult-daughter relationship. But it had been wrenched from me, never to be enjoyed again. A million new regrets flooded my soul.

While I mourned my loss of her, at the exact same time I felt an ultimate relief knowing she was gone. It's so difficult as a parent to figure out if your child is really getting it. Understanding God's love. Getting the whole repentance and forgiveness thing. Being willing to fight against devilish peer pressure. I knew she was involved in the leadership of our youth group, but as evidenced by the many seats *without* clothes in them, being involved in church or the youth group or even being on staff hadn't guaranteed anything whatsoever.

Holly had never been especially outspoken or demonstrative in her worship or faith like some were, so I had just *hoped* she had the right kind of relationship with God. But now, sitting here with her precious, dainty clothes nestled in my arms, I had proof positive that she had given up the easy, comfortable way of life on earth for a better, eternal life. I cried with thankfulness and relief for a daughter whom I knew for sure now, loved God and had been a true follower of His.

It was going to be a long, excruciating process, the hardest journey I'd ever taken, trying to come to grips with the fact that Holly and Mark and Mom and Dad were gone. But the other side of the coin quickly reared its ugly face. Although I felt comfort with the thought that Holly would not be tormented in the way I was already experiencing, the discovery of her clothes meant beyond a shadow of a doubt, no question about it, I was totally and completely alone.

An orphan. A widow. And childless. All in less time than it took to blink.

CHAPTER NINE

Sunday, five eighteen p.m.

IT TOOK ME a little while to compose myself after finding her things. I sat on the floor in front of her chair for maybe thirty minutes, allowing memories of her to flood my mind, from the time she was a baby, to graduation, to a myriad of times in between, while at the same time desperately trying to stop the same hurtful thoughts. Because with every memory came the heartache stubbornly tagging along. For a few moments I had gotten much needed privacy by crouching between the rows. And in that brief respite, the pain I felt from missing her was more overwhelming than the deep shame I had been previously wallowing in. My only child. The one we had prayed for before we even knew we were pregnant. In God's presence. Separated from her forever. Now I completely understood how people lost their will to live.

My only desire now was to get out of this place. It was bringing me no comfort, and I didn't want to be seen or to see anyone else. I just needed to gather my family's things before I fell to pieces. Holly's oversized purse easily held her clothes, jewelry, and shoes, so I stuffed them in. I felt like I was visiting a morgue, forced to identify the remains of loved ones, inside my own living nightmare. The emotions accompanying my trek around the auditorium were a jumbled mess. I had always been the *responsible* one; maybe you could call me the *Martha* of the family.

Overly distracted with the details of life. But now was not the time to critique my many faults. I just needed to gather the last things my family had worn on earth. I couldn't bear to leave their things here for people to look through, talk about, or plunder. Who knew if this place would even be locked up tonight, or if in a few hours it would be stripped bare.

It was amazing the speed with which wild thoughts raced in and out of my mind. Conversations with myself, both accusing and full of fear. From debilitating, painful memories to ramblings of curious wonderings of what the future would hold. I found myself wondering if this building would even continue to be a church. I doubted seriously that my Dad had ever discussed what might happen if the majority of the church turned up missing. Because why would they care? Surely no church had ever broached that subject in legal resolutions, so I guess that would ensure that most Christian churches around the world would soon be facing foreclosure. I looked around at the beautiful building Dad and members had lovingly planned. It upset me to picture total strangers occupying this place or creating some generic community center out of it, or worse, letting it slowly disintegrate.

But responsibility wasn't the only feeling I was experiencing. A war was going on inside me, doing its best to convince me the opposite of what Jeremy had told me had happened. Wasn't being taken in the rapture and going to heaven one of the major reasons people chose even to serve God in the first place? I felt like a consummate failure. And I had known shame, had struggled with it my entire life. From a young age I had felt as if I was on display, which wasn't a good thing from my perspective. If I didn't follow every rule my parents, teachers, or friends put out there, if I didn't seem to be making everyone happy, or wasn't the most obedient, I felt like a failure. I was always begging for mercy, never fully reaching for or accepting the grace. I felt like I had to walk a chalk line, and the line seemed so blurry at times. I couldn't stand out in a bad way—sure couldn't let everyone think the preacher's daughter was a *bad girl,* but, ironically, I also wasn't supposed to stand out in a good way either. Don't go for the glory, don't be an attention seeker. I couldn't seem to win and didn't know how to balance the two extremes.

I never did figure out why anyone, including myself, would think just because my Dad was a minister, I would, should, or could be perfect or better than the average kid. Regardless of whether I was supposed to feel that way, I failed miserably. Yet I wondered now if that had really been the truth, or if my heart or the enemy had bombarded me, deceiving me. I remembered hearing back in youth camp that you could get a new heart.[1] Had I been stubborn and somehow held onto my old one, unwilling to give it up? My mind was finding it hard to accept that the epitome of everyone's hopes and fears had come to pass today. The big hurrah. The finish line. The final ta da. And yep, here I was. Left behind. With all my imperfections now screaming to be discovered by the world. That I had been a holier than thou co-worker. A nagging wife, a micro-managing mother. A lifetime church member who hadn't been able to get it right in the end. My self-accusing voice was in full swing now, and I was hitting them out of the ballpark. Only to find that none of the hats I'd attempted to wear over the years had been enough to score in the end.

I thought back to the moment I walked up to Jeremy and how he had looked at me strangely. I had assumed it was because he was hesitant to be the bearer of bad news about Dad. But now that I'm so much wiser, I realize his face was barely hiding his own questions about why I was still here. Just like I was now wondering the same thing; why our associate pastor was here. I could only imagine what it was going to be like from now on whenever I saw someone who knew who I was and what I had purported to be. Would this day forever hold such pain that most of us would pull back from contact with each other because we couldn't bear to see each other again? I dreaded experiencing the amazed stares, unspoken questions, the whispering, sneers, outright sarcasm, and finger pointing that would follow. Life was going to be unbearable. I knew it.

A couple of hours ago, I would have described myself as a pretty positive person. But like a strange metamorphosis, almost a physical sensation, I could feel my personality changing. If I didn't know better, it was almost like an evil presence in the air, biding its time, beginning to surround me, ready to fully overtake at a moment's notice. And I didn't have the faintest idea how to combat it. I glanced around, wondering if anyone else was experiencing the same dread. What was life going to be like now?

When all hope is gone, when your belief system has been tested and come up short, when your world is turned upside down and the future is filled with trepidation and questions, what are you supposed to do with that? How were we supposed to cope? I heard myself taking quick, gasping, unfulfilling breaths. I felt like I was under black, murky water, desperate to take a breath, but with the surface exasperatingly too far away. I needed to be alone before I lost it.

I went behind the platform and found a trash bag to gather the rest of the clothes. Walking back into the sanctuary, I began wondering if I could be having a stroke or a heart attack, or if it was all in my mind. I would welcome dying right now.

Except...I hadn't fixed anything yet. And that sent a bigger seed of fear straight to the root of my heart. I shook my head, trying to get rid of that thought while I walked over to Dad's clothes and picked them up, then to Mom's and finally to Mark's. Lastly I put Holly's purse on top and slung the bag over my shoulder. Sorrow overwhelmed me as I touched their things. My head was pounding as I tried not to dwell on my physical actions, but it eerily felt like it was my last possible act of love for them. And none of it even mattered.

Straightening back up, I saw people still coming in and out of the sanctuary. I did my best to stay in the shadows. Some people I recognized, some merely looked familiar, and some you could tell were just gawkers who didn't even belong to our church. I found myself getting angry at them. Couldn't they see we were all in pain and disillusioned? Could they be kind enough not to shove this helpless situation in our faces? Every few seconds I saw other church members popping up from corners or between pews where they had probably been stationed for hours now. With a sentimental eye, I looked around the dark sanctuary a final time, wondering if I would ever want to return or have the need.

Then, suddenly, my eyes sprang open, remembering the reason I entered the sanctuary in the first place. It seemed like hours ago. With a snort of self-derision, I remembered being intent on warning the whole *prayer meeting* that the church was about to explode and go up into flames. But instead? The surprise had been totally, completely on me. No wonder those inside hadn't been worried about a silly plane. I found myself wishing the plane *would* fall and end the throbbing in my heart. All reminders of this place would forever be painful.

Deciding it was past time to leave, my eyes caught Jeremy's across the room. I was too exhausted to let my emotions get out of hand again, but I owed him a goodbye. Who knew if I would ever see him again. I couldn't imagine my life ten minutes from now, much less months, years... Another painful sigh escaped my lips, and I couldn't bear to complete the thought. I walked toward Jeremy, carrying the sack slung over my shoulder and feeling like a vagabond with no home. I felt guilty for not asking about his wife, but then had to assume she was also gone, otherwise he wouldn't have been so distraught. So with his wife and newborn baby gone, he was alone in the world, just like me.

Matching step for step, we met in the middle of the sanctuary without motioning or saying a word. As we got closer, we avoided each other's eyes. I wondered if this kind of awkwardness would be alive and well long after the current shock was over. When we were within inches of each other, we finally looked eye to eye. I saw sympathy in his eyes and mine mirrored his. Pity for each other and pity for ourselves. I knew if I didn't fight it, it would easily turn into a pit of deep depression that I wouldn't be able to escape. I wasn't yet sure I would be strong enough to fight it...or if I even wanted to.

I took the lead, laying my sack down and giving him the proverbial "Christian" side hug while patting his shoulder. But then suddenly we both realized it wasn't enough, perhaps because we knew neither one of us might ever get a real hug in this life again, so I opened my arms and gave him a bear hug, like his own mother might have done if she'd been here. Except I knew his mother and I could guarantee she wasn't still here. As our faces touched, I felt the tears on his cheek that he'd gotten tired of wiping away. Myself? I was wept out at the moment. Numbness was settling in. We hugged like long-lost relatives for several seconds, and in an odd way it made it better to share our sorrow. Our pain. Our regret. I knew for just a moment our empathy connected as we attempted to comfort each other as best we could. Then, suddenly, the depth of despair I was feeling started coming too near the surface and it scared me, so I pulled back. As we separated, we must have both decided to not even try coming up with more empty words, so I picked up my bag and turned quickly with a half wave.

But before taking more than a couple of steps, I turned back and whispered lamely, "I'm *so* sorry, Jeremy." I paused, searching for more words, but they wouldn't come. Then, remembering that I usually called his wife, Jessica, when I needed to get in touch with them, I said, "Since we don't know what's going to happen, do you want to exchange phone numbers?" He barely nodded, and, without a word, took out his cell phone. After we saved each other's numbers, we both knew there was nothing left to say or do. A thought crossed my mind that we could both probably use some company or something to eat, but I couldn't bear the thought of either one, so I merely said, "Keep in touch, Jeremy" with a tiny, forced, wry smile.

I picked up the bag of clothes and walked down the interminably long aisle toward the back door. If I was lucky, maybe the airplane would crash down on me as I walked underneath it, or maybe the fuel would find a spark and explode, killing us all instantly. It frightened me to ponder how many suicidal thoughts had gone through my mind in just the last hour. I wondered if these feelings would get stronger and harder to ignore, and if I should be alarmed if my destructive thoughts tried to find an avenue of escape, as I walked directly under the still-dripping plane in the foyer.

Feeling the finality of my movements, on a whim right before leaving the church, I decided to follow Jeremy's angry advice and go to the children's center. Meandering in that direction, I still occasionally heard doors open and close as people continued walking in and out of the sanctuary. Someone behind me entered through the front doors of the church and I could hear them walking through the slivers of glass spewed all over the foyer. I had absolutely no desire to run into anyone else I knew. The few bits of conversation I'd already shared had been extremely painful, so I lowered my head while I walked the same path I used to take years earlier when I would drop Holly off in the nursery.

I gratefully reminisced about every single nursery worker, every Sunday School teacher that had patterned for Holly what true Christianity was all about. Holly had learned God's way from early childhood, and I was so thankful to know she had followed what she'd been taught. The old scripture encouraging us to be childlike came back to me,[2] and I found myself wishing I'd followed Holly's path as well, instead of just remembering Scripture verses.

What once were joyful memories only brought pain now. My heart fell when I heard someone coming toward me through the narrow hallway. I didn't want any more small talk, so I did my best to shield my face with the bag of clothes slung over my shoulder. I must not have done a great job, because even though the person didn't stop, it didn't keep them from letting out an audible gasp as they walked by. There was no question I had never experienced true humiliation before today. This shame would never be compared to anything anyone had experienced before. The old phrase "airing your dirty laundry in public" just barely scratched this surface. Everyone's biggest secret was no longer hidden.

It was a surreal experience from the moment I walked into the Children's Center. I wasn't at all prepared for what I saw. What I had innocently *expected* to see was an exaggeration of the darkened sanctuary. Perhaps a few people here or there mourning, or maybe not even one person at all since I knew every young child, baby, or toddler in the entire universe was unequivocally in heaven at this very moment. What a sobering thought that was. But immediately upon opening the door, I regretted my decision and almost changed my mind. The area was definitely somber, but everywhere I looked I saw parents. There must have been over a hundred people lining the halls and in and out of the nurseries. It seemed that moms and dads and couples had rushed the Children's Center soon after it happened. The few adult-sized chairs were filled, but most were just sitting on the floor in the maze of hallways and nurseries with their backs to the wall, staring at nothing in particular with a now familiar glazed look on their faces.

The strangest thing was not hearing one child's voice. No giggles, tired cries, or first words. Despite the crowd, there was almost total silence, except for an adult whimper here or there. I sighed for parents who would never experience the joy of their child's first day of school or teaching them to ride a bicycle, much less graduation days or giving hands in marriage. What was the world going to be like without children to keep us young, cheer us when life was overwhelming, and, most importantly, give us a purpose to keep going? Then I closed my own eyes as a tear escaped, realizing I would never experience the joy of spoiling future grandchildren, never feel them hug my neck with the kind of unconditional love only a child gives.

Looking at the empty faces of these young parents was disturbing. And just as disturbing was the fact that no husbands or wives were comforting each other. I scanned the first hallway and then the other, and although I saw the occasional husband and wife sitting side by side, not one of them was hugging or leaning into each other or even holding hands. Every single one of them was obviously in their own private hell, with not even enough sympathy left for their spouse.

But I understood. Although we were all sharing the same shame and shock and loss—and everyone desperate to be rescued—there was nothing in any of us that felt like participating in group therapy. No matter how empathetic I momentarily felt as I observed each hopeless person, I knew none of us had enough comfort to give others, because, inexplicably, each one of us was here for different reasons. Husbands and wives couldn't even fully share the grief they were feeling. This was going to be like solitary confinement without bars. In a way, I felt sorrier for those going home *with* someone experiencing the same pain and unbearable bitterness. It might be worse than the loneliness I knew I was going to experience.

The only reason I didn't turn back around was that I didn't see a single person look up when I entered the area. No one seemed curious or cared. I was shocked that they wanted to stay here. Then I knew. They were dreading the moment they had to go home and see the empty nurseries and cribs. I continued walking unnoticed through the middle of the hallway toward the nurseries.

I reached the door of the infant nursery first. There were rows and rows of dainty white cribs with pink and blue blankets and beautifully painted murals. It was a serene, protected atmosphere, and I knew parents had always felt secure leaving their precious bundles of joy here. As I walked in, the door's spring hinge silently closed behind me and I was alone.

Surprisingly, I was welcomed by the quiet, peaceful, softly lit room that didn't feel as hopeless as the sanctuary had. There were probably twenty-five cribs in the room and on first glance they'd all been full. I walked over to the first one, touching the pink blanket and dainty white lacy long dress. Then I remembered. Today had also been "Dedication Sunday." Each year they planned a special celebration on Mother's Day to offer a prayer of blessing over new babies. I wondered if this baby's parents had joined their daughter when she escaped this world.

Each crib had a miniature marker board attached to it with the baby's and parents' names written on it. I didn't recognize the first name or the second. I didn't even know the exact time "it" happened yet, so maybe they hadn't even gotten to the dedication part of the service when it happened. I slowly walked, crib by crib by crib. Every single crib had its own story. I recognized some of the names. One couple had gotten pregnant after fifteen years of marriage. The whole church had celebrated when their baby was born. I hoped they were with their precious boy now.

The next to the last crib was the one I had subconsciously been looking for. Jeremy's sweet, cherished daughter, Cassie, had been in this crib. Her parents had dressed her in a simple pink and white dress and tiny white patent leather shoes. And then I looked down. Right in front of the crib on the floor was a ladies pair of high heeled shoes and a beautiful, bright sundress befitting a mother on her first Mother's Day.

It wasn't the nursery worker's clothes because they wore special smocks, and there were several of those scattered around. These clothes had to belong to Jessica, Jeremy's wife. She'd probably been saying goodbye to her baby daughter when she dropped her off in the nursery. I wondered if Jeremy had run in here as soon as he figured out what happened, or if he hadn't been able to come yet. What was the use? I pictured the mayhem that must have taken place seconds after it happened and it chilled me to the core. I was glad I hadn't witnessed it.

I decided to make one more stop before I left. It almost felt like I was making a final lap of the church in case I never came again. I left the infant nursery with decisive steps, passing by each of the toddler rooms, seeing no purpose in even glancing in. I opened the miniature sanctuary that was decorated for the elementary children, and it seemed so bizarre that I caught my breath. It had obviously been story time because there were rows and rows of almost perfect half circles of solid heaps of clothes starting mere inches from the platform. There must have been at least a hundred children sitting, listening to a story about Jesus, when suddenly, they were with Him. If I hadn't been currently mourning my own regrets and failures, I could have enjoyed the thought of millions of babies and children entering heaven at the same moment, the King of Kings welcoming them with open arms. It must have been a beautiful sight, and tears slipped out again.

I sat down on the platform stairs facing the floor where every child's new spring clothes were gently piled. Deep down, I was glad the ultimate plan included every single, innocent, pure child. Not a single one left behind. God had lovingly accepted those not yet accountable for the fact that we were all born into sin. He had let them escape what was going to be the most fearful times any of us would ever experience. How appropriate, I thought.

I had assumed that I was alone as I pictured their heavenly reunion, when I heard a sob in a far corner. I tried to squint unobtrusively, and although I didn't recognize her, I now saw a lady sitting in one of the small children's chairs in the back corner of the room. And she was rubbing her stomach. I sighed deeply, comprehending her horror. She looked like she had been maybe seven or eight months pregnant. Obviously unconcerned that she had an audience, she started moaning louder, "He's not moving! God, no, No, NO, please give me back my baby."

My heart could take no more. I would only keep getting more and more morbidly depressed if I saw any more. Ignoring her desperate cries, I tiredly lifted myself up from the steps, turning to leave the room, when my eye caught another movement on the opposite side of the platform. I instantly regretted being distracted, when I recognized a young man, one of Holly's friends, who I knew helped in children's church. I couldn't imagine what this day had been like for him. To be in a room and literally see hundreds of children and fellow workers disappear while you stand motionless in front of them. I knew how sensitive the young man was, and I feared he would have nightmares for a long time to come.

I wasn't sure any of us would escape them.

CHAPTER TEN

Sunday, six twenty-four p.m.

I WENT OUT the back door of the Children's Center. There was no way I could walk back through the hallways filled with grieving parents. I was flustered myself, lightheaded from the mental agony, and weary of carrying my trash bag. I was drained. Inside and out. I longed for the privacy of my dark bedroom.

Rounding the outside corner of the side building, I headed toward the main parking lots, still shocked at the sight of all the cars as if church was going strong. I wondered if there would be parking lots full of unclaimed cars for days or weeks all over the world. How appropriate, I guess, that it happened when so many were actually worshipping Him. And how inappropriate for those of us who hadn't been.

I wanted to run one final errand before I left the property. I knew there was a good chance this place would be ransacked and maybe even burned to the ground if the plane fell. Whether by fire or smoke or vandals, right now would probably be the last chance to get anything from my Dad's office. I was close to the rear entrance and welcomed the chance of slipping in unnoticed. As I put my hand on the doorknob, I was reminded by the pain that I still had a sliver of glass from my front window lodged somewhere.

I wasn't exactly sure why I needed to visit my Dad's office; I just knew I had to. If I had all the time in the world, I would have gotten someone to help me move every book and piece of paper to peruse at a later date. At the moment, though, it felt eerie and lonely and a tiny bit disrespectful to be heading into my Dad's office, knowing where he was now.

Reaching his office, I saw the door slightly ajar and knew something wasn't right. Dad never left his door open; in fact, I had been afraid it might be locked. I tiptoed the last few steps and saw that the wood had been dug out around the lock. I hated the fear that seemed to have moved in and set up shop inside me. Was it growing bigger because of my imagined vulnerability or the fact that I was actually in danger now? I wasn't sure, but I didn't like it.

The fear told me to forget it, go home, and hide out until I figured it all out, but anger at whoever had broken into Dad's office won out. So without thinking through any possible consequences, I did my best to startle whoever was in there by shoving the door open so hard it banged back against the wall. But instead of fearing the occupants, I saw the pitiful group of young people who had been huddled in the corner of the sanctuary. They were sitting on Dad's love seat, his chairs, and the floor. It was obvious they were just trying to protect themselves and stay together. Needing to touch another human being; to delay the abject loneliness the orphaned kids were already experiencing.

It was obvious I surprised them, and I was a bit embarrassed myself. I looked around, seeing a myriad of expressions. I knew all but a couple of them. Some looked heartbroken, upset, and needy. Others were looking at me with "HELP" desperately written on their faces. But a few surprisingly looked hardened, perhaps even more rebellious than before, despite what had just happened to all of us. The remaining ones? I knew that look well. It was mixed up pieces of pride and sarcasm and resentment but with a big dose of regret. The overwhelming vibe I immediately gleaned was that they felt they belonged in my Dad's office as much as I did, since I was a loser just like they were. And they were right on all accounts.

I wasn't going to prolong it, so I meekly said, "I just need to get a few things and I'll get out of your hair." It must not have been what they expected, because no one said a word, although every eye followed me.

I felt like an intruder. I walked behind Dad's desk, picking up a journal he used and another one of his Bibles. I gathered some CDs and pictures from his credenza. There were simple reminders of him that upset me just by looking at them. His penmanship was unique, and I would never forget it. I wished I could do this privately and contemplatively, rather than feeling rushed and anxious as they stared at me. It was strange because, on one hand, I felt sorry for them because I knew some of what was ahead for all of us, but, on the other hand, I had a sniggling fear and was keenly aware they could do anything to me they wanted to. I just wanted out.

I opened a couple more drawers, saw a personal folder and a book he was currently reading, and began grabbing all that would fit in my bag. Almost finished with my scavenging, I opened his top drawer and saw some cash underneath a paperweight. It was obvious the kids had only wanted privacy otherwise they would have already confiscated it. I grabbed it, deciding I had enough. I was done.

Walking toward the door, I said, "You guys are welcome to stay in here," as if I had the authority to make them leave, "but I have to warn you—there's a good chance that plane is going to fall soon, and when it does, this whole building will probably go up in flames. You really need to find a better place to stay." Carrie, Holly's friend, immediately burst out bawling and one of the boys impatiently tried to shush her. Another one told her, "If we have to, we can go to my house, so just shut up." I felt relieved, because although I felt extremely sorry for them, I wasn't prepared to be a dorm mother right now. Mainly because I couldn't take care of what I needed to if I was taking care of them as well.

With my hand on the door, I said, "Should I get one of your numbers?" Carrie jumped up, obviously wanting me to have *her* number, giving me a sad look. We exchanged numbers and I hugged her. On a whim I handed her the cash that had been in Dad's drawer, and said, "You'll probably need this, call me if you need anything else." The words seemed too lame and too empty. Of course they needed something. They needed parents, they needed money, they needed protection and advice. They needed God. They needed a second chance. But every one of us needed all those things. So I gave them a half wave and shut the door behind me, handing them back their privacy.

Walking back down the hallway toward the exit, I had the distinct feeling it would be the last time I walked this path. Opening the outside door, I was reminded that dusk was almost here and began quickly walking toward the main parking lot. Without my car here, I had lots of choices, but the easiest would be Mark's since I knew where he always parked, so I headed in that direction. Thankful for the cool spring air, I took a deep breath, hoping it would clear my troubled mind. It seemed incongruous that, while I was experiencing this tragedy, the weather was unaware of how foreboding it should be. It made me wonder how many pieces and parts of life would go on as if our very being hadn't been yanked out from under us, or if, alternatively, not one solitary thing would ever feel the same.

Maneuvering my way through hundreds of parked cars, I still saw the occasional car pulling in and out of the lot. I assumed many were just curious and knew no one would stop them. I felt all of our personal business had been opened up for the world to examine and at some stage we would be mocked as having professed to love God but found wanting. I had been so overwhelmingly dazed I hadn't even begun to apply this unexpected twist as an explanation for my bizarre morning. It was obviously the missing puzzle piece. But despite feeling stupid, now wasn't the time to figure out anything.

I finally spotted Mark's car and was relieved because my arms were aching from lugging the awkward trash bag. But I wouldn't have left it behind for a million dollars. These things were my last ties to those I loved, and I knew I would shed tears over them later.

With a deepening sadness overtaking me, I opened the car door that should have been driven by my husband as we celebrated my Mother's Day lunch. And now I couldn't even buy my *own* lunch if I wanted to. It was now a holiday I would never celebrate again, not only because of the pain, but because there was no longer a reason. In a surreal way it was like Mark had driven to his own funeral and left me behind to drive his car home. Getting in the car, I almost angrily threw the trash bag in the back seat and started the car, hearing loud static. I looked down and saw the radio was set on a local Christian station. I wasn't naïve enough to think every Christian station was comprised only of true Christians, but my imagination began to run in that direction. If *enough* Christian companies were missing owners or employees, their businesses would be the first to close. I thought of church employees, just like Jeremy, who suddenly had no job. I wondered how many unexplainable things in the world's eyes had already begun to happen that would make complete sense to those of us who understood the truth behind this day.

I put my hand on the gear shift, ready to put it in reverse when my eyes glanced at the dashboard and through my pain I had to smile. The gas tank was bone dry and the amber warning light lit. Mark loved to get as many miles out of the tank as possible, and none of our teasing had changed his habit. It was a potent reminder of the little things I would miss. How many heart twinges would I be able to stand without being suffocated by the pain?

It took only a moment to decide my next step. Since I didn't have any cash, and hadn't had a chance to look through my family's wallets to see if they had any, I decided to drive around the parking lot, find Holly's car, and just leave Mark's behind for now. Hopefully she had more gas in her tank to last until my debit card began working again. After all the problems I'd encountered today, I didn't think I could stomach running out of gas and having to walk again or trying to hitch another ride. I was sure at some point the wrecker business would begin removing cars all over the city and I didn't want any of ours mistakenly towed, knowing I might never see them again.

Mindlessly putting Mark's car in reverse, I began slowly backing out, but slammed on the brakes when I heard a screeching noise as a car sped by. My heart beating furiously, I whipped my head around in time to see it barely make the corner, running over the edge of the curb and scraping the side of a huge tree. Once the car disappeared, I turned back around, just in time to hear a loud crash telling me that whatever the guy's problem had been, his headache was bigger now.

The sound of the crash inserted a new fear inside me. This day was handing me a special type of headache. No longer did I have a partner, a daughter, or parents to help whenever there was trouble, but from now on all of life's minutia would have to be reconciled by myself, with no one around to ask for help. Life, bills, accidents, sickness, crime, pain. And the strange thing about it was that, before today, I quite often felt overwhelmed with life, thinking it was too hard. But in the last hour I had figured out that life before the rapture, no matter what it had ever handed me or anyone else, had been a piece of cake compared to what this would be like. I felt unprepared and defeated before the real struggle had even started.

I backed out more tentatively this time, purposely turning in the opposite direction of the crash I'd just heard. Whoever had careened out-of-control was in a desperate frame of mind, and my fear factor was growing enough to know I needed to avoid desperate people. This all-encompassing fear felt different than anything I'd experienced before. Instinctively, I knew all barriers were removed, all rules gone. Everyone was out for themselves. I knew it, because that attitude was already rising up inside of *me*, and I was a "good" person. Now that evil was unrestrained, I couldn't begin to imagine what it was going to do to some people. Frightening, that a person's character could begin to change in a matter of hours. It was like an invisible force had been removed and we were all laid bare and available for attack. Then I thought the most sobering thought.

Perhaps I was feeling this physical and mental heaviness because the presence of God was missing. I had no idea how this was going to affect us all. I just knew it already felt awful.

Unlike Mark, Holly didn't seem to have a favorite parking spot, so I drove down quite a few rows and sections, looking left and right, hoping I wouldn't run out of gas trying to find her car. Over and over I encountered cars where drivers had disappeared while they were in the middle of backing out, cars still running after having hit a curb or hitting another car, or cars blocking an entire row. Except now I knew why they were there. I became more and more envious knowing those drivers had escaped, the old adage "you can't take it with you" becoming more real every time I saw something out of place. I was beginning to get tired and frustrated in searching for Holly's car, and I began regretting my decision. A couple of times I had to completely back out of a row I couldn't squeeze through, so I was relieved when I finally found her car at the end of one of the rows near a side door.

There was an empty space not too far from her car so I pulled in, grabbed the trash bag and locked up Mark's car. Walking toward her car, I opened the bag and grabbed Holly's purse, found her keys, unlocked the car, threw my stuff in, and slammed the door. Impulsively I locked it when I heard a motor start close by.

I felt my emotions on the verge of lurching out-of-control again, and I became a bit concerned about how I was going to react once I was alone. I was pretty good at controlling myself in front of people. But I would soon be alone. Expecting no reunions. Ever again. This was uncharted territory. Not one person on earth had ever experienced this before, and I knew I was completely unprepared. Talk about trial and error. I had made plenty of mistakes, but there was now no doubt what my biggest one had been.

Starting Holly's car, I was relieved to see she had a half tank of gas, so at least that was in my favor. Perhaps when her car was almost out of gas, I would come back and trade with Dad or Mom's car. I just hoped they wouldn't be stolen before I could come back for them. I felt like a scavenger myself, but pictured the property being overrun with desperate people once they got an inkling of where major disappearances had occurred. Because right now they would find two things here, empty pews and the *rejects of heaven* hiding out. As those words filled my mind, an unbelievably sickening feeling enveloped me.

I knew I didn't want to be anywhere in public when the sun went down. I needed to be inside my own personal fortress. But without warning, the mocking voice inside my head reminded me of how insecure my so-called fortress *was* at the moment. I recalled with a sinking feeling how impatient I had been earlier when I realized I didn't have my keys. With my front door busted and glass all over my front porch, I might not be safe there either. The seed of fear inside me was blossoming.

While driving toward the exit, I began wondering, did I *really* want to go home just as the sun was going down? Where someone might have walked in my house while I was gone? I didn't even know if we had any planks of wood in the house or garage to repair the door. Then I remembered my earlier glib statement, "I'll have Mark fix it," and, with tears surfacing, I couldn't bear to focus on the fact that he would never fix anything again. In the past I hadn't been intimidated by being alone, but this was a different type of solitary loneliness that was bringing along its friends, futility and despondency and failure, like nothing I'd ever experienced. My worries and fears were just like a vacuum, devouring all remaining crumbs of hope.

Relieved to finally reach the exit, I paused, looking both ways, before seeing a disturbing sight. Two cars full of loud teenagers looking too much like a gang, were pulling in right where I was about to exit. Their windows were open and their loud, vulgar music filled the air. But it was their blatant looks of carefree defiance that was alarming, because it told me they weren't despondent or here looking for their parents, but for trouble. I double-checked my doors, wishing for Mark's protection again.

He never seemed to back down to fear but rose up underneath it. I was going to deeply miss him. But I no longer had a caretaker. I fled the scene, hoping they weren't planning to hurt someone. But my conscience immediately began nagging me, so after driving only a few hundred feet I forced myself to pull over.

I wasn't totally heartless. I could at least text Jeremy and warn him. I found his number, thankful we had just exchanged them. I texted, "leaving parking lot-2 cars full of kids pulled in, might be trouble. Be careful." I felt better, hoping it gave him time to gather help and protect the remaining people. Pulling back onto the road, I heard my phone make a strange noise and looked down in time to see "Message Undeliverable."

My frustration at a peak, I slowed down and tried to call him. Even if he'd already spotted them, I needed to know if he needed help. I heard the fast busy tone telling me either his phone was off, or service was still down. I sighed, wondering what to do. Should I just go on my way, knowing I wouldn't be much help anyway, or should I go back and warn him in person? I decided I had to at least try. I did a U-turn and drove back, warily entering the parking lot again.

Keeping to the main drag so I wouldn't have to dodge stranded cars, I paused, looking down each parking aisle to see if I spotted either of the cars I'd seen. Nothing appeared out of the ordinary, so it gave me hope that they'd just driven through and exited out the rear of the property.

But as I rounded the final corner before the front drive, I saw both of the cars and a jolt of adrenaline went through my veins. I slammed on my brakes, hoping the squealing hadn't brought attention to me and that I was sufficiently hidden from view. Peering through the windows of a car I hoped was shielding me, I tried to see if they were still in their cars. Then I saw that both cars had actually driven up onto the sidewalk positioning themselves perfectly between the two major sets of doors, effectively blocking the main arteries in and out of the church. My heart sank.

My eyes darted to and fro, looking for someone that could rescue them better than I. This could get dangerous. They hadn't looked like kids just wanting to have fun or even punks trying to rifle through old ladies' abandoned purses. With my cell phone in hand, I tried Jeremy's number again, then on a whim dialed 911. It felt strange realizing I'd never had a reason to dial that number before, and I wondered if it would become a normal occurrence now.

I heard the same fast busy signal and closed my phone. We were on our own. I needed to think clearly, but it was so hard. I couldn't make a hasty decision, or, not only would I not help them, but I'd put my own life in danger. And I wasn't yet ready to die. While contemplating my next step, I heard three gunshots from inside the building. Things were already going downhill, and I was at a loss. I didn't have the faintest clue what I should do.

I had just about decided to drive around to see if I could find someone to help, when I heard more gunshots, this time sounding like a machine gun, with the volleys so fast and furious I couldn't count them. My heart sank for Jeremy and the others and for the group of kids in Dad's office. I found myself wishing I'd stayed inside with them. Since I was looking at a hopeless future, if anyone had to die today, I wished it would be me.

Before I could put my car into gear, I heard shouts and watched both cars slowly pull forward, unblocking the front doors, and I could see that drivers had been in the cars all along. Suddenly, without warning, the front doors burst open and the rest of their gang exploded out, motioning and screaming, "Move! Move! *Move!*"

Before their last car door was even shut, I heard engines gunning, one backfiring as they burst forward, almost going airborne off the curb. Then my heart lurched as they whipped a U-turn heading back in my direction. One of them swerved back over the front sidewalk, its oversized tires hitting flowers beds, propelling dirt, flower petals, and mulch into the air, creating a mini-tornado of debris. That flurry was exacerbated only by the scraping sound each car made as it bounced back over the curb onto the street.

It all happened so fast my mind hadn't computed the fact that I should be hiding instead of staring. By the time my brain figured it out, both cars were passing mere feet from me, and my eyes widened in disbelief as one guy looked straight into my eyes. In one fluid motion his arm came out the window, and before I could run, hide, dive to the ground, or cover my ears, he fired a shot directly over my head, as he stared straight into my eyes, reminding me he could have ended my life.

I fell back into the car, breathing a tiny sigh of relief when neither car stopped but instead sped toward the exit. When I heard the familiar backfire several blocks away, my heart rate began returning to the abnormal beating I'd grown accustomed to over the past couple of hours. But right as I turned back around, I heard the foreboding sound of hundreds of panes of glass shattering alongside wrenching, twisting metal being torn from its brackets. My ears pointed me toward our state of the art, beautifully designed foyer, and I knew what the result from the machine gun fire was.

Whatever havoc the boys had wreaked inside, apparently in their militant mood they hadn't been able to resist a final act fully intended to bring the airplane down from its resting place. With horror I watched as, in one final crescendo, the rest of the glass ceiling panes, along with each finely etched metal brace, crumpled in a loud climax as the plane crashed through, landing on the imported Italian ceramic tile underneath. Even a hundred feet away, I involuntarily jerked, immediately knowing I needed to shield myself from whatever would happen next.

Perhaps from the sudden pressure, or amount of debris falling at once, about a second later, it created a cause and effect that sounded almost like a sonic boom. Every single one of the thirty or more twenty-foot tall foyer windows and glass doors shattered simultaneously, like they were exploding in anger by an unseen force. This time I reacted with a mere split second to spare, diving headfirst into the front seat as the first several rows of cars up and down the parking lot were pelted with splintered shards of glass.

I waited with baited breath for several seconds until follow-up crashes and shifting wreckage eventually quieted. I now wished I had just driven home rather than being stuck here now. But as dangerous as every inch in the surrounding area was, I knew I had to find out if Jeremy and the others were okay. I couldn't just drive away now. Carefully extricating myself from my prone position, I sat up and looked through Holly's cracked windshield. I grabbed the paper towels in her back seat, inching my way out, holding tightly onto the car door as my feet immediately hit glass. I was glad for flat shoes; otherwise there was no way I could have made it into the building. Standing up slowly, I surveyed the unbelievable damage. It looked like a bomb had hit. By this time my mouth was wide open.

It was almost impossible to believe that just a few hours earlier the shattered building I was now looking at had been beautifully decorated for Mother's Day, intact and full of people worshipping God with no hint of what was to be. What a difference a few hours had made. Then, abruptly, through the now open air of the foyer, I heard a cry. I had been wondering if anyone had survived, but now that I had my answer I had no choice but to go and help. Except I wasn't sure what kind of help I could be. The voice inside my brain kept screaming how tired *I* was and how many of my *own* problems I needed to take care of and how, for now, I needed to ignore the voices.

But my mothering instinct kicked in. Before closing the car door to begin the treacherous walk across the street, I spotted a mop in the back seat that my daughter had bought for me yesterday. I figured I could use the handle for a walking stick and even mop away some of the glass so it didn't puncture my shoes. Walking cautiously, I saw glass and miscellaneous debris strewn for what looked like hundreds of feet in every direction. As I got closer, I even saw the shrubbery and lawn had a coating spread over it.

It was sad and strange not to hear sirens or see people running toward the church. There was no way the neighbors hadn't heard the explosion, but looking around, I didn't see even one curious person, and for sure no one coming to help. I also didn't see people running out of the church and that concerned me even more. I finished crossing the street gingerly, stepping onto the sidewalk and smelling the bigger danger I had temporarily forgotten. The fuel. What had been a slight drip and an earlier puddle, was now a fully ruptured fuel tank eager to explode. In the middle of the church building. But I sure couldn't leave now that I'd heard someone cry out.

I toyed with the idea of going through a safer side door rather than what used to be the front set of doors, but that would add several precious minutes, and by the time I made it back around, there might not even be anyone left to rescue. The sensation of sleepwalking hit me as I walked right through the middle of the disaster site. I was amazed how the shattered remains of the plane had almost completely filled our foyer as it disintegrated. I wasn't an expert on combustion, but any idiot could figure out that something bad was going to happen soon.

Now that I was inside, the navigating was even more treacherous. My intuition was dead. Where should I look; how was I going to be able to help anyone? I wondered if any of the people in the sanctuary were even left, since I didn't see anyone. I couldn't imagine Jeremy still being in the sanctuary, but I had no other ideas of where to look, so I began navigating carefully toward the door leading into the sanctuary. From thirty feet away I could clearly see all the damage done to the doors and walls. I stopped in my tracks when I heard a distinct moan not far from me.

There wasn't an empty spot anywhere in sight, so it wasn't obvious where the voice had come from. I yelled out, "I'm trying to find you; where are you?" then stopped walking, hoping they would moan again. But I heard more than that.

"Here." The voice was muffled and sounded as if it took all they could muster to get that one word out. It actually sounded as if the voice was coming from underneath the plane, and that scared me. I was pretty strong for a woman, but not *that* strong. I bent down and began looking in the nooks and crannies of debris for any movement, but the long shadows of the afternoon weren't helping.

To reassure them, I yelled out, "I'm coming!" And just then I saw a slight movement to my right and, to my horror, saw part of a body underneath the tail of the plane. I stepped away from the cab of the plane where I'd been looking and headed back toward the tail. Ignoring the danger but choked by the smell of fuel, I was now more nervous to see what kind of shape I would find this person in, and how much they would expect me to be able to help. I almost tripped as I stepped around the crumpled wing of the plane, and then I saw someone's legs and feet and a torso completely smashed by the plane's tail. I pushed one of the plush foyer chairs out of the way to get to the other side, and then saw his face. Struggling to maintain composure, I cried out, "Jeremy!" not even knowing if he would be able to respond.

No longer worried about myself, I knelt down beside his head, my mind desperately trying to come up with a plan. I grabbed a chair cushion and placed it underneath his head as a makeshift pillow because I could hear the gurgling sound as he tried to breathe. His lungs were filling with fluid and it scared me. My makeshift walking stick still in hand, I looked for something I could leverage against to lift the rubble from his legs and give him some relief. "I'm going to get help Jeremy, hang on." I had no idea if my cell phone had started working or not, but if nothing else, I hoped it would give him hope to hang on. Before I could dial 911, though, with his one free hand he grabbed mine with a grip that surprised me. The intensity of his grasp hurt, but it did its job because my eyes were forced to stare deeply into his. Before he even spoke, I intuitively knew this would be our last conversation, and my heart ached. Not just for him, but for me as well.

I will never forget his labored words. "Annie," I didn't say a word or breathe so he wouldn't be interrupted and so I could hear every word. There was a long pause as he tried to breathe, and I was afraid he wouldn't be able to finish. Right when I had disappointedly assumed it was all he could muster, he slowly forced out the rest of his message. "Kids came in and robbed us all. They shot me in the stomach when I tried to stop them, and then they tied me to the foyer table so I couldn't avoid being hit when they shot the plane down."

I moaned out loud and heard his gurgling increase. I felt hopelessness, and started to mumble platitudes that wouldn't have helped him or satisfied me, but he imperceptibly shook his head.

He whispered, "It's okay; I know I'm dying and no one can help. That's not why I called out. I was hoping you were still around so I could see you again." He stopped and coughed, a stream of blood spurting from his mouth, and I knew his time was short. I needed to hear whatever message he was anxious to give.

I looked expectantly, urgently, hoping beyond hope he wouldn't breathe his last breath before he delivered it. He barely opened his eyes this time and seemed to struggle with the words he wanted to say rather than with his physical injuries. It made me even more desperate to hear them. I didn't want to miss one word or nuance, so when he opened his mouth, I leaned my ear closer until I could feel his labored breath on my cheek.

It seemed forever before he rasped, "I'll be gone in a minute. I don't know if I've done it right this time or not, but I obviously wasn't right with God this morning…and neither were you." Tears sprang to my eyes, and I caught my breath at his cruelty, even if I couldn't dispute its truth. Before I could react, he continued, "I am *begging* you to do what I did a few minutes ago. Whatever it was that kept *you* from going to heaven, find out what it was and make it right today." He paused and I wasn't sure if he was done or if he was waiting for my response. As he stared at me, I saw an unspoken question in his eyes and a completely different kind of pity because he knew he was about to escape this world's mess, while I was the one being left behind. Again.

Before I could squeeze his hand, say goodbye, or assure him I had already decided to do what he had asked, his eyelids lowered, a tiny, gentle sigh escaped his lips, a soft smile settled on his face, and he was gone.

CHAPTER ELEVEN

Sunday, six fifty-nine p.m.

MY MIGRAINE WAS back with a vengeance, but I also knew it was much, much more than that. Death was heavy on my mind. It had always seemed more like a remarkable journey in the past. I was always moved by it, whether it was a close loved one, a mere acquaintance, or even a celebrity I'd never met. I believed beyond a shadow of a doubt that life after death existed. With such a strong belief system, it was totally contradictory for me to still be here. But neither irony nor contemplation of the hereafter had been enough to guarantee me a spot in the location of my choice. So many thoughts were demanding their turn. I felt dizzy trying to sort them out.

Jeremy's last words were still ringing in my ears. Crusty, blunt criticism of my spiritual condition, ending with a begging admonition. I felt like I'd been slapped in the face with the obvious fact I was wishing everyone would ignore. I was simultaneously missing my friend desperately and experiencing self-pity, anger, and jealousy. And if he had really been able to make it right with God, I was stunned to realize he was in heaven right now while I remained in this hellish pit, wallowing in a bottomless supply of loneliness and fear.

If possible, an even new faceted shame dug in its heels, mocking me, mainly, because it still wasn't obvious to me why I was here. Apparently it had taken Jeremy very little time to figure out his reasons for not making it. A touch of self-righteousness sprang up inside me, thinking he must have been living in obvious sin, making it easier for him to repent, while that just wasn't my case. I shook my head, disgusted with my own thoughts, knowing my emotional roller coaster ride wouldn't be over any time soon.

Not knowing what else to do, but feeling the need to do something, I ripped off a paper towel and gently wiped the blood from the corner of his face. I wished we could have talked at length, without self-consciousness or embarrassment. Despite our mutual shame, it would have been helpful to share bluntly and truthfully about our spiritual condition and what had prevented us from going.

In a clear and strangely lucid moment, I realized life was going to be even more fleeting now. An hour ago Jeremy never imagined he would die within hours of the rapture. I determined right then and there, I would not let twenty-four hours pass before I followed his advice. It was disturbing to know I had already lost the one friendly soul I had been assuming I could count on. With my whole heart I hoped Jeremy had done it right and that somehow, some way, I would be able to find my way as well.

I was at a loss as to what to do next. I felt bad about leaving him there, but I knew I could never disentangle him without help. I believed the Bible enough to know that the Jeremy I was seeing now was no longer him.[1] It comforted me to know that if he'd really made it right with God, then he had joined everyone else already. This was going to be so strange. All of us openly mourning, yet no funerals to attend. No memorials. It made me think of people over the years whose family members were abducted and never found. Life in limbo. Without closure. What a sad state of affairs dropped in our laps. With those thoughts, I realized I had no choice but to leave him where he was. Looking wistfully at him for a moment, I imagined his slightly delayed reunion with God and his family. I touched his face with one finger as tears filled my eyes again and whispered, "Goodbye."

Both of my legs were cramping, and as I flexed slightly, I felt a pain in my hip. Lifting myself up with one hand, I saw I'd cut myself on a piece of chipped tile. Looking around I could see that as the plane fell, it had shattered almost every ceramic tile underneath, making the entire area not only a mixture of glass, plane parts, metal braces, and foyer furniture fragments, but also dangerous, large, jagged edges of broken tiles. A beautiful church that I couldn't ever picture being usable again. No one would be interested in paying for costly renovations or repairs.

Even surrounded with the overpowering stench of fuel thick in the air, I slipped off into another world again, fixated on tiny details of the mirage around me. I saw an old fashioned sock monkey hanging half in and half out of the cockpit, telling me there had been children on board. I saw brochures advertising our next semester of classes that had scattered everywhere when the plane fell, and I realized those classes would never be attended now.

I thought back to what Jeremy said the gang had put him through. What a nightmare. First being shot, then cruelly forced underneath the plane as it and the glass ceiling collapsed. The problem was, I was the only one left holding that picture in my mind. Jeremy sure wasn't thinking about how he'd died now. I was utterly envious. He had been forced to experience a few hours of terror. I, on the other hand, had been left to live in the midst of what I feared would soon be an all out war to survive.

Lost in my thoughts for several seconds, I would have sat there in my introspective fog longer if dusk wasn't ushering its sinister shadows into the room. Because then I heard it. The familiar hum. My eyes grew wide and I sucked in my breath, not moving a muscle. I knew all too well what that sound was. When our church designed this state-of-the-art foyer, they searched for the most beautiful, unusual glass chandeliers, placing them throughout the huge foyer and each long, connecting hallway. The problem was, they were set on timers to come on at dusk every single day and, unaware of the surrounding disaster, the timer was poised to finish the damage. The original idea was that the most visible part of the church would be glowing each evening.

Dear God, I thought frantically. Glowing was not going to adequately describe the building in a few minutes. I had been in the foyer many times when the now familiar hum began, and I knew in about two minutes, one by one, the lights would begin to flicker on.

But this time would be different. When the fuel tanks punctured as the plane fell, they had sprayed their potent mixture of fuel around the entire room. Looking up toward the jagged, gaping hole where the plane had been, I saw dangling live wires where most of the chandeliers had been ripped from their sockets as the plane fell to the ground.

I have never moved so quickly. I looked around wildly, deciding where to go first. With the front doors gone, I could have easily run out, saving myself, but as my final act I felt I should warn anyone else still in the sanctuary. The entire building was going to explode, and I would never forgive myself if I didn't give them a heads up.

Attempting to calculate how much time had elapsed, I figured I had used up about twenty seconds, which meant I had a little over a minute and a half before the first chandelier came on at the far end of the hall. By the time it hit the first dangling live wire, I might get an additional minute's reprieve. On a normal evening, it was a beautiful sight to behold, but tonight the destruction would more than likely be complete. I could only try to keep the devastation from killing any more people. In the same instant I jumped to my feet, I yelled loudly, "Get out! The building's about to explode!" to anyone within hearing range, while doing my best to reach the sanctuary doors.

My non-athleticism chose to appear when I was within reach of the doors. In my haste I hit an unwieldy batch of crushed glass mixed with fuel, and my walking shoes failed me. In a split second my feet slid out from under me and I painfully landed on my rear end with a loud thud as my tailbone connected with a piece of chipped tile and metal. To make matters worse, I had tried to shield my fall with my hands and felt sharp pain in both of them. But I didn't have time to baby myself, since my fall had stolen another ten precious seconds. Picking myself up, I could see more slivers of glass in the palms of my hands, and now mixed with fuel, the pain radiated until my hands felt like they were on fire. I figured my hip was bleeding as well, but there was no time to check.

While jerking open the door, my peripheral vision caught the first light toward the end of the hall blinking on, and the pain in my hands was forgotten. I began yelling even louder while I ran down the aisle, trying to see if anyone was left in the now darker room. I was frustrated to see a few people still sitting scattered throughout the sanctuary. Were they crazy? After the shooting and the plane falling, why on earth were they still here?

I yelled again, giving no one a chance to misunderstand. "The building's about to explode! Get out now! You only have seconds!" But it was as if they were all deaf. I saw one older couple in the back jump up hurriedly and run out a side door, then a couple of teenagers leave through another. But what bothered me most were the people congregated at the front of the sanctuary, standing in a circle and not responding to my yells.

Angry that they were putting us all in danger, I ran closer, still yelling. When I was right behind them, I raised my arms, incredulously asking, "Why are you still here? Didn't you hear me? I'm trying to save your lives!" Yet the moment the words left my mouth, time froze, and they didn't have to say a word. I knew exactly why they weren't moving.

Because there was no saving to be done. We had *all* missed it. None of us was either ahead nor behind another. For the first time in history, every single person on earth was even. Just plain lost. There was no more pretense or need for anyone to be judgmental. We were all in the same boat. There were no hypocrites, no pretenders. And since I hadn't been able to save myself, how could I expect to save anyone else?

I was one moment away from running back up the aisle, knowing I would never see any of them again, when she spoke. An older lady with her back to me turned around, and I was appalled to recognize Mrs. Cook, a precious sweet pillar of the church I'd known since I was a child. I couldn't believe it. I was shocked to silence. But she was looking at me with cold eyes, and when she opened her mouth, words came spewing forth from a dark, lifeless voice holding absolutely no emotion. I knew the face well, but the voice was not hers.

"Missy," she began, "your days of thinking you have anything to offer anyone are over, don't you think? Have you forgotten we're all in the same mess? There's nothing for us to live for and we *want* to die, so leave us alone." I stared at her, knowing she was crazy and not in her right mind, hoping I had misunderstood her. I couldn't believe those words were coming from the mouth of a lady who had taught Sunday School for years and, in her retirement, helped run a local food bank. She had been called the "mother of the church" for the past decade, basically put on a pedestal. Without realizing it, my mouth had fallen open until she snapped her fingers in my face, saying with an even colder tone, "Are you deaf, girl? Go save yourself if you think you can!"

I turned, running for my life. My hip was burning, my hands sore and bleeding, but my heart was hurting the most. Not caring how much noise I made at this point, I hit the back doors of the sanctuary hard, with one hand flat on each door almost as a sign of my anger, the sound reminding me of a clap of thunder. As my feet left the carpet and touched the tile I began sliding again but was able to steady myself after slamming into the remains of one of the foyer tables. I knew it would leave a vicious bruise, but at this point I almost welcomed physical pain. I took a split second glance to the left and saw that a total of five chandeliers had come on and the dangling live wires were mere seconds away. I didn't wait, didn't falter. I ran straight through glass, debris, and puddles of fuel, my only priority to get away from this unending nightmare.

The moment my feet reached the edge of the sidewalk, I heard what sounded like a sparkler being lit and knew my chances of survival was getting slimmer and slimmer. Adrenaline kicked in, and I found a fresh spurt of energy surging through me and getting me across the street. I was thankful I'd parked close and hoped I wouldn't fall before I got there or that the explosion wouldn't demolish the car before I could speed away. Reaching the edge of my car, I opened the car door and in one motion sat down and turned the key.

Pushing my foot to the floorboard, despite hearing crushed glass under my tires, I sped away, preemptively cringing from an inevitable blast. As I reached the street and began my turn, I glanced in my rearview mirror, seeing a brief flash before I heard the sound. It was even bigger than I'd feared. The explosion jolted my car, the blast sending the oncoming darkness temporarily away. Turning around to look, I saw it illuminate the horrible damage and destruction while the sound of the explosion sent all semblance of silence away. There was no point in looking back, so I began driving as I continued to hear perfectly timed explosions as one by one the next live wire offered itself up as additional fuel for the deadly inferno.

CHAPTER TWELVE

Sunday, seven fourteen p.m.

WITH VISIONS OF flames continuing to play in my head, I breathed deeply, unsteadily, as I drove toward my house, my haven, my hope of security. My mind couldn't get rid of the picture of Mrs. Cook and her gang, hoping they had changed their minds before succumbing to the inferno. I had done what I could. Warned and begged, but I was glad to be gone now. At least I had taken some of Dad's things and my family's effects. Everything left behind was rooted in sadness. Maybe one day I would see if anything survived, but probably not for a long time.

Then the strangest, fleeting question tiptoed through my mind, wondering what I would do on Sundays from now on. I looked off into the distance, choking back a sob. Thinking of Mrs. Cook's words confused me. Did they not understand I wanted to die just as much or more than they did? The difference was I didn't want to just get burned or hurt or paralyzed. If I could be assured I would be killed and this torture end, and more importantly that there would be no *eternal* torture, it would be more than tempting. But until I had a heart to heart with God, I had to be sure I stayed alive. And I wasn't quite ready for that talk yet. If only I could go back in time. I would give up trying to live life my way, on my own terms, so I wouldn't miss the greatest opportunity of my life. The problem was, it was too easy to promise myself these things now after I'd been slapped in the face with reality with no chance of changing the past.

I realized now why so many people had been sitting in church for hours. There was no place to go. Very few people had been with family members. I'd only seen maybe four or five intact couples. But mostly? Mostly, I'd seen lonely individuals. I thought of Mrs. Cook and the elderly people I'd seen. Many of them had lost children and grandchildren, even great-grandchildren, and now faced a lonely, hard future with no one to comfort or help them. The most heartbreaking had been the teenagers and young adults without parents or siblings. Of course, then there were us middle-of-life failures who had lost both children and parents. And it had happened exactly as I'd warned Holly. I could remember my exact words because I'd used them many times.

"Holly, you have to make sure your own heart is right with God; because families don't go to heaven together. There's no package deal. We won't stand in front of God together. It's a personal decision and a personal journey." My eyes stung as my words came back to taunt me. I couldn't believe I had preached them, yet they were ringing in my own ears.

Had I only lived the Christian life vicariously through family members, but subconsciously never fully committing to Him myself? I was dumbfounded that a family like ours could love each other, live together, go to church together, and even pray together; but somehow not be on the same page in the end.

In my mind's eye I pictured the moment Mark and Holly realized I hadn't joined them, and the deep ache and embarrassment that thought brought to my heart made it feel like it was going to explode. It was bad enough picturing my husband figuring out I hadn't made it, but Holly? That hurt even worse. I felt shame and loss of pride well up, picturing the exact moment they put two and two together, realizing I was nowhere to be found. That had to be why the Bible said God would get rid of tears in heaven.[1] I could see why that was good for them, but the distressing part was that now there were even more tears here on earth.

Just like all those around me, there was no place I needed to be either. I knew beyond a shadow of a doubt I didn't have another relative in the entire State, and at this point, I hadn't had a moment to wonder about any extended family around the country. The phones being down weren't helping the matter. My life felt like it was crumbling around my feet. I honestly wasn't sure I was going to survive one night in this foreign world. I felt destitute and homeless, despite the fact that I now had two houses and five cars at my disposal if you counted my parents' things.

But with one car broken down, one out of gas, and no cash to get gas or fix any of them, I didn't quite feel ahead of the game. At the moment, even if I was starving, I wouldn't have been able to buy one bite of food, and I wasn't positive I still had a job. Jeremy had accidentally found the easy way out. But me? I had an almost impossible path ahead. Serious choices with a multitude of different paths to choose from. And not one of them would be easy.

Getting closer to my neighborhood, I figured I would at least drive by my house to see if it looked safe. I wanted to curl up in bed and sleep this new life away. We lived in a pretty quiet neighborhood, with trees hiding our front porch, so I had hopes that no one had driven up the long drive to discover the smashed door which had been open for hours now, available for anyone to enter. Driving without concentrating on the street, I contemplated my morning. Now that my eyes were opened, every bit made sense now. It didn't make it easier, just made more sense.

What all of us on earth *should* have been doing the past few hours was falling on our faces and repenting before God. I had a funny feeling, though, that the world as a whole hadn't done it yet, and amazingly, neither had I. What was heart-wrenching, if you stopped to think about it, was picturing a world where all the truly "good" people had left. I knew no one was really "good," but apparently there had been a distinct difference between those taken and those of us who were left. I could only imagine how those differences were going to become more and more evident. The few people who I knew were gone for sure had been honest, hard-working, kind, and generous people. Not perfect, not even professing to be, but trying to follow a perfect God. I was frightened to fathom an entire world full of nothing but unforgiven sinners. For the first time ever in history. And I belonged to that world. How had this happened?

There was barely a sliver of sun left, giving off the impression that even the streets were depressed. It reminded me of Super Bowl Sunday, with no one out on the streets once the game starts. I wondered where everyone had gone. How were other people coping? I had no way to estimate or imagine how many people were gone. I tried to imagine friends of mine who never professed to know or love God, almost taking pride in the fact that they didn't believe in God, and I imagined their lives had probably not changed as much as mine had already. Not yet at least. But I knew as much as I knew anything that this event was sending history down a path where it would never return. Events set in motion that no one but God could stop. And He wasn't going to.

Despite the warm spring evening, the blood in my veins felt cold, and I shivered. I was reminded of a sermon series Dad preached years ago. He had studied the Bible since he was a teenager and for this series had hung a prophecy chart across the front of the church. Teaching what the Bible said would happen after the rapture.[2] My interest in the subject then was short-lived which now meant I was pretty much in the dark as to what I should expect now.

Driving past the earlier bus accident, I pondered it with new eyes. The confusion and impatience I felt earlier disappeared now that I knew. I realized with relief that the bus really *had* been empty since the kids had exited the world before the accident ever happened. The truck driver and the fireman had quickly followed them into eternity, but more than likely not ready to meet their Maker. I wondered if the fireman's young son had ever shared the gospel with him, and perhaps, just perhaps, as he held his boy's Bible in his hands he was making it right with God before he was killed. Which led me to my own million dollar question… Was there any way *I* could recover from this, the biggest mistake of my life?

That reminded me of a conversation I'd had with a friend about an end times book she was reading. She'd commented on how she thought it would be so interesting to experience the end times after the rapture. But as an unwilling participant now, what I was feeling and experiencing just a few hours after the rapture was not in the remotest way interesting or exciting. And even in my ignorance, I knew it would only get worse.

And I didn't have to be a rocket scientist to know that if I hadn't been able to live a Christian life in America, where I still had religious freedom and wasn't persecuted for my beliefs, it was going to be virtually impossible for me to live for Him in this new scenario. I was now in a world as a whole that wouldn't respect or obey any of God's rules, and there would be inevitable persecution. I thought back to just the past few months and years. Christian attitudes, morals, and ideas had begun to be fought against politically and in the media, with new laws beginning to limit churches and some of the freedoms we had taken for granted for years. There was no predicting how much more difficult it would be now that there were absolutely no true Christian politicians, religious leaders, or voting Christians who would have the guts to fight for truth or moral issues.

Those thoughts depressed and frightened me, so to get my mind off that train of thought, I looked again at the still-smoking rubble of the bus and truck below me. Then, almost uncontrollably, my eyes were drawn like a magnet to the missing guardrail. A large portion of it had gone down when the vehicles fell, and with the absence of city emergency workers, no barriers were up. As I stared, I distinctly heard a voice in my head encouraging me, telling me all I had to do was gun the motor, hold my breath, and my pain would be over. But I was pretty sure whose voice it was. The problem was, now that people had actually been raptured, it proved beyond a shadow of a doubt that there really was an eternity. So I couldn't afford to seal my fate just yet. I felt like I already had one foot in the evil place, and that my torment had already started.

I turned my head and slowly drove by, refusing to think about it again. Then the voice reminded me I could come back in the middle of the night if I changed my mind. The shadows were lengthening and I dreaded the darkness and that voice. Passing by the gas station, it was worrisome that the intensity and agitation of the customers was obviously growing. People without cash were angry at being turned away and were screaming and cursing. I had to imagine vandalism tonight was going to be at an all-time high.

If it hadn't been so serious and wasn't also affecting me, the cash situation would almost be humorous. In the last few years the entire world had almost stopped using cash by design. I thought of the commercial showing how the world stopped turning when someone tried to use "old fashioned" cash instead of a credit or debit card. We had been taught for years cash was archaic and a bother and dangerous to carry around. So even the hold-outs, grandparents and people who didn't even use computers, had switched to debit cards, which even meant ATM machines weren't used as much. It had been years since Mark and I had used checks or cash regularly. We all felt so cosmopolitan, taking it all for granted. And now most of us were at least temporarily penniless. Angry people seemed dangerous to me. And that added to my anxiety and the unnerving loneliness that was settling into my soul.

I was sorely feeling the communication void and withdrawal from having no contact with family or friends, and it was disconcerting. It had been a surreal awakening to realize every person I had tried to reach earlier today was already in heaven. So even now, I still wasn't sure if I had been having cell phone issues, if the satellites were down, or if I had just been trying to reach people who were no more. Then after calling 911 with no success, I had to assume their system had crashed or was overloaded. Amazing how our advanced technology had made us all helpless now.

And to think most people had given up home phones or land lines because we had been told for years they were unnecessary. Until today. How ironic that the world had become so proud of its sophisticated technology, advancing so far, virtually everything was wireless and cable-free. Yet it was crippling us. Making each one of us into a virtual island. Disconnected, detached, and penniless, yet with money in the bank and every imaginable high-tech gadget we could afford.

Pulling into my own neighborhood, the two-car accident was also ready to be viewed in a different light. It helped knowing my friend's little girl hadn't been on her bicycle when the accident happened, but had already been in heaven. Nestled in the arms of Jesus. What a thought. But I couldn't afford to follow that vein of thought either without getting choked up. As the final blocks to my home flew by, my anxiousness increased. Would I be lucky enough to find a neighbor nearby to walk through my house with me? Then the mental vision of Daniel running down the center of the street returned. Except now I, too, had experienced that awful moaning. To think I had foolishly judged him, thinking he had gone crazy. Instead, I now wondered who had disappeared from *his* life to send him over the edge. I felt so dangerously near that very same edge.

CHAPTER TWELVE

Slowing down to a crawl a couple of houses before mine, I scoped out the territory. I saw absolutely no movement on the block, and it frightened me, while at the same time bringing relief. I wasn't sure what I feared. But seeing my neighborhood looking fairly normal gave me courage, so I pulled into my driveway.

But before I was fully past the first bend, I slammed on my brakes, biting my tongue as my chin met the steering wheel.

There, directly in front of my garage door, was the same pick-up truck I had approached for a ride this morning. Then I remembered their last words, "We'll see ya later!" My heart dropped to my feet and my fear-filled imagination had no trouble picturing them scavenging my home or, even worse, waiting for me to return. With intermingling emotions of panic, sadness, and anger, I backed my car up as slowly as I could, praying the gravel under my tires wouldn't give me away. Feeling totally defenseless and alone, tears welled up in my eyes. I was so desperately craving a private, safe place to think and cry and pray and plan my next steps.

Looking both ways before backing out of the driveway, I saw a movement out of the corner of my eye from across the street, and there he was. I could see Daniel, sitting on his porch. Even though his house wasn't far enough away to make me feel very safe, I at least knew him, and now that I understood his frightening behavior from this morning, figured he could provide some protection if I needed it.

I wasn't dense though. I realized the last thing he wanted right now was company. I didn't really want company either, yet was craving contact with a safe human being for just a moment. While pulling into his driveway, I avoided his eyes. I didn't want to see them tell me I was unwelcome. We weren't extremely close, but I could hope he wouldn't turn me away.

Still not wanting to make unnecessary noise in case my interlopers were outside my house within hearing range, I opened my car door as quietly as possible, barely latching it closed. I finally ventured a sneak peek to see if Daniel was looking, but instead recognized the familiar dazed look of hopelessness. I wasn't sure he was even aware I had pulled into his driveway. He was sitting with his elbows on his knees, his head in his hands staring at the porch floor. Normally it would have embarrassed me into skulking away, but today I wasn't going to be deterred. I walked up onto the porch and quietly sat down in the empty chair inches away from his.

Finding the wherewithal to give him a moment, I sat in contemplative silence, deciding to let him make the first move, if he even chose to. On a normal day, under normal circumstances, his silence and act of blatantly ignoring my presence would have made me feel so awkward I might even have been offended at the rudeness. But would there ever really be another normal day after today? Instead it felt entirely appropriate sitting side by side, not saying a word. A full ten minutes later, I heard him clear his throat and whisper my name. "Annie," he said, through clenched teeth. I was a bit startled but chose to patiently wait, afraid if I spoke, my own voice would crack.

After a long sigh, with one fluid movement he unexpectedly lifted his head from where he had been resting it, and leaned toward me looking me straight in the eye, our faces now mere inches from each other. "Today has been the worst day of my life," he said guardedly. I stared into his red-rimmed eyes, wondering if he thought it had been a joyful day for me. "And quite frankly, I'm surprised you're here." My concern for him turned quickly to hurt and a new kind of humiliation and anger, making me regret my decision to stop. People's judgment of me before I had a chance to fully judge or berate myself, was hurtful and embarrassing.

But before I could think to stand, much less walk away, which is what my offended spirit urged me to do, he spoke again, grabbing my attention with his first words. "I don't know how you found out, Annie, but I was standing right beside my wife. She woke up sick, so she didn't go to church. She was on the phone with our daughter, postponing our Mother's Day lunch. I was inches from her face. As close as I am to you now. Close enough to hear my daughter's voice on the other end of the phone. I was staring into her eyes, when for just a fraction of a second her eyes opened as big as saucers and she cocked her head and was gone. Disappeared." He stared off into the distance a few moments before beginning again. "Her clothes fell to the ground and her phone hit my foot." He paused, looking intently at me to see if I understood.

112

All I could do was barely nod before shutting my own blank, sad eyes, because I more than understood.

"I thought I was dreaming or hallucinating," he continued. "I just knew I was losing my mind. I bent down and picked up the phone and could hear screaming. I yelled into the phone over and over, trying to get someone's attention, when finally Rick, my son-in-law, picked it up. When he realized it was me, he began sobbing, telling me he had just seen our daughter, Debbie, disappear. My wife and daughter talking to each other, then both of them gone. In the same instant. And the bad part is her husband and I both knew exactly where they'd gone." He caught his breath with a quick intake and a half sob. "I cried and cried, trying to make sense of it or explain it away. After watching the first news reports, I couldn't deny that what my wife had warned me about had actually happened. I felt I was going insane and couldn't stand to be in the house anymore. I ran screaming down the street, finally coming back hours later, but I haven't been able to go inside the house yet." He sat back again and I could tell he was done recounting his painful story.

There was no point telling him I had witnessed his uncharacteristic jaunt down the block. Nor admitting it had taken me several hours before I found out what happened. I was overwhelmed again by my own foolishness. But now, hearing his story and seeing his desperation, there was no need to bother him with my own worries or fears, and the urge to leave returned with a vengeance.

I was wondering how to come up with a polite way to leave, when he turned and said, "What about you? Are you alone?" All desire for human companionship disappeared in that instant and I stood up abruptly, not trusting my voice, but nodding my head yes as I walked down the steps to Holly's car, getting inside with one fluid movement. It was a strange way to end our visit, but it was all I could handle at the moment.

Putting my car in reverse, I realized how rude I'd been, and I snuck a look, intending to wave or mouth the words "I'm sorry," but he had returned to his original stance, and was completely unaware of me. As much self-pity as I was living with, I still managed to feel sorry for him and was glad I hadn't seen anyone disappear in front of me. I knew that would live with him forever.

If I took myself out of the equation, I knew it had to have been a most glorious experience. Millions of people raptured in less time than it takes to blink. True Christians rising up to heaven excitedly anticipating meeting God face to face for the first time. I pondered Daniel's description about his wife's disappearance, when she cocked her head as if she had heard something. I wondered if he had witnessed her hearing the first note of a heavenly trumpet beckoning her.

My jealous heart broke again.

CHAPTER THIRTEEN

Sunday, seven thirty-five p.m.

BACKING OUT OF Daniel's driveway, my thoughts wandered again to the hoodlums who'd invaded my home. While I was sitting next to Daniel, my issue seemed unimportant compared to his shock and misery. But now I was back at square one in the middle of the most regrettable life situation I would ever face. Strange how Bible tidbits I had not thought about in years kept coming back now. And at the moment, in an ironic way I was the only "Bible scholar" I knew. I was experiencing a once in a lifetime event that had been predicted thousands of years earlier, never kept a secret, and with an invitation given to every human being on earth, never just a select few, with plenty of time to prepare for it. And yet…it had caught me off guard. Unbelievable. Amazing. Humiliating. Devastating.

The biggest lesson I was learning in the shortest amount of time was that it mattered not one infinitesimal bit how much a person had *acted* like a Christian. I was learning the costliest lessons I could have and *should* have learned as a child. That no matter what you do or what you say, God can still read your heart. And if He finds your heart not right, then *you're* not right. Unlike humans, and enabling parents and friends, He doesn't cover for you, overlook the obvious, or even grade on a curve. He doesn't give extra credit so that your good deeds balance out the bad things you've done. And even though I still hadn't figured out why I was here, in my pride-filled, deceived heart, I must have stupidly, subconsciously thought if I acted like the real Christians were acting, that it would count for eternity.

But I had an immediate predicament. To find a safe place to spend the night. I would have loved to check into a luxury hotel with a jet tub, order a seven course room service meal, and end with about three Ambien® to send me directly to sleep for a long, long time. Minus any dreams hopefully. I *knew* I couldn't afford to dream tonight. But right now, without cash I couldn't even buy a bottle of water or a gallon of gas.

Not wanting to run into the kids parked in my own driveway, I turned the opposite direction from my house in case they might be leaving or watching for me. Reaching the end of the block and remembering my earlier shock from seeing my friend's burned house, I decided to drive by just in case she had returned or a neighbor could tell me if anyone had survived the fire.

It seemed long ago when I'd walked by Tanya's house, and at that time I still hadn't known what had happened. But now that I did, I had to wonder if my friend's house fire was a coincidence or not? Was she a Christian and I hadn't even known it? We had met at a neighborhood garage sale months earlier and quickly formed a friendship. We sometimes walked together in the neighborhood or met for lunch or shopping. But the subject had never come up. Surely her house was just a casualty of the day and nothing more? Pulling up I had to admit it was a stark sight and dusk was doing it no favors. I had been in her house often, and the smoldering darkness was almost frightening. We had baked cookies here just a couple of nights ago when my oven had been on the fritz. I really didn't want to find out that she'd died in this fire.

I wasn't sure how this visit would reveal more than the first, but I felt compelled to pull into her driveway. Glancing around sadly at the pieces of brick and metal that hadn't burned, I was startled when I noticed a young man sitting in the shadows on the edge of what was left of the porch. Given that it was the last moments before full-blown nightfall, I should have been more careful, but the young man seemed more heartbroken than frightening, so I took a gamble. I turned my car off and got out without over-thinking it. The young man looked up with a wistful expression on his face almost as if asking me to wake him up from an awful nightmare.

I wanted to be gentle, but my main intent was to find out whatever he knew. I had to assume he had a connection to my friend or he would have parked himself anywhere except a nasty, smoke-filled lot. "Excuse me," I started tentatively, "my friend lives here and I was wondering if you knew…" I trailed off purposely, hoping he would fill in the blank without me presupposing what their outcome had been.

He looked at me with empty, soulful eyes a fraction of a second longer than necessary before merely saying with dismissal, "They're gone. All of them."

Well that gave me a tiny bit of information, but not nearly enough. What did he mean? Gone like to a hotel because their house burned down or…gone because they died in the fire…or gone because they disappeared? I was tired, but would have to pry. "I'm really sorry to bother you," trying to give him my most empathetic look, "but did they die in the fire, or…?" I trailed off again. I wasn't going to give him my opinion about what had happened today.

He looked annoyed as he said, "Lady, if you *really* had a friend who lived here, surely you know they were a part of all the people who disappeared?"

I sighed, because of his news and the embarrassment of my lack of knowledge about them. I was also disappointed I hadn't guessed they were Christians. I didn't say anything, but now it was his turn to annoy me when he said, "You really didn't know, did you? Then lady, I can guarantee you she was praying for you!" I had been avoiding his eyes by pretending I was interested in the burned rubble until he made that statement, and then I whipped my head around until I was facing him. The question marks in my eyes were as plain as day and my mind was screaming, "Why would she even *think* she needed to pray for *me*?" I was reminded that he was a teenager when he chuckled sadly as he saw the confusion on my face.

"I'm Ryan; I was dating your friend's daughter." He paused long enough for me to recall Tanya telling me she wasn't excited about some guy her daughter was seeing, and I surmised this was the "boyfriend."

"She told me she had been praying for me and said she did that for all her daughters' friends and hers," he nodded, not realizing he was giving me new information. "She told me she never pressured anyone about their relationship with God until He gave her the go ahead. Isn't that crazy? Like she actually talked to God about me." Then the chuckle and flippant attitude disappeared as he dipped his head so I couldn't see his face, but not before two tears fell to the porch. When he looked back up he didn't bother wiping them away, "I don't think anyone else had ever prayed for me before," he said contemplatively. "Last night about eleven o'clock when I brought Ashley home from the game, her mom came up to me and said God had told her to talk to me about my future."

He paused, and I knew no matter what he said next, the ending wasn't good. "She told me about God's Son, Jesus, and how He died to *save* me so I wouldn't have to die for my own sins. Until last night, I didn't even know I *needed* saving!" He pursed his lips, nodding for emphasis, then stopped and stared out into the street before speaking again. "She told me I needed to ask Jesus to forgive me of my sins and to come into my heart. It wasn't the first time I'd heard His name, but it was the first time I'd ever had a girlfriend's mom talk to me like that. In the strangest way she made it seem really urgent that I make the decision last night." He paused, then added, "I guess it's obvious I turned her down." He looked down at his hands and the level of his voice dropped dramatically. I had to step closer to hear his whisper, "I didn't realize it would be my first and my last chance."

My heart ached. He was just a kid who still didn't realize the finality of what he'd turned down, so he rapidly collected himself, then I watched as the strangest look composed of inquisitiveness but a little spite settled on his face before some of the more hurtful words I'd heard that day came out of his mouth. "I guess God hadn't given her the go ahead to talk to *you* about Him yet, huh?" I stared silently at him, digesting his painful truth. But his words began burning a hole inside my mind, wondering if God had in fact *ever* talked to her or anyone about me and my spiritual condition. Had she known I wasn't right with God? Or had I fooled her and the majority of people in my life? Or was it worse? That deep down I had to admit that if she *would* have approached me, I would have quickly assured her that I'd been a Christian for years and years.

CHAPTER THIRTEEN

My eyes glazed over and my mind went blank again. I felt on the verge of going into shock and without consciously making the choice, felt I needed to worry only about self-preservation. Too much pain, emotion, regret, and anger kept surfacing. And I couldn't start down the path dissecting soul and spirit until I could finish uninterrupted. In private. After all, there really was no rush now, was there?

Standing up, I forced a tiny, dry smile, asking the obligatory questions, "Are your folks still here? Do you have a place to go?" His flippant attitude and answer proved his sensitive moment was over, "Oh sure. I live with my mom and stepdad and my dad and stepmom are still here too, both sets of grandparents and my two sisters and all their families. I'll be fine. This whole thing is sort of weird, you know?" Watching his nonchalant attitude made me consider a whole different perspective of this tragedy.

His story was of at least three entire generations left intact with not a person missing. That is if you wanted to call being left behind "intact." And they were all so far from knowing the truth they didn't even know enough to be appropriately frightened or appalled. Yet there was a good chance each member of his family had at some point in their lives consciously made a choice to not accept God's offer. And amazingly, God hadn't given up on their family. Right up to the night before it happened.[1] But Ryan had followed his entire family in their generational ignorance, and turned God down too.

My story, on the other hand, was exactly the opposite. Everyone *but* me. I guess there was no wondering who "the black sheep of the family" was now. And there was no joy out of the knowledge that until this day no one would have labeled me with that title. Amazing how good I must have been at playing the game. The one I hadn't realized I'd been playing. And to find out it hadn't been a game. I had been *so close. So close* to living the life that no one had wondered about me. *So close* to finally getting serious about God again. But yet "so close" had ended up being so very far away and completely out of reach of the end result I wanted.

"Well, Ryan," I said flatly, "I live on the next street over if you ever need anything." He didn't say anything but gave a half wave as he turned to head toward the sidewalk and down the block. I found myself shaking

119

my head, contemplating our discussion. Here I was, just as lost as Ryan who had never accepted Christ in his life, almost upset with the fact that he hadn't the faintest idea what his indecision had cost him.

It was easy to figure his main sadness or regret was from mourning the loss of his girlfriend. But he had lost much, much more than that. To think how close he had come to having a different ending. All it would have taken was a sincere, repentant prayer. I found myself jealous of the fact that Tanya had confronted him, yet never confronted me. What a difference today would have been if I would have truthfully reexamined my heart and life last night. But it didn't matter now and there was no point in dreaming. My stomach was upset and my head was hurting from life and from the smell of smoke.

Staring off into the distance, I had to ponder Ryan's last few hours. He'd been given a most important last chance. That thought sent me down a mental road trying to dissect my own previous forty-eight hours. Doing my best to figure out where *my* last chance warning had been hidden. Surely I'd had one. I thought of the moment I left work on Friday evening, tired, but with my usual "glad it's the weekend" attitude. Nothing unusual in the air at all. We had met our church friends, the Perrys, at Chili's for a loud but leisurely dinner. We had driven home with the windows down, enjoying the spring breeze, and watched the news at home together until I fell asleep and dragged myself to bed. I thought long and hard but was sure I hadn't dreamed at all Friday night. No, the more I thought about it, there had been absolutely no warnings on Friday.

My mind turned to Saturday morning, my only lazy day of the week. Determined to find the moment I must have ignored, I did my best to scrutinize what I could remember of my thought processes yesterday. I remembered slowly waking up around eight thirty, pouring a cup of coffee, and watching some shows on the cooking channel while I read the newspaper. Mid-morning Holly and I had gone to work out, then we'd gotten pedicures and enjoyed lunch at a nearby sandwich shop afterwards. The morning had flown by and I didn't remember a single introspective moment. Nothing whatsoever out of the ordinary.

After lunch Holly had cunningly convinced me to go buy a new Mother's Day outfit, both of us fully aware she would end up getting one as well. After we finished our successful shopping spree, we headed back home where I did a couple loads of laundry, then sat down and read a magazine beside Mark as he watched the end of a spring training game. There was nothing. I was sure of it. Everything I recalled seemed so average, so commonplace, and so very normal. Then I remembered dozing off on the couch late Saturday afternoon, and when I woke up, Mark suggested we grill steaks for dinner. Afterwards we sat outside in the cool air talking about possible vacation spots in the summer, completely unaware we would never again visit any of the places we contemplated.

Then an old friend had called Mark and while they were talking I had decided I was tired enough to go to bed. And that was it. I was sure of it. There were no lightning bolts, no audible voice. Not even a whisper from God, I thought, feeling abandoned and completely left out. And while I slept, there were no nightmares demanding I awaken and get right with God or else. And that's all I remembered of Saturday night before sleepily telling Mark about my headache as he got out of bed the next morning. I remembered dozing back off this morning, but then, wait! I *did* have a dream, and I struggled to remember it. And then, with a slight frown, I remembered. It was a silly dream about Mother's Day and how Mark and Holly had surprised me with a puppy. And the next thing I knew, I had awakened at 10:58.

I didn't know whether to be shocked or angry. I was a little of both. How could I have dared to sleep or dream a silly dream at the very moment I should have been a part of the most important and exhilarating journey of my life? How could I have not *felt* something in the air the past few days? Had I really not had *any* inclination? Was that possible? But try as I would, I couldn't remember even one enlightening or warning moment. Not a convicting presence or a nagging at my soul. And then I tried remembering if I had spoken *about* God or *to* God yesterday, but to my chagrin I couldn't remember doing that either. Maybe if I would have…

A deep emptiness overtook me as the reality hit me that, once again, I hadn't believed what the Bible had clearly warned. My own mind had deceived me into thinking there would be *some* kind of warning, giving me time. The strange part was that I knew all kinds of warnings were in the Bible, but now that I was in a kind of hell on earth, I couldn't recall that the Bible ever promised a personal, final warning.[2] Had I thought I could outsmart or out-time God? That I was so smart or that my intuition was so strong that I would just know when the time grew close? That I would somehow miraculously be able to sense when this event was about to happen in enough time to get serious with God and make it right? I was disgusted and upset with myself, disappointed, almost to the point of hating myself.

Ironically, my biggest problem had been not even being aware of the fact I wasn't right with Him. Had I gotten so used to tuning out His voice so I wouldn't feel bad all the time, that eventually He had become the background noise of my life and hadn't been able to get my attention when it mattered most? The thought shattered me.

By the time I shook myself out of my reverie, there was no sign of Ryan, so without any more hesitation I got back in the car, locked the doors, bringing my gloom along with me. Today had been a grueling day and I was dog-tired. There was now no more light left, and the darkness infiltrating the car with a heaviness was more than just a lack of light.

Hard to express, and even harder to admit, but I could definitely feel a void of the presence of God. Until His presence had come up "missing," I hadn't realized that the essence of God in the Christians that surrounded me must have fooled me into believing I was actually sensing His presence for myself. But it must have been a mirage and it was now becoming more apparent that I had primarily been experiencing God through the overflow of Christians around me. But now that His people were gone, there was a barrenness and void that no one had ever experienced since God created the earth.

I began mindlessly driving out of the neighborhood. Then it came to me. I would stay at my parents' home tonight. *Deep breaths*, I thought. My nerves were frayed and were craving a safe place as much as my body was. Or at least as safe as any place on earth would ever be now. I was thankful that in the midst of my earlier shock I had thought to gather my family's belongings so I had their keys and wouldn't have to break into their house. Now that I knew where I was going, I had about a ten-minute drive past the church again in the other direction, and I'd finally be safe.

CHAPTER THIRTEEN

As I drove, my thoughts strayed to my parents, and it brought pangs of mourning and wrenching, guilt-filled thoughts. Although I knew exactly where my family was, it was as if they'd all died together today. Most of all I was mourning my loss and questionable future and feeling guilt from not having spent much time with my parents lately. I thought of the times Mom had suggested we join them for dinner on their back porch, or for an evening playing games. But lately I'd been busy or tired, putting them off. What I would give...

I had to wonder now if I'd had a self-conscious fear that they would somehow discern my spiritual condition. Had I been avoiding an inevitable sermon? If I would have listened, would the outcome have been different? My mind was exhausted from pondering, so I pushed the thoughts aside to put my mind back into auto pilot. As I headed in the direction of their house, the car basically drove itself. They had lived in the same house over forty years, contentedly settling in. I remembered hearing Mom tell Holly the other day how she was looking forward to babysitting her great grandkids someday. But today, history had ground to a halt. There would be no more overnight stays or family get-togethers. No kids, grandkids, much less great-grandkids to ever spend time with.

As I drove past a neighborhood elementary school, I noticed the school's flag was lowered to half mast, and mentally agreed that it was totally appropriate under the circumstances. It was like a veil was being lifted from my eyes, bit by bit, as I understood another piece of what this day's event would impact. Realizing there would be schools all over the world basically standing empty, now that God, in His mercy, had taken everyone from earth not yet held accountable for their sins.

Every single baby on earth, born and unborn, every toddler, every young child, was gone from the face of the earth. Even if that was the only thing that had happened today, it would have been devastating to life as we knew it. To think in one moment life could change so drastically that there was absolutely no need for nurseries, day care centers, or, for the most part, elementary schools. It was hard to fathom the effect of this one part of the phenomenon. I couldn't imagine a world without children. And for at least the next nine months, the world would be without even *one* child. No need for maternity wards, pediatricians, children's clothing, or toy makers. I couldn't comprehend the enormity of it.

Thinking back to the flag, in the strangest of ways I felt like my own heart was at half mast. Still in shock and in the beginning stages of missing each person forever absent from my life, I was overwhelmed by the whole set of circumstances in which I found myself immersed.

With no radio in my car and the electricity going off just as I was about to catch the news, it felt strange that I still hadn't heard one news report. With mild curiosity I wondered if the flag had been lowered for someone famous, or just a sign of respect for all the losses today. I wondered if anyone would bother putting out a paper tomorrow. How could anyone select which piece of which story to report? And with Christian reporters gone, which explanation would get the most attention? Christians in the past had wondered how the world would react after the rapture, how they would try to explain it away. Except I hadn't counted on *experiencing* it myself. Now I would know the answer to all those questions.

By now I'd made it to the main thoroughfare and would soon be passing the church and would see how far the fire had spread. I had hoped to be holed up in my own home now, but instead was still on the prowl for my safe place. I could see a few cars up ahead pulled off to the side, parking to watch the sight. Night had fully fallen, and with electricity off in several areas surrounding the church, it was eerie. Before I even got close, the glow from the fire lit up the sky. If it wasn't so devastating to my heart and soul and a grim reminder of how my life had changed, it would have been rather amazing. The plane's fuel tank must have been full because the fire's original starting place was alive and well, a full thirty minutes after it had begun.

Except it hadn't stayed there. Joining the blaze was virtually the rest of the church, flames finding sources of fuel everywhere they touched. I saw the church's library blazing, and the choir room with all its music and drama costumes. I was sure it was thriving in the church office with all records soon to be destroyed. Carpet, upholstery, and draperies over the entire campus were willingly feeding the frenzied flames. The fire seemed bent on destroying every bit of evidence that God had ever been worshipped there. I felt sorry for those who hadn't yet considered going to the church to collect their relatives' things, because there would be no verifying or collecting now. The final traces were disappearing.

CHAPTER THIRTEEN

I felt like a reluctant witness to the complete eradication of a church. Except it wasn't any church, it was *mine*. This was *personal*. I couldn't believe there wasn't at least one fire truck on the property. It was a towering inferno and a wake at the same time, with no one in attendance protesting or fighting the inevitable. The majority of those who *would* have protested were now in a faraway place. I barely even slowed down as I drove by. I was resigned to its unavoidable obliteration and it was out of my hands.

In an odd way, I had always been a follower of disasters. I always read and watched news programs about them, empathizing with those affected. Today reminded me of a mixture of all other disasters, except none would ever compare. I mused about how long the media would focus on *this* one, since they couldn't report the *true* story.

Still driving, I welcomed distracting thoughts flitting through my mind. Anything that diverted my attention from my own present circumstances took the pressure off my aching heart. My thoughts wandered back to what had previously been the disaster of all disasters for our country, September 11th, 2001, or as it began being called, 9/11. I clearly remembered that Tuesday morning, sitting at my desk, checking email, offering "good mornings" to friends and co-workers as they wandered into the office. When my subconscious finally realized my music kept being interrupted with special news reports, I turned the radio up and heard about the first plane crash.

Over the next few hours we congregated in a break room where we watched in horror as the Twin Towers fell, eventually sent home because no one could keep their minds on work. I had been transfixed and heartbroken by the tragic stories and personal life experiences for days, and even years later found it hard to believe. I remembered the next morning waking up honestly wondering if it had been a dream. We had never been the same, or as safe, after that. But life had gone on.

I could see a day where people would hint at the similarity between that day and this. The problem was this was touching every single town, country, or huge metropolitan area around the world and we were *all* experiencing this life-changing pain simultaneously. There would be no unaffected locales who could help shoulder the pain, because everyone was going through their own hell. In the past, lots of people, and especially Christians, would generously care for others in need, except now everyone's hearts were breaking, and the Christians were gone. Even for myself, I couldn't think of anyone to call who would truly care for me or provide the concern, security, or love I was suddenly craving.

While that stinging thought was in my mind, adding insult to injury I remembered an old song my mom used to sing when I was young. The one line in the song that came to mind was:

No one ever cared for me like Jesus.
There's no other friend so kind as He.[3]

I sure didn't need to remember *that* song right now, as tears sprang up again, because today it brought no comfort, just condemnation.

Glad there was little traffic on the roads, I mused that there were two huge differences between previous disasters and this. First, this was a worldwide disaster with global implications and with an impact no one could yet begin to fathom. I knew there would be no "getting over" this.

Second, there had never been an incident where this many people were affected in exactly the same way at exactly the same time. There were probably very few people on earth at this moment totally free from *some* kind of pain or life situation affected by this. If not missing one or all relatives, then bosses, co-workers, neighbors, or friends. Everyone was experiencing severed relationships, financial ruin, worry, and stress for the future, and that didn't even take into account those who knew enough of the Bible to know what was ahead for all of us. No matter what they ended up labeling it, it was a widespread catastrophe. Millions dead or missing or whatever they ended up calling it, yet mysterious and up for debate since there was no proof or bodies. No funerals to be held, no graves to be dug, no autopsies to perform. And we were stuck here, left to pick up the pieces of life.

And to think that all those missing were together, safe, in one happy place. Imagining that sight made me think of another old song I had learned as a child.

CHAPTER THIRTEEN

"What a day that will be,
when my Jesus I shall see,
and I look upon His face,
the One who saved me by His grace;
when He takes me by the hand
and leads me through the Promised Land,
what a day, glorious day that will be."

Songs I had sung over and over to the point of being able to easily recall the words forty years later were coming to mind. I could even remember that poignant second verse, describing what my loved ones were experiencing at this moment.

"There'll be no sorrow there,
no more burdens to bear, no more sickness, no pain,
no more parting over there; and forever I will be
with the One who died for me,
What a day, glorious day that will be."[4]

Although tears seemed forthcoming, my eyes were dry. Instead, I honestly thought I was going to be sick. Wishing I was experiencing the peace my family was enjoying now, I wistfully remembered the zeal I'd had when I'd first become a Christian. I found myself wishing I had died earlier in life, when I had been right with God. I hadn't thought of those days in years. I remembered right after high school when I contemplated going to the mission field. Those days seemed like eons ago.

Part of my consternation was the coldness I felt inside. But I was afraid the feeling wasn't brand new, that maybe it had taken up residence inside of me and I'd just been ignoring it. The coldness hadn't infiltrated my spirit immediately. I had been on fire, brightly burning for God before, but hadn't recognized when the fire began to go out.

I had to think the chill had come on gradually while I was focused on life challenges, sidetracked, or caught with my guard down. Was I over-analyzing myself, just desperate to figure out why I was here? No, I knew the feelings I'd been experiencing had actually felt comfortable after a while. I wasn't feeling the daily pressure, the constant conviction reminding me God was watching. I thought back to a time years earlier when I wasn't exactly sure what was wrong, just felt disconnected.[5] And rather than fight it, or realize it was a cunning deception, I had been lulled into believing I was okay, just going through something and had figured I didn't need to worry about it. I remembered telling a friend things with God didn't feel quite right, and she had said that everyone went through cold spells and not to be concerned. But now I knew I should have been greatly worried. What I hadn't realized was that I should have fought my way back, because staying still only made my heart stagnant and entrenched me deeper. And every day the coldness remained, the less I even wanted to fight my way back.

I wondered if my meandering thoughts were trying to tell me why I was still here. Because back then, years ago, when I first felt the distance, it seemed like such a minor detail that I had plenty of time to focus on later.

I had forgotten that the God of the Universe was also God of the tiniest of details.[6]

CHAPTER FOURTEEN

Sunday, eight twenty-one p.m.

IT WAS AMAZING how many conversations I had with myself in the time it took me to drive to my parents' house. Introspective thoughts were flowing in directions I hadn't had time for nor allowed in years. I wasn't going *there* yet, but after a significant day like this, it was virtually impossible to avoid *all* memories. The problem is, life happens. Never fair. Full of joy or sorrow, frustration or peace. Everyone getting a portion of each. Like a lot of people, I had quite often felt out of place. A strange combination of introvert and extrovert. Thinking things through to the extreme or detriment of a peaceful existence at times.

That's why the anti-climactic result of this day was such a puzzle. I wasn't a surface thinker or a simple person, but somehow, some way, I must have treated the potential of me leaving this earth in the rapture in a less than serious way. I was more than shocked, more than disappointed. I was so very angry at myself. I was now an elite part of one of the saddest groups on earth at the moment. Those that had fully expected to have gone with the others.

Pulling into my parents' neighborhood, I had an unsettled feeling. I was thankful to have a place to land since my home was compromised, but felt like a wimp for giving up so easily and not storming in, demanding that the punks leave. But the feelings of failure didn't stop there. It was ironic turning onto my parents' street how many childhood feelings swept over me. Old voices that had convinced me my parents weren't proud of me, always disappointed, irritated, or exasperated, arose again out of nowhere, mocking me. The strange part about it all was that my parents had never expressed those feelings verbally, but I had been fully convinced of them and they returned with a vengeance. Except this time the feelings had proof.

Mom and Dad's house was in an older neighborhood, with detached garages in the rear of each property, most of them down long driveways. I didn't have their garage door opener, so I was thankful the spring sunset was completely gone. I planned to hide my car so it wouldn't be obvious to anyone that I was here. The houses were fairly close together, so I was determined to park as close to their garage door as I could get. Stepping out of the car, I reached into the back seat and grabbed the sack of clothes, pulling it out onto the driveway. Not wanting to draw attention to myself, I quietly latched the car door so the inside light would be extinguished. With no street lights nearby, I intended to try to manually open their garage door and get my car fully hidden. I rummaged through the sack of clothes, trying to find their keys. Once I found my mom's purse, I grabbed her keys and ran around to the small door on the side of the garage, leaving the sack in the driveway, desperately hoping no one would drive by or that a neighbor wouldn't glance out a window.

Just as I reached the side door, I heard a sound and froze, crouching, trying not to breathe. The house was so close to the neighbor's I could hear their television and hoped they were sufficiently occupied. Almost convinced it had been a squirrel or a branch in the wind, I was about to stand up again, hoping my creaking knees wouldn't give me away, when I heard it again and turned my head toward the noise. As my eyes became accustomed to the swaying shadows from the porch lights occasionally flitting between the leaves, I squinted. Then I heard a soft laugh and an unusual flicker in the backyard of the neighbor's house just thirty feet from where I was standing. When I moved my head to get a better look, I could see several young people whispering, sitting on the ground with candles or lighters.

Mom had told me many stories about this family over the years, so I was more than a little wary. Not only because of their family's history, but because this day had invited the presence of evil stronger than I'd ever experienced. I had the distinct feeling that these people could be a potential threat. I knew most of the neighbor's young adult children had been in and out of jail since they'd graduated from high school, and when my parents had experienced a break-in last Christmas, they'd been pretty sure who the culprits were. All of that knowledge kept exploding in my brain, reminding me how important it was that the neighbors not know I was here. But since they were mere feet away, hiding the car in the garage would have to wait.

My knees were shaking from crouching in one position so long. It was a strange sensation, realizing not one soul on earth knew where I was at the moment, and that if something happened to me, I wouldn't even be missed. Yet it felt safer living in the dark for now. I had already figured out that if no godly people were alive, then any and everyone on earth had the capability of harming me. I knew that I'd better never forget that logic and keep reminding myself that no one would be trustworthy from here on out.

Thinking about trust seemed so incongruous now, since in the past, *Christians* were the ones considered untrustworthy and suspicious. Although I knew no perfect Christians, I knew most had spent their life *attempting* to do the right thing, to continue letting God change them and following God by loving others and treating them right. But now? Every person on earth had every reason to be paranoid. My joints were screaming in anger by now, so I began crawling away from the side door out of the immediate view of their backyard. Hoping their ears weren't attuned to our yard.

I crawled as slowly and quietly as humanly possible, until I felt a blister start to form and stood up. But if pain was necessary to keep me from being discovered, I had no problem with it. Walking on the opposite side of the garage back to my car, I wasn't about to leave the sack of my loved ones' things, so I knew I would have to take my time in order to not be heard. Hurrying would only endanger my life. I took several minutes tiptoeing back to the driver's side of the car and my precious garbage bag. Then I sighed when I saw I'd forgotten to get my purse out of the car, so I carefully opened the door, reaching in with lightning quick speed, then lifted the handle of the door as I gently shut it so only a moment of light was visible if anyone was watching. I stayed in that position for another minute and listened.

I was convinced I hadn't drawn any attention to myself. When I heard a car coming, I grabbed my bag of clothes so the passing noise of the car would cover for me and took off toward the door. The problem was, I hadn't counted on the same car pulling into my neighbor's driveway, but I was already on the run by then and knew it would be even harder to get inside the house with more people arriving, so I kept going, thankful for overgrown shrubs. It ended up not mattering how much noise I made, since their car had a bad muffler. I ran up the porch steps, reaching the back door just as my parents' motion sensor light on the corner of their garage detected movement and kicked on.

In full light of whoever might be glancing my way, I had no choice but to stand up, fumbling with the keys as I unlocked the door. My hands were shaking so badly I dropped the keys on the porch and my heart sank. Right about that same time, someone slammed their car door, and I prayed the noise covered me. I didn't hesitate but grabbed the keys with no pretense of hiding now, sticking the key in the door just as I remembered I didn't know their security code, but I had no other alternative, so I unlocked the door, grabbed my purse and sack, then tripped, falling into the kitchen. I shut the door and locked it, then held my breath, praying Mom hadn't set the alarm. Miraculously, that one thing went my way.

When I didn't hear any noise, I cautiously moved to the back window of the house overlooking the driveway and the neighbor's house, hoping the noise of their car and the abundance of trees had somehow kept me hidden. Peeking through the blinds, I saw the once flickering lights in their backyard moving. My mind began picturing the worst possible scenario of my sanctuary becoming some sort of torture chamber. With that new fear joining the myriad of previous ones already running rampant, I felt like a gate had been opened inside, letting every possible fear out of its pasture, free to roam, since I had lost all control.

I held my breath as I watched several young adults walk toward the driveway, waving at the new group that had just pulled in. But then, all of a sudden, one of them glanced over at Holly's car and said something to the others and they all turned to look at it. I jerked back from the window into the shadows when I saw a couple of them look toward the house. My heart sank, thinking my only safe place had been compromised. I still hadn't breathed when their screen door slammed and the neighbor lady walked out her back door yelling, "Ed's back! Come get the food while it's hot!" My eyes shot back to them, *praying* the food would grab their attention and distract them from anything related to me. It seemed like time stood still while I waited to see their verdict. I was never more thankful, almost to the point of choking back tears, when their hunger won out over whatever might have been intended for me. I finally breathed when the last one walked into the house barely thirty feet from where I stood.

As soon as their back door closed, I didn't hesitate for a second, grabbing my keys with barely a formulated plan. I knew once it was set in motion, there was no turning back. I only had one car at my disposal at the moment, and couldn't afford for them to harm it—or because of it, discover me. If it was no longer in the driveway, they would have to assume I had driven away while they were inside. Quietly opening the back door, I half ran, half walked back over to the side garage door, keeping my eyes on the neighbor's back door. Opening the door, I walked in the darkened garage, remembering the last time I'd been here when the garage door squeaked so loud I could hear it down the block. I had no idea if Dad had ever fixed it, and I couldn't chance it. I released the garage door mechanism so I could manually lift the door, hearing the tiniest of squeaks. With the light of the moon shining in the windows, I spotted a can of WD-40® on one of the shelves and with one fluid motion sprayed the springs closest to me, running to the other side and doing the same. I closed my eyes and slowly began to inch it open again, thankful when it was obvious the spray had worked its magic.

As soon as the garage door was open enough, I ran back to Holly's car, glad it was a small sports car because I couldn't take a chance and start it. Opening the car door, I placed the car in neutral, and with one eye still on the neighbor's door, started slowly pushing it into the garage. I was amazed how much adrenaline the fear of being caught gave me. Within ten seconds the car was inside the garage, although I had to dig my heels in to stop it so it wouldn't hit the paint cans Dad stored at the front. I put the car back in park and ran back, inching the garage door closed. After latching and locking it, I held my breath and didn't move, hoping I had completed my mission without being discovered.

When I didn't hear anything, I inched back toward the side door in the darkness, almost slipping on a pair of pliers, sending them sliding underneath the car, but I didn't stop. Just as I opened the door, I heard the squeak of their screen door and voices. I wasn't about to let them catch me outside or be stuck outside the house again. So I ran back behind the garage, through the edge of the back yard, dodging shrubs and praying they would think the motion detector light had come on again because of *their* movement, finally reaching the back door and locking it behind me.

I immediately moved back to my lookout to watch. Peeking through the blinds I knew this was the critical point in my subterfuge. Would they believe I'd driven away or figure out what I'd done? They were standing in the exact spot where my car had been, looking up and down the driveway, talking amongst themselves but quiet enough I couldn't make out a word. Then, simultaneously, all five looked up at the house, almost directly at the window I was peeking through. I felt like I hadn't taken a full, deep breath in days and hoped I wouldn't have to cough or sneeze. I couldn't afford to. My heart stopped when one of the guys started walking toward the garage. I prayed the dark windows would keep my car hidden from their view.

The relief that swept over me can't be described, when once again the screen door came to my rescue. It opened and the familiar raspy voice yelled out, "We're going to Tim's to play poker, wanna come?" It was a ray of hope I could hold onto. In my wildest dreams I couldn't imagine how someone could think about a card game on a night like tonight, but I hoped it sounded irresistible to them.

They talked amongst themselves again; then looked back in my direction, finally turning toward their house. My eyes followed them like I was holding onto a lifeline, and I found myself whispering, "Go, go, GO," as they slowly shuffled into their house. I felt a tad bit safer, until the last one—the one who'd almost peeked in the garage—paused with his hand on their back door and turned back.

In the bright porch light I clearly saw his face as he squinted in my direction, even shielding his eyes from the porch light. He looked back and forth the length of our house, looking for any lights or signs of life. I could almost see the wheels turning in his mind; my heart felt cold and the sick feeling in my stomach rumbled. Why did he care so much if someone was here? Did he hate my parents? Or after what had happened today, had he automatically assumed they were gone and planned on robbing the place? His interminably long look continued for several seconds until a guy inside his house yelled, "Come on, Toby, we're leaving!" With one final look toward the garage and back up the driveway, the guy they called "Toby" reluctantly let the screen door clank shut, closed their door, and I watched through his window as he turned their kitchen light off.

I didn't move a muscle but watched the progression through their house. One by one, each room's lights were extinguished. I moved to the front of our house so I could watch them walk out their front door, without a care in the world. The neighbor lady, whose desire to party had saved my life, finally walked out on their front porch along with what must have been her latest boyfriend.

My mom had told me that she had asked the lady over and over to go to church with her. Mom and Dad had lived beside her through her first, second, and third divorce, and Mom knew her struggles inside and out. She had even helped her pay bills she couldn't pay and invited her to our church's divorce care meetings and all the women's lunches. Mom had never, ever given up on her and being the proverbial cookie baker, used cookies as an excuse to visit, but apparently in her case never getting the reaction she had prayed for. Amazingly, it didn't look like the lady had been fazed at all by the events of the day. At the moment, however, I was just thankful they wanted to play poker.

Watching them pile into the same SUV Mom had told me they struggled to pay for, I hoped when they returned they would have forgotten all about my car in the driveway. I wistfully observed their carefree attitude through the window as they obviously anticipated a hilarious night out with friends. I couldn't understand how anyone could feel that way when my own life was crumbling. As I watched them drive away, the relief I felt brought more tears, and I sat underneath the living room window and cried. Utterly exhausted, but not even close to being sleepy, my stomach was as jittery as if I'd drunk a whole pot of strong coffee.

I refused to turn on any lights for fear of giving my hiding spot away to anyone else and suddenly felt the need to secure my asylum. I set the deadbolt on the front door then walked to the back door, rechecking it since I couldn't even remember if I'd locked it moments earlier. I placed both hands on my heart, trying to will it to beat slower. Carefully thinking through all the possibilities, I decided not to turn on any lights in any rooms along the front or sides of the house so no one would guess anyone was here. My parents' bedroom was toward the rear and had darkening shades and a good television, so I decided that's where my retreat would be.

Walking into their bedroom, I shut the door behind me and the familiar scent of my Mom's lotions, powders, and soaps wafted around me like a blanket. I took an even deeper breath, amazed that in the few hours she had been gone I could miss her as deeply as I did. It's a hard thing losing your Mom. Even if you go days without seeing or talking to someone at times, once you *can't*, it's totally different.

The room brought back many memories. Days of staying home sick from school years ago while Mom nursed me in her own bed. Evenings propped up on pillows sharing school problems or my latest flirtations. The back rubs, the toe polishing sessions, and even the get-it-off-my-chest crying times. The memories not so sweet at the moment were the ones where she would talk to me about God and her impromptu prayers that always seemed to be on the tip of her tongue. More recently I had been too busy with work and my own home and responsibilities to come over that much, but the room brought me a little comfort just by walking in.

I wished I could ensconce myself in their bed, never having to leave, and then noticed with a wry smile that Mom had made her bed her last morning on earth. I craved deep sleep so I could awaken to find this was a horrible nightmare. If it was, within seconds of awakening I would fix the situation so the end result would be different. But sleep wasn't in the cards. And all the wishing in the world wasn't going to make this a dream.

On a normal Sunday evening I would be a little melancholy by now as the weekend wound down with the work week soon on its way. But there would never be another Sunday like this, and the melancholy was thicker than usual, more far reaching and completely invasive, and had nothing to do with Monday morning coming. I was embarrassed now at my earlier stupidity in listening to the voicemail message canceling work. Amazed it *still* hadn't entered my mind that something earth shattering had occurred causing my company to close down. And to think I'd been convinced it was terrorism. But now that I knew, I needed to see if there were updates on our website. I greatly regretted my earlier response to my firm's request for contact information. It meant everyone knew I was still here now. Perhaps I hadn't fooled any of them, but I was still deeply ashamed.

My Dad's laptop was on his desk in the corner of the bedroom, and I grabbed it and the remote control and climbed in the middle of their bed. I looked over at my Dad's nightstand and saw a half-empty bottle of water, his reading glasses, and the remains of a chocolate chip cookie that must have been his midnight snack. On the floor beside his nightstand was a stack of current books he was reading, maybe ten high. He had never been intimidated by other writers, nor did he accept everything they said hook, line, and sinker. He always weighed their words carefully, sometimes recommending a book to the congregation, but sometimes closing a book, shaking his head, and not even finishing it. I admired him for that, and knowing I would have a lot of time on my hands now, I wished I knew which ones he would have recommended and which ones weren't worth my time. *Especially* at this crucial stage of my life.

As soon as Dad's laptop warmed up, I noticed his home page was our church's website. I had actually been a bit surprised and proud when my Dad became involved with computers at his age. But he had seen early on how many potential church attendees searched via the web, and I remembered him diving into the process headfirst. As the site came up, I realized I hadn't looked at our church's website in awhile and did so nostalgically now. I wondered if it would ever be revised. Or if someone did, what on earth would they put? "The pastor and most of the members disappeared on..." Or, "The church burned down several hours after the rapture and is now a community center with Bingo on Wednesday nights." Then I wondered if any of us who had attended church there would ever go to *any* church again.

My morose thoughts were exhausting, so I logged onto my company's website. This time it looked like it normally did, so I logged into my email. One of the hardest things about this day was that everyone's personal business was out in the open. I wondered how many of us had been successfully living a lie but had their choice taken out of their hands this morning. I recollected being close friends with a young couple years earlier only to find out later that he'd been cheating on her with several friends. His whole life a lie. And now I was beginning to think mine had been just like that too.

After I'd become an adult myself, I saw that, to a certain extent, every single person hid who he or she was. No one is totally, brutally, unequivocally honest about thoughts, feelings, insecurities, motives, or actions. Mostly because we all feared rejection and knew no one was trustworthy enough to risk becoming fully transparent. Except God, I supposed. But now a firm line had been placed in the sand. I sighed deeply. The genuine permanently separated from the pretenders. The hypocrites supernaturally separated from the sincere. I guess, if nothing else, this day had proven once and for all that not all churchgoers were hypocrites. But yet some of us obviously were. Again, an old scripture came to mind—something about separating sheep from goats.[1]

I really didn't think I'd been outright lying about being a Christian. Maybe cutting a few corners, maybe not as devoted or completely sincere all the time, but didn't everyone feel that way at times? Should I have been honest and told someone I didn't feel what others were feeling? Or admit how cold and unmoved I was at times? I just assumed it was better to at least act right, even if my inner self wasn't feeling it. Because if I would have been truthful…what would people have thought of me?

It was a crushing blow realizing I had cared more about fooling people than apparently seeking a true relationship with God. My mom's voice invaded my thoughts and memories again, reminding me that no matter how much we hid from others, nothing was ever hidden from God because he knew even our thoughts and motives.[2]

I thought back to those I'd seen at church today. I wasn't stupid, and knew some had just been kind enough not to say what they were thinking when they saw me. Some had disguised the shock on their faces, while others hadn't even tried. I detected a sneer and a hint of glee a couple of times, as if to say, "I knew you weren't what you pretended to be." Or, "So much for your 'holier than thou' attitude, huh?" To be truthful, I was probably treating others the exact same way. Surprised and outright dismayed to see many still here, I'd inwardly become their judge and jury. I'd been saddened and shocked to see Jeremy, one of our pastors of all things. Then, on the other hand, I'd been astounded to discover that a different staff member was *gone*, mainly because I had really doubted her sincerity. I shook my head in disgust, realizing my judgmental attitude hadn't died with the rapture. In fact, if I left it unchecked, I knew it could grow by leaps and bounds.

Looking back at the laptop, I could only imagine our entire firm was overloading our system, which had to explain why it was so slow. When my email finally came up, I was nervous as well as curious, wondering what I would find out. Several emails had come in during the day, but first I scanned the list, searching for an official looking email or perhaps the first email I received after the rapture. Then I saw the email from our firm's President and an attachment entitled "Remaining Employee List," and I knew this was the email I had been dreading. My heart sank, knowing that seeing my name in print would somehow make it more official, squelching the dream possibility and solidifying my nightmare.

I opened the email and began reading words that seemed too easily written without the emotion it warranted. Amazing how someone could make a life-changing email seem like the most mundane correspondence.

"To all Employees," it began coldly. "As everyone must now be aware, the world experienced unusual disappearances today that will undoubtedly affect each of our offices in unique ways. Our past track record of surviving obstacles throughout our firm's fifty plus years assures us that we will survive this as well and we expect a continued bright future. We are a thriving company and were excited to discover the majority of our great board members, managers, and employees are still with us, eager to return to work. To those employees who might be dealing with a loss of family members or friends, we give you our sincere condolences. If you feel you need to take an extended unpaid leave to deal with any life situations, please contact your supervisor.

"Rather than inundate our server with thousands of emails while employees attempt to discover which friends have survived this disaster, we have compiled a master survivor list. As you were previously informed, none of our offices will be open this week, and you should wait until you are personally contacted by a member of management before reporting back to work. Meanwhile, enjoy your impromptu vacation. Once we have completed financial audits and our assessment on adjusting our staffing needs, we will be in a better position to predict future needs."

Just like that. So matter of fact. Like it was nothing. I was offended, disappointed, and appalled. Words like "unusual disappearances" and "affect us in unique ways" told me they saw this as just another business hurdle, and were mostly interested in how this would affect our bottom line, rather than caring that lives had been torn apart. Words like "obstacles" and "bright future" told me they were either trying to feed us the biggest line of garbage in history, or we had foolish people leading our company. Words like "excited to discover" and "ready to return to work" told me they had no earthly idea what had really taken place. And finally "survivor list" and "enjoy your impromptu vacation" told me they didn't know the *real* survivors were the ones in heaven, nor that none of us would ever have a carefree vacation again. I had been abandoned inside a world with no awareness of reality.

The moment I had dreaded was here. With my cursor on the attachment, I hesitated, almost hoping they had accidentally left my name off the list so no one would have every right to call me a hypocrite, wondering if I had the nerve to just disappear and never go back to work and just find another job. I opened the document and, for some reason, had almost expected to see that someone had scrawled names on a piece of paper and scanned it to get them out quickly, but instead the offensive document that popped up on my screen looked way too professional. It looked like a word processor had labored over the words, organizing names in a pretty font, with titles under each proper city's office location, and even alphabetizing them all. I was sure the person had stopped to spell check as well. As if the words were the important part. When in reality it was a list of lives forever changed.

Looking blurry-eyed at the page, I sensed the column headings were all wrong. One column should have said "Those in Heaven," and the other, "Living in Hell."

CHAPTER FIFTEEN

Sunday, nine fourteen p.m.

I STILL COULDN'T help but fume at the flippant attitude ingrained in my firm's email. Since I had yet to see news about today's bombshell this was my first foray into how others might twist the truth. I was insulted to see they were trying to make this horrendous day palatable somehow.

In the oddest way, every few minutes something would grab my attention, and for a brief second I could actually forget. Then when the knowledge rolled back into my consciousness like a huge wave, I became sick to my stomach. It was so hard to believe what a life-altering mistake I had made. How on earth could I not have realized it? Had I somehow known deep within my subconscious, but been willing to gamble that there was plenty of time? Had I been lulled to sleep assuming I was on the right side of the fence? Had I been so proud I couldn't imagine anything I was doing would be considered *that* bad? Had I thought I could set the bar as high or low as I wanted, instead of acknowledging God had the only deciding vote? Or in my foolish, deceived heart had I stupidly assumed the Bible didn't mean *exactly* what it said? How dense could I have *been*?

I thought of the Bible story about the wise and foolish virgins awaiting their bridegroom.[1] The story had warned, "...because you do not know the day or the hour." I guess I was the poster child for that story. There had been a time in my life when there had been plenty of oil in my "lamp," plenty of fire in my relationship with God. But it had been awhile since I had been full. Not that it even mattered now, except for the further bruising of my pride, but I kept going back to the question of whether anyone in my family or at church had doubted I was right with God. Had it been obvious to *everyone* around me that something wasn't right, making *me* the complete fool? Or were they as shocked as I was? Then I closed my eyes and realized I was doing the same thing I'd done for years. I was still worried about what others were thinking of me. And all the while, God had known. This hadn't surprised God at all. The problem was I still couldn't quite put my finger on what God knew that I didn't.

I was caught in a strange situation and just beginning to understand the bigger picture. A frightening clarity was beginning to emerge that perhaps I hadn't fully belonged to either side of the fence. God had made it painfully clear to the world that despite living side by side with other Christians, even emulating them, you could miss the mark. I almost felt like I'd let myself become inoculated against the truth God had been trying to get through my thick skull. I wondered if it was possible that the minutiae of life[2] had tied me up until nothing had been able to penetrate my heart.[3]

I tried to think that concept through as I examined myself. As we had gotten older and more comfortable financially, as Holly had started branching out, beginning her adult life, we had begun to enjoy the nicer things of life. I had to admit I spent quite a bit of time thinking about vacations and entertainment and enjoyable things. Things I felt we deserved because we worked hard. Surely my desire to enjoy life to its fullest hadn't suffocated God out of my thoughts?

Thinking back, though, I had to acknowledge there were many church services and classes I had daydreamed through. Yet, as if mocking me now, I clearly remembered warnings I'd heard over the years. Was this what hell would entail? Remembering in minute detail every chance I'd been given to make it right, while being tortured?

Then I remembered a time in high school when our youth pastor warned us that the path to heaven was not a wide path, and how the

Bible dared to say few people would actually find the path and stay on it.[4] I hadn't bothered to focus on it back then, but now, with a strange new understanding, I began to get a visual picture.

I saw God's path, a very narrow, uncomfortable path at times. It seemed almost too straight and regimented, not as free or easy or relaxed as other ways and paths were. With my eyes closed, I imagined the two different paths and pictured something I hadn't contemplated before. It was frightening and I was afraid it described my situation.

The one path was so narrow that there was rarely room to walk side by side with someone, making it lonelier than any other path. It also seemed extraordinarily bumpy with hills and valleys. And then there was the confusing part. Changing my focus to the other path, I was astounded. It wasn't miles or even hundreds of feet away from the straight path. The wide, comfortable, smooth, and beautiful path ran almost side by side the narrow, confined, bumpy one!

I now saw with such clarity how those on the straight and narrow path were able to talk and touch and embrace and live with the ones on the wide, destructive path, all seemingly going in the same direction, with the same goals and plans. But while those on the narrow path struggled at times, panting while desperately working to get around obstacles, struggling up hills, trying not to slip on the downward trails leading into slippery valleys, their companions on the wide path seemed to have an effortless time of walking their path, unaware of the troubles those on the other path were having. I could see couples were able to walk hand in hand with one on the straight path and the other on the wide one. The visualization sent a chill up my spine and an arrow deep into my heart.

That had to have been my story. I had been on the wide path, yet walking stride for stride with friends and family who were on the narrow path. Close enough that I could *see* them, hear the same exact things they were hearing, enjoying their presence as if…as if we were on the same path, belonging to the same world. I had fraternized with them and talked their lingo. A tear slipped from the corner of my eye as the perfect descriptive word settled into my mind.

Vicariously. In a strange way I had lived vicariously through my Christian family and friends, experiencing *their* relationship with Christ through *their* eyes and ears rather than having my own, full-blown, intimate, genuine, first-hand experience of my own. All along assuming we were experiencing and living the same things, without actually embracing what the real Christian life entailed.

I closed my eyes, picturing the two paths again. The whole problem with the picture was that, toward the end, the paths slowly began to separate. Not immediately, or drastically so as to alarm those on the wide path, just slowly but surely a chasm grew between the two ways. By the time it became obvious that the paths were splitting, when those of us on the wide path observed the differences between our paths, the narrow path looked confining, restricting, even dangerous and uncomfortable, and not at all inviting. Those who had been walking side by side were no longer quite as close or in one accord. Those holding hands had been pulled part. Until the very end, when those on the narrow path took their final step into eternity this morning, while I awoke only to discover my path hadn't even been pointed in the right direction.

And to think I had quite often taken a "hit" for being a Christian. How stupid had that been? Taking the hard knocks, but in the end not being in a position to receive the ultimate benefit of being a Christian! And now, by default, I was aligned with the world, the unbelievers, and now the dark, wide path we'd been on seemed foreign and frightening.

I knew now that everyone didn't *accidentally* make it to heaven. The absolute truth couldn't be clearer. No one made it to heaven by default. Only those who specifically chose Him and, especially lacking in my case—stuck with Him, following His path all the way to the end— made it.[5] My mind had no other direction to go but down a deep, spiraling, dark hole of despair.

I rubbed my eyes, trying to awaken myself, not from sleep but from the funk in which I felt myself getting lost. I began looking in earnest at the list my company had prepared, hoping they might have just posted the names of those who *hadn't* responded to the voicemail so my name wouldn't be in print, but as luck would have it, there was a side by side list for each office. The ones accounted for and those who had disappeared. In black and white. No punches pulled. I couldn't bear to look at the list that held my name, so I began looking at the "missing" lists first. It was quite a bit shorter than the other one.

CHAPTER FIFTEEN

To begin with, I hated the title they'd chosen, "Remaining Employee List," because they obviously didn't realize it was a shame to be listed on the "accounted for" list. I looked at the first name on the "missing" list: Trent Adler. He worked in our computer department. And it puzzled me because I hadn't once heard him talk about God or admit to being a Christian or necessarily even act like one. He hadn't hung out with "known" Christians. Nagging at my own soul was the knowledge that so many knew I went to church, and I could hear the embarrassing questions. Unbeknownst to me, Trent must have been a Christian no matter how much it surprised me. But looking at the list, the surprises for the most part went in the other direction.

With a strange twist of fear and knowing I had no control over my previously controlled life, I wondered if I would ever work side by side any of my co-workers again. I had always been slightly bored with prophecy or sermons about life after the rapture, so at this awkward juncture I really didn't remember what I should expect next. I did remember that over a third of the Bible was made up of hundreds of prophecies foretelling intimate details of Christ thousands of years before He was born, giving irrefutable proof He was the promised Messiah.[6]

And now that the rapture, one of the most dramatic prophecies God had given, had occurred, only a fool would think the rest of them weren't also going to come to pass. The immediate problem was that I knew a specific timetable—a certain number of days had now been put in motion, which was unique to most prophecies.

It wasn't going to take thousands of years for the next predictions to come true, and I was already dreading every moment of my terrifying future. At some point I would have to get out Dad's Bible, with all his notes, and actually read Revelation as if I were interested this time. But I was fearful because I knew it would be like reading a future diary. I shuddered at that thought because I figured it would frighten me more than I already was. I hoped people wouldn't assume since Dad had been a pastor I was ready or able to help them. Because I desperately needed help myself right now.

Sighing and realizing that once again my thoughts had carried me far, far away, I looked back down at the list, thinking of the employee everyone admired at work, Julie. She'd been with our firm longer than

I had and everyone thought she was the epitome of a sweet Christian lady. Then my eye caught her name on the *wrong* list! What on *earth* was she still doing here? Seeing it took my breath away. I felt her pain and was angry and frustrated. I could feel my blood pressure rising and my pulse quickening. Suddenly I was angry that there was even a list. It was as if someone had ratted us out, putting us on display to be ridiculed.

Each name brought a pang. It didn't matter which list. Jealous of some, judgmental of others, surprised, or bitter. A twinge of "well, of *course* they would still be here if *I* was," or the incredulous, "what was God thinking to take *them*?" There was no mere curiosity left, just raw emotions. I abruptly closed the attachment before scanning more than twenty of the names. I didn't care. I *couldn't* care. It hurt my heart and my head to care. No one on either list could help me now. I closed the email and attachment with a sense of finality. I didn't care to ever look at it again.

When my list of unopened emails popped up, all I saw through bleary eyes were messages I instinctively knew I didn't want to open. Looking at the time stamp showed me most of them had been sent after the list was posted, so they had known I was still here. Almost under duress, I opened a couple emails, alternately making me so angry I wanted to do bodily harm to the sender, or making me so desperately sad and ashamed that I wanted to do bodily harm to myself.

Then I opened Christie's email, which said, "I'm SO glad you're still going to be on our floor! I was afraid I was going to have to go to lunch by myself now that Jane's gone!!" After deleting it without answering her, I felt a tear drip down the side of my face. I wanted to be where Jane was now. In my heart of hearts I didn't want to *ever* go to lunch with anyone again. Oh God, why couldn't they be talking about *me* because I wasn't here? I saw no need for the trite chit chat life had revolved around before today. After closing her email, the next one popped open automatically, and I saw with chagrin that it was from smart aleck Rudy a few offices away from mine, who said, "I KNEW you were always just a good old hypocrite like me!! Ha! See you next week when the office reopens, sucker!"

146

Grinding my teeth, I realized I had been gnawing on the inside of my mouth when I tasted blood. I closed my eyes, longing for more innocent days, or the day when this life would be over. If I ever figured out what I had done wrong, would it even be possible to live a Christian life in front of everyone after today? It would be so much easier to just disappear from life. Quit my job. Hide out somewhere and never return to the life I had previously spent way too much time thinking about. With a strange, determined calm, I deleted the rest of the emails without reading any of them. There was no way they were work related, and each one brought more pain than the previous one. I couldn't bear any more. I was busy chastising myself enough without needing people who didn't care about me joining in. I closed my eyes, trying to calm myself when I felt a vibration.

My eyes popped open at the unexpected intrusion, surprised that my phone was working, while wondering who could be calling. I looked around on the bed, finally seeing the edge of my phone peeking out of my purse. Apparently cell service was still intermittent because I had missed the call and had a voicemail message. Not recognizing the number, I checked the message and heard Sue's voice, a friend from work. Her sweet voicemail message said she was just checking up on me to see if I needed something. Even before today I had the potential of being a loner, and now? I felt myself literally moving headlong in the direction of becoming a complete recluse and just letting the depression, the shame, the regret, the fear, and just plain sadness have its way and take over my mind.

But then her message sounded so innocent and kind and I needed kindness, so in an out-of-character whim, I called her back. But instantly regretted it. From the beginning of our conversation she sounded a bit odd and stilted, and although she was trying to be tactful, first asking politely how I was doing and did I need anything or want company... then coming out and saying it. The most painful question of all. The one I dreaded *anyone* asking. The one I was viciously refusing to even allow *myself* to think about because I was afraid it would make me lose my mind. But she caught me off guard before I had a chance to steer the conversation to a safer place. Right when I was about to hang up, she blurted it out.

"So Annie, is your husband and daughter with you? And how about your parents, or the rest of your family?" She couldn't see my eyes clamp shut, or the tears that managed to squeeze through. Perhaps she heard my quick intake of breath before I moved the phone in an effort to keep her from hearing the slightest sob that escaped. I would *have* to get better at answering this question. I wasn't going to be able to fall apart the rest of my life every time someone mentioned my family. That phrase "the rest of my life" now seemed so final. There had been a day when that phrase brought up pleasant thoughts; like planning my daughter's wedding, spoiling precious grandkids, and spending a lazy retirement in the backyard. The same stuff most people work themselves silly for their entire life. But now "the rest of my life" was more of a death sentence, but without a welcome electric chair to end my misery.

I took a deep breath, thinking, "I'm an adult. I'm a professional woman. I can control myself. I can do this." Then, with almost a scary determination, I forced my eyes open, hardened my gaze at nothing in particular, gritted my teeth, and in an unnaturally flat voice said, "No, Sue, all my family is gone. Everyone. I'm alone."

The silence on the other end was deafening. Two seconds might as well have been two minutes, with her pause being longer than mine. But my self-preservation mode kicked in with the hope of catching her before she said something empathetic to make me cry. I knew if I waited to hear her response, I might embarrass myself by openly sobbing, so I quickly added with what I hoped came across as light-hearted sarcasm, "I guess working overtime won't ever be a problem for me again, huh?"

My attempt at lightening the mood either let her off the hook, or fooled her into thinking I wasn't as devastated as she expected. She seemed relieved, and gave a perfunctory giggle saying, "You're right! We can all make boatloads of money now that we'll be shorthanded, huh? Okay, I'll let you go; I'm sure you're tired. Enjoy your week. Call if you need anything!"

My dull, fraudulent voice was able to spit out only three more words, "Sure thing, Sue," before collapsing in a heap. I had barely been able to press the button to end the call before an ugly, guttural half scream, half moan came from deep inside of me that I couldn't have squelched even if I'd wanted to. And it lasted unimpeded for two or three minutes.

CHAPTER FIFTEEN

You know the release you normally get after a good cry? That was no longer available for the taking. The rules had obviously changed. There was no deep, shaky final breath with the thought, "I'll feel better in the morning." There was no one around to offer a hug or a pat or a promise of, "Don't worry; I'll take care of it; I'm here for you." Life as I had known it, just a few hours earlier, no longer existed.

A cloud seemed to be tucking itself around me with one mocking thought. I had been quite pleased with the fact that I had fought my way out of bouts of depression during my life. There had been normal life challenges that had gotten me down, from which few are exempt. Feelings of extreme insecurity, feeling unworthy of love or attention, feelings of being untalented, unwanted, unneeded, and unappreciated. Nothing highly unusual, but private emotions people rarely share with family or friends. And seldom God. There were times of being hurt by people I loved or trusted. It had been so easy to worry about what people thought of me and to let those feelings rule my life, but barely did I give a thought to what God was thinking. I'm not sure I had fully concentrated on the fact that He even *was* thinking about me. But assuming He had been, I definitely hadn't reciprocated those feelings.

About those periods of depression I thought I'd experienced before? Times so desperate I daydreamed about what it would be like once life was over? Well now those times of depression seemed like a walk in the park with a rainbow in the sky, pretty music, and balloons scattering in the breeze, because now I knew the accurate definition of depression. It's being completely alone in the world while it prepares to fall apart. It's knowing you are totally responsible for the situation you're in, with no way to change the outcome or the inevitable and no "do-overs."

Although I had promised myself throughout the day that as soon as I was alone I would start my self-psychoanalyzing, I was still not ready to go there, still unwilling to begin examining why I'd been left behind. Most of my reservations stemmed from the fact that it still wasn't obvious to me why I'd been left behind. It was the elephant in the room, but to me it was still invisible.

I figured I had hours and hours of catch-up news to watch, which would help keep my mind off me and my situation for awhile. I hoped the satellite wasn't down because I was now at the point that I *wanted* and *needed* noise to distract me. Finally feeling secure and entrenched in my parents' back bedroom, no longer fearful the flickering light would give me away, I reached for the remote.

Within seconds it became crystal clear that my day of ignorance was officially over and I no longer lived in the same world.

CHAPTER SIXTEEN

Sunday, ten twelve p.m.

MY SELF-PITY HAD been in overdrive for several hours now, and until this moment I quite honestly hadn't cared or focused on how this day had impacted anyone but me, much less the entire world. When the blank screen disappeared, the first thing I saw was an announcer with a picture of the Vice President to his right, and I wondered if he was about to give a special announcement. My adrenaline began pumping. I knew this was one speech I should actually pay attention to. Seeming completely odd for a news program, however, was the quiet, somber music playing in the background and then the reporter, with a formal demeanor, announced we would be joining the other networks for a special announcement from Speaker of the House, Kathryn Medulla. Without even realizing it, I slowly inched closer, sliding off the bed until I was sitting on the floor, barely a foot from the television, my arms hugging my knees. Wondering if I should be afraid.

As the camera focused on the Speaker of the House as she walked to the podium, the ticker tape across the bottom of the screen began announcing well-known facts about the Vice President, reminding us he was a previous Nobel Peace Prize winner, champion for Children's Rights, and similar accolades which confused me. They hadn't said he had died, but it sure sounded like a memorial. Or were they celebrating some heroic effort of his during this horrible trauma? Then I remembered the flags at half-mast and wondered if they had been lowered because of him. This day had been so traumatic personally. I hadn't yet even begun to imagine all those outside my world who might have disappeared. Maybe the Vice President had been in an accident or had a heart attack.

I couldn't have been more wrong.

Stifling a yawn, through tired eyes I saw the flicker of a banner that said, "Repeat of Previously Aired Press Conference," and wondered how long everyone else in the world had known what I was about to hear. By this time the Speaker of the House had reached the podium and was being introduced. In a plain black, designer suit, she seemed diminutive behind the large podium. As she began to speak I wondered if I really wanted to hear what she had to say or if it would just depress me further.

"Good afternoon fellow Americans, Congress, Senate, press, and friends around the world. It is with great sorrow that I must announce that in addition to our earlier shocking announcement, I must inform the world that it has been confirmed that my good friend and fellow leader, Vice President Donald Edwards, was a part of the world-wide disappearance and loss we've all experienced today." I gasped out loud as she continued, chillingly stone-faced. "Our deepest condolences go out to his wife, Jeanette, and sons, Timothy and Elijah, and their families.

"Just as every family, neighborhood, business, and branch of government around the globe is doing, the leaders of the United States of America are doing their best to verify the existence or disappearance of every member of our government. After the Vice President's disappearance was confirmed by his wife, and as stipulated by law, the President pro tempore of the Senate will be named Vice President."

I was flabbergasted. Not just because we had lost our second in command, but because he had gone and I hadn't. Just like the rest of his family. We were left to pick up the pieces. But she wasn't stopping, so I had to listen.

"I want to assure the American people as well as our friends around the world that our country is strong and we have weathered many past disasters and have many safeguards in place to ensure we remain a viable force in the world. Every branch of our military around the world is on full alert, and we expect nothing more significant to occur than supporting those searching for loved ones and helping those whose lives have been disrupted through various reasons because of the tragedy.

"Because the unusual disappearances have created a likelihood of looting and crime, we have been forced to declare a "National State of Emergency" and martial law has been declared for an indefinite period of time."

My mouth fell open and I didn't have the strength to shut it. I remembered distinctly after 9/11 all the arguments for and against the same declaration. Some thought it must be approved to keep us safe in case terrorists infiltrated our country, while others fought against us losing our basic American freedoms.

And to think it wasn't a terrorist at all that had infiltrated our world this time. It was much, much worse and no country was prepared for this. *God* had chosen to infiltrate our world. He had come and gathered His own, with no one being able to stop Him.

Amazing how over the years more and more people used the excuse that they didn't believe there was a God. But not believing in Him hadn't kept this from happening either. It didn't matter what we thought about Him on earth, apparently. No one had been able to escape His touch today. I clinched my eyes together as hard as I could, pressing my face into my knees until it hurt. My eyes were raw from wiping them, and I was surprised tears could still come. I shook myself so I could concentrate on what else she was saying.

"Every state government has been given autonomy to do as they see fit for the immediate future, and the majority of state governments have passed on that same authority to city governments and townships so that individuals needing government subsidy must contact their local officials. There will be *no* federal declarations of disaster, as our government does not have funds to help every citizen needing assistance. Preliminary estimates seem to indicate that perhaps 25% of the population is missing."

My mind tried to absorb her estimate of 25%. I couldn't fathom a worldwide number that large, then thought back decades earlier when our country still considered itself a Christian nation, wondering if the number would have been higher then. But no matter what the percentage ended up being, it was enough to devastate the world. No wonder my stomach was tied up in knots. I was thankful there was nothing in it. But she kept going.

I saw her shuffle several papers, settling on one of them before continuing. "As the hours have passed since this happened, it has been determined that in addition to martial law being declared, additional governmental limitations are going to have to be enforced. To give you the background on why the United States government has decided to take these steps, you must know the unfortunate news we began receiving several hours ago from areas close to the International Date Line.

"One of the first reports to hit regarding this incident, causing chaos in the business world, came from a city by the name of Anadyr, which is part of the Russian Federation located on the Date Line. The disappearances hit them just a few hours before their normal work week was to begin, as they are seventeen hours ahead of America's Eastern Standard Time. Exacerbating their problem is the fact that most areas in their particular time zone are bustling fishing seaports and adventure tourist hot spots, so their work day begins in the pre-dawn hours, which meant their work day was already starting when the disaster hit.

"Within thirty minutes after it became known, as more and more news reports surfaced telling of world-wide disappearances, every automated teller machine in their area and every local bank branch with early morning hours were emptied of cash, as people withdrew entire checking and savings accounts. By 6:30 a.m. their time, grocery stores, gas stations, and insurance offices were overcome with hundreds of frantic customers beginning to riot.

"In addition to cash flow problems, credit card limits began to be maxed out as reported by every major credit card company as people frantically emptied stores of emergency supplies and survival equipment. This wasn't an isolated fluke, however, for as time went on and subsequent time zones were hit, and as the sleeping world awakened to find their world drastically changed, the scenario was repeated time and time again until it was apparent there was a certainty a world-wide financial system breakdown was on its way."

I didn't know what to think at this point. I knew my own debit card hadn't worked and it was a scary feeling knowing the government had the power to keep me from using my own money, but that made me wonder what other safeguards the government would think were necessary. Ones I had no power to stop. But the Speaker of the House kept going as she turned to her next page of facts.

"The final straw was broken just a little over three hours ago at 7:00 p.m. Eastern Standard Time, which was 9:00 a.m. Monday morning in Japan, when the Tokyo Stock Exchange opened. Not only was their city also experiencing the same cash withdrawal issues as previous cities, but even worse, within seconds of the Stock Exchange opening, it was overwhelmed with massive sell orders, dropping a shocking 39% within the first minutes, precipitating the exchange officials to close the trading session after twelve minutes, with no promise whatsoever of when they might reopen."

I couldn't process what I was hearing at this point. I tried in vain to remember what kind of numbers the Stock Market Crash of 1929 had experienced. All I knew was that stock markets worldwide had already been experiencing severe downturns over the past several years, so a 39% loss on top of what we'd already lost would be devastating. I knew everyone was already uptight about losses from 401k funds and IRAs, some people having already lost over fifty percent of their nest egg. When our New York Stock Exchange opened, it would be catastrophic to the retirement system of America. This day had sealed the fate for pretty much every investment fund. And then she dared to touch my world.

"Fortunately for us in America, we were able to learn from our neighbors across the world, which is why our government chose to implement safeguards to keep us from experiencing the long-lasting effects of this day on our economy as other countries have. Effective immediately, and until the government has stabilized the situation sufficiently, banks have been closed until new regulations can be put into place preventing complete withdrawals of funds. This mandate also temporarily includes the freezing of assets, limiting of trade, and possible confiscation of property if deemed necessary."

I cocked my head, thinking I'd misunderstood what she'd just said, but she wasn't pausing, so I just watched.

"Our immediate desire is to limit the fear of the unknown and to assure American citizens and the world that within days our financial foundation will once again be viable, stabilized, and we will be conducting business as usual. Wall Street is an integral component in this action and has been suspended from opening for a minimum of one week to conduct a complete assessment and create stabilization features that can be installed before it opens for business again. The pressing need right now is to ensure that panic withdrawals are not allowed, or the impact will be felt the world over.

"In further news, we have been forced to immediately implement the reinstatement of our military draft. Although only a rudimentary estimate of those missing has been established, unlike the general population, the military has the ability to more quickly account for their members. Previous to this morning, the latest numbers for all our armed forces, including reserves, was not quite 1,500,000 members. Although the final audit numbers may change, at this point approximately 417,200, or around 28% of our armed forces have disappeared.

"Those young men already registered and in compliance with the draft laws will be contacted within three days and informed where they should report. Those previously in noncompliance with the law will have a one-time, one-week reprieve before the existing penalty of a $250,000 fine and up to five years in prison will be imposed. It has not yet been determined if this draft will be sufficient to replace those missing and to further bolster our military as is needed, which means a female draft will more than likely be considered."

There was no room left in my mind to absorb anymore shocking information. I thought of Holly's friends still here who would be eligible for the draft, and I was further saddened. The speaker was straightening her papers now, so I hoped she was ending.

"Rather than go over every national concern that has arisen because of this catastrophe, I urge each and every person in America to log onto the government website listed on the bottom of your screen for things you need to be made aware of and answers and solutions that have been compiled.

"In closing, I assure you that the FBI, CIA, as well as world renowned scientists, engineers, terrorist specialists, and theologians are at work, making an accurate evaluation of today's events before announcing their explanation of this occurrence. With all the security, video, and technological information available to us, rest assured we will be able to provide a plausible explanation within hours. We urge you, if at all possible, to remain in your homes, obeying martial law in your area so that you will not suffer additional consequences.

"Lastly, because of certain global implications, the United Nations is convening the first thing in the morning so that world leaders can come together as we uncover this mystery and make future plans. Good afternoon and God bless."

Although I had grabbed a blanket when I slid off the bed, more for comfort than warmth, I shivered uncontrollably as if I was outside unprotected and the weather had just dropped twenty degrees. The screen went black for several seconds, and the echo of her words "...and God bless" rang in my ears. I whispered angrily to the blank screen, "How can you dare say "God bless" now?" I greatly feared the window of His blessing had forever closed and only my nightmares would give me clues as to what we could all expect next. To think that people still thought, just like the Speaker of the House did, that you could use that term so glibly or that it meant anything or would do any good. At least I now knew enough to know that mere words weren't and had never been enough.

My mind was in a muddle. I wished I would have thought to record the speech because I had so many questions. I wasn't sure if I'd missed the answers or that she hadn't given them. First of all, had they said why she was making the speech instead of the President? Was he in seclusion because they thought terrorism might still be involved? But wouldn't the Secretary of State have been the one to take the place of the Vice President? I wasn't sure. Many words I'd just heard were rolling around, mixing themselves up in my thoughts. Martial law being enforced, no national emergency funds given, financial worlds reeling, and stock trading halted. And all of these decisions had been put into place just hours after the rapture. I could only imagine what other government straitjackets would be installed as soon as they had time to reconsider the cause and the ramifications.

Before I could go too far on my own mental tangent, the television mercifully lit up with two different national announcers. You could immediately tell they were on a roll, similar to news reports after previous disasters. With no time for news writers to have scripts written, they were instead listening in their earphones, deciphering what news video or report would be shown next.

It made me wonder what the first news reporter had said right after it happened, or if someone had even disappeared while on camera. I knew something like that would eventually be online. If I could even bear to watch. My planned exodus from earth. The one that I'd missed. I was still so disgusted with myself and the fact that I had slept through it like a baby. I knew that would be the last good sleep I would ever have for the rest of my life. But now I needed to listen to every word they said. I had twelve hours of information and news to catch up on.

I caught the tail end of them reminding people to visit the governmental website, although they immediately chuckled obnoxiously, with a smile to each other, remarking how millions of people trying to visit the website had brought the site down several times. Then they proceeded to say that since so many people were calling in panic because they couldn't access the site, their station would give a synopsis of each of the major points found on the website.

Rather than follow my usual instinct of grabbing a piece of paper to take notes, my body was frozen while I stared unbelievingly at the screen. I didn't want to miss a word, yet I wasn't fully comprehending any of it. I breathed shallow breaths as they ushered in new layers of fear with each word. They first reiterated everything the Secretary of State had already announced, informing us what martial law exactly entailed. Reminding us that everyone in the United States, except for military personnel, police, and fire fighters was under a curfew. Nightshift work had been suspended across the country until further notice. I thought of my next door neighbors who had slipped away to play poker and wondered if they could get in trouble. I almost hoped it meant they wouldn't be coming back for awhile. I felt safer thinking they weren't over there wondering about me.

Then the announcer began listing items of interest on the governmental website, beginning with our bread and butter, cash. He reiterated that all ATMs had been turned off and emptied as a precaution and to prevent looting. But he wasn't finished.

"Any retail facilities that manage to stay open will not be accepting checks, debit or credit cards, but only cash. All banking accounts have been temporarily frozen, with no exceptions, so that no one can wrongfully empty a joint or individual account until verification of missing parties is completed. Limited banking transactions may begin in a few days once the federal government's protective measures have been installed."

I couldn't begin to imagine how quickly panic would erupt. Most people, like our family, kept very little cash on hand and it had been that way for a long time. The convenience of debit cards was coming back to bite us. I wasn't as concerned as some people since I had two houses with food and several cars at my disposal, but this would create extremely desperate people and they were the ones who frightened me.

I wondered if looting had already started in earnest for those needing to buy groceries or gas for their cars. For some reason I had this fear that I'd never had before today that someone was going to commit a crime against me. And that fear grew each time I contemplated the fact that any semblance of Christianity had disappeared. Decades ago the general public seemed to all share good old-fashioned morals, living by the Golden Rule, but year by year, decade by decade, any ethical code had basically disappeared. I had to face facts that every tiny shred of those earlier principles would more than likely disappear since those who had let God be their conscience were gone. And there was no assurances that even the laws would be followed for long. It made me crave a hiding place where I wouldn't have contact with anyone until things settled down. If they ever did.

My shoulders and neck were aching and an old-fashioned migraine had begun in earnest. I desperately wanted to get an ice pack, turn out the lights, and sleep it all off. But I had been in the dark figuratively way too long today and couldn't afford to be any longer, especially since some of it already impacted me personally. I longed for a back rub and an iced tea, and the solitude was already deafening and threatening my sanity. The announcer continued droning on, his forced professionalism convincing me the words he was spouting didn't concern him. I tried to quit analyzing and just listen.

"For governmental purposes, we must begin updating our national missing persons lists. To do so, each American citizen has three days in which to log on to the governmental website previously provided by selecting the large 'Register' icon that appears on your screen. Each person should first log on for themselves. If you are positively aware and have made visual contact with and can legally vouch for your dependents and/or spouse, you may then log their information into the system as well.

"If it is discovered that you erroneously vouched for someone who is, in fact, missing, it will be considered a felony and liable for prosecution. Those without a computer need to call the 800 number on the bottom of the screen. At present there is a four hour wait, however, more lines will be added shortly. It is highly recommended that you remain holding to secure your spot and ensure that you meet the three day deadline.

"Until lists are compiled, verified, and doubled-checked with social security numbers, all government checks will be put on hold and checks not already deposited have had stop payments issued for them. Anyone attempting to cash a governmental check since the time the incident occurred will be arrested and prosecuted for theft. This process will more than likely take a minimum of two months to complete before checks can be reissued.

"Lists of governmental agencies affected are on the website, but as a general rule, every kind of government subsidies are included, such as social security, welfare, unemployment, disability, and food stamps. At this time, in addition to the discontinuation of those checks, payroll checks for all federal, state, and city government and judicial employees will also be delayed. Each person affected by this stoppage will need to appear in person with two forms of verifiable identification before payment can be reinstated.

"The government is encouraging people not to panic, because these are only temporary holds, and the government will be working around the clock to ensure our financial base is back on its feet quickly."

What they were saying was so unbelievable I had to convince myself it wasn't a cruel joke. Could the world have changed this much in twelve hours? Just then a new ticker tape began across the bottom of the screen, announcing that the original emergency announcement would be replayed as soon as this report concluded. I couldn't imagine what else they needed to share. More than the Vice President's disappearance, or the financial collapse of the world? I missed having someone to discuss important things with, or to commiserate with.

But the announcer continued by dropping his next bombshell. "Previous to today's tragedy, our country had approximately 125,000 people on its active missing persons list. Once this three day registration period is completed, those who haven't registered or had someone vouch for them will be placed on this list, which will then be distributed to nationwide gathering stations who will inform governmental departments, financial institutions, and the medical community, so that no one can illegally claim a missing person's benefits or assets. If surviving members of the missing parties can be located, they will be notified when someone has been assigned to their case. Although we obviously have no exact numbers at this point, preliminary estimates give expectations that possibly a little less than 2 billion people worldwide will be found missing, with no less than 85 million of those added to our missing persons list in the United States."

I was dumbfounded. I knew this early they couldn't absolutely *know* how many were missing, but what if they were even close to being right? There would be no surviving something this devastating, or even maintaining any kind of normal. If just over 3,000 people died in the 9/11 tragedy and it paralyzed a city and, to a broader extent, a nation for a time, how on earth could we handle a loss of over 85 million people?

I tried to remember the last figure I'd heard quoted as the world's population. I grabbed a calculator from my mom's nightstand. I thought I'd recently heard the number 7 billion worldwide, and I started punching in their estimate of those missing, and saw they were figuring 27% or 28% missing worldwide. Unbelievable. It had actually happened like we'd been told. Ironic how just recently our country had been having vicious word fights about not wanting to be called a "Christian nation." I guess this day would prove whether it was the truth or not.

I had recently read in a magazine that around 33% of people worldwide considered themselves Christian. But I noticed they weren't predicting that percentage was missing. I knew this meant there were a whole lot of people in my exact situation. Maybe 6%, who might be low-balling it, who said they were Christians, yet were stuck here on earth with me. I plugged those numbers in my calculator and stared.

Positive I had entered the numbers wrong, I punched them in again. Six percent of the worldwide population sounded like such a small number. But it wasn't. I saw the number 420,000,000 come up on the calculator's screen and felt sick. Possibly *four hundred twenty million* people shocked to find themselves still here. I knew that also meant there were at least that many people with a good idea of what had happened today, no matter what their denomination. And the fact that our country had purported to be a "Christian" nation, I wondered if an even bigger percentage of disappointed people were in America. Then besides that horrific number, there were the people who didn't *profess* to be Christians but had moms, grandmothers, or friends who were and who had possibly talked to them, warned them, maybe even pleaded with them. So they knew too. We had all been lulled to sleep.

The announcer wasn't running out of bad news. He was now droning on about welfare checks, government charity organizations, government feeding programs, and suspension of government housing, educational funding, and other programs I'd never heard of. The bottom line was this—no one should expect help for awhile. And they had dumped the problem on cities that were also cash poor.

There weren't enough food banks in the world to keep people afloat, or mortgage companies willing to be lenient when homeowners fell behind. It didn't help that our economy had already been in a downturn for a few years. I wasn't a financial analyst, but even I knew this was going to send the world into a tailspin. If this news report didn't steal the last bit of hope, it would make people angry enough to riot. And sadly, I was going to be around to see the fallout.

While I waited to hear information that might apply to my situation, my mind continued wandering as I figured imaginary numbers. If they were predicting a less-than-30% missing rate, since I lived in the suburbs of a large city, it meant at least 800,000 people were missing in our immediate metropolitan area. I lived in what was called the "Bible Belt" and wondered if that would mean our percentage would be higher or lower, since I was now painfully aware that wearing a name didn't mean a thing to God. It would forever be disappointing to realize this phenomenon known as the "catching away,"[1] or what the church called the rapture, hadn't included everyone that had expected to go.

I already sensed that a line was going to be drawn in the sand. Out of the huge number of us who should have known better, we would have to choose whether to admit our failure and sin and humble ourselves to get ready for the hardest ride of our life, or decide out of pride, anger, disillusionment, or deception to further harden our hearts to the truth, refuse to repent, and forever join the enemy's side. I no longer trusted myself, unsure of everything at the moment, and honestly wondered on which side I would end up.

I tried to remember if I had ever heard of *any* disaster effecting 30% of a population. I remembered the Asian tsunami that hit several years ago, killing over 300,000. But the fact that this loss wasn't contained in one locale would disrupt life across the globe. I could picture the depression, loneliness, and financial ruin that would soon overtake people, very possibly myself as well. I wondered how long I could last on my paycheck, or our pitiful savings account if I never got a check from my company again. It felt odd to even be thinking these thoughts. Me. The planner. And to think that planning could have gotten me off the planet. Which was becoming a very dangerous planet. The announcer began again, and I stared without seeing him.

"Another major job ahead is to estimate the immediate loss of tax revenue from the missing millions as well as previous tax-paying businesses that will no longer be viable, which is why the government cannot promise that any previous funding or agencies will continue as before. In addition, those not having yet received their tax refunds for the past year will instead be given a credit on their taxes for the current year." I sat stunned, remembering all the political promises we'd heard from both sides in the last election, promises of new programs and benefits guaranteed to bring our economy back from the depths. Promises many were counting on that had just been shattered. And to further place my life up in the air, we hadn't yet received our refund, so there went any money I had hoped could fill the gap.

Although I didn't count on very many people acknowledging that God had kidnapped 2 billion people off the face of the earth, I *did* know that this was exactly what legal contracts called an "Act of God" or an "uncontrollable or unexpected event" that most contracts included in the fine print so when something unexplained ever happened, then all bets were off, contracts and agreements would not be binding. Meaning, basically? We were all sunk. For a moment I truly pitied people who desperately needed assistance and would not survive without it. But I was having trouble focusing on his words again.

"Most people are aware that the majority of satellites controlling cell phone systems and internet access have been not working properly or at best intermittently. Repair departments for these systems have been given permission to work around the clock to get systems up and running, given that these are the mainframe systems used to inform employees of working arrangements, locating missing family members, and notifying the general public of policies and procedures."

I thought it ironic that for quite some time the popular thing to do was to let go of land lines, but yet those were the few forms of communication working properly now. And it was like he had read my mind as he continued.

"Because so many people no longer have land lines but are using cell service completely, a master list of individuals in the United States still having land lines is being created by the government as this broadcast is being aired. The government will be informing those individuals that there is a probability that homes or offices with existing land phone lines will be commandeered by local or national governmental offices to be used as command centers until cell service has stabilized. Displaced individuals will be provided living quarters in the nearest military barracks or hotels."

My mouth fell open again. That *had* to be a joke. I might lose the possibility of living in my own home because of my stupid phone line? Amazing how a little decision to keep a house phone a few months ago might now lead the government on a straight path to my door, with no way of hiding or escaping.

CHAPTER SEVENTEEN

Sunday, eleven thirty-eight p.m.

THE NEWS I'D watched over the last hour and a half disturbed me
at such a deep level I found it hard to concentrate on what most of it
would mean to me personally. I tried to calm myself down, but knowing
I had missed the bulk of the news made me nervous. I missed Mark's
calming presence. I knew we all needed to know the nuts and bolts of
how to get through the next few days, and for those without a Christian
worldview, there was nothing else on which the world needed to focus.
Because of my choices, I was now stuck in a world where the majority
would rule. Whatever *they* decided, I had no choice but to live with it.

Incredulously, in just a few short hours, people I previously thought
had *little* authority over me had grabbed it, and were rearranging my life
willy-nilly. With regret, I recalled in the past how I usually felt it was a
waste of time to vote, especially for local leaders, thinking my choices
either didn't count or didn't matter. But the problem now was that
the politicians whom *someone* had voted for, were making all kinds of
decisions affecting every single piece of my life. I had naively thought
I was insulated from government interference and politics for the most
part. I had always thought as long as I worked, paid my taxes and my
bills, and didn't break the law, I was in charge. Perhaps when I did vote, I
didn't always vote the way God would have wanted, but I never actually

dreamed these people would control the details of my life. I had never researched their beliefs because I had never anticipated a day like this. My eyes felt tight and swollen and I was tired of the depressing, negative news CNN was spewing. I picked up the remote and changed channels to one that usually offered more human interest news.

Unlike the professional newscasters on CNN, I felt a twinge of empathy for this woman. Although she looked the part, wearing a smart gray suit and pink pin-striped silk blouse that probably cost the equivalent of a week of my salary, her face told a different story. The other newscasters had smiled, paused appropriately as they read from the teleprompter, and articulated properly as they were taught when they got their high-priced journalism degree. But although this announcer looked the part, you could tell she *knew*. She knew the truth and it was killing her. Her makeup almost looked intact, but her eyes were swollen and it was obvious she had been crying recently. I allowed myself to ponder who *she* had lost. She looked young and hip, so perhaps she was grieving for her parents. Maybe she'd had a praying mom, like I'd had, yet was intent on living life, being successful, and probably not quite living the way her parents had prayed and hoped. And now both of us were left with no one to pray for us.

She couldn't have moved up the journalism ladder by stuttering or not being able to control her emotions, so it was painful to watch her struggle now. You could tell she wasn't faking her distressed persona. Her voice was shaky and on the verge of cracking, almost having the power to drag me along with her. It seemed to be taking all she had to sit and read words she couldn't bear to consider. I knew where she was coming from, and I was glad I didn't have to do any public speaking at the moment. I even spotted a folded tissue beside her papers as if she knew she needed to be prepared. I was surprised her producer hadn't pulled her from the heinous task, but if they were shorthanded, there was probably pressure to have all hands on deck, as if this was a normal disaster. The problem was that in the midst of our own personal disasters, who was really interested in hearing about other people's problems?

I noticed that rather than commercials being shown, apparently they were using normal advertising time slots to repeat the government phone numbers for registration. It made the surreal seem even more bizarre. Quick blurbs reiterating government program stoppages, the "no checks until further notice" policy, and other benefits we shouldn't count on, as if they were announcing something as blasé as the weather instead of words guaranteed to bring havoc.

Then she was back. It looked like her makeup was freshened, and she seemed a bit more composed. I wondered if her producer had screamed at her to pull herself together or she would lose her job. I knew at this stage of the game we all needed to keep the jobs we had and pray that we got paid. I continued to watch and listen.

"As most of you are aware, we have been reporting on this phenomenon beginning mere moments after it happened, but for those who might have missed our earlier emergency broadcast, we will now replay the previously aired program followed by updated videos of major accidents that have occurred today. Over to you, Frankie."

This was what I'd been waiting for. I knew my morning had been extremely strange, and that was before I had a clue about what had happened. With so many accidents in my own neighborhood, I couldn't begin to imagine the extent of worldwide devastation there would be. I wondered what the world as a whole looked like now. Had the rapture already drastically changed it? My gut told me what my mind was afraid to consider, that my worst fears would come true.[1] If the government blatantly shut itself down, even temporarily, knowing that their decision would cause widespread panic, then nothing should surprise me. We were about to see how crazy this world could get.

The video that must have originally been shown hours ago began to replay, the camera focused on Frankie, a reporter I'd watched before. Although he always appeared to be a young, cocky kind of guy, I saw a seriousness and formality on his face and leaned in close to see what I'd missed from earlier today. The ticker tape on the bottom of the screen said: "Original broadcast from 11:00 a.m."

It was strangely odd realizing I still didn't know when *it* had actually happened, but now, at least, I knew the rapture had happened sometime before 11:00 this morning. But there was no point in focusing on that once he started speaking.

"As many of you are already aware, and as we will report in greater detail later, there were many plane crashes today, some immediately after the disappearances and others later when automatic pilot features failed or planes ran out of fuel. We will be reporting on some of these accidents at length as we receive detailed information, however, at this time I must turn the broadcast over to our national headquarters." I knew that had to mean it was a bigger story than a local reporter would cover, so I listened up. As the screen shot switched to the national news desk, I saw it was the regular 10 p.m. news anchor ready to speak, and he didn't hesitate.

"It is with extreme sadness that we must confirm that Air Force One crashed into the Washington Monument not long after takeoff this morning."

Involuntarily I screamed, "What?" Surely he wasn't saying…?" I just had to shut up and listen.

"According to preliminary reports released by the CIA, President Walker, his entire extended family, various media representatives, government employees, and secret service agents onboard were all apparently killed instantly."

I breathed, "No…" thinking I wasn't really hearing this.

But he continued, "Since at thise time there is no way of knowing if this tragedy is somehow related to the disappearances or if it is terrorism, or unrelated to either, our government has placed our entire country on alert with an investigation into possible causes. The crash site has been closed off for several city blocks surrounding the Monument until damage and loss of life is assessed and the investigation complete."

Almost immediately, so rudimentary it seemed thrown together by novices, they began showing a brief historical video montage memorializing his presidency. As always, they showed highlights and strengths, ignoring struggles or failures that the same media would have harped on yesterday, instead making him out to be a saint today.

But I was having trouble following them as the shock settled in. I closed my eyes for a moment, unable to believe what I'd just heard. What else did I not yet know that would turn my life upside down? No wonder the government was overly skittish now. With the President dying in a fiery crash coupled with the Vice President disappearing off the face of the earth, for the first time in history we had lost both top leaders in two freakish ways within moments of each other, and our country was now being run by people not one person had voted for. I was very frightened.

I slowly opened my eyes, fear deciding how fast my heart would beat, and watched as pictures of the Washington Monument were shown just minutes after the accident, and the sight was astounding. As the camera panned the large area filled with wreckage, they began to include random historical snippets long forgotten, such as "Constructed to Commemorate the First President of the United States, George Washington," then, "Completed in 1888, proudly standing over 555 feet in the air." Except that it wasn't standing proudly at all now.

Then, suddenly, the announcer seemed to fall out of character. As if he'd forgotten he was on camera, he stared for a second at the sheet of paper in his hand, then said in an almost derisive tone, "Oh, here's another lesser known tidbit about the monument. Apparently the Latin words 'Laus Deo' were carved on the highest point of the monument, which means 'Praise be to God.'" Then he shook his head and let out an angry little sigh, before almost saying under his breath, "That doesn't quite seem to fit the day, does it?" I just stared, letting it all sink in.

They then began showing "before and after" pictures side by side, and it was unbelievable. I could see that Air Force One must have been in a dive to be so close to the ground that it basically sliced off about two-thirds of the monument. As the helicopter cameras panned closer, you could see what had once been one of the wings maybe a hundred feet past the monument, and then they showed the tail and how it landed right in the middle of the "Reflecting Pool," the normally serene, beautiful strip of water, famous for its reflection of the monument.

I remembered pictures showing the rows of trees on either side of the water and could see that several of the trees on one side had been partially mowed down by the second wing and then caught fire from the burning fragments. Because the trees were so near each other, the fire had spread to every single tree on one side, scorching them completely. As the camera panned in and out, you could see huge haphazard piles from the chunks of marble, sandstone, and granite created when the monument toppled. On top of the remaining section of the monument, there were wires and pieces of metal structure sticking up randomly, and then I winced as I remembered. The metal pieces had to be the remains of the elevator that took tourists to the top. And since this was Mother's Day, the famous tourist attraction may have been even busier than normal.

As if the announcer had read my thoughts, the pictures on the screen changed from the scenery to the affected people. The first pictures showed the late President and his wife, and as the names and titles of everyone they believed had joined him for the trip scrolled across the screen, the accident became even more gruesome, if possible.

The President's two grown sons and daughter had been on board with their entire families, as well as both sets of grandparents. My mouth slowly fell open again. In one moment our President and his entire extended family had been snuffed out.

I wanted to stop and consider each tidbit as it was thrown to me, but each seemed worse than the previous revelation, and the overload began to stockpile in my mind. I could feel my pulse. Like a methodical online morgue, they began showing pictures of employees they knew were working at the Monument today. For some reason when they showed the pictures of teenagers, obviously part-timers trying to make weekend money, all I could do was shake my head. The next group of pictures showed various people who had been invited on Air Force One. Obviously, a fun Mother's Day trip had been anticipated as they had reportedly left Andrews Air Force Base in Maryland earlier that morning, headed toward a Mother's Day afternoon brunch at Camp David.

As they switched back to live pictures of the salvaging process, I saw twenty or thirty fire trucks, ambulances, secret service, and army personnel swarming the area. Then, almost so nonchalantly I missed it, he said that the bodies of the pilot, co-pilot, and flight engineer had yet to be found.

But of course that explained it. There had been no sabotage, terrorism, or equipment malfunction. If no one else had figured it out, I sure knew they didn't need to find the "black box" because, in a strange twist of fate, all three of them must have been Christians. I tried to imagine the absolute terror in the hearts of the air traffic controllers as they realized their most precious cargo was off track and no one in the cockpit was responding. No warning, no one screaming "Mayday" or there to turn on the automatic pilot. Instead I pictured a cockpit as three people silently, calmly, joyously left the earth's atmosphere in a fraction of a moment. And perhaps it was several minutes before their most important passengers even knew anything was amiss. Or maybe they never did. Nevertheless, without giving their passengers a choice, they had seen to it that the entire group entered eternity moments after the pilots.

That made me contemplate the horror of those dying because of accidents immediately after the rapture. Realizing most people had probably been oblivious to what had taken place before they died, without a second chance to make it right, being in hell right now. No matter how desperate of a place I was in at the moment, they had it worse than I did. I still had a slim chance. That fact didn't do much to cheer me, though, because my regrets were growing by the minute. I couldn't see how the stress of life would be possible to bear now. Often feeling over-burdened with life before, now my mental burden was heavier than any physical ones had ever been.

I was glad when the announcer seized my attention again. "As you can imagine, every news agency keeps downloading video after video shared by other news agencies and audience members, and we are doing our best to compile them to show montages of this unusual day's events from around the world. You will now see an assortment of the more terrifying and unusual accidents caught on video."

Waiting for them to cue it, I whispered, "*What* are we going to do?"

I watched with a combination of horror and sadness at the physical and emotional wreckage we had been left to clean up. It was as if hundreds of million-dollar horror movies had been filmed at once and merged together. Except this was real life. With lightning-like speed, and no time spent in the editing room, I began watching videos filled with horrors multiplied many times over.

The first video was obviously a home video of someone at a men's softball game in a small town in Ohio. It must have been filmed by a girlfriend or wife, as she yelled encouragement while he was batting. The second he struck out, while the camera was still on his embarrassed face, there was a strange, horrendous, indescribable sound in the background. Before her viewfinder had time to follow the noise, the man's face turned upward and by his expression you knew something horrific was about to happen. The lady finally woke from her trance to follow the sound and in a moment the entire camera's frame was filled with an American Airlines plane not more than a hundred feet off the ground. In the next second, the most terrifying mixture of screams was combined with sounds of an explosion as a fireball filled the video screen and it went black. My heart was pounding again and my thoughts went off on their own tangent as the announcer gave minor details of an accident that no longer mattered.

Missing from my memories flooding back, was a distinct lack of talk about the rapture, the nuts and bolts of it. From what now seems like a completely naïve viewpoint despite my upbringing, I had honestly mistakenly figured that when the time came, there would be an obvious "great divide" between the Christians and the non-Christians. No gray areas. Very little wondering or surprise from either side. I had even pictured that after the initial shock, life wouldn't be much different for those left behind. In fact, I had figured the world would be happier without Christians around. But I had been wrong. I was now convinced that probably millions had been living in denial just like me, fully assuming they were heaven bound but now finding themselves unexpectedly left behind. And barely twelve hours later, life had drastically changed for every one of us.

What was catching me off guard now was what I could only describe as "residual loss of life." The world wasn't just missing the millions or billions who had been swallowed up off the face of the earth. But how had no one predicted or discussed the fact that thousands and thousands of people would die from every imaginable type of accidents and mishaps as the Christians disappeared? Because now that I fully considered it, I saw how common sense dictated that for all those Christians driving or flying a vehicle, there would have been a corresponding accident. And across the globe, accidents of every kind and type had to have occurred, and I knew of only a fraction of them so far.

A little surprised I hadn't yet heard any "plausible" explanation for what had happened, I wondered if the truth would ever be acknowledged, or if prognosticators were still busy spinning their explanations and responses. It was reminiscent of the time of Jesus' resurrection. Would this great disappearance be coupled with all the other lives lost through accidents and crimes and eventually be lumped together and ultimately blamed on God? I had a feeling people would be encouraged to quickly move on with life.

In fact, I could almost hear a quiet, beguiling voice in my own ear explaining how I could create a new life on my own terms now, without anyone looking over my shoulder. It sounded almost peaceful but scary, and I knew I dare not focus on that voice. I was going to have to fight to remember how I got in this position in the first place.

The plane crash beside the softball game was just the start, so I braced myself. Next, they showed a huge overpass interchange in Atlanta called "Spaghetti Junction" because of its intricate highway exchanges, and the giant mix-master looked like parking lots on top of parking lots set on fire. I saw at least four jack-knifed semi-trucks strewn across the highways, some having completely gone down over barriers, with hundreds of cars in haphazard locations and directions, dangling off edges, others smashed and on fire. An occasional camera zoomed in on people wandering aimlessly in both directions on the highway, seemingly in a trance, with others trying to use non-working cell phones.

From that scene the video moved to Las Vegas and the upscale Bellagio Hotel. As the picture filled the screen, I sucked in my breath. If this would have been a movie, I would have been impressed by the special effects. But it was real. I knew it used to be a beautiful hotel built in a half circle with a crown in the middle and elaborate fountains in front. It contained four thousand rooms. But now a hovering helicopter showed another airplane had crashed into the hotel, almost as if it had attempted to knock the crown off its stand, crashing right into the center. Somehow the angle with which it had entered had prevented it from going all the way through, and it was still easily identifiable as a plane despite the huge fire and horrendous smoke. And just like most crash sites, what the collision didn't obliterate, fuel tanks were finishing. As they ruptured and spilled, it was as if they had spread enough of their poison to invade all the hotel rooms. All but a few windows had flames licking out of them. It was a sight to behold, if you ignored the fact that thousands of people had probably been caught unaware, sleeping in late after a night of gambling, planning a relaxing weekend ending with a fancy Mother's Day brunch.

The video shifted awkwardly with a split second of black screen and then a picture of a burning helicopter dangling from a metal structure. When the camera pulled away, I could see that of all places it was the Eiffel Tower. I shook my head in disbelief, wondering if God was making sure we were never again in awe of anything as mundane as a structure. But down deep I knew that instead of all this being representative of God being vindictive, all He'd done was determine the moment in time to call His family home, something planned since the beginning of time.

My original thirst for news was more than overwhelmed by this time, and although my eyes were still pointed toward the TV, it was hard to comprehend everything I was seeing. The next thirty minutes of video showed picture after picture of depressing, unbelievably heart-wrenching loss of life and property. From watching television footage in major cities throughout the world, then switching to home videos taken from someone's roof, showing an entire neighborhood, in a tiny, unassuming town, totally engulfed in flames.

The next clip began with more helicopter footage as the announcer took us to a beautiful, large rural ranch in South Texas called "King Ranch." I faintly recognized the name, but the ticker tape on the bottom of the screen reminded me it was one of the largest ranches in the world, made up of almost 1,000,000 acres, famous for raising thousands and thousands of cattle, horses, and exotic animals. As the helicopter flew over magnificent homes and multiple barns, it was so impressive I tried to imagine what they might be about to show. Then the camera changed directions and I saw billows of smoke past one over-sized, modern barn. When the helicopter passed over the barn, I saw with horror where yet another commercial jet had crashed in the largest pasture I'd ever seen.

Apparently the jet had been gently angling toward the ground when it hit because it looked like it had skidded for hundreds and hundreds and hundreds of yards, scraping a path, or actually creating its own highway in its wake until reaching its final resting place. The bloodbath was so overwhelming it was implausible. Not only had the plane crash immediately killed and obliterated what looked like hundreds and hundreds of cattle, but the jet's fuel tanks had burst, splattering in all directions, spewing fuel the entire length of the trail so as soon as sparks from the broken wheels scraped the countryside, the streams of fuel had lit, and there was no containing the damage.

I couldn't even imagine the sounds the remaining terrified cattle had made as they were caught in a stampede of burning cattle stumbling over those already dead from the original impact. It was obvious burning cattle began running from fright because everywhere you looked there were burning streaks headed in every direction as far as the eye could see. I saw no grass left unscathed. But even worse than the loss of beautiful land and homes, was the pitiful burnt carcasses and charred bones lying everywhere with an occasional scorched cow bleating in shock. The gruesome sight made me want to cover my eyes.

The helicopter continued moving toward the area where the jet stopped, and I could see how little by little the jet had disintegrated as it lumbered across the countryside. As they hovered over it, it looked like the Boeing cockpit had blown to shreds first, also contributing to the fire. I could only imagine the abject terror of passengers after the cockpit split in two right in front of their eyes, leaving the front of the plane open and them unprotected as the plane catapulted across the land. It must have begun to tilt at one point because the right engine and wing had snapped off after only a hundred feet or so, which then sent the plane tilting in the other direction and its wing deep into the earth, starting a giant splintering effect, eventually shattering the wing off.

The announcer felt compelled to horrify his listeners further by telling them how bystanders reported that the final trajectory of the plane caused it to spin out-of-control, turning end over end and sending passengers flying in all directions. The details made me nauseous, and I shut my eyes, trying to get the vision out of my mind. The segment ended when he announced that the "black box" had not yet been located.

I heard myself screaming at the television, "It doesn't matter! None of it *matters*!" As if by explaining that the pilots were in heaven would make living on earth more palatable. For the black box would only reveal that there was a second in flight where everything was perfectly normal, and then silence.

I lay face down on the floor crying, pounding the floor with my fist, fully feeling an agony I'd never felt before. The problem was, when I closed my eyes, my imagination focused even more on my own situation, and the horror intensified. After a minute or so, I grabbed a tissue, forced my eyes open, and sat up, hoping whatever I saw next would distract me from the deepening depression overtaking me.

CHAPTER EIGHTEEN

Monday, one forty a.m.

I RELUCTANTLY LOOKED back at the TV in time to see a reporter stick a microphone in the face of some executive. It seemed silly watching people try to conduct a normal interview while the world was falling apart. I noticed the United Airlines logo behind them, and leaned forward to hear him promise they were trying to assess the overall damage, although it would take days to fully evaluate the situation. He continued with a sober expression, "On a normal day our airline alone has around 3,500 planes in the air throughout the world, and today's schedule was no different. We positively know about several *hundred* accidents, and we still have a number of missing planes, so that number will more than likely rise. We are devastated by the loss of life around the world, and the financial hit our company will take will tally into the hundreds of billions of dollars."

I tried to imagine what the skies must have looked like this morning with pilotless planes in the air from every commercial airline in the world, much less private planes and helicopters. The man went on to explain that there were normally about 5,000 commercial jets from all airlines in the air one time in the U.S. and between 40,000 and 50,000 commercial jets flying throughout the *world* at any one given time. I knew that meant if an average of twenty or thirty percent of the pilots had disappeared, and a smaller percentage had both pilot *and* copilot gone, there might have been 10,000 airplane crashes around the world today. And if an average of 200 people were on each plane, it would be easy to estimate up to two million people dying in airline crashes alone. And that didn't account for the loss of life on the ground when they went down.

The executive began sharing losses they were already aware of, showing video after video of unbelievable crash sites. Some from airport security videos, showing collisions occurring during takeoffs or landings, others occurring at odd times throughout the rest of the day after automatic pilot settings became irrelevant once fuel tanks ran dry when it was past time to land.

The next detail they shared was just as chilling. The CEO solemnly explained that exacerbating the problem was the fact that hundreds of air traffic controllers around the world were also missing, leaving stations in a quandary as they attempted, suddenly shorthanded, to locate off track airplanes while frantically trying to understand where their co-workers were, just like the rest of the world had been doing. As he continued to explain details and issues they were facing, it sounded like a nightmare for every airline and airport around the world.

I breathed long and deep. There were so many convoluted layers of problems and issues created by what happened, there would have been no way anyone could have considered the possibility of the subsequent ramifications. It didn't seem fair. We were stuck here. Left to deal with so much.

They finished the interview, but the woeful saga was far from over. The announcer continued and it was obvious the problems with planes had been a major issue. They showed another airline with an equally dreadful crash in Brownsville, Texas, at a major border crossing between Texas and Mexico. The crash had closed the entire thoroughfare between the countries. From what I could tell, it had actually crashed on the Texas side, smashing the long line of cars waiting to pass over the border, the momentum pushing its wreckage through the border plaza, crushing the customs offices beyond that, then obliterating maybe another fifty cars on the other side. I was sure there was heightened traffic at the border because of Mother's Day, making it even worse than it might have been. I felt another surge of anger, but knew it would do no good being angry at God. We had all made our choices, and now had to live with all the consequences.

The journalist awkwardly held his hand to his ear mid-sentence, saying they were switching to a New York affiliate station. The screen clumsily changed, showing a flustered older newscaster shuffling papers, unsuccessfully attempting to organize his thoughts. I watched as he yanked his ear piece out in anger, tired of listening to the voices yammering in his ear.

As he began to speak I saw another heartrending sight. One of the Staten Island ferry boats, the *Andrew J. Barberi* had crashed into a pier soon after the disaster, and although they had not yet verified the number of customers on the ferry, they had estimated from the amount of money collected that day, that there might have been close to 6,000 passengers on the boat. The possibility of a high death toll was probable. I looked closer and was horrified to see no recovery teams or emergency crews in sight, even though video crews were reporting the carnage. Thankfully the reporter didn't bring attention to the gruesome sight the video also clearly showed, the large number of bodies floating in the water. I felt like a voyeur, and was repulsed and saddened.

My thoughts were muddled and I felt like I was trying to think through a thick fog settling over my brain. I felt devoid of hope, as the new world unfolded before me. One that was ugly and desperate and raw and terrifying. A loud, sad sigh escaped as I wondered if my husband and daughter and missing friends had thought upon this day more than I had, and maybe that was why they weren't here.

Concentrating again on the television to break my train of thought, it was obvious technology had outdone itself. A good majority of the world's entire population had a cell phone or video camera or both, and added to all the security cameras everywhere, it was providing an unlimited supply of the carnage and proof of what had happened today. I would never have dreamed there would be this much death and destruction on top of the disappearances.

We knew how long it took cities to recover from disasters, but there was no timetable and not enough money on earth that would accommodate for the repairing, recovering, or restoring that would be necessary after what had happened today. No combination of hurricanes, tsunamis, tornadoes, earthquakes, or evil events inspired by terrorism would ever compare to the loss that was evident so far. I had to surrender to the terrifying idea that life would never be the same. There was no place to deposit the hopelessness I was feeling, no one to turn to. I needed to talk to someone, but couldn't think of who.

I barely watched as odd accident after accident appeared on the screen. Then they showed a video of a tourist attraction in Bangkok called The Floating Market. A fuel truck had crashed down into the canal, leaking a full load of fuel into the water which had then spread the length of the river, catching on fire. The wildfire that spread minutes after the accident hadn't limited itself to the miles of fuel-tainted water now in flames, but had spread to every individual market on each side of the river. Everyone's livelihood gone up in flames, and probably lives lost as well. I saw houseboat after houseboat with barely a few shreds of metal as a reminder of what used to be.

I was just thankful that in all of the accidents I'd seen, I knew no children were experiencing these horrors. I kept thinking of past disasters, when civilized countries would pitch in with millions of dollars and relief efforts to help hurting countries. But that wouldn't happen this time. Every single country, almost every single family, had its own burdens to bear. Benevolence had gone out the window, with selfishness the new rule.

Although seeing the shocking stories took my mind off my situation for a few seconds here and there, it didn't help my mood. Every story added a new layer of despondency on top of my already darkened mood. But I couldn't tear my eyes away from the screen. The aftermath of this phenomenon had been so unpredictable and terrible and bizarre. If only I could divorce *myself* from the situation, it would have been an astonishing display of what happened as God's plan had touched the earth. But being in the middle of it, it was threatening my sanity.

The cameras then jerkily moved to a huge fire in Dublin, Ireland with an entire neighborhood up in flames. Blocks and blocks of homes, with only a couple not yet totally engulfed. A second later they moved on, with a video of a Celebrity Cruise ship. As I curiously watched, something seemed different, until I realized there was no announcer, no music, nothing. At this point all we had was a running caption at the bottom of the screen.

I stretched, feeling cold and stiff and exhausted. I twisted around to look at Mom's bedside clock and saw it was 3:25 in the morning. No wonder. They must have run out of replacement announcers and figured it didn't matter, and they were right. Pictures were enough to portray the utter destruction and desolation, and I had a feeling we were just being shown the tiniest pieces that had garnered attention.

The sad news was announced by the ticker tape, saying the cruise ship had been in the middle of a fourteen day cruise out of Sydney, Australia. As the ship had rounded Westernport Bay near Phillip Island, it had gone off course, running directly into the concrete piers of the bridge. The picture, taken a few hours earlier, showed a large hole, the size of the width of the bridge, torn into the front right side of the ship, causing it to sink. But then when they switched to a current view, I saw no recovery teams and the ship was almost lost from view now. The final ticker tape said many of the life boats had still been attached as it went down.

I was worn out. I had been awake about seventeen hours but that wasn't why I was tired. The adrenaline and fear and disappointment coursing through my body had kept any intentions of sleep away. My emotions were attaching themselves to each and every disaster scene. As sorry as I was feeling for myself, I was also hurting for everyone else. And all the while the analyzer inside me kept trying to get a grip on the impact this was going to have on my immediate life. Not knowing the answer to that question was upsetting my stomach, my heart, and my mind.

It was obvious the loss of life was quickly becoming more than an astounding number. I wondered if they would ever get a grip on it or figure actual numbers on how many had gone "missing." Somehow I doubted it. When the government and the media fully recognized how widespread this had been, it would almost be *too* frightening to report the numbers. Too unbelievable. Proof that no human being had been in control of the day. Those who never knew God couldn't handle the truth. And those, like me, who had known God, were in worse shape. I had a small picture of what the future held, and frankly, it scared the wits out of me. I determined to stop letting my emotions follow each heart wrenching story, and just store up information I needed to survive. I just needed to think clearly.

My hand found the remote and I mindlessly surfed. Several major channels were off the air. It felt like the world had ended, and I wished it had. I found another news channel still trying to act like life was normal, and I laid the remote down. My attention was drawn to what looked like a group of animal rights protestors holding signs around a facility saying "Save the Animals." I shook my head saying out loud, "You've *got* to be kidding me," as I wondered how anyone could focus on any kind of an "issue" now. When the protestors moved, I saw they were standing in front of a wildlife animal sanctuary.

The ticker tape at the bottom of the screen announced it was northeast of Denver, in Keenesburg, Colorado. Apparently a large truck without a driver had run off the road, mowing down major sections of fencing, barreling through the sanctuary's outside fence, then through several inside security fences on the property. Two families visiting the sanctuary had been immediately killed as they stood in the truck's path. But what the protestors were concerned about now were the animals that had escaped. Apparently the sanctuary had positively discovered that no less than fifty wild animals, including bears, leopards, lions, and wolves had escaped, already killing several teenagers as they tried to run from them. I thought it a bit sad the picketers were more concerned with saving the animals than the people who had been mauled.

I felt numb, remembering how people had talked about the coming tribulation and the seven years of prophecies soon to be coming true. Because if life after the rapture got any worse than today had been, then it was only a prelude to hell. I had been sufficiently warned, and it hadn't helped. At this moment in time I *hated* the fact that God had given us total autonomy to make such a serious choice on our own, especially now that I was in the group that had made the wrong one.

My eyelids half closed, almost in an effort to shield myself from the barrage of carnage, yet I couldn't stop watching the continual litany of tragedies. Any kind or type of accident you could dream of had happened. Several train collisions, one with an Amtrak train that had departed from Chicago early Sunday morning headed to New York City. At this point the details were sketchy, but I saw the entire train, every single car, had turned over on its side, some upside down in a deep ravine, and the majority of cars had caught on fire.

I thought of the jobs people held that ordinarily wouldn't be considered dangerous at all, but how they had suddenly turned dangerous today. Like the person responsible for switching train tracks, or watching a monitor to prevent a deadly accident or the air traffic controllers or 911 operators or anyone driving a vehicle. In one moment's time, war had broken out. The sad part was that it was a one-sided war, and by the time we could pick up any weapons, it was over.

Apparently this news channel was trying its best to cover every aspect of our changed world, so it now brought out some high-powered business guru, a consultant who seemed to have figured out the world's problems and had all the answers. He pronounced with great fanfare what anyone with a brain had already figured out. That every business would have to step back and reevaluate their future and, depending upon the consumers they served, figure out if they needed more or less of their products or services. Some whole groups of potential customers were gone and certain businesses were no longer needed. Some businesses would have severe layoffs, while others wouldn't be able to find *enough* qualified employees.

He acknowledged that the possibility of business failure was enormous. I thought of businesses that catered to churches or Christians. Would people flock to them with the hope that they had the answer? Or would their product be useless in a world with few people attempting to find God? I thought of church and ministry employees. For those left behind, they suffered embarrassment, much less the added financial pressure of losing their job and benefits.

I knew exactly which businesses would grow exponentially. Anyone providing anything to numb the pain. Alcohol, tobacco, and pharmaceutical companies would be needed now more than ever. Illegal drugs would be in greater demand and those who for years had urged the legalization of certain drugs would find little or no argument now. But that scenario sent my mind down a scarier path because with heightened usage of substances, came more crime, accidents, addictions, overdoses, and health issues. However, feeling numb sounded really good now, and that temptation would be very real. Even for me.

I was tired of hearing this blow hard nonchalantly explain how he was sure our economy would eventually survive and bounce back and how no one should panic. Self-absorption and pride exuded from him and it was obvious he was going to use this opportunity to get credit and attention for his so-called wisdom. I turned the channel and found a local station that had come back on the air.

I saw a local news celebrity I had watched for years looking pale and unusually somber. It gave me strange comfort to see someone looking sufficiently serious, though. When I heard the emergency warning beep that usually only sounded during tornado or storm warnings, I turned the volume up. She announced how our local State and City government officials had declared that we were in a state of emergency just like the majority of cities nationwide and were under a strict curfew from sundown to sun up. She then said they would be replaying the national message with new regulations that would affect anyone living in the United States. Although I could now partially understand our government's knee-jerk reaction, I still felt it was premature and more devastating to the economy, civilization in general, and our wellbeing.

Then she began saying things I hadn't heard yet. I numbly listened as she announced that the state of emergency included a suspension of property insurance policies and payments for accidents of any kind, retroactive to the exact time of the disappearances. It was obvious who they were protecting. I imagined thousands and thousands of teenagers and young people who had been living with their parents and how they would soon be homeless, and even many who had lost a spouse and perhaps their entire household income in one moment. Those whose houses had burned down and now didn't know when or if they would ever receive compensation now without a place to live and perhaps no income. Those who had lost a vehicle in an accident and were now stranded with no expectation of a settlement. I imagined the utter chaos that one flippant sentence was going to bring to many lives. I gave a tiny sigh of relief, knowing at least I didn't have any property loss to worry about.

But then it suddenly turned personal. I had purposely not allowed myself to focus on what life was going to be like without my husband, daughter, or parents. Even outside my immediate family, I knew there was a good possibility I was all alone in this new world. What a complicated mess this was going to be.

It might sound cold, but I have to admit it had crossed my mind during the past couple of hours, and had given me a small level of comfort knowing I had life insurance policies on my husband and daughter. That if nothing else, that money would pay off our house and debts in case my company went under or I lost my job.

But the announcer wasn't finished and her next words turned my heart to cold, hard stone. She calmly informed us that not only was liability insurance suspended, but life insurance was as well. At that point I just closed my eyes and listened. She explained that because of the extreme number of accidents, even if insurance companies *could* determine liability, most would have to declare bankruptcy if forced to make settlements. They would probably never be expected to even research details on who had died and how. An administrative nightmare as she described it. Then she pounded the final nail deep into my mental coffin.

"And for those who have "missing" family members, you should be aware that life insurance companies *rarely* pay for missing individuals even during normal times, and only then after several years of investigation, or a minimum of seven years." My eyes opened and I stared straight ahead, shivering as I realized with one sentence she had destroyed the only bright spot I had found.

I took a deep, slow breath as I stared at the ceiling, thinking about what she had just said. Seven years. It was a rather magical, terrifying number. I wouldn't be here in seven years, and by then none of this would matter. That thought was staggering. But with Mark's income gone, and the possibility of mine as well if my firm didn't reopen, I might as well say goodbye to my home and any other security I had. I began to think random thoughts, wondering if my parents' house was paid off or if authorities would even let me legally stay here if it was. I realized everything was up in the air and I couldn't begin to imagine what other laws and restrictions would be placed on us next. I was afraid to refresh my memory of what the Bible predicted for my new future, and because God knew we couldn't handle it, I had to assume He probably hadn't even given us the entire horrible, frightening picture.

Then I heard a noise and held my breath. While in the back part of the house I had convinced myself I was in the safest location, and the quiet had surrounded me like a cocoon, giving me a false sense of security. Until I heard the noise. I was petrified. I heard it again and turned the television off, welcoming the dark. I listened carefully, trying to figure out where it was coming from. Then I knew. It was a familiar creaking. Someone was in one of the rocking chairs on the porch. Dad and Mom loved their sprawling front porch and had two of those old fashioned wooden rocking chairs. Upon listening closer, though, I was dismayed to realize it sounded like *both* chairs were rocking. One would have been frightening enough, but I had no chance against two people.

Were they going to break in? Could I not be safe from harm for just *one* night after this traumatic day? I knew Dad didn't have a gun and I wasn't sure there was anything else in the house worth finding to protect myself with, so I sat quietly, fearfully waiting. After what seemed an interminably long time, I heard loud laughter and heavy steps that sounded like boots. For a second I couldn't tell if they were walking toward the front door or off the porch. Please, I prayed frantically. Please be distracted. Find someone else to harass. I heard laughter again but it seemed farther away and I allowed myself to hope. Then I heard a car door slam and a loud muffler. I desperately waited for them to drive away, out of my life. Inside my head, I was begging, "Please give me time to figure everything out before I have to fight for my life!" After what felt like an eternity, I heard the car drive away and it was quiet again. I felt thankful and relieved as tears sprang up. The smallest thing could feel like a miracle now.

But did any of this really matter? My hopelessly doomed financial situation? The isolation and loneliness already engulfing me? My physical well-being or the lack of it? What did any of those things matter when I had been found spiritually wanting, and hadn't even figured out yet why I was still here?

With that thought I began crying in earnest.

CHAPTER NINETEEN

Monday, four a.m.

MY SOBBING AND heaving reminded me of my prepubescent days after I'd been disciplined. It forced me to wonder if today would have had a different outcome if I would have taken Dad's discipline to heart, allowing it to change me permanently. But this was quickly turning into a life or death situation, so I had to force myself to stop making noise, or I would never last long enough to get right with God. That very real fear stopped my tears cold. I put one hand over my mouth and one over my beating heart, willing myself to be quiet. By the time I heard another car door slam in the distance, my silence was complete.

I was so very tempted to sneak out of my parents' house and go get a hotel room before sunrise so I could be in safe seclusion. My nerves were shot and I couldn't bear imagining someone attacking me. Someone being as close to me as the front porch was unnerving. Tomorrow I needed to find someone to help me kick those kids out of my own house so I could go home. Then I would barricade myself inside and buy a gun if I had to.

Then my tidy plans suddenly fell apart. With chagrin I remembered that I had no cash, and with credit cards not working until the banking system was up and running, I was stuck here with no other choices to choose from. If I left, I might never make it back to any semblance of security.

The thought of being defenseless in a world filled with people who didn't acknowledge God scared me. Although I'd held a secular job most of my life, in a strange way I had still isolated myself within a Christian cocoon of family and friends, and this was the first time I'd been this alone in my life. Loneliness added to fear becomes unbearable, and I was living smack dab in the middle of both.

My heartbeat finally began to calm down enough so I could hear if there were any other noises. I took a quick, deep, uncontrollable breath, the kind that comes without warning after a hard cry. Then I forced myself to pause. No breathing, no crying, nothing. If I wasn't safe, I wanted to know it. I wanted no surprises. I wished I could pray and get it over with, but I was struggling with those thoughts. It didn't seem appropriate and I didn't know what to say to the One I now knew was the most powerful being in the Universe. I was seeing Him in a totally different light than I'd seen Him before. I wondered if it would ever feel appropriate to talk to Him again.

With the TV off and the room dark, I was alone with thoughts I'd been avoiding for hours. I had known this time would eventually come, but I didn't feel like sobbing again as I contemplated my future and my past. I couldn't now, and this time it was because of the fear of someone knowing I was alone in the house. How had my safe, suburban life gotten so screwed up in a few short hours, finding me hunkered down behind a bed in the dark? I had to think it would only get worse.

But why *was* I here? How was this possible? And why was I having such a hard time judging myself? The most recent times I had briefly pondered the rapture, I had complacently pitied the obvious ones, the *sinners* whom everyone, including themselves, expected to not make it. There'd be people openly flaunting atheism, agnosticism, or those living in blatant sin, never accepting Him, taunting God to strike them with lightning. Criminals, thieves, murderers. The *obvious* ones.

But I had never pictured so many people, especially not *myself*, in this situation. I had no starting point for these thoughts. Was I absolutely positive the rapture had happened? Or would those contemplating theories find another explanation that made more sense, and I was just being paranoid? Had our enemies or some terrorist group come up with a way to abduct people? And just as that thought entered my mind, the most unusual thing happened.

I physically felt what can only be described as a gray suffocating cloud beginning to hover over my mind and an equally eerie feeling of peace come over me, instantly making me feel better, and I almost smiled. It was such an odd, physical sensation that it made me look around the room, and I shivered despite the blanket. And then I knew. Something ungodly had just invaded my space and instinctively I knew I had just a moment to fight it off.

My heart began beating desperately, and I jumped up faster than I'd moved in years, blanket flying, and screaming "*No!*" momentarily unconcerned about being heard. I felt I was in a life or death struggle for my sanity and future. Was this what it felt like to go crazy, or be possessed? A split second later I began crying, "*No! No! No! No!*" Then suddenly remembering the danger, I stopped, going back to my hunched state in the corner, still trembling, still rocking, cuddling my blanket in the dark as I continued whispering, "No...."

Scattered thoughts reminded me of a time Dad prayed for a minister who had "changed his mind," believing there was no longer a devil or hell. His explanation was that hell was merely living on earth without the presence of God. I wondered if that preacher was still here like me, pondering his own fate now. I would have to agree with one of his skewed facts, though, because I most definitely felt like I was in hell on earth now, and didn't know if God would listen to my belated voice calling Him. But at the deepest core of my barely living spirit, I *knew* that if the rapture, the most alarming, preached-about, controversial thing the church discussed, had really occurred, then the rest of the things in the Bible were also true. This day proved beyond a shadow of a doubt that there really was a hell and, as unbelievable as it seemed, it would be worse than what I was experiencing.

So many bits and pieces of sermons came back now. Why they hadn't seemed to penetrate my psyche at the time, I don't know. But they had no trouble coming back now. I remembered Dad harping on the fact that the devil could send darts in the form of thoughts into your mind, but we had the choice of which ones we accepted as truth, making them our own, or totally rejecting them. Then I remembered the important part. He had said we would never get rid of thoughts by trying to replace them with "good" thoughts or just deciding to reject them in our minds.

Rather, the only way to stop bad thoughts from overtaking us was to speak out loud. I had thought it sounded like embarrassing preacher talk back then. But I remembered he said they had proved something physically happened to your brain when your own voice spoke out loud against a thought. And then He said there was always the extra benefit that it informed the devil that you hadn't fallen for his lies either. So I guessed if nothing else, screaming "No" showed I wasn't going willingly.

I felt so helpless. If I hadn't learned or conquered lessons with Christians on every side of me, how would I be able to now? I almost pictured the devil and his demons laughing in unison as I tried to take a stand to fight them now.

But what did I have to lose? I had lost everything on earth that mattered today. And just as the words "on earth" flitted through my mind, I realized that was one of my problems. Pretty much everything that had ever mattered to me had been...on earth.[1]

That reminded me of my sweet, stubborn Mom. For years and years, she had added the scripture reference "Matthew 6:33" to the bottom of every single card or letter she ever signed. It was almost a part of her signature, and I had virtually ignored it for years. But I could quote it verbatim now. "But seek ye first the kingdom of God, and His righteousness; and all these things shall be added unto you." I wasn't convinced *that* was the answer to my question now, but I *did* have to recognize I had been seeking my own perfect world and comfortable life more than I'd been seeking God or His kingdom. I wasn't even sure what that meant at this point.

Finally quiet and everlastingly alone, I started to wonder about that fog and heaviness that had attacked earlier. What had brought it on? Then I recalled how I'd been wondering if the rapture had really taken place. And I knew it was that seed of doubt I had been toying with that inserted a tiny crack in my mind that now convinced me could break into a huge chasm if I allowed it. Why hadn't I been this diligent with thoughts festering in my mind for years? And then I knew. Because I hadn't been this quiet in years. Literally years.

CHAPTER NINETEEN

I had been so busy trying to be super mom, super wife, super employee, super daughter, super church attendee, perfect human being, that I had filled every waking moment to the brim, then medicating my sleeping moments until I had little time left for real, genuine God-thoughts to even sneak in. I was a goal oriented, list-making, pie-chart creator that felt inferior if I didn't accomplish my day's goals. I had forever worked toward the "Atta girl," the "Job well done," or the "We couldn't do it without you," so much that it must have squeezed out the most important thoughts and actions that would have ensured an eternal "Well done, my good and faithful servant" by now. My head dropped in shame, hot tears flowing freely again.

With all the energy I had left, I jerked my head up, deciding I would do the tiniest bit of fighting I could muster. Opening my mouth I said in a trembling, but stern voice, the kind I usually reserved for chastising someone, "God I *know* you are real and you have taken your Christians in the rapture and any explanation the world comes up with will be a lie." Even in the dark, all by myself, I felt embarrassed for saying it out loud, even if the only ones in hearing range were God or demons. So I just squeezed my eyes shut and got quiet.

The strangest thing happened. There was no flashing light, no noise penetrating the awful quietness. But the chill and heaviness left so quickly I even loosened the blanket from around my shoulders. And then I physically felt it. Like I'd had a too-tight headband on my head, and someone gently lifted it off. The heavy cloud that had prevented me from thinking clear thoughts lifted. Like an evil warning system, I had been inundated with a strange, almost demonic false peace that had flooded my soul and now it was gone; replacing it with the original fear! But in an ironic twist, it felt good because I *knew* fear was a natural emotion. The strange peace, however, had been seductive and foreboding, and even in my spiritual state of limbo, I knew it hadn't felt right.

For the first time in hours I felt the tiniest bit of comfort and hope. I had been having trouble remembering whether there could be hope for anyone who missed the rapture, so I began with the most elementary of thoughts. If there *was* a chance for me to make it now, where should I start? Now that I had no distractions, no friends, no family or church to attend, was it even possible to become strong enough to withstand evil? I remembered hearing someone once say that "If you can't live for God *before* the rapture, chances are you won't be able to live for Him after." And my fleeting hopes were shot back down. But just in case, I figured I would have to take a lot of time and consider it.

Then as if the window of my soul had been wiped clean letting me finally see through, I had the most sobering thought. If I was here now, it meant that if I had died at some point before the rapture, I would be screaming in hell now. Or if I had been a part of the huge number of casualties today, I wouldn't have a second chance to reconsider and change my fate and future. That thought sent chills down my back and reminded me how important it was that I stay safe and alive until I was sure where I would spend eternity.

I was quiet again. My soft breathing was the only sound I heard, giving me hope I was still hidden and undetected. I thought about the fog that had enveloped me earlier in my brain and heart and realized good and evil was truly battling for my soul right now. I felt like maybe for years I'd been sitting on a high fence several stories high, attempting to straddle it, not fully on either side, struggling with all my might not to lose control, yet unwilling to tumble over the other side into God's arms.

I didn't know nearly enough about heaven. Was it possible for those on the other side to still pray for us? Once my family realized I was nowhere to be found, did they, *could they,* say a prayer for me? Were there people all over heaven searching aimlessly for loved ones exactly like we'd been looking for them down here? Were groups of friends congregating, sharing news of who had made it and who hadn't? Were people there as shocked as we were here? Were they sad and upset for me? Or not surprised and just resigned to what they had detected a long time ago? Had it been painfully apparent to them? Would their memories of me and the pain it brought slowly dissipate like when people mourned on earth? Or had their memory of me been mercifully taken the moment they entered His presence? That thought left me so empty. As if I no longer existed for them. Why couldn't we have gone together...?

I had to stop with the questions. There was no comfort or answer to be found. All the thinking in the world wasn't going to change the outcome. My only hope now was to change the future. I wasn't positive

God was going to talk to me now since I must not have been trying to hear Him before. Or was it that I had heard but was ignoring Him? That was probably even worse.

I knew certain questions would never be answered here. But on the other hand, I didn't want a placating, evil presence deceiving me with *his* answers or opinions either. At this point I preferred human fear to evil possession. I heard a siren several streets away and my train of thought was broken. It reminded me that self preservation was my top priority now. I had to formulate a plan, and this brought another of my Mom's favorite quotations to mind. Anytime I would tell her about some plan I had, she would remind me, "We can make our plans, Annie, but the Lord decides our steps."[2] I wondered if that could apply to me now, or if I was truly, totally on my own.

I was learning that sounds meant danger or the possibility of being discovered or even worse, so when the siren faded off in the distance I felt some relief. I needed a strategy to protect myself. I had depended on my husband or Dad for so long, I wasn't sure where to start. I shook my head, realizing if I had transferred my dependence over to God a long time ago, I wouldn't even *be* in this position.

And that reminded me of the still unanswered question haunting me. I needed to confront it now, before the day was over, for once I was engrossed in preservation mode, it might get lost in the shuffle. I needed to know. If there *was* a second chance, was it possible I could be strong enough to make it? But before worrying about that I had to figure out why I was in this position or there was no hope.

But how do you judge or critique yourself when you thought you were okay? What huge roadblock had I missed? If I had been deceived, then I must still be deceived. Sitting with my mind devoid of answers, but feeling my introspection was complete, I thought, "I don't think there was *anything* wrong! I *should* have gone with them! It's not fair!" And with that thought, I felt the tiniest bit of anger rise up. Resentment for being misjudged and for the embarrassment and newly cemented shame I would forever endure. I heard a voice inside agreeing, even sympathizing. It felt good, like I was being validated.

Then I knew the evil presence had come in the back door again. I wasn't sure I could keep mustering the energy to fight it, but then I also knew I couldn't tolerate it. So before it had time to take root, or the daunting fog to descend, I said out loud, "God, I'm not sure if You are even listening—but I know I must have not been right or I wouldn't be here because You are perfect and don't make mistakes.[3] Help me figure out why I was left behind, so I can make it right."

I kept my eyes tightly shut, and miracle of miracles, just like before, the new root of self-pitying anger dissipated, and I felt calm. I also felt regret and remorse that I hadn't gotten in the habit of talking to God like this about everything before, with honesty and humility instead of depending upon myself or putting pressure on others or worse, just accepting the continual onslaught of "darts" sent my way. I'd obviously never understood that true Christians knew it was imperative to fight against certain thoughts instead of meditating on them.

An old scripture I had memorized came to mind. I could actually remember standing on stage, proud to be the one chosen to recite for a program. Wearing a little pink flowered dress, saying ever so clearly, "James 4:7: Submit yourselves therefore to God. Resist the devil, and he will flee from you!" Now decades later, I would have to do more than quote it. I was going to have to live it, or die.

At that moment something made me curious to see if Mom had written anything beside that scripture in her Bible. I had a feeling if I had any chance of making it in the coming days, I might have to live by not only every Word in the Bible, but every word *she* had written as well. She was a Bible writer, taking every word to heart, using it as a guidebook with handwritten notes on almost every page. I felt around blindly on her nightstand, and then remembered she used to keep a flashlight in her drawer. My hand located the Bible and I quietly opened her drawer and felt around. I found the flashlight and then brought both to my lap, looking first toward the window. The curtains were heavy; I just had to hope they would cover any light that might escape. I had never been in a situation where every action I took meant possible life or death. I would have to adjust quickly.

I turned on the flashlight, further obscuring the light with my hand, and opened her Bible to James 4. I saw that the Bible version I'd found in the dark was *The Message Bible,* and I half-smiled, knowing Mom had about every version of the Bible ever printed. I always wondered why she needed so many versions. But after finding the verse I was glad it was in this version because the meaning was expanded and gave me a sliver of comfort.

I read it silently and marveled. But that didn't seem enough. I decided to read it out loud so my own ears would hear it, so it could sink in, so I could maybe learn to obey it now. I quietly read:

"So let God work his will in you. Yell aloud 'No' to the Devil, and watch him scamper. Say a quiet 'Yes' to God and He'll be there in no time. Quit dabbling in sin. Purify your inner life. Quit playing the field. Hit bottom, and cry your eyes out. The fun and games are over. Get serious, really serious. Get down on your knees before the Master; it's the only way you'll get on your feet."

My eyes had never been as wide open as they were right then, physically *or* spiritually. I wondered if God had arranged long ago for me to have *this* version at *this* time so I would get the entire message. And all my Mom had written in the margin was, "Do it!"

Fighting the enemy seemed larger and more real than ever now. I looked again and saw that the verse actually said to "yell!" Continuing on, I noticed I was told to "quit dabbling in sin" and to "purify your inner life." And then the words "quit playing the field" hit me square between the eyes. I would never have dreamed that by the time I read this verse, the phrase "hit bottom, and cry your eyes out" would already be happening.

There was no time to waste. I needed to obey the rest of the scripture. It was now or never. The rest of my life was now. I'd been so arrogant in the past, assuming I was smart enough to *time* whatever final repentance might be needed. Thinking that somehow I could live life the way I desired and make corrections just in the nick of time for the great event. And in all my wisdom and pride, I had slept through it. Like a baby. Without the slightest hint of a warning. And now? Although there wouldn't be another rapture to surprise me, life itself would be unpredictable from now on. My life could be taken from me at any moment. It was imperative I get right with God and never be distracted or turn away from Him again.

I sat up straight and did what the rest of the scripture advised. "God, I'm really, really serious, finally." I started crying a flood of tears and could barely get the words out, but fought to finish. "I admit I have lived apart from You and I'm so sorry and I don't want to mess this up. I want to finally make You Lord and Master of my life. If You can still help me, even though I waited too late, I want to live the rest of my life for You. Please show me what kept me here. Show me my sin."

So with nothing better to do, I started at the beginning.

CHAPTER TWENTY

Monday, five o five a.m.

THIS WAS BRAND new territory. Had everyone else in my position been able to immediately know what their blind spots had been, or their sin? And despite grasping what the future would now hold, still manage to sincerely repent? I knew better than to make just an outward show of being sorry now.

I wondered if God really would help me figure out why I hadn't heard the call. Thinking about that moment, made me wonder if my family had actually heard the sound of a trumpet or if it was all just a figure of speech. I hoped they had heard one. What a magnificent moment it must have been. I thought of all the explanations given over the years explaining away miraculous events from the Bible so people wouldn't believe or take the Bible for what it said. There were stories of bringing people back to life and splitting the Red Sea wide open, miracles that seemed impossible or improbable, ones that required an actual God to perform them and actual faith to believe.

Perhaps there *were* parts of the Bible not meant to be taken literally, meant more as metaphors and to be taken figuratively.[1] The second that thought passed through my head, I felt it again, hitting me with lightning speed now. The same twinge of doubt. Like a familiar friend, commiserating with me and the condition I was in, agreeing with my misgivings, coddling me, taking my side. These were things I craved, someone to take my side even if I was wrong. I hadn't realized how quickly a thought could take root in my mind. And after planted, the thought invariably propelled me in the direction *it* chose, rarely the direction I was intent on heading. And the thoughts never seemed to send me in the direction of trusting, believing, or obeying God. Was my current vulnerability and desperation allowing me to have more insight and discernment or was this God answering my prayer in the middle of the night?

Except I knew I hadn't grown leaps and bounds in the last twenty-four hours. I wouldn't always recognize his trickery, and would fall for it again. I wasn't sure of anything else at this point, but I had a sneaky suspicion I was going to have to fight exactly the way it was spelled out in Mom's Bible. So I quickly yelled "No!" glad no one was watching the spectacle I was making of myself. And in case it wasn't enough, I followed it with "God, I know everything in the Bible is true! Whatever it says I'll believe it and won't try to explain it away or make it fit what I want it to say!" I couldn't think of anything else to say so I sat quietly again.

It almost felt like a fresh, cool breeze blew into the room, and I took a deep, refreshing breath. It didn't chill me to the bone like the earlier one, and the heaviness lifted. I wasn't sure what this was that seemed to come and go, but it was frightening. Deep inside, however, I *knew* this voice and was afraid I'd obeyed it more often than God's voice in the past. It seemed to know my reactions and my weaknesses, and it was the only voice I was hearing at the moment. Evil's competition had stepped way back into the shadows.

I remembered hearing a warning from the Bible that our enemy actually came to steal God's Word from our hearts. And the most frightening part was that the *enemy's* words were *never* stolen from our hearts. So unless rejected, they stayed in there, festering, embedding, spreading, grounded in my heart. I had let every last word of the enemy remain in my heart, and the words had taken root, growing profusely, accepted as the truth without any fact checking. It exhausted me to think of how much work was ahead of me. Without anyone to help or give encouragement. I would have to seek God harder than I'd ever sought

Him or anything else in my life before, developing a kind of faith I'd never even tested before. It sounded next to impossible.

Never having experienced a failure this public or final, my first instinct and the urging in my heart was to lie down and give up. And not just physically. But I had skirted the issue long enough. I had no idea where to start other than to think back to the earliest time I could remember hearing about Jesus. All I knew from an early age was that our lives were surrounded by God. I remember back in the day when churches couldn't support a pastor and Dad sold insurance on the side. In retrospect, I realized that might have kept him grounded more than some pastors who never touched the real world or even unsaved people. All I knew was that we attended church all the time, had daily family devotions, and what little entertainment we had usually involved family or church.

Perhaps I had gotten so used to being *around* God over the years that when I stopped letting him *be* God to me, I hadn't even made the connection or felt a difference. I had gone and done what people hate to have done to them. I had taken God for granted.

It was amazing, but I could remember the moment I first asked Jesus into my heart. It was a Wednesday night in the fall, a few months before I turned six. Our family was getting ready for Wednesday night church, but about an hour before we were supposed to leave, all of a sudden I felt an urgency. The lights in our living room had been dimmed and the natural light from the day was gone. While everyone else was busy, I called my Mom into the living room, telling her I needed to ask Jesus into my heart. She stopped right then and prayed with me. I had known I was right with God.

But that was over forty years ago. What had happened since then? I knew I hadn't lived a perfect life. But that wasn't expected or possible was it? I tried to think of all the sins the Bible talked about, and wondered what great one I had committed. I started getting a little angry, thinking of other people I knew who were gone now, *knowing* they weren't perfect.[2] It seemed outright unfair.

I recalled an older gentleman I knew who worked part time at the church. He had been in prison for twenty years after killing a grandmother and her two grandchildren while driving drunk. After getting saved in prison, and getting his life straightened out, when he got out he began a compassion ministry for widows and single mothers. Jeremy had mentioned that this older gentleman also disappeared. So it was obvious God forgave heinous sins.[3]

I thought of the lady who ran a recovery ministry at church. Abused as a young girl, turning to prostitution and leading a promiscuous life, she had several abortions and ended up getting hooked on methamphetamines. She had perhaps the most checkered past of anyone I personally knew. After coming to Christ, she started a ministry helping ladies with their recovery. But when Jeremy said he was the only staff member left, he must have meant she had gone too. After *that* kind of life, she had made it! I was becoming painfully aware that certain sins weren't worse than others. Or sinning a lot didn't keep you from accepting Christ and being completely forgiven. Instead my thoughts strayed to the question: was God really fair?[4]

I knew the danger the direction of my thoughts were taking me and warning bells were going off inside my heart, but I almost stubbornly continued full speed ahead. I was convinced my own family hadn't surpassed me in *their* perfection. My husband wasn't above getting angry, and my daughter had made the usual teen blunders. I could even point to instances where I thought Mom and Dad missed the mark. So why me? Had God not loved me as much as He had them?[5] It felt like the ultimate betrayal. I was hurt thinking of God not wanting me or caring about me or treating me the same as he had others.[6]

I was already down the path of self-pity and kept going. I began comparing my weaknesses, faults, and temptations with some who had disappeared. They always came up wanting, while I sank deeper with every pathetic sense of reasoning. And then, miraculously, somehow I stopped myself. I couldn't afford to go down this path again. Even if I never figured out why I was here, there *was* undoubtedly a reason I hadn't made it. Only the biggest idiot could watch millions disappear from earth and not believe in God. And after pulling this off, if He wanted me to know anything, I was convinced He could find a way.

So that left me back at square one, hoping God wasn't too busy in heaven now that all His children were there, and forget about us poor souls on earth. I let my mind wander back to my elementary days, remembering when I was about eight, loving God deeply, thinking about Him and talking to Him in my bedroom. I would write things about Him in my diary and even wanted to be a missionary to China. I wondered if that was where I went wrong. Had I been out of "God's will"? Could I miss the rapture because of that?

In a millisecond I felt like someone had read my thoughts[7] and chimed in on the conversation I was having in my head. I "heard" the thought, "I would never do that." My eyes opened wide. The words seemed that clear. And I knew that wasn't my thought because this voice had contradicted my *own* thoughts, and I was convinced it was God's voice. A gentle reminder that He was alive and well, fully aware of me and where I was right now, even though His intention had been for me to be with Him now. I felt slightly comforted, hoping He would stay close, especially now.[8]

So if I hadn't been left behind because I wasn't in His will, where had I gone astray? Had I been headed in the wrong direction for years without knowing it? I thought of my teen years. Times when I didn't obey my parents, didn't always make wise choices, but then I also remembered precious times with God where I cleared it all up and sincerely repented, something I couldn't remember doing for awhile now. I knew my heart was tender back then though. Had I required too much forgiveness? Had God become frustrated or irritated or impatient with me? Had I annoyed Him because I hadn't been able to get it sooner?[9]

Then mid-thought, I heard something that sounded like gunfire rather than a backfiring car. Again. And it sounded closer. My heart rate doubled and my hand began shaking. I would have to return to my private judgment seat later. This time I wasn't satisfied hiding in the corner of the back bedroom. I needed to know if I really was in danger or if it was just stupid kids roaming the streets, ignoring curfew. Half out of curiosity, half out of abject fear, I grabbed the flashlight I had been using earlier and headed toward the noise. Deciding to only use the flashlight if I had to, I slowly shuffled my feet so I wouldn't bump into anything or make a commotion. I hadn't looked at the clock in awhile, but figured it wouldn't be too long before daylight began peeping through the blinds.

My shuffling proved to be a bad idea because before I even got out of my parents' bedroom I stubbed my toe so hard on a bookcase I was certain it was broken. I had the sense not to scream, despite the pain, but inadvertently squeaked out an "Ohhh!" louder than I would have liked, and froze mid-wince. I heard a shout somewhere outside and my heart skipped another beat. Already angry at myself for the situation I was in, I was now disgusted by my clumsiness.

I figured if I had been discovered, I might as well get a glimpse of them before they figured out how easily they could overtake me. I was a bit more careful as I eased myself out the bedroom and down the hall toward the living room. Did I have the guts to confront someone? Would strange kids listen to a "mother" figure telling them to shut up and obey curfew or get off my property? Probably not. I thought about the kids in my *own* house and was reminded of my previous lack of bravery and my heart sank.

I was nervous and exhausted and lonely. I could only imagine how high my blood pressure was, and I felt I might be sick again. My body had never had to process this much adrenaline and fear and anxiety before, and I'd been doing it now for eighteen hours straight. Moving inches at a time toward the living room picture window, I thought back to how dense I had been the previous morning. But did it really matter? Would anything have been different if I had been at church? Would it have made any difference if I had seen them disappear in front of me, knowing what happened? I would have still been left behind. No rearrangement of the day's facts could make it better. And to think that just a day ago I had been fully in control, my life ordered as I saw fit, feeling fairly fulfilled and pretty proud of myself.

By this time I was only a couple of inches from the window when I heard another gunshot and my hand flew to my mouth to stop any sound. Danger was no longer imagined. The shot was within feet from where I was standing. God, was this it? Had I lasted such a short time before my life would end? Then the most unbearable thought filled me.

I hadn't yet figured out why I hadn't made it, hadn't really repented, didn't feel I was ready yet. If they killed me now, my last chance of spending eternity in heaven was gone. I had prayed a prayer earlier, but was it enough? I closed my eyes and the only prayer I could think to pray was for safety. I still had a lot to talk to God about, like emptying my heart of the sin I must have been harboring, but I couldn't focus on that now. I promised Him if He would keep me safe, I would make it right.

I took a deep breath, steadying my feet so I wouldn't stumble again. My toe was still throbbing, but the pain was nothing compared to the one in my head and my heart. I moved my hand slowly toward the window and paused when my fingertips touched one of the wooden blinds close to my eye level, and I circled it with my thumb and forefinger. My eyes were barely an inch from the blind as I lifted it up a quarter of an inch and froze.

Not ten inches from the slit in the blind were two guys standing on the porch. Trying to size them up while forcing my hand not to shake, I could see one of them was maybe six and a half feet tall and 300 pounds. Even with the dark shadows and only a tiny bit of street light filtering through the trees, he looked rough and intimidating. His hair was unkempt and down to his shoulders and looked like he had something in his hand, maybe a bat. He said something to the other guy, and I saw he was a little shorter and scrawnier. But the problem with him was that he was the one with the gun and he kept waving it around as he talked.

Between my head throbbing and heart beating, I was almost afraid they could hear it through the window. But someone could have tackled me and I wouldn't have let go of that blind. I was in a life or death situation with no clue how it would end. Their heads were so close to me I couldn't believe they hadn't seen the blind lift, but I sure couldn't take a chance of dropping it now. All it would take would be the glint of the street light as the blind moved and I would be at their disposal. Without any choice but to watch whatever unfolded, I thought of the familiar, comforting scripture in Psalm 23 that pretty much everyone could quote. "Yea, though I walk through the valley of the shadow of death, I will fear no evil: for thou art with me..." I shut my eyes just a moment and silently mouthed, "Please be with me."

I opened my eyes and their whispering suddenly stopped as if they weren't concerned about being quiet any longer. I was glad since it meant I could hear what they were planning, that is, until their words were actually out there. The scrawny one said, "I'm telling you Jake, I *saw* a lady go in here! Let's bust in and have some fun...C'mon! Nobody's going to stop us!"

My knees felt weak and my heart sank because I knew he was right. I had never felt so close to being violated and the fear deepened when I looked between them and saw the *rest* of their gang in the middle of the street. There were another fifteen or twenty guys drinking, shoving, and laughing. One of the guys fired a gun into the air, causing the big guy on the porch to yell, "Cut it out you morons, are ya *tryin'* to bring people out of the woodwork?"

His words must have inspired them, because one guy yelled back, "We've got the guns and the manpower! The police aren't helping anyone! *No one* will stop us! What do *you* guys wanna do? Let's go in and have some fun!"

For a split second, the guy they called "Jake" paused as if seriously considering it, even slightly turning his head to look toward the house. If I didn't know better, I would swear our eyes met through the slit of the window. You couldn't have paid me to blink, and in my heart I knew I'd been caught. If the guy focused, he could tell the blind was skewed and not aligned with the rest. I begged God in my pitiful way, awaiting my fate.

The sound of the explosion was deafening but made even more intense by the flash that lit up the sky, and I let out a shriek before realizing it. The only thing saving me was that most of them had also screamed, and my yelp was indistinguishable from theirs. The blast illuminated the sky, the street, and the entire porch, indelibly imprinting their faces on my brain. And then the torrential rain began. The guys in the street immediately ran toward their cars across the street, and both guys on the porch paused just a second before taking off in a steady run, shielding themselves from the driving rain.

Once they reached the street, I lifted the blind a full two inches and stared. Directly across the street from my parents' house was a huge oak tree that probably stood fifty feet in the air. One we'd played in and around as children. It had been struck by lightning and literally split down the middle and, regardless of the downpour, the tree and surrounding grass was entirely ablaze in flames. My mouth dropped open in disbelief. It was hard to take my eyes off of it, as most of the gang drove away. But at the last second the two who had been on the porch paused before getting into their car. In spite of the heavy rain, one of them yelled something and they both looked back toward the house. I instantly regretted my courage in lifting the blind, and prayed they couldn't see it from where they were standing.

Then, as amazing as the first strike, another flash of lightning with an accompanying clap of thunder sounded at that same moment, hitting the *same* tree again. I heard their volley of obscenities before they jumped in their car and sped away.

I shuffled to the front door, opening it without a second thought and stepped out onto the front porch. With my mouth open, I stared at the awesome sight of the neighbor's blazing tree. I was almost drawn to it in the strangest of ways. I stood mesmerized for maybe thirty seconds, and then miraculously the downpour slowed and within seconds completely stopped. Not even a sprinkle. A frown barely creased my brow as I processed what had just happened. I stepped down off the porch, looking up into the sky as if to verify to myself that we'd even had a rainstorm. But all traces of it were gone.

God had just made an appearance.

CHAPTER TWENTY-ONE

Monday, five fifty-two a.m.

ALTHOUGH THE SUN had not yet risen, the sky was beginning its slow metamorphosis, changing to lighter shades of darkness. I knew the night would soon be transformed. Even after such a traumatic day and night, I was almost disappointed to realize the sun was coming up just as if it was a normal day. The only relief I felt came from knowing daylight usually meant less crime. But now there was no usual.

The few minutes of rain had brought a distinct freshness to the air, and I breathed deeply. Slowly scanning the street in both directions, I saw no sign of the earlier perpetrators. At the thought of the terror I had just experienced, my eyes were drawn back again to the tree. What had been a colossal blaze a few minutes earlier, although still impressive by its mere existence, was now just smoldering with a few insignificant flames flickering here and there. I marveled at a tree that large and majestic being split in half by lightning right in front of me. A slight smile settled on my face as I wished I could read God's mind right then. Had He decided after His lightning and fire did its trick by chasing off the hoodlums that He didn't really need to show off any more and just as quickly turned the waterworks off, displaying another miracle by doing that?

I heard a siren in the distance and, although I was getting used to them, it reminded me that I needed to get back inside before someone saw me. I turned around, walked back up the porch steps, and went inside after one last look back, not forgetting to double lock the doors behind me. I was aware that God had rescued me, but unsure if my heart could stand much more, even if it *was* a miraculous feat. I knew without a shadow of a doubt that after what I'd just experienced it was past time to finish my talk with God, to completely, utterly, and honestly judge myself.

I walked contemplatively down the long hallway back into my parents' bedroom. I felt mellow, almost melancholy, after what I'd just experienced. Walking through the bedroom door, I shut and locked it as well. I eased myself back onto the floor in the corner, somehow feeling safer there. Closing my eyes, I tried to remember where I'd left off. I knew myself way too well. I was a great procrastinator and my self-talk had already been put off for hours, even though it was the most important thing in life I needed to accomplish now.

Then why did I suddenly feel the urge to turn on the news? I fought it for a moment, assuming it was another one of my stall tactics, but in the strangest of ways I felt like I would be obeying God, so I reached over and turned it on. A fresh face had come in to replace the exhausted crew from the night before. The time in the corner of the screen said 6:06 a.m., and before thirty seconds had passed I knew exactly why I was meant to turn the TV on.

A young rookie announcer seemed to think this was his chance to prove himself to the network. He was bright and overly-polished and doing his best to sound chipper and professional. It was clear he didn't have a clue as to what was going on in the world, but after his first sentence, he had my complete attention.

"I'm being told we are about to show the first released eye-witness video of the events that transpired less than twenty-four hours ago, so this should be exciting..." I started holding my breath when he said "eye witness video," assuming they were going to show some grainy security camera footage, but when he announced where the video had been taken, my heart leaped. "Apparently a church by the name of The Christian Cathedral right here in the mid-cities area had begun broadcasting live streaming video for their Sunday morning services for the very first time yesterday. Our station just obtained this video, so I haven't had a chance to see it myself yet. Let's watch it together."

I knew I was about to see the rapture caught on tape. I shivered. I didn't really *want* to see this most wonderful phenomenon, but felt I needed to. So my heart could never question it again. So I would know beyond a shadow of a doubt it had been real no matter what happened in the coming days.

Before I had time to fully prepare myself, the video started. My thirst to get a glimpse of what my family and friends had experienced was growing and I was determined to watch carefully, no matter how much it hurt. This was as close as I would ever get to this terrible, wonderful moment. Just as the sound started, I pressed record on the remote, not wanting to miss one microscopic detail.

It was obviously a small, country church. They must have had a techno whiz in their church who wanted to try out his video equipment, and to think his first video had been his last. My smile disappeared as I felt the weight of the importance of what I was seeing. There was only one angle from a camera in the back corner of the church, so in the beginning, I saw only the backs of people's heads. Everyone was standing up for what looked like the conclusion of their worship service. I saw a few people raising their hands. When I looked beyond the audience members' heads, I saw a young worship leader on the platform in the front, facing the camera. He was just finishing up the last notes of a song I couldn't quite place.

Then he turned it over to what must have been the pastor, an older gentleman, close to retirement age. He had a pleasant, trustworthy voice, and I felt compelled to actually listen to what he was saying, not merely watch for the sight I was afraid to see.

The camera awkwardly zoomed in to get a close-up of the platform area, and as the minister started, he immediately began apologizing for what he imagined wouldn't be considered the best subject to preach on Mother's Day, but said that he had no choice but to obey God. That made me lean in closer and I turned up the volume. With a profound sadness and regret overwhelming me, I wondered what subject my own Dad had preached for *his* last sermon. The one I'd missed because of a little headache and the desire to keep my toes from being stepped on while he preached. I wasn't about to miss *this* preacher's last words though. I had to imagine what a wonderful thing it had been to be actually preaching the gospel the moment His Savior called him home.

After his preemptive apology, he began speaking in his laid-back, country twang. "Let me go ahead and read the scripture God wants me to read, and then I'll explain what He impressed on my heart for you today. It's found in Revelation 3, verses 2 and 3, and says:

"Rouse yourselves and keep awake, strengthen and invigorate what remains and is on the point of dying; for I have not found a thing that you have done, any work of yours, meeting the requirements of My God or perfect in His sight. So call to mind the lessons you received and heard; continually lay them to heart and obey them, and repent. In case you will not rouse yourselves and keep awake and watch, I will come upon you like a thief, and you will not know or suspect at what hour I will come."

He paused and looked tenderly, almost lovingly at the crowd, as if he were letting it sink in. Not embarrassed by the silence. In a strange way, I felt like I was part of his audience as I watched. If I would have actually been there, before I knew what I knew now, I wondered if his odd scriptural warning would have penetrated my spirit like it was doing now.

Just at the moment his pregnant pause was coming to an end, the camera man slowly zoomed back out, showing the entire auditorium where perhaps fifty or sixty people were in attendance. And without warning, it happened. Before the minister could spit out one more word, an extended altar call, or a simple persuasive, convicting plea, it happened. Words will never describe it or give it justice.

One moment everything appeared to be normal with the minister's mouth opening to begin his next sentence. I barely heard what sounded like a hushed, split-second "whoosh," and then I saw the slightest glint of light like a flash from a camera. In the next instant the auditorium was almost empty with a slight movement near the floor. I wrinkled my brow, thinking, *Wait! What was that? Maybe it wasn't what we thought?* When my gaze turned to the floor, my mouth slowly opened as I saw the movement had been clothes falling to the floor all over the room. I had been distracted by the falling clothes and had missed the first responses from those left behind. And a moment later, the camera slowly began panning upward to the ceiling, telling me the camera man had also made the impromptu trip.

It had happened so fast, I wanted more. Goose bumps were already rising on my arms when right before the video turned off, I heard the beginning sound of a guttural "Noooo…" and felt physical pain shooting through my heart. I knew that moan, for it had come out of my own mouth, my neighbor, and others who understood the day's impact. I was relieved when the video stopped. I couldn't bear to see faces mirroring my own devastation.

I dreaded hearing the announcer's frivolous explanation of what we'd just seen, but was too stunned to turn the television off in time. The station hadn't scripted his next remarks, and he made some offhand remark, saying he bet we hadn't seen anything like that before. And then he stupidly went on to say, "That looks like the perfect example of alien abduction or some type of voodoo magic to me!"

Then he foolishly continued, "I don't know about *you*, but I'm glad *I* wasn't whisked off into no man's land, aren't you?" His insane comment brought my anger back to the forefront and I reached for the remote, but not before I heard his next words, "And in case you didn't get a good look at that tape, I'm being told that our video department recommends we see the same clip in slow motion!"

This I had to see. I was so hungry to see if there was a glimpse of anything. A heavenly sign, *something* to give me hope for my own future. As they restarted it, they didn't begin at the very beginning of the tape, which wasn't surprising since the minister's scripture had actually *given* the explanation for where everyone had gone if anyone actually listened to it, but instead they began in the middle of the pastor's scripture.

His words seemed even more ominous now with the slow motion effect, making his voice lower and drawn out, "*…I—will—come— upon—you—like—a—thief,—and—you—will—not—know—or— suspect—at—what—hour—I—will—come.*" And then they showed his eerie pause, made longer now since the tape had been slowed down. I carefully watched the pastor's eyes as he remained silent, and now I could easily see he seemed to be attempting to make eye contact with every single person in the audience. It felt supernatural, like he was begging each person to contemplate the verse and its blunt language. It was like he was on an urgent mission and couldn't afford for them to ignore him or misunderstand, afraid if he spoke, his words would muddle what God was doing inside their hearts at that moment.

I couldn't help but wonder if any person in the audience, in that last brief moment after the scripture was read, during their last possible respite, had become a true child of God and was raptured because of it. The final possible moment. I was so jealous of his or her opportunity.

But I was waiting to see that next moment, and if possible, was even more attentive now, wondering if I would see any clue. As the now slower "whoosh" started, my eyes opened wider as I saw with absolute amazement that there was a strange movement preceding it! Like someone had opened a door behind the camera, and a breeze had entered the room before anyone was aware anything was happening. I saw definite movement! People's sleeves moved in the same direction, forward and upward, I saw strands of hair shifting with the momentum and saw a Kleenex box fall from a side chair with no one touching it.

And then! In the most remarkable way, I saw the most supernatural phenomenon so thrilling I marveled as I watched. I was thankful I was taping it, because I knew I would replay this portion of the tape over and over for encouragement when times got rough. Right after the slight movement and the "whoosh" began, it looked as if the majority of the audience were puppets with strings attached, because, as if choreographed, I saw heads slightly jerk upward, cocking them toward the ceiling, as if they had heard something! I heard nothing, knowing full well now that the marvelous sound had been reserved for only His children's ears.[1] And in the next millisecond, those whose heads had shifted, simultaneously began to lift their arms ever so slightly, almost like little children expecting their Father to pick them up.

And then? The barely perceptible, tiny flash I had seen before? In slow motion, it was the most beautiful, brightening glow and couldn't have come from an ordinary light source. And unlike the breeze that had blown from one direction, streams of bright lights seemed to be coming from everywhere, but No! It wasn't just light! It was great moving swirls of light, almost like—was it the outline of *people*? Was it Angels?

CHAPTER TWENTY-ONE

I couldn't be sure, but they were swooping from the ceiling, followed by beautiful light streamers trailing behind, almost like there was one for each person. Then, just as suddenly, the light streams shot through the ceiling like boomerangs. In real time, it had happened in less time than it took for a person to *blink*.

And it was over. The breeze. The light. And God's people were gone. I wished they would have stopped the slow motion replay right then. But they didn't. I continued watching as pain radiated through every cell of my body, tears streaming down my face. I will never again watch the next part of the tape because it was so painful. I counted six people who had been left behind. The falling clothes no longer enamored me, even though it was an astounding sight as clothes fluttered to the floor around the entire room. But this time my attention was elsewhere.

I first caught sight of an older lady, whom I'd noticed before because she had been sitting down with her head nodding, having an early Sunday nap. She was still in the exact same position, still enjoying her rest. Ironically, not too different than what I myself had been doing when it happened this morning. She had totally, completely missed every part of it. I wondered who ended up having to explain to her what had happened when she finally woke up.

But the rest of them. Although I had experienced yesterday's spectacle from an entirely different perspective, I empathized with their unexpected trauma. I saw a businessman in an expensive suit, respectable and polished. He was obviously shocked and dumbfounded as he slowly turned around, trying not to draw attention to himself, obviously not having the faintest idea of what might have happened. Probably coming to Mother's Day service just to appease his wife, and now he looked dumbfounded, appearing out of control for perhaps the first time in his life.

The three teenage boys on the back row broke my heart. From the moment I saw the group of teens in my own church, I instinctively knew it would be hardest on young people left without parents or family. All three of them jumped up, turning their heads back and forth, looking first to each other then back to the front where their families had probably been sitting. One of them started to head to the front of the church. The other two were looking at each other with shock and dismay and the beginning of a sick recognition of what had occurred. As desperate as they seemed in that brief moment, they didn't have the faintest idea of what life was getting ready to hand them. And now that it was hours since it had happened, I wondered where they were at this moment.

But the sixth person. She's the one who immediately understood. She got it. A twinkling of a moment too late, but she instantaneously knew what had happened and what it meant. *She* was the one I heard making the low, guttural moan. And I knew why. I had noticed her momentarily during the beginning of the service. She was an attractive, thirty-something lady standing beside a husband who seemed to idolize her, while on her other side were four "stair-step" kids. Three girls and a boy. They had been standing on their chairs worshipping along with the adults just moments earlier.

She immediately knew she was utterly alone. Trauma, regret, fear, self-pity, and horror were clearly written on her face. The second after it happened, her mouth was open and aghast, horrified as she looked around the almost empty room. In one motion she slapped both hands on her ears, starting the half scream, half moan I now despised. It made me want to join her. Tears burned a hot path down my raw face. Unstoppable. Some for her, but most for me. And the moment the camera began its upward tilt without a camera man to hold it steady, I saw the young mother grab her children's clothes and begin shaking and sobbing, before falling to the floor.

I pictured the same scenario being played out over and over across the entire planet. Different time zones, different settings, but all the same. People across the globe defying gravity as they went to their eternal reward laced with peace and joy and untold mysteries unfolded.

Leaving behind the epitome of despair and hopelessness.

CHAPTER TWENTY-TWO

Monday, six fifty-one a.m.

AS THE VIDEO ended and the screen went dark, I found myself craving quiet and solitude, which sounds funny now that I'll have plenty of both forever. But the video brought it all to life. Solid pictures were embedded in my mind now, and it made the tragedy more real than ever. We were such a visual generation, with digital images advancing so far it was sometimes hard to tell the real from the fake. For those of us left here, it was evident the words in the Bible explaining the future hadn't been real enough for us. But that video snippet had brought the Bible to life right before my eyes. If possible, I was even more disappointed with myself now.

My eyes were flooded and by the time I located the remote, the announcer's face had already filled the screen. I wondered if the slow motion version had affected him anywhere near how it had me. Not that I cared what he *thought*, but I was curious how the world would react once the facts were thrown irrefutably in their face. Was it possible people all over the world would fall on their faces to repent because they couldn't deny there was a God now? Would people have to acknowledge there was a deity so powerful He could abduct millions of people from the earth with no one having the power to stop Him? Or would they accelerate their belittling and denial of the truth, giving lame excuses for the most celebrated and anticipated Christian event since the resurrection of Christ?

It was like my eyes were opened just a bit as I pondered how Christians had been waiting for this very event for thousands of years. Impatiently. Wondering why God was waiting so long. But now I realized with such clarity how amazing it was that God patiently waited until this particular era to rapture His church. If it had occurred years earlier, it could have been more easily hidden, and the impact to society in general almost minuscule. In fact the shock would have been completely lost.

I remembered being convinced the rapture was imminent when I was in high school. But if it had happened in the day before faxes, internet, satellite cable, or worldwide television coverage, before cell phones, email, texting, twittering, and worldwide security coverage, people could have easily assumed or been duped into believing a wide variety of excuses. It would have been easy to deceive people. Convincing them it was a local issue, or fabricating stories of mass kidnappings, criminal activities, terrorism, or people disappearing by choice. And those who had actually witnessed a disappearance would have been convinced they were insane, perhaps not even admitting to others what they had seen. But in His wisdom He had waited until it was virtually impossible for people to deny that such a momentous worldwide event had happened.

Almost like God had done it on purpose, I thought with a half smile. Waiting until international communication and time barriers were demolished through 24/7 satellite and worldwide internet coverage. Almost every human alive had access to some type of technology, internet access, television coverage, video or camera footage; even in the most backward areas on earth there were internet cafés, and because of that there had to be untold thousands of pictures proving His handiwork. I could only imagine the first few seconds after it happened. Wireless systems must have been on fire. Billions of texts, calls, tweets, social networking sites screaming the news, and web surfing bringing down most systems. And that didn't even account for security and television cameras that had recorded the entire thing.

Because as crime had increased over the past years, almost every single place of business was secured with cameras, from the corporate world to stores, malls, restaurants, churches, government buildings, and even highway interchanges and intersections. I thought of nanny cams in homes and daycares. All the proof anyone would ever want caught on tape. I imagined those tapes being alternately pored over then hidden or destroyed. Because there would be no comfort found in them. Proof? Definitely. Comfort? None at all.

I felt a tiny morsel of empathy for the announcer as the camera studied him. He seemed a bit shaken, less cocky, and more vulnerable than just a moment ago. Shuffling unnecessary papers while staring at them, he finally looked toward the camera with a subdued, "Well! That video makes you sort of wonder where those people are right now, doesn't it?" As he looked back to his papers, he muttered under his breath as if talking to himself, "Not sure who can explain that one away..." His voice was suddenly frightened, lonely, and shaky.

Watching his reaction made me consider many of my own friends, and multiplied millions already on anxiety medication and antidepressants before this catastrophe hit. From several lips to my ears, their medication never quite completely repaired or transformed their lives, and I shuddered to think how much more medication would be needed now by an even larger population in order to even survive the stress that was to come. The economy that was already worsening, health issues that would be exacerbated from the stress, and the pressure of strained relationship issues, would cause people to need something to numb their pain. And then there was the fact that we all needed something to assuage our consciences and diminish our newly discovered fears. Loneliness would be rampant, and medication would have to be used to help us forget that we had no one to turn to, no back-up systems or plans to rescue us. I had several friends who before this happened already refused to spend a night alone because of fear. But most of us had no choice now. We would either live with our fears or die with them.

I now had my own personal set of fears to deal with. My mind continued to run rampant, imagining every possible scenario every time I heard a noise. I had a feeling that without God's intervention less than an hour ago, I could have easily been gang raped or killed or at the very least thrown out of the house with no place to land.

How totally useless security systems were now, since no one was caring or paying attention to alarms going off, and none of them were being monitored. I had heard several going off throughout the night, most of them continuing for long periods of time, and not one time did I hear a siren respond. With so many empty homes, and insurance not paying for property loss or death benefits, why would the police even want to endanger their own lives? It was scary contemplating a society that had already been throwing away its moral compass combined with the removal of the threat of being caught or punished. It could only result in an entire civilization run amok.

In my mind's eye, I saw the economic fear alone evolving into widespread panic and eventual catastrophe. Over the past few years there had already been thousands of banks, lenders, mortgage companies, and investment houses collapsing all over the world as owners, attorneys, or advisors were found guilty of fraud, misconduct, or plain bad business management. I had recently read an article about how some parts of our country were experiencing a 19% unemployment rate, and my own state was considered better off than most at 12%. The government had been pretending for a long time now that they had enough money to pay unemployment to millions of people indefinitely. And if you added to those numbers the people already receiving social security, disability, food stamps, or other government help that would no longer be received, you had a world already in trouble less than twenty-four hours after it happened.

It was a bit shocking to realize that our government had been so callous as to immediately stop all assistance at the moment of our country's greatest need. The numbers were going to be astounding when you added those who were already jobless to those who had lost their family's breadwinner. To make matters worse, possibly millions of new people might be losing their jobs because of this day. Our government was just validating people's fears. And if the banks were frozen for long, there would be mass rioting and vandalism like our country and the world had never seen. The coming economic devastation would be across the board at every societal level.

In an epiphany I saw why the media and government would never be able to tell the truth, even if they figured it out and were so inclined. I could see what would happen if the government put out an official proclamation saying they regretted to inform us that they had determined the reason millions of people disappeared was because God miraculously took them all to heaven. Because if they admitted this event had been predicted thousands of years ago and that it was recorded in the Bible how every man or woman had been invited to join this mass exodus, there would be a revolution. Because the government would then be accused of misleading our country years earlier when they methodically began removing all signs of Christianity from government, schools, and the media, including their ongoing attempt to scientifically refute anything pointing to God as our Creator and eventual Judge. I knew one of the first decisions was in the early '60's when prayer was banned in schools.

I shook my head, thinking how sad that the government couldn't dare tell the truth now without bearing the brunt of the blame and being accused of everything from causing the collapse of the economy and family structure, to health and mental problems, and our entire way of life. I thought about decisions our government officials had made, thinking they were promoting freedom when all the while they had been trying to force our country to disavow God. Now they wouldn't have the fortitude to recant their position.

It was hard for *me* to admit when I was wrong, but an entire country or government or world structure wasn't about to admit anything that big. So we were stuck in a world that couldn't help us and couldn't tell us the truth.

I reminisced how the United States had helped other countries get through worldwide disasters over the years. For the most part we were a sympathetic country. But lately it had seemed like *we* were the ones needing sympathy and help. Our country's greed and hunger for materialistic things had slowly but surely begun skewing our whole financial system. And times were going to be drastically different now. There would be no collection of famous celebrities performing a "We are the World" fundraiser. There would be no announcement of federal disaster areas. But then no federal aid could help me in my situation anyway.

I barely noticed the television screen as it started showing more shocking videos again. I was weary of it all, wondering when I would be able to shut my eyes or find relief. But I was afraid if I tried to shut my mind down, I would literally go crazy. Then something caught my ear.

The announcer was back, appearing subdued. If I didn't know better I would have sworn his eyes were red and puffy now. But it was his tone that caught my attention. He sounded shell-shocked. "The network has been poring over hundreds of hours of tapes from news agencies around the world, and have uncovered another very serious, unexplainable predicament our society is facing. Despite the uncomfortable nature of the subject, the network feels the need to report it."

Well, *that* got my attention. What further horror had been discovered that made them hesitant to report it? What could be worse than untold millions missing? And if you added the probable financial collapse of the world, topped off by disasters and accidents killing another big percentage, what was left? But a minute into his report, I understood immediately. Because the very same thing had crossed my mind.

"As everyone is now aware, our world was shocked yesterday at 10:27 a.m. Central Standard Time when millions of people around the planet disappeared at the same second."

So, finally I knew the exact moment. That time would be tattooed on my brain forever. Now I knew positively. I had been sleeping the very second it happened. But he continued.

"The most respected scientists and educators around the world have been hesitant to make a pronouncement or educated guess as to what it was that occurred. But after much consultation, argument, and research there is a general consensus that this could very well have been an advanced, elite terrorism group with powers and abilities we do not yet understand, possibly with spatial connections. A much smaller, less discriminating group of scientists have opined that they believe this might be some type of religious phenomenon. But in any case, those theories will more than likely be argued and perhaps never be completely satisfied for quite some time.

"But the new troubling report is above and beyond the issue of the missing individuals. This new concern began coming to light mere moments after the disappearances, but is continuing and emerging as a frightening trend without apparent contact or word of mouth between the groups. Authorities and agencies have begun receiving reports of suicides occurring at an alarming rate around the entire world."

I closed my eyes and sighed, instantaneously identifying with the shock, sadness, remorse, regret, shame, and hopelessness prompting this trend. Apparently others had carried through with thoughts that had been flitting through my subconscious since I'd been told what had happened. But he wasn't stopping to give me time to commiserate, so I just listened.

"News agencies began picking up on this strange tagalong tragedy in different locales, originally thinking they had a unique problem. Soon, however, agencies began sharing information until it eventually became obvious this was developing into a worldwide calamity. Reports have indicated via first-hand witnesses that there were a shocking number of suicides across the globe that occurred within minutes of the disappearances, appearing to have been committed with little or no previous deliberation, no communication with anyone, and no notes or explanations left behind." I stared hopelessly at the screen, but he wasn't done shocking me.

"But, if possible, something even more shocking than those suicides is happening over and over again across the world and apparently are not considered copycat tragedies since many occurred simultaneously before the news got out. The unspeakable horror we are referring to are multiple reports of large groups committing group suicides." I closed my eyes and groaned softly. Knowing. Successful deception by voices screaming hopelessness and fear inside my own brain had gotten to them and they had obeyed those voices.

"Apparently these mass suicides have continued to increase through-out the day as mass hysteria continues." I sucked in my breath and held it. I *knew* exactly what had gone through their minds. I identified with them! Because the same voice had been whispering to me. I felt sorry knowing they hadn't been able to resist the evil voice, or realize their fate was now worse because they obeyed it.

The fact that anyone was confused or surprised by the hopelessness engulfing the world merely showed their ignorance. I had most definitely felt that same hopelessness. Even if you believed this great disappearance had no spiritual connotations, the fact that parents had lost children alone would be enough for them to not want to live.

But if you add the knowledge that you missed out on eternal paradise shared with loved ones who disappeared, the mental anguish deepens.

This was what I was currently trying my best to fight off. I wondered if they would ever analyze the trend, finding out that a majority of the suicides were from people with religious backgrounds.

Ending it all had crossed my mind more than once, and if for one second I thought it would help me escape this situation, I would end my life in a heartbeat. But I knew better. I knew now beyond a shadow of a doubt that every word in the Bible was true. And that knowledge scared me to my core, increasing my helplessness and out-of-control feelings. There was an eternity and, whether I liked it or not, it was going to last forever and ever.

I found myself wishing this life-altering decision hadn't been completely up to me. I wasn't trustworthy! I was fickle! I hadn't thought it through! I hadn't counted the cost! I remembered hearing celebrities spew their gospel with absurd things like, "*My* God is a God of love, and wants me to be happy." But I knew now that no matter how important or smart I thought I was, I had no say so in God's rules about life or eternity, and He alone had decided who joined Him in heaven. The only choice *we'd* had was deciding whether to follow Him and then *continuing* to make that decision every day.

I knew that killing myself would only make eternity come quicker, and until I was right with God, I didn't dare listen to any voice but God's. Something deep inside assured me that God would never tell me to kill myself so I couldn't afford to listen to any other voice. Eternity seemed more real now than it had ever been.

Something the announcer had said was troubling me, but my thoughts were so tangled I couldn't even remember what it was. So I just focused on his voice again. He started with the usual disclaimer, admitting the numbers they had were still preliminary, but indicated the estimates had been made with positive numbers influencing them, and as new reports surfaced, their estimates were holding up.

"For years government and medical journals have kept statistical reports of suicides in an effort to study and prevent them, not only in the United States, but also internationally. The latest published reports are dated a little over a year ago. At that time, statistics said that *each* day in the United States there was an average of eighty-nine suicides, with worldwide figures showing 28,000 suicides *daily*."

Wow. I could never have dreamed up those numbers. *Every single day*. That number of people feeling so hopeless they didn't want to live. And I knew over the last ten or twenty years suicides kept increasing dramatically, so those numbers might even be higher now. From your average person to the most famous celebrity, hopelessness hit all types of people at every level of living. From senior citizens to elementary students, blue collar workers to the most elite.

I already knew that suicide didn't drastically discriminate between races, or become more pronounced in big cities. People with lots of money or no money, it didn't seem to make a difference. Pain was pain. One of the biggest lies was that death brought a guarantee of happiness.

I remembered about four to five years ago, when an uptick in suicides seemed to coincide with the onslaught of economic problems. All kinds of sad trends began to appear with one spouse killing the other and their children before committing suicide. And even stories about children killing their parents.[1] The lack of respect for life was rampant and seemed to leave everyone at risk.

The announcer did the math and it was worse than I could have ever imagined. "Most of us are shocked to hear the suicide rate was as high as it had been for the past several years, because even with eighty-nine suicides a day, that adds up to a little over 32,000 suicides in the United States *each year*, and figures out to approximately one million suicides around the world. But after today, those numbers will never be considered high again."

"Oh no…" slipped out, as I held my breath again, wondering if I knew anyone who had fallen prey. But he first continued with a strange request.

"Before we announce those numbers, however, the federal government is asking for the help of everyone hearing this report. Since suicide seems to have become a common solution for a huge number of people, authorities around the world are asking those who are physically able, to create neighborhood groups and canvas local neighborhoods door to door. The intent is to discover and locate people who might have committed suicide so their bodies can be taken care of, before a pandemic of disease adds to the current catastrophe. The fact that a majority of the suicides seem to be among those whose families disappeared is creating further problems since no one is left to report the suicides or take care of the bodies."

The reporter seemed to have aged several years in the span of this telecast. There was no life left in his voice as he continued, "Until we get reports from neighborhood watch groups, we can only report on the number of suicides already turned in thus far. For many reasons it is important that suicides be reported and placed into the national database to facilitate the creation of reports and revised population estimates.

"As stated earlier, the number of daily suicides previously reported in our country was eighty-nine; however, less than twenty-four hours after the mass disappearances, it appears that close to 44,500 individuals in the United States have been reported as having committed suicide thus far. More than *five hundred times* the previously recorded daily rate."

I gasped aloud, whispering "No..." at the television. It was too staggering. In my wildest dreams I couldn't have imagined a number that high. But before I could even digest that, I knew it would increase. With only perhaps a fraction of suicides discovered or reported so far, and people all over the world still desperately trying to process what had happened. I knew there were people right now on the cusp of joining those 44,500. Then he did the math again.

"Communication is at best sporadic with foreign countries, but if our U.S. figures are even similar to those worldwide, we are looking at the possibility of over fourteen million people around the world who may have committed suicide."

I thought I was going to faint.

CHAPTER TWENTY-THREE

Monday, seven seventeen a.m.

WERE THEY SERIOUS? Fourteen million people might have entered eternity by their own hand on the *same* day an additional two *billion* were spirited away? And then if you added the thousands upon thousands killed through accidents and disasters, this was a nightmare. Life could not have turned this distressing and full of this much trauma in one day. Then my mind thought of the majority of those fourteen million and where they probably were at this moment. Knowing beyond a shadow of a doubt that they had immediately regretted their action after discovering they were in a hellish infinity.

Then I remembered a strange scripture, and it clicked. It talked about suicide, of all things, and I had always wondered why God had included it in the Bible. But now I realized it was a gift of grace from our Creator. The scripture said, "And in those days shall men seek death, and shall not find it; and shall desire to die, and death shall flee from them."[1]

I wasn't sure when "those days" would begin, or when God would invoke that promise, but it would have to happen soon. Because in the strangest of ways it would be a gift God knew we would *need* during the coming years of suffering; otherwise the whole world would want to end their life and few would ever have the opportunity to find their way back to Him.

The announcer began speaking again, and in a daze I watched and listened. "Continuing on the painful subject of suicide, we return to one of the more disturbing facts emerging, and that is the large number of group suicides."

I frowned as I tried to imagine what kind of scenario they were going to show. Totally catching me off guard was the next picture shown on the screen. I saw a church sign I recognized in the city next to mine. I squinted at the screen, turning up the volume. I had driven by that church many times, and was pretty sure someone I worked with attended there. "We have a first-hand report from relatives of members who attended the local Mercy Gospel Fellowship Church. After the initial news of mass disappearances became common knowledge, this young lady immediately drove to her mother's church. She lives about forty-five minutes away from the church, and although she is obviously shaken, has agreed to speak with us.

"Ma'am, could you tell us your story please?" the reporter began sympathetically.

The young lady despondently began, "I've actually visited here with my Mom before," she said as she slightly turned, pointing past the sign to the medium-sized church building behind them. She wiped her eyes with the bent knuckles of both hands before continuing with a trembling voice, "My mom had asked me to go to church with her this morning." Her eyes avoided the camera's glare. She looked like she was gritting her teeth to keep from crying, but finally said, "I was feeling guilty about turning her down, until I got here and saw this."

She had my attention now, since her words reminded me of the promise I'd made my *own* mother. She almost successfully stifled a sob, and then composed herself as if on a mission. With a wild-eyed look she gazed straight into the camera and started again, "As soon as I heard that people had disappeared, I knew exactly what it was. My mom had warned me about this day for years." She looked away again, this time with a faraway look, staring into the sky, "She said no one knew when it would happen, but one day God would take all the Christians out of the world. She kept warning me I wasn't ready." She looked away from the camera again, but continued to talk, almost as if to herself, "I just liked my life the way it was, so I kept ignoring her." She shook her

226

head and looked back at the camera, and I saw a tear slowly roll down her face, "But as soon as I heard people were missing, I drove here to see for myself if she really was gone. I got here about forty-five minutes after it happened, about 11:15, and ran right into the church, and that's when I saw it."

The reporter took back control of the microphone as if to tell her he'd heard enough of her religious mumbo jumbo, and she needed to get to the part his station wanted to hear. "Exactly what *did* you see when you entered the church?" he asked.

She shook her head as if trying to forget the sight, "No one was in the pews, but as I walked farther down one of the aisles, I saw something on the carpet at the front, so I ran up the aisle to get a closer look. There were about fifty people lying face down. I wasn't sure if they were praying or what. They were all holding hands, each one with the next, connected like a long chain. But then I saw something dark on the white carpet underneath the head of the one closest to me, and when I looked closer I could see that none of them were moving." She paused gasping for breath and a sob escaped again. "I was the only one making any noise. I bent down to the young girl closest to me who had the longest, blonde hair. I was about to touch her shoulder when I saw a bullet wound in the back of her head. I was mortified, and then looked at the guy beside her, and he had one too."

The announcer didn't pull back the microphone this time, but patiently waited so as not to break her concentration. She stared off in the distance, and then began again, "I was horrified, and wondered who on earth had killed all these people, thinking maybe it wasn't the rapture like my Mom had talked about. But then my eyes were drawn to the stage where a guy in a suit was half sitting, half leaning against a wall with a gun in his hand. He was dead too. I had to assume, since he was the one with the gun, that he had killed them all, and then himself."

The reporter contemplatively took the microphone back, quietly saying, "Since you'd only been to this church a few times, I don't suppose you recognized the shooter?" In a weird metamorphosis, the girl's persona changed from pensive and shocked to defiant. She jerked her head around, staring straight into the reporter's eyes, and with an insolent tone she enunciated clearly so no one would misunderstand, "I know exactly who the killer was. It was the *pastor* of the church," she finished with a flourish, not breaking her stare.

The reporter took a moment to recover from what was obviously an unexpected answer. You could see the wheels inside his head turning, knowing he had a coup on his hands, expecting to be congratulated for his exceptional reporting skills. "Well!" he said almost too excitedly, "Were you shocked when you realized what you had discovered?"

The girl's despondent attitude had returned and she looked at him without hiding her disgust. "What do *you* think? When you walk into a church expecting to find your mother and see that the pastor has killed the members?"

He looked sufficiently dressed down, but quickly came back to his senses, finally asking an appropriate question, "Did you find your mother?"

She turned her head, almost looking through him. A softening of her gaze was evident. "No. I had to go to each and every person who had died, just to be sure. But no, my mom wasn't killed, and I *know* she was there. So she was one of those who had disappeared. I'm happy for her, just sad for me."

It was obvious the reporter didn't want to lead her down a sentimental path again, and decided the interview was over. Looking into the camera, he said, "Well, you've heard another unexplainable event that will take days, if not weeks, to figure out the underlying motive." He paused for a breath, and in that half second, you could clearly hear the voice of the girl off camera, saying, "It actually *won't* take that long."

It was an awkward moment for the reporter, and the camera man recovered first, zooming out so both the girl and the reporter were once again in the frame. The reporter, a little ticked off at being embarrassed, said in a thinly veiled, belittling tone, "So you think you know why this happened? And how is that?" he asked snidely.

You could tell she knew she had the winning hand in their war of words because she ever so slightly rolled her eyes, looking right into the camera, pulling the microphone closer. "Because I read the suicide note the pastor left," staring at him with an almost hostile boldness.

I could only imagine that his superiors were yelling in his earpiece after hearing how he'd missed the biggest morsel of her story. In a lame attempt to recover, he said, "Well, *please*, tell us the *rest* of the story."

"After I made sure my mom wasn't killed, I went up on the platform where the pastor was to get a closer look at the kind of person who would do such an atrocious thing. It was horrible, though, because he'd shot himself in the mouth. There was blood on the wall and all around him. I was about to leave when I noticed something in his hand. His hand was still in a fist, but it made me curious what he had been holding as he killed himself. I pried open his fingers and pulled out a crumpled piece of paper." She paused, closing her eyes as if wishing she could get rid of the image. "When I straightened out the paper I saw it was their Sunday bulletin and was about to throw it away since there was blood on it, when I noticed handwriting on the back."

Then she shocked everyone, including the reporter, by reaching into her pocket and pulling out the wadded, stained piece of paper. She saw his expression and said, "Maybe I shouldn't have taken it, but we all know there won't be an investigation, right?"

His impatience was more than evident as he interrupted her, "Can I see the note please?"

Clutching it between both hands, she said, "How about if I just read it to you?" and before he had a chance to respond, she began. "Just a few minutes ago there were some Christians who disappeared, including some in our own congregation. As the pastor, I knew I had been left here for a purpose to help the distraught members who had been left behind. Out of the kindness of my heart, I comforted them by explaining how God had told me we could still join our family and friends today. We do not want to live in this world any longer, but took charge of our future and joined our loved ones. God Bless." As the young woman finished reading the letter, she looked up with the most inscrutable expression on her face. She seemed needy, her eyes begging for someone to make sense out of the gibberish she'd just read, wondering if it were true.

For me it was a tragedy taken to a whole new level because it was a pastor who had lied to his church. A leader, a shepherd, one they should have been able to trust. Someone like my Dad. I knew enough to know this man had *not* heard from God, but had stolen their last chance to make themselves right with God while trying to make himself look good. I thought of a sermon I'd heard about leaders leading people astray.[2] I felt I had just witnessed a false prophet's words and felt sorry for those who had believed him.

The reporter took back the microphone, stated his name, and signed off. I figured his producer must have put the kibosh on his reporting, or he was out of lame explanations and didn't feel like trying anymore. The announcer back at the station started off by saying the church suicide we had just heard about was not an anomaly.

"Not only have there been an enormous number of individual suicides, and hundreds of families ending their lives together, but the internet and blogs have been overloaded with similar stories of large groups throughout the world ending their lives together. Authorities are struggling to figure out why so many churches have been the location of mass suicides and if they are related in any way, or are part of a particular cult or denomination. If anyone had contact with any of these groups or has information about the mass suicides, they are asked to contact authorities.

"Religious educators are attempting to compare the two situations we are facing today to see if there is a connection. It appears that an extremely large percentage of the population that disappeared were either in church when it happened or known to be very religious, making people believe it is an extremely organized or terroristic cult even more horrific than the Jim Jones tragedy over thirty years ago."

I now knew an answer to a question I no longer wanted to ask. For years Christians had prayed for Christ's return, and I had even thought what a wonderful escape it would be from the hard knocks of life. Most Christians had fully expected and begged God to start this next phase, becoming almost impatient when He seemed to delay it unnecessarily. But after seeing just a tiny portion of the worldwide devastation it had left behind, the horrifying loss of life through accidents, and this avalanche of suicides, I knew the answer.

I was full of reverence and wonder and awe of a God of the entire universe who had all the knowledge and wisdom necessary to first create it, then maintain it. But the unexpected answer to the question was the reminder that I had only partially been serving a God who knew everything, everyone's past, present, and future,[3] which meant He knew ahead of time every tiny thing that would happen once He set this ball in motion. And if it were really true that He loved each person He had ordained to be born, then it made sense for Him to wait until the last possible moment, giving every conceivable chance for us to be with Him. Because He had not only known those who wouldn't make it when He gathered His children home, but also knew those who would immediately lose their lives and forever be damned.

I felt like such an alien. Forgetting the fact that I was still here, I had still lived in a religious cocoon, and this new world already seemed so bizarre. I was in limbo. In between two distinct worlds. Between a world of people like me, who knew exactly what had happened, overwhelmingly knowing it would be the hardest thing they'd ever do to live for Jesus now. And then there was the rest of them. Those who were completely lost, alone, and still oblivious.

I felt so smart…and so stupid.

CHAPTER TWENTY-FOUR

Monday, eight forty-five a.m.

AS I FINISHED watching what the station probably considered a fine exposé, only to begin their next piece on widespread crime and vandalism unchecked throughout the world, I slowly and deliberately turned the television off. I needed no more pictures to convince me the world was a different place than it had been twenty-four hours ago. I needed no more ideas of crimes that could be committed against me, nor more opinions of what had caused this or what might happen next. I scooted further back into the corner, leaning my head against the wall as my eyelids dropped. Why couldn't this be a dream? I wondered how many others around the world had struggled with their thoughts and regrets as much as I had throughout the night, and I knew I hadn't even started coming to grips with it all.

I considered how we'd been taught all our lives to "grow up" but how I'd gotten it so mixed up. My mind had skewed the concept of maturing, convincing myself growing up meant "becoming responsible for" or "being independent" and "in control." But I had a funny feeling now that God had never intended on me becoming independent *from* Him or fighting for control of my life. Now that our pseudo-control had been ripped from us, it left us unsettled and at the mercy of others.

At the moment, it seemed like my life was inside a snowball at the top of a mountain, rolling down whichever path *it* chose, picking up debris and tragedy in its way, going at a frightening speed. There was no steering wheel in my hands and no brakes. Everyone's life plan was off track now. All the goals and lists and budgets I was so proud of? Out the window.

Amazing what kind of chaos had emerged within seconds of the rapture. I thought of people in high positions of power, politicians, heads of states, kings, or CEOs. Those accustomed to power and pride and wealth, believing they were on top of the world, setting the rules, everyone at their beck and call, everything going in their favor, used to success. And then something like this happens, and they can't even fix their own little world now. I imagined how drastically financial statements around the world had changed today.

I heard a truck lumber by in front of the house, and I came out of my reverie. Rubbing my eyes, I could see the sun was about to rise and light was bleeding through the blinds. I hadn't slept one moment yet, and was exhausted. With my company closed I had nowhere I needed to be. With strangers having overtaken my home, even if I had wanted to freshen up, I would have to borrow clothes from Mom's closet. At the thought of her, I closed my eyes again, but decided I wasn't going to the morbid, dark place in my thoughts this time. I had opened and shut that door so many times throughout the night that I was physically tired from the exertion.

Instead, my mind began thinking of heaven and curiously wondered how many people before the rapture had entered heaven's gates each day. No imagination could comprehend how the hosts of heaven rejoiced as they welcomed each arrival. But I knew yesterday had been different, because everyone in heaven had been waiting for this parade. What all the Christians—all the saints of God—had lived and died for. I imagined God summoning everyone so that the welcoming party was bigger and better than any previous one. With a slight smile, I pictured throngs of people who had been raptured, joyously dancing, praising God, excitedly looking everywhere, trying to take it all in, grateful that the blood of Jesus had made it all possible. I almost chuckled, picturing an old Hammond organ playing the old song:

When the saints go marching in,
Oh, when the saints go marching in,
Lord, how I want to be in that number—
When the saints go marching in.

Thinking of the song was silly, but daydreaming where they actually were was a comforting thought if I kept my mind off myself. My mind traveled to Mom first. She was always such an excitable person, uninhibited, loving Jesus with all her heart, unabashedly unashamed. She could cry or laugh at the drop of a hat and if we protested, she would quickly remind us that God kept track of her tears.[1]

I imagined the exact moment she became cognizant of what had happened. I imagined her sprinting to find Him, the one she had talked about, sang about, preached about, loved, and lived for. And when she found Him, I pictured an all-enveloping hug lasting as long as she wanted. I envisioned the loving words He spoke to her.[2] Until she was healed. Of worries, fears, insecurities, regrets, and yes, even her famous tears. Many of which had been for me.

And then I pictured it. When Jesus and Mom finished their love fest, she would excitedly wander around heaven reconnecting with old friends, meeting new ones, finding church friends she had just been worshipping with moments earlier on earth. I pictured her finally finding her parents, and other long lost relatives,[3] squealing with delight each time. My mind couldn't imagine her having any more energy than she did on earth, but I bet He found a supernatural dose to give her, while taking away all her aches and pains so that not one physical malady would ever slow her down again. And after that, she would look up the older saints, ones she'd read about, who had gone on before, prophets and apostles from the Bible. I could see her having long conversations, learning from them, yet never shy about sharing her own experiences with them as well.

Then I thought of Dad. Somehow I imagined his journey would be a little different. Having been an evangelist and pastor for over sixty years, he had done a lot of talking in his day! I pictured him now with a bright, calm, peaceful smile as he entered heaven, knowing he was about to meet the one he had conversed with every single day. I sensed he would be overcome with a quiet anticipation. As a little girl I would hear him praying in the early mornings. And to think that every word he'd spoken to God had been remembered.[4]

You would think they would have a lot to talk about now, except for the fact that I was sure Dad had already given his cares to God that very morning, so in a way they were already caught up. I knew from observing my own Dad that pastors quite often ended up on the receiving end of hurts, wounds, and disappointments that they had to continually give to God before bitterness set in. I could imagine God showing him each and every purpose for the pain he'd endured, and how He really had "worked it all together for his good" and quickly, effortlessly, healed every single one, making him all the better for the hardships he'd borne. He had taught and talked about Him so long I couldn't imagine how full his heart was as he anticipated meeting his Savior. Yet, I saw him quiet. A huge smile on his face, but completely contented, knowing he had completed his journey successfully and was finally home.

I thought of the different books the Bible mentioned God kept, and how big they would *have* to be just to include Dad's life. His life from a young man had been spent serving God in one capacity or another. He had never been afraid to mention His name, encourage someone in the Lord, pray for someone, or even help the Holy Spirit convict them if necessary, I thought with a smile. If everything we did was really recorded, I couldn't imagine how much evidence they would have to show for Dad.[5]

My mental picture switched to an impromptu parade after Dad met with Jesus. They'd be walking down the street as those who had come to know the Lord from his years of ministry up until his very last service, yelled out, joining him as he walked, hugging and thanking him. I smiled at that thought. He had worked hard for God while he was on earth. I had to wonder if his one regret was that his own daughter hadn't made it? I buried my face in my hands, weeping as I hoped it would get easier thinking of this day. Because if it didn't, if I couldn't think of my loved ones without this deep, wounding hurt, I would have to push those feelings under, refusing to ever think of them again.

It was a different story when I pictured my husband entering heaven. I only felt a deep, profound sadness that I couldn't shake. No matter how hard I tried to visualize him being thrilled or excited, I couldn't. Even though I knew he would greatly enjoy rekindling friendships and reminiscing with friends and relatives. We had shared many, many years together as well as our relationship with Christ. But it was clear now that you could sit side by side someone in church, sharing prayers and attending the same classes, but it said nothing about the condition of your heart.

Perhaps my husband had had no idea, like me, that I wasn't ready, or perhaps he'd clearly understood. I will never know. But whichever it was, I knew it distressed him to realize I wasn't there. I could see a crestfallen, incredulous look on his face, knowing this was one thing he couldn't fix for me, and had no control over. My protector, my best friend, the love of my life, but he couldn't change my situation. I knew over the years he had prayed for me, worried about me, and even nagged me occasionally. But apparently my spiritual blindness had overshadowed his discernment and my pride and the lies I'd believed didn't allow me to think my husband knew something I couldn't recognize. Pride was such a dangerous force. I felt deceived.[6] I couldn't blame him. But I also couldn't continue thinking about him. The wound was too raw.

My vision of my daughter entering heaven was one of complete pride and relief. To know that she had sincerely been living for God and wasn't stuck in this scary world gave me peace. I would have welcomed anyone to stand beside me as I tried to finish this daunting journey, but I wouldn't have wished that upon her for a moment. All I knew is that I would miss her desperately and wished someone could *promise* me I would see her again. But I knew no one could make that promise because it was up to me. And since I had failed the test so miserably the first time, I wasn't sure of anything.

I continued thinking of Holly, picturing her finding her beloved grandfather who had died a few years earlier, and meeting other grandparents she'd never met. But I pictured her first moments with mixed emotions as well. She had many, many friends. Some friends she knew loved God, but others she knew were on the proverbial fence. Too busy spreading their wings, trying to fit in with friends and experimenting with life that they never saw the need to really commit to serving God. She knew they were trying to play the Christian game just enough to get their parents off their back. They even sometimes fooled the youth pastor or their friends for a time. But invariably it slipped out.[7] True feelings, true yearnings, and struggles usually weren't hidden forever.[8]

So I knew until God freed Holly, she would have a lot of sadness, because she would be searching in vain for many friends. Starting with the ones I'd seen huddled in church yesterday. I knew she had never imagined her life would end so early, but I was so thankful she had made the right decision rather than using the excuse about wanting to live life first. Perhaps that was what I had been doing. They were all so fortunate to have escaped whatever it was I would have to live through.[9] I hoped God would help me escape from at least some of the terror to come.

Tired of thinking of the place I should have been, I thought of the song I'd always liked by the band called the Los Lonely Boys entitled "Heaven." I started humming one of the lines, thinking of the words:

> *Save me from this prison, Lord,*
> *help me to get away*
> *Only you can save me from this misery*
> *I've been lost in my own place,*
> *And I'm getting weary*
> *How far is heaven*
> *I know I need to change my ways of living,*
> *How far is heaven.*

Then my eyes got big and my humming stopped. Even in that song there was a message for me. Singing to God that they knew they needed to change their way of living, but just wanted to know how long they had until they got to heaven. How long could we stay the way we were without missing out on heaven? And that's what I'd done. It had been an exhausting way of life, guessing, trying to time it, but for what? To keep from fully surrendering to God?

The urge to lie down and sleep was strong. Mainly because I just didn't want to be awake. The light was beginning to invade my privacy, my secret hiding place, and it took the mystery out of what had happened yesterday, bringing it into the broad daylight. It wasn't pretty. The devastation was brutal and all encompassing. Life had no attraction now. There wasn't one career goal, one purchase I wanted to make, not one person I wanted to talk to.

I could hear a regular traffic pattern outside, hoping it meant a little more safety. Surely someone wouldn't try to break into the house in broad daylight. I wearily climbed upon the bed and laid my head on my Mom's pillow. I took a deep breath and smelled a combination of hair spray and face cream. I missed her.

The loud ticking on the bedside clock got my attention and I glanced in that direction. Was it a coincidence that it said 9:27? Exactly twenty-three hours to the minute when my world crumbled. I was too numb to think, regret, or worry for the moment. I noticed Mom's CD player beside her lamp and randomly wondered what she had last listened to. More because I needed a diversion rather than because I cared, I pressed play.

Mom had turned the volume up loud, and the music completely filled the room. I didn't even reach to turn it down. I shut my eyes, recognizing the chorus of a song I'd heard by the group Casting Crowns, immediately knowing it wasn't by accident this song had been cued. I closed my eyes and let it preach. The song's title, "Slow Fade" seemed to tell my story:

> *It's a slow fade—When you give yourself away*
> *It's a slow fade—When black and white are turned to gray*
> *And thoughts invade, choices are made*
> *A price will be paid—When you give yourself away*
> *People never crumble in a day...*

Then if possible, the verse drove the sermon deeper.

> *The journey from your mind to your hands*
> *Is shorter than you're thinking*
> *Be careful if you think you stand*
> *You just might be sinking*

And there it was. My cue to get back to business. I had one hour before twenty-four hours ended. Had others in my shoes already discovered why they missed it? I sat up in bed, starting with a simple prayer. I didn't even close my eyes. For the first time there was no reason to fake it or try to impress. No reason to pretend to be praying if I wasn't, to care about God if I really didn't. I now knew beyond a shadow of a doubt that there was no pretending with God.[10] Since it had gotten me nowhere before, I had lost all desire to try.

I prayed with as sincere a heart as I could. As I began to pray, I grabbed Mom's other Bible off the nightstand, staring at it while I talked to God. "God, I'm embarrassed and saddened and confused that I wasn't ready for You. I'm not questioning You now; I'm just asking You to show me where I went wrong so I can make it right."

I had nothing else to say so I stopped. And waited.

CHAPTER TWENTY-FIVE

Monday, nine thirty-two a.m.

I KNEW MOST people never heard God's audible voice during their lifetime, and I didn't expect to now. But I was in a strange position at the moment because now I really needed to hear from Him, was actually *desperate* to hear from Him, and wasn't quite sure how to go about it. I mean I couldn't *make* Him talk to me, so I wondered what my next step should be. I tried to think of the last time I had purposely attempted to listen for His voice. I mean I talked to Him and prayed, at church or with the family. I breathed prayers of protection when I knew Holly was out late, but as far as asking direct questions and needing direct answers…it had been awhile.

It made me think of a sad situation that seemed to happen at work over the years. After working side by side people for years at a time, many of them were my best friends. Yet, when a good friend would leave, changing jobs or moving, no matter how good of a friend they had been, the friendship invariably suffered unless great care was taken to keep it going. We never intended for it to happen. We swore it wouldn't! No harsh words were ever spoken, no disagreements, nothing to hinder our continued friendship.

The only thing askew was that daily contact had been broken. I wouldn't bother them with a few of my family stories; they wouldn't share their latest heartache. After a few days of not speaking, we would try to catch up, but the next gap would be longer, and then another, until our catch-up time became awkward with too many stories to recount, too many missed experiences. Then excuses would be abundant, until we stopped seeing each other and rarely talked. I deeply missed some of those friendships, but the only remedy was to begin spending time together again.

It felt *exactly* the same now. I felt sheepish, because I had known the antidote all along. I had missed many daily talks with the God of the universe. He had been more than ready, willing, and able, anxious even, to hear from me, and the gap had been totally created by me. Strange how we have high expectations of fellow humans, expecting and needing them to be there for us when we need encouragement, help, or attention and become incensed, disappointed, and even resentful when they're unavailable or don't provide the *exact* emotional support we crave. Yet the Creator, limited by nothing, the one much more able to help than any friend or loved one, had openly made Himself available to me around the clock.[1] He had been completely at my beck and call, but quite often cast aside as unworthy of my attention. I was disappointed, thinking it had been my choice and I had made the wrong one.

But now? There was plenty of time to wait and listen. No plans. No distractions. For days or weeks or months perhaps. So I sat and waited. It was awkward. Uncomfortable. I was embarrassed and ashamed that suddenly I was interested in hearing what He might say. I wasn't one hundred percent convinced He would talk to me again. But I had no alternative but to wait.

The song I'd just heard kept floating in and out of my thoughts. A slow fade. I wasn't sure, but I wondered if that had been my problem. I became aware again of the Bible I was holding. It had been my grandmother's, and after she passed away Mom had begun using it, so it was well-worn and barely in one piece. It felt like I was holding her heart and soul in my hands. It wasn't one of those Bibles you carried around for looks, because this Bible wasn't pretty. She studied it, pored over it. I remembered her telling me how every word in it was like a seed.[2] Depending on what you did with it, it would grow and produce whatever He said it could,[3] or alternatively, it could dry up and die.

That was another nagging point she used. She was a big believer in reading straight through the entire Bible. Over and over. She had told me if I would do that, read every word in the Bible, then every possible seed God wanted available to me would be planted inside my heart and mind. And then, if I made sure my heart was good soil,[4] it would begin producing fruit.[5] It had all seemed like a lot of mumbo jumbo when she went on and on like that. I remembered her telling me the Word of God had an answer to every single problem in life[6] and how He was the answer for every sin we couldn't overcome.[7] I wondered if everything she had said would work the same now. I felt a familiar cynicism rise up inside. Outwardly, I rarely spoke against what she or any other Christian purported was the truth, or what they told me would "work," but my inward voice was sometimes screaming back at them because it didn't seem that easy for me,[8] and I had been too stubborn to admit that I had doubts, and too much pride to humble myself and ask for help.

But Mom was gone and I was here, so there was a good chance she knew what she was talking about. I knew I would have to stuff the pride, the holier-than-thou attitude I'd had and maybe still did, and return to square one. Maybe God would be kind enough to let me remember things Mom and Dad had told me over the years. Things I'd previously chosen to let slide.

I figured if I opened her Bible and started flipping through it, *surely* a verse would jump out at me. It seemed like nearly every page had some kind of markings or notes or arrows on it. Maybe I could find something that applied to me and would help me start the process. I was getting anxious to get it out in the open. I felt a deep urgency to be clean before twenty-four hours passed. I needed to finish this part of my tough passage. I had a feeling there was something in my life I had ignored for awhile, covered it up, rationalized it, demanding that my conscience stop bothering me about it. But what was it?

I opened the Bible, and was drawn to some pink highlighting, so I looked down, my eyes alighting upon Matthew 6:14, 15. I remembered hearing Dad talk about how "newborn" Christians sometimes opened the Bible, pointing to a scripture like it was a game of chance, hoping to randomly find a verse that blessed them rather than thoughtfully reading His words. His statement stung when I realized the inference now included me. Perhaps I remembered it because I was guilty. I read the verse, hoping for something to build my hope and encourage me in my torment, but I hadn't found one to bless me. Instead, it was God's way of answering my prayer in a blunt way. I read:

"If you forgive those who sin against you, your heavenly Father will forgive you. But if you refuse to forgive others, your Father will not forgive your sins."

I read it quickly, brushing it off because it was a familiar verse and I had read it many times, so I just figured I needed to keep flipping until I found a verse that could really help. I even had my hand on the Bible ready to turn the page, when it almost felt like someone in the room whispered, "Read it again…" So I did.

I was *pretty sure* I had forgiven everyone. I thought of shows where people who had been harmed through horrible crimes would proclaim to the world that they would never, ever forgive the perpetrators. But I knew *I* had never said those words!

So surely it didn't apply to me… I frantically began scanning my memories. Looking back at Mom's Bible, I saw she had circled a footnote leading to another scripture. I followed the pointer and read:

Luke 17:4—"And even if he sins against you seven times in a day, and turns to you seven times and says, I repent, I am sorry, you must forgive him (**give up resentment and consider the offense as recalled and annulled**)."

I was tempted to be irritated, thinking Mom had underlined it just for me, even though I knew better. But at the moment, it was the only hint I had. My only hope. I couldn't get lost in what would have been a previous course of irritation or self righteousness. With a sinking feeling, I thought if *that* was what it actually meant to forgive, how had anyone been able to do that? So people who had been raptured had truly forgiven everyone? But it was *hard,* if not impossible, to act as if an offense had *never* been committed. To give up the right to even be angry about it, nor harbor bitterness, dislike, or hatred for the offender. And it also probably meant I wouldn't have told others about what someone might have done to me...since you wouldn't talk about something that had never happened.

Pondering forgiveness in this new light and with a fresh heartbroken honesty, I realized there were probably fewer people I *had* forgiven over the years. My heart began to be stricken and a new shame surfaced as I began remembering instance after instance where I had not fully forgiven friends or loved ones, holding things in my heart, remembering them, recalling them, recounting them, and holding others accountable—whether in my mind or face to face. Bringing up the past, doing my best to eke out fitting punishments that would satisfy my hurt or their guilt.

I felt foolish now admitting I had wondered if this scripture had meant *exactly* what it said. That God *couldn't* or *wouldn't* forgive my sins if I didn't forgive others? There was no point in delaying, so I laid my heart bare before God, asking Him to fully show me my innermost thoughts and sins no matter how ugly.[9] And as sad as the outcome was, He was faithful. In a most revealing, albeit ugly, way, various memories began flooding my mind, working the work God needed to do in my heart, reminding me of my sin of unforgiveness.

I remembered silly things, hurtful things, times betrayed, times ridiculed, imagined offenses, real offenses, things I'd held against people in church, coaches, teachers, so many things I couldn't seem to let go of. Like a windshield wiping away muck and mire, I saw things inside my heart I'd held against people for years. Although they were usually well hidden, occasionally a hateful, judgmental thought erupted at the mention of a name or the sight of a face. I thought of stupid misunderstandings, people I felt had maligned me, minor events filed away in my heart, still holding people responsible for actions and judging them long after the time had passed.

I thought of church members who had hurt my parents over the years. How I'd criticized them, gone to friends and shared my accusations, even slandering their name, pulling innocent people along with them. Now that I was willing to admit it, I was amazed how the bitterness still felt fresh and raw no matter how old the wound. But amazingly, I knew that my parents, the ones the offenses had actually been committed against, had worked hard to fully forgive them all. I shook my head, clearly remembering a Sunday dinner when I mentioned that I'd run into a particular couple, the same ones I knew my Mom had cried and prayed about, and as I began to recount it, Dad had stopped me, saying, "Annie, you must let it go; *we* had to. Let God be the one who handles the situation." I hadn't even considered taking his advice that day; instead I continued imagining how I hoped they would be punished.[10]

When I fully felt the conviction of my sin of unforgiveness I finally admitted to harboring in my heart, I felt ready to pray. Except suddenly I realized His work wasn't complete. I began crying as new memories kept flooding back. God had plenty of examples, plenty of ammunition on this one. I remembered a situation where I felt that my actions were justified because it had hurt so much. This act of unforgiveness had been buried the deepest.

The tears flowed as if it were yesterday. I was a senior in high school. Seventeen years old. Vulnerable, soft-hearted, hungry for acceptance and love. That same year Larry and his family moved to town and joined our church. The sight of him had taken my breath away. His personality was infectious and his sense of humor garnered him crowds of friends, making it all the more miraculous when he asked me out. To think that a good looking, Christian guy with a great personality would want to be with me, won me over without him even trying very hard.

By the time we both graduated from high school, my mind had convinced me we would go to the same college, marry, and our beautiful life would fall into place. Except for youth camp. That summer we were both camp counselors. I could still remember the night I was walking my group of girls back to our cabin, down a dark trail, and stumbled upon Larry kissing a new girl who had just joined our church. Even the little girls with me gasped, as much for the kissing part as for the shock of knowing my boyfriend was cheating on me. I could still picture his face when he looked over at us. Without an apologetic look or any sign of embarrassment, he grabbed her hand and walked away in the opposite direction.

I remembered the girls gathering around me, wondering if we'd broken up or if he was cheating on me, consoling me in their childish way as I tried to save face by showing them I wasn't going to fall apart. I silently cried myself to sleep that night, hating him for betraying me and wondering about my unknown future, glad that camp was over the next day.

CHAPTER TWENTY-FIVE

That summer was a blur. I remember taking an impromptu trip to my grandparents' home in the mountains. My heart was bursting, my dreams and future shattered. By the time I came home, news was out that Larry had gotten his new girlfriend pregnant and they were going to get married. Larry's father had been on the church board for years, and I remembered doing my best to talk my parents into kicking him off. My furor against the family grew to new heights when I heard he'd broken up with his pregnant girlfriend right before they were set to get married. He'd instead moved out of state to go to college. The day they were supposed to be married she committed suicide. I remembered the uproar it caused throughout the church. I was appalled that neither Larry nor his parents had gone to her funeral, and I'd made my outrage known to everyone.

Even after going off to college myself and meeting Mark, falling in love, and beginning my own life, time and time again when I would meet a new couple in church, or be in a Sunday School class and someone would mention Larry's family, my mind pictured what he had done over and over again. I would invariably lower my voice, looking slyly left or right, then I would tell them about *that family*, explaining how their son was a traitor and a backstabber, how he had caused the death of a sweet girl and her baby. All the while his parents continued to act as if they were all innocent and stood behind him rather than doing the right thing. I could go on and on ad nauseam to any willing listener about how unbelievable it was that they could still come to our church or hold their heads high. And the last time he was up for renewal as a board member? I clearly remember with chagrin how I had taken it upon myself, like a personal vendetta, to go to enough friends and acquaintances until I was sure his reputation was ruined and that he would never be reelected. Feeling vindicated when my grassroots effort to derail him was successful.

The evidence against me was overwhelming. But God wasn't done. Despite what anyone had ever done to me throughout my life, if my unforgiveness toward others meant I couldn't be forgiven *my* sins, then I stood condemned with the guilt of my own sins fully on my shoulders. The burden was heavy and unbearable. I wasn't sure now how Jesus had been able to accept every sin from the beginning of time on His own shoulders, when the weight of my own sins, ones I hadn't even considered that "bad," were too heavy for me to bear. I glanced back down at the scripture, and sure enough, there was another footnote leading me to another verse to confirm it again.

> "And when you stand praying, if you hold anything against anyone, forgive him, so that your Father in heaven may forgive you your sins."
> —Mark 11:25

And it led me to another:

> "Bear with each other and forgive whatever grievances you may have against one another. Forgive as the Lord forgave you."
> —Colossians 3:13

And finally, in case I didn't feel convicted enough, the next scripture reminded me that even my *thoughts* had been sinful. Not only had I chosen not to forgive, but the next scripture attacked the hateful, judgmental, and prejudicial statements shouted inside my head when I had enough self control not to spew them out.

> "...Your heart is not right before God. Repent of this wickedness and pray to the Lord. Perhaps he will forgive you for having such thoughts in your heart. For you are full of bitterness and captive to sin."
> —Acts 8:21-22

I felt like a fool having thought I could get away with anything. I figured at this point I might as well read them all. Every scripture listed. Bombard myself with the full effect of the truth. Everything my heart had previously rebelled against. So I tried to read with an open heart, as a brand new Christian would. What I should have fully understood and been practicing the past forty years. I concentrated so I could understand and apply it to my heart.

> "Jesus began to preach, crying out, Repent (change your mind for the better, heartily amend your ways, with abhorrence of your past sins), for the kingdom of heaven is at hand."
> —Matthew 4:17

"Truly I say to you, unless you repent (change, turn about) and become like little children (trusting, lowly, loving, forgiving), you can never enter the kingdom of heaven at all."

—Matthew 18:3

"O Lord, they meant to please You outwardly, but You look on their hearts. You have stricken them, but they have not grieved; You have consumed them, but they have refused to take correction or instruction. They have made their faces harder than a rock, they have refused to repent and return to You."

—Jeremiah 5:3

"And forgive us our sins, for we ourselves also forgive everyone who is indebted to us, who has offended us or done us wrong."

—Luke 11:4

"Do not judge and you will not be judged. Do not condemn, and you will not be condemned. Forgive, and you will be forgiven."

—Luke 6:37

And then it got down to the nitty gritty...

"In anger his master turned him over to the jailers to be tortured, until he should pay back all he owed. "This is how my heavenly Father will treat each of you unless you forgive your brother from your heart." (NIV)

—Matthew 18:34-35

It was time. To first admit it to myself, then to God. The plain, bare truth that I had harbored unforgiveness in my heart. Without a second thought. All the while assuming I would be forgiven because I was a "Christian."

I had to shake my head with a sad smile. The term was overused. I had to think a lot of people, just like myself, had felt a false sense of comfort being raised in a Christian family, going to church, knowing the lingo and what was expected of us. All the while forgetting the ultimate goal was not to convince *others* I was a Christian, but letting God transform my heart and following the one who had given me the best example of forgiveness. I needed to do it right this time. I had no way of knowing how long I had before my life would end. I was frightened to the core knowing life was going to get crazy and dangerous fast. My days of coasting had to end. I looked back down at my mother's Bible. I saw a little piece of paper poking out of her Bible pocket and pulled it out. Anything with her handwriting seemed precious now. In her own blunt way she had written:

When someone is ready to accept Christ:

"The Lord is close to those who have a broken heart and saves such as are crushed with sorrow for sin and humbly and thoroughly penitent."
—Psalm 34:18

And then the old familiar:

"If we confess our sins, he is faithful and just and will forgive us our sins and purify us from all unrighteousness."
—1 John 1:9

I was beginning to understand there was a difference between blithely saying "I'm sorry" to God and the Bible's version of repentance. When I read the words "crushed with sorrow for sin and humbly and thoroughly penitent," I had to wonder if I'd ever experienced those feelings over any of my sins. The even harder fact to swallow was that He *knew* my motives so there was no hiding or pretending. This was going to require a new way of living. Carefully monitoring even my *heart's* words. Listening and immediately judging my motives and intents without delay. Actually feeling sorrow whenever I sinned, recognizing my need for repentance, and immediately asking for it each and every time I sinned. No more postponing it or bypassing it or saving up things for when I remembered to pray.

I thought of all the energy I had expended over the years trying to hide real feelings and weaknesses, giving fake "Christian" responses, refusing to acknowledge my own struggles. When all He required was that I continually, daily acknowledge my need for a Savior and accept the forgiveness only He could offer. And no matter how desperately I wanted to pretend I was perfect, to get commendations from people, I hadn't been able to reach perfection, and the strain and weight of the farce had been backbreaking. God had known it all along, had still held open arms in my direction, but I had been busy trying to be good on my own, and looking good for others. But failing miserably. Amazing how one word from God at exactly 10:27 yesterday morning had automatically either validated or solidified people's reputations, or alternately ruined them. In one second's time.

I closed my eyes, breathing deeply, reverently this time, prepared to fully ask for His forgiveness, even to the point of naming names, listing the offenses. I felt a tear slip from beneath my closed lids. Why hadn't I felt this same tugging on my heart when there had still been time? I was afraid now that I had squelched the tugging of God's voice too many times over the years.

Self pity kept rising, and I felt like I was treading water in my mind, exhausted. But continually kicking myself wouldn't help or get me out of this mess I'd created. I sighed deeply, wiped another tear, and began with a desperate throb in my voice, "God."

While considering my next word, the color drained from my face as I heard a loud thumping on the front door.

CHAPTER TWENTY-SIX

Monday, nine forty-two a.m.

MY HEART RATE went out-of-control and began beating as fast as the knocking. Unbelievable how it took only a split second for fear to reinvade my body. I had felt on the verge of finding a tiny shred of peace in the midst of this horrible nightmare. And now this. Then my next thought was, "NO! I haven't finished praying!" Except the pounding wasn't stopping so I desperately tried to concoct a plan, or an escape, but the situation was made worse when I heard someone yell, "I know you're in there!"

I was petrified. There was no one to rescue me if something went wrong. No one to call, or have on the phone as I answered the door. How was someone so sure I was here? I didn't recognize the voice, but wouldn't most people have assumed my parents had disappeared? I understood the hooligans wanting to rob the place or break in just for the fun of it, but this didn't sound like them, or at least I hoped it wasn't, but apparently my cover had been blown. I had no idea how to get out of this mess.

I kept the Bible open but laid it on the bed, edging off as quietly as possible. I would at least go to the door and see if I recognized the person. I remembered begging my parents to get a peephole put in their front door, and I could still hear Mom responding, "I'm going to open

the door for everyone anyway, so why do I need to see who it is first?"
I would always shake my head at her. It must have been her love for
people that made her act that way, making her lose all common sense
in my opinion. I sure didn't want to open the door, but on the other
hand I was smart enough to know if I didn't stop the racket, they would
bring attention to me just by standing on the porch yelling.

I was in the front room, almost to the front door when I glanced
through the dining room and saw the big clock on the wall. I could
even hear the tick, tick and it spurred me to do the foolish. For some
arbitrary reason I was desperate not to let twenty-four hours pass without
being right with God. I craved the peace I knew would come. The clock
showed 9:45. I had less than forty-five minutes. I felt the fear turn into
anger and impatience with whoever was interrupting the most important
thing I would do today.

If I would have thought twice, and not have glanced at the clock, I
would have cautiously peeked through the blinds, maybe even biding my
time, hoping they would give up and go away. But I had just begun my
crucial nuts and bolts reconciliation with God, knowing it was a life or
death situation, and was determined to finish it, strangely forgetting that
whoever was knocking could actually keep me from *ever* finishing.

So without a pause, I boldly walked up to the door, unlocking it
loudly, *jerking* it open with an angry, but fake bravado, while barking,
"What do you *want*?" And then my mouth fell open and I froze.

Standing not a foot from me was Larry's father. And even though
I had just been on the verge of crying out to God to forgive me for
my thoughts and actions and bold unforgiveness for this man and his
family, the vivid memories came piling on top of me as I stared into his
face. The humiliation and depression and vindictiveness I'd felt over the
years after being unceremoniously dumped by his son. The disgust of
hearing about the pregnant girl, her suicide, and their family's apparent
callousness. Years ago I had spent many evenings in their home, assuming
they would be my in-laws one day.

My mind was whirring a hundred miles a minute, embarrassed
that he and his family had just moments earlier been fighting their way
through my thoughts. I wondered if God had prearranged this meeting
to see how serious I was about my desire to obey Him and truly forgive.

My heart hurt, knowing that I had to overcome this hurdle because I now knew it was at least part of what had ruined my life. If I put aside my feelings, this wasn't just Larry's father standing in front of me. He had been a friend and confidante of my Dad's, a board member and teacher of my teen Sunday School class years ago. And as much as I already knew how much it hurt having someone stare incredulously at you under the current circumstances, I was having trouble breaking my gaze.

I decided not to speak. I was shocked and angry and frustrated and impatient. Anything I said would only prolong our painful conversation, and I was already wanting it to end. It was obvious he wasn't shocked to see me, and that made me even more mad and hurt and embarrassed. I realized my mouth was still open so I closed it and just stared back.

After an awkward silence I watched as his previous nerve and audacity melted before my eyes. He was the first to look away, out into nothingness off the end of the porch, and I could see that his eyes were shiny. "Just come in quickly, Steve, but I have something important I'm doing so I can't talk long," I whispered.

Waiting for him to speak, the intense feelings I'd felt for years every time I thought of his family merged with the newfound conviction that had erupted, and I felt like I was going to explode. My world had been turned inside out. Privacy was no longer mine, and our existence on earth had given everyone permission to meddle.

He had a confused look on his face, perhaps wondering why I was in such a hurry, but I didn't think I could tell him what I'd been doing when he knocked, so I kept silent. I was still trying to recover from the fact that out of all the people in the world, *he* was the one standing in front of me. I had no idea why he was here, and wasn't prepared to talk to him about what God was just confronting *me* about. I also knew I hadn't yet gotten rid of years of venom I had been storing inside me for this family. It was an awkward moment and there was nothing either one of us could do to change that. Then I saw tears spilling out of his eyes as he hesitantly began.

"It was the most horrible thing I've ever experienced," he said as he looked away again. "I was looking at your father when he disappeared right before my eyes, along with hundreds in the auditorium. I knew immediately...I thought I was going to have a heart attack...Then I wished I would have. I...I never imagined it would end this way. I wanted to go home and end it all."

At his admission, there was no doubt his past twenty-four hours had been as hard on him as they'd been on me. I touched his arm gently, even empathetically. For him to be here, I knew his wife Marty must be gone, and I wondered about Larry. But there was no point in assuming anything anymore.

At my touch he looked directly in my eyes, and I detected a hollowness and hopelessness that went all the way to his soul. When he spoke again, it was apologetically, "I'm sorry. I shouldn't have barreled in here like this. I might have frightened you. But when I got a call from someone who saw you at church earlier, I knew I needed to stop by." He paused and my mind started working overtime, wondering who had told him, and feeling the shame and embarrassment return. I could tell he was clinching his teeth as his jaw muscles moved back and forth. "I thought maybe you needed to know I was here, just in case...you know, when things get bad. In case you ever need help or something." A tear slipped out and I had no power to stop it.

I thought he was finished until he took a long, deep, shaky breath, trying to gain his composure, and then broke my heart. "But that's not the main reason I'm here."

I so wanted this moment to be over. I nervously looked down at the carpet, waiting for him to continue. "After the first few minutes of shock wore off...after everyone disappeared, I knew I needed to pray so I drove straight home and stayed there for hours." He snuck a look in my direction and our eyes met and I was deeply afraid of what he was going to say next.

"I was pretty sure I knew why I hadn't gone in the rapture. And you were one of them." I couldn't help but suck in my breath at his revelation and bluntness and I looked down again, feeling my heart beat out of my chest. "I've known for thirty years that Larry didn't treat you right, and treated the mother of his child even worse, but I was so proud and couldn't bear to think my son wasn't perfect and we did wrong by covering up for him and allowing him to not have to pay the consequences for his actions. But while that probably didn't keep me out of heaven, the bitterness and resentment I've felt toward you and my refusal to forgive you for things I thought you'd said about our family over the years ended up turning into a hatred that I've let fester for years."

My heart was beating so fast by now I was amazed he couldn't hear it. "So I came here to finish what God's been talking to me about, and to ask you to forgive me. I know God has now, but once I heard you were still here I knew I had to ask you too. I was wrong, Larry was wrong, and I will spend the rest of my life trying to fix it. I'll leave now. I'm not done searching my heart because I have a feeling there are other things I've been ignoring, and I can't take any chances now.

"Please be real careful though. There's no telling what will happen now. I drove by your home before I came here," he looked tentatively at me to see if it was a shock, "and I saw a strange truck sitting in your driveway with a bunch of young kids hanging out in the front yard. That's when I guessed you might be staying here. Here's my home number." He handed me a piece of paper he'd written on earlier. "Call me if you need anything, okay?"

By this time tears were making a steady stream down both my cheeks, falling wherever they desired. All brought about by the shock of his coming, his confession, utter exhaustion as well as his confirmation that intruders were still camping out at my home. Perhaps the tears were also for his unexpected kindness when I needed it most. I knew my voice couldn't be trusted, so as he reached for the doorknob I touched his arm again to catch his attention, barely whispering, "Thank you for...you don't know...I have to go. Take care," as a half sob slipped out.

His eyes were also full by now and he nodded his head without blinking so his tears wouldn't brim over. He turned to go, and with my hand on the door I felt my heart jump as if to get my attention, and I knew what I had to do. "Wait... Steve?" I said tentatively. He suddenly looked worn out and older than he had just a few minutes earlier. He looked back expectantly, but not helping *me* this time.

"Steve," I began, not knowing how I would finish. "I've also been searching my heart and I need to ask you to forgive me too." My last words were whispered because my chest was heaving so violently. Pent-up feelings from the past thirty years were fighting a war inside my soul. "I was so hurt when Larry did that years ago, but I should have given it to

God, and there's no excuse for me holding it against your whole family and doing my best to ruin your reputation." The ugliness of my actions suddenly hit me as I felt true sorrow for my actions that should have been there years earlier. The next words came a bit easier as I half sobbed, half blurted, "I'm so sorry, Steve, for hurting you and your whole family. I repent and hope you'll forgive me." He hadn't said a word while I was giving my speech, and since I hadn't dared look at him, I had no idea if he was accepting my words or not.

When I finally had the guts to look in his eyes, his face was contorted and tears were streaming down his face, drenching his shirt. He nodded his head and mouthed the words, "I forgive you," and turned, walking off the porch. I gently closed the door behind him, wiping my eyes so I could see again. Sympathy for him overwhelmed me at that moment. Steve, once a family man, a business owner, and respected leader in the church, now probably holding none of those titles. In twenty-four hours, both of us had lost our identities.

As I locked the front door, I breathed a prayer, "God help us to keep hearing Your voice so we can both get it right." At this point, I wasn't the least bit curious if there were other reasons he hadn't gone to heaven. For perhaps the first time in my life I was realizing sin was sin, and I didn't have to be a mass murderer to not be allowed into heaven. Any sin, supposedly hidden, unforgiven sin, unrepentant sin, even if it was what some of us might call "lite" sin was the same as if one were *filled* with the most heinous of transgressions.

I hated being lumped into that group. But perhaps that was another one of my issues. I hadn't looked at sin the same way God did. I had created this imaginary dividing line in my mind. Rating sins by degrees of unacceptability, totally ignoring the fact that God saw all sin as disobedience and willfulness, whether a "simple" lie or murder or adultery. And even worse, when I had sinned it had been against *Him,* not others.[1]

I was thinking now that one of the biggest deceptions the devil had perpetrated was to imply there were white and black lies. Big and little sins. That embezzling millions from investors was worse than not acknowledging extra change from a cashier. That having an abortion was worse than refusing to forgive or gossiping or lying. I was beginning to feel the weight of the truth that for a righteous God, all sin broke His heart because He knew it would ultimately separate us from Him eternally. Only now did I realize that because of His holiness and perfection, He couldn't allow the sin I'd refused to give up to infiltrate heaven.[2]

Without that full understanding, I had developed a false sense of peace over the years. I wasn't sure where I'd gotten the idea that *outward* sins, ones you could be caught *doing*, ones requiring action or inaction, were the only ones that counted in God's eyes. Ignoring evil attitudes, sinful thoughts, motives, and plans that His Word promised were equally as evil. It was obvious He saw them all the same, because our thoughts were screaming out to Him.

I knew there had to have been a boatload of surprised "Christians" yesterday. People only had two choices. They were either seeking Him, following Him, living a repentant life, or rebelling against His system and His way of doing things.[3] I was still shocked at a God who had arranged Steve to visit right at the moment I was confronting my own heart and its first attempt at forgiving a thirty year old resentment. Thoughtfully heading back toward the bedroom, the clock caught my attention again. Ten o'clock. I was still unbelievingly astonished at what happened almost twenty-four hours ago, and how I had been sleeping like a baby while it happened, totally oblivious. Back in the bedroom, I climbed on the bed, not even tempted to close my eyes now. I was on a mission. Without the slightest pause, I continued as if the last fifteen minutes hadn't happened. "God." A deep sob started immediately, but no matter how much my voice cracked or the tears rolled, I wasn't about to stop. "I'm so sorry I didn't believe Your Word when You clearly said I needed to forgive others in order to be forgiven. But I'm asking You once again to come into my heart and forgive every single instance of the unforgiveness I've hoarded in my heart."

Like a dam had been broken, names began to roll off my tongue, as if I was reading from a script. I remembered instances from church, fellow students, neighbors, even Sunday School teachers and family members. I fully repented over Larry and his dad, Steve, and their family. Any name or memory that popped in my head, and there were many, I took as a sign that I needed to confess. There was absolutely no reason to hold anything back now. So I didn't. Then for good measure I quoted the words that had opened up the wound in my heart earlier, "God I give up all resentment and consider every offense taken back as if it never happened, because I desperately need for You to be able to forgive *my* sins."

I took a deep breath and was amazed how good it felt getting those things off my chest. I thought of those who had offended me in the past, realizing they had also been responsible for their actions and had either been taken or left behind yesterday as well. But I had only hurt myself by condemning them.

I felt better, but for some reason didn't feel finished. There was something more. I knew it. Funny how I had felt self-righteous because I hadn't been living in adultery, or stealing from my company, and wasn't a common criminal. But I was becoming painfully aware how thought patterns and mindsets had turned me against obeying God, so I knew the possibility of me having something else out of whack was extremely high. So I asked Him again, and waited. The ticking on the clock seemed louder and faster, but I refused to look at it again since time didn't matter if I wasn't right with Him. I had to wonder if the fact that I'd been a "Christian" for so long had been a hindrance rather than a blessing in the end. Had I known the ropes so well, gotten so complacent, that I wasn't even aware I'd had sin in my heart? Now that I knew God couldn't, and wouldn't, look past any sin, I needed to keep searching. Nothing else mattered. So I got quiet again and waited.

I heard a vibration and it startled me in the midst of the quiet. I realized I must have missed a call earlier while I was praying, and reached for my phone. I had a voicemail and with a bit of trepidation pressed the button. When the voice began speaking I immediately felt empathy. It was Carrie, Holly's friend I'd felt impressed to give my cell number to in Dad's office. She was sobbing and I had to turn up the volume to be able to understand her. "Miss Annie," she sobbed, "All the other guys decided to go partying and I'm all alone in a strange house and I keep hearing noises. I don't want to keep living the way I was. I don't want to mess up my chances of seeing my parents again." She paused and I could hear her breaking down again, and I covered my own mouth as

I heard a groan coming out. "*Please* call me or tell me where you are so I can come see you. Please?"

My heart was stricken for the helpless girl I could tell God was dealing with. I knew that God had not destined me to miss the rapture and it sure wasn't His fault, but somehow, some way, I determined right then and there to begin planting the right seeds for perhaps the first time in my life. I had nothing else to live for now. But I had to make it right myself first. Then I would help her.

I picked up Mom's Bible, knowing His Word was what had convicted my heart earlier. I regretted avoiding it as much as I had lately. It hadn't seemed that necessary or alive or interesting just a day ago. But now it was a precious diary and a map and a lifeline to God. If only I'd let His voice penetrate the brick wall of my heart earlier. Opening the Bible again with no idea where to begin, I felt a bit foolish, but just then a folded piece of paper fell from her Bible. Not surprising, since Mom was a note writer with all sorts of papers tucked between the pages, however, I know this one ended up being something prepared for my eyes for this particular moment in time. It was written on the back of a Sunday bulletin.

I was going to desperately miss her. Again. I brought the note to my face, taking a deep breath, assuming. And I wasn't disappointed. It was there, the same familiar hand lotion Mom used. *Warm Vanilla Sugar.* Tears flooded my eyes. Unfolding the note, I half expected to see a scattered "to do" list, or what she needed to buy at the grocery store. But *absolutely nothing* could have prepared me for the words she'd written. It was as if she had written an intimate prayer to God and I was eavesdropping. I bit my lip as I read the painful words:

"God, please rescue my lukewarm daughter."

My first inclination was to wad the note up and throw it across the room. Tears spurted, as I whispered, "You didn't know *anything* about me, Mom," and buried my head in my hands. But apparently she had. And had even been praying about it. A few seconds passed as I tried to compose myself. "Oh God," I thought, embarrassed that my self-righteous anger was still showing its ugly head, "Had I been so bad that my family was having prayer meetings for me?" I looked down at the note burning a hole in my heart and saw another note in the corner, as if proving why she had written what she did. It said: "Rev. 3:15-17."

This was one of those times when I desperately wanted to prove her wrong. But the proof wasn't on my side. I was here and she wasn't. Then I heard the replay of my own piercing words asking God to show me where else I might have gone wrong. Did he *have* to use my mother's scrap of paper though? I didn't even want to look up the scripture. I felt insulted and slighted, like when you walk up behind someone, catching them talking about you. I felt my own Mom had been judging me, and it hurt.

But had she been right? Was that another reason I was still here? I abruptly reminded myself that God was also listening to my strangled thought processes, waiting to see how I would respond to His nudges. I would have to get over hurt feelings and figure out why Mom had prayed that prayer over me. I thumbed to the back of the Bible, searching for the scripture, and then reading the words:

"I know everything you have done, and you are not cold or hot. I wish you were either one or the other. But since you are lukewarm and neither cold nor hot, I will spit you out of my mouth. You claim to be rich and successful and to have everything you need. But you don't know how bad off you are. You are pitiful, poor, blind, and naked."
—Revelation 3:15-17

And she had highlighted it. But if I was going to use her Bible as a roadmap to get where I needed to be, I had to stop getting mad every time something in the Bible pointed to me because the same familiar, chip-on-the-shoulder feelings desperately wanted to rise up inside. I had to abandon my right to doubting, confusion, anger, remorse, and give it all up, begging Him to change my thoughts and show me how to live now.

The problem was I hadn't really considered that prospect very often. I wasn't always sure what God would want me to do in most of my day-to-day situations. This would be tough. I remembered a sermon about conquering my thoughts by renewing my mind and heart,[4] and to become holy[5] or sanctified,[6] but hadn't been able to do any of that before, and wasn't sure if I could now. And the fact that there was not one single person on the face of the earth at this moment that had gotten it right scared me. I feared we were all in trouble.

On a whim, I decided to look up the word lukewarm. My Dad did that a lot. He had a whole library on his nightstand. I looked over to his side of the bed and sure enough, I saw two versions of the Bible, a dictionary, a concordance and, ironically, a book on prophecy that I was afraid to read now.

But as I opened *Webster's Dictionary* to the L's, the definition hit me harder than the Bible verse had. It said, "Just slightly warm, *especially when expected to be hot.*"

I paused, fully deflated. That defined me. God, the world, my church, my parents, and husband and daughter, had all "expected me to be hot" but instead I had been just slightly warm, if that. And in case I hadn't understood that definition, the next one hit a homerun: "Showing or having little enthusiasm, interest, support, or conviction." I figured I might as well get the whole sermon over with, so I even read the words the thesaurus suggested: "Tepid, unenthusiastic, halfhearted, unexcited, indifferent, subdued, apathetic, and lackadaisical."

The Bible still open beside me, I noticed Mom had drawn a star beside the verse. I looked at the bottom of the page, and she'd written several lines in the margin.

Lukewarm = No Ears
(you stop listening or hearing God's voice);
Lukewarm = No Tears
(your heart is hardened,
conviction no longer reduces you to tears);
Lukewarm = No Fears
(you lose the fear of God, forgetting He
knows all, sees all, and judges
according to His standards).[7]

My eyes glazed over for a moment, looking at nothing. When I tried to focus on the pages again, I saw an arrow pointing to another note she'd written, "A person might take twenty years to backslide…Just as we physically grow old gradually, we backslide gradually."

The words were like coals, burning through me. I read another quote, recognizing the name of a famous minister, "Charles Finney says

263

it's possible to be active in Christian service, even maintaining forms of religion and obedience—all with a backslidden heart."

I gave up, resting my case. There was no point in arguing with myself *or* God. Prior to yesterday, my tears had all but dried up, except for an occasional sad story or movie. And the fear of God? Had I ever *really* had that? Had I taken advantage of grace and mercy to an unhealthy, unscriptural extent? So much that I had forgotten He doesn't bend rules for anyone and eventual judgment comes for everyone if they have unforgiven sin?

If God was saying being lukewarm was despicable to Him and He preferred those who were cold rather than the lukewarm, then He had to have been disgusted with my attitude. "Showing or having little enthusiasm, interest, support, or conviction concerning God?" Yes. "Tepid, unenthusiastic, halfhearted, unexcited, indifferent, subdued, apathetic, lackadaisical?" Yes again. Every single word of the definition hit me at some level of my character. And the verse said that God saw me as "wretched, pitiable, poor, blind, and naked."

I forced myself to look back several years, wondering when my stagnant journey had started. I pictured an especially hard period of time. I had been experiencing struggles at work, had some health issues with distracting symptoms, wasn't sleeping well, and all of that was contributing to irritations at home. I figured the "healthy" thing to do was to withdraw from life just a bit, take care of myself. I remembered consciously doing that, withdrawing physically from a few things, mentally from others, emotionally from most. Now that I was actually trying to honestly judge myself, I had to admit I probably withdrew spiritually as well.[8]

I wondered now if I would have thrown out my pride, asking my husband, friends, or parents to gird me up in prayer when I first felt the mental and emotional fatigue, if it would have made a difference. Because those nonchalant, blasé feelings I experienced must have bled over into my spiritual life as well. Now that I analyzed it, I saw that perhaps instead they *started* spiritually and moved outward. Nevertheless, I remembered feeling like I was receiving the "cold shoulder" from God when the prayers I actually took time to pray felt like they weren't making it through the ceiling. And now that my eyes had been at least partially opened, I had to admit that my habit of unforgiveness had more than likely opened the door for and influenced the beginnings of lukewarmness in my spirit.

Most times I felt *nothing* while talking to God, like I was trudging through a foot of mud. I distinctly remembered a time when I knew the right thing to do would be to pray about a situation, but even the energy needed to put forth the prayer was too much and too hard, and over time the concern and impetus to even pray about things waned. I remembered thinking, "Who cares?"

I'd heard other people talk about going through cold periods with God, so I figured it was normal and nothing to get hyped up about. When I didn't see results from prayers, or barely felt God's presence even in church, prayer ended up being one more thing on my to do list that got lopped off when I ran out of time. And I usually did.

But in my newfound desire to understand and seek God's opinion, I had a feeling that during those times when I had not felt hungry for Him, even downright cold, those times were partly from the enemy to distract me and dissuade me from serving God, but also *meant* to inspire me and push me through the fog to seek Him out, forcing myself to go deeper because of my desperation and need for Him, instead of pulling back and letting my heart stagnate like I'd done.[9]

Sort of like when a girl feels taken for granted, so she doesn't call her boyfriend, hoping he'll miss her more because of it, deep down expecting him to move heaven and earth to spend time with her.

But instead of moving closer, I had gotten used to the feelings, eventually accepting them. Seeing the note written in Mom's handwriting shocked me, but I had to admit she was probably right. I had become lukewarm. A chill had snuck in, camping out in an enticing, familiar way inside my heart.

And stayed.

CHAPTER TWENTY-SEVEN

Monday, ten seventeen a.m.

I WAS ABOUT out of time. My self-imposed deadline was looming. The clock said 10:17, reminding me that twenty-three hours and fifty minutes ago, my life had forever changed, and a new time clock had started. I didn't want to start the second day the same way I had begun the first, by experiencing shock, sorrow, and regret for the present, dread for the future, and looking into the past, unsure of what sins had kept me here. There was no point in reminiscing about what once was, or what could have been, because if I ever fell in that deep hole of self pity, I might never climb out.

As I was about to close the Bible, another footnote caught my eye, so I quickly followed the path again. It began leading me where I hadn't dared to tread before, persisting with gentle chastising and much needed corrective work:

> "'You have rejected me,' declares the LORD. 'You keep on backsliding. I will lay hands on you and destroy you; I can no longer show compassion.'"
>
> —Jeremiah 15:6

"'Your wickedness will punish you; your backsliding will rebuke you. Consider then and realize how evil and bitter it is for you when you forsake the LORD your God and have no awe of me,' declares the Lord, the LORD Almighty."

—Jeremiah 2:19

"For the backsliding of the simple shall slay them, and the careless ease of self-confident fools shall destroy them."

—Proverbs 1:32

"Then shall you return and discern between the righteous and the wicked, between him who serves God and him who does not serve Him."

—Malachi 3:18

"But now You number each of my steps; and take note of my every sin. My transgression is sealed up in a bag, and You glue up my iniquity to preserve it in full for the day of reckoning."

—Job 14: 16, 17

"…Make me recognize and know my transgression and my sin."

—Job 13:23

The word "backsliding" had always seemed such an old-fashioned word, but there seemed to be bright lights pointing me to it now. I imagined over the coming days, if I survived very long, God would have to help me recognize many things inside my heart that He had implored me to let Him work on over the past many years. Things that should have disappeared from my life long ago. I remembered another scripture about God changing us little by little,[1] all without being a bully and even allowing us to stop the process if we dared, and I must have done just that. But for now, he had shown me two glaring areas I had blatantly disobeyed Him in that could have kept me from being raptured.

Strange how my heart had deceived me into thinking I could decide how I would be judged by God. Or perhaps the enemy had convinced me that because of God's love, He would look at me through rose-colored glasses, be a bit lenient, overlook some things since He had to know I meant well. I had rationalized that certain things were tolerable in *my* case. But whether He ever showed me anything else or not, I knew that He would not accept an unforgiving spirit or a lukewarm heart. Ironically, these were things no one had ever seen me commit. But God had.

For some reason, the final verse I read stung the worst, like a hard slap on a cold day.

> "Laughter conceals a heavy heart, but when the laughter ends, grief remains. Backsliders get what they deserve; good people receive their reward. Only simpletons believe everything they're told! The prudent carefully consider their steps." (NLT)
>
> —Proverbs 14:13-15

That hurt. "Backsliders get what they deserve." I never dreamed choices I willingly made could affect me so tragically. I must have convinced myself that when life was less hectic and when it was more convenient, I would get serious about God again. I had all the necessary spiritual tools at my fingertips and no one had coerced me into turning back. And my payback for not keeping my heart committed to God was loneliness, embarrassment, fear, anger, and shame and the ultimate gift of being left behind.[2] I wasn't feeling mere embarrassment though. Disgrace and dishonor are far different animals. They had traveled to a deeper, more permanent place.

A strange part about this new adventure, if you wanted to call it that, was that I was aware God had not *taken* my salvation from me.[3] God promised He would never renege on His Word, but the problem was He also didn't create robots. Sometimes I found myself wishing He had, because I always had really good *intentions*. I just didn't carry through with them. Because in His design, He chose to allow humans to choose whether they would love Him fully and totally of their own choice and volition, and would never force them.

So His freedom incredibly had included the freedom for me to turn my back on Him.[4] And that had happened slowly but surely as I let my love grow cold. Disobeying His clear instructions, not taking His Word seriously, not realizing I continually needed forgiveness for sins

I was ignoring, and choosing to ride the fence rather than becoming a follower of Him.

It wasn't just one errant sin I had committed at the last minute before He came. In my heart I knew that a just God wouldn't keep me out of heaven if I had developed a pattern of repentance and hadn't yet had the chance to ask for it and receive it. No, I had been harboring long-standing patterns of sin that I had trivialized. I had gotten used to stuffing conviction so deep that I couldn't feel it any longer. And His perfection, purity, and holiness couldn't allow the evil connected to my unrepentant sin to come into His presence.

I was reminded again how the Bible said God kept several books. When we had asked Him into our heart and our sins were forgiven, our name was placed in one of those books. A glorious day for the person, and it even said the heavens rejoiced over each and every one.[5] There was only one possible glitch. The problem was if *we* turned our back on *our* original decision, *we* could choose to leave His family. This was where His family dynamics were different from ours. *Our* name, through *our* choice, could actually be taken out of His book, never through *His* choice but rather ours.[6]

I realized immediately what my problem had been. God hadn't made a huge announcement when my name was removed, and I somehow knew it had taken a long time before it had been removed because of His mercy and grace. I was sure I hadn't been the only one who had ignored His still small voice as it tried to convict me, attempting to warn me more urgently as yesterday had gotten closer. But the voices I was used to focusing on were louder. I hadn't even been concerned or paying attention when my name had finally been blotted out.

I remembered hearing of Christians who believed that, since God didn't punish them immediately for sins they were committing, they were getting away with disobedience, or God either wasn't aware or didn't care.[7] And I was one of them. I knew the verse so often quoted that God would never leave us or forsake us.[8] So since He couldn't lie, the truth was that I had left *Him*. And because He had made me a "free moral agent," He allowed it no matter how much it pained Him. Because that's the kind of God He was and will always be. Today, I hated my free will.

I was ready to pray again. With just a couple of minutes to spare, I closed my eyes, sucked in a quick breath, and shakily said, "God, I've sinned. Thank You for already forgiving me of the unforgiveness I've stubbornly held for years. Please keep showing me how to forgive. Now please forgive me for letting my heart become lukewarm and losing the first love I had for You years ago. I've ignored You, and taken You for granted. I'm going to do my best to obey You and follow Your plan, to abide close to You so You can abide in me. I want You to live inside of me and be first place in my life above everything else. Thank You for giving me another chance. Help me to never turn my back on You..."

The tears streaming down my face now were different, and my heart felt just a tiny bit lighter. As I closed the Bible, my eyes glanced down and I saw a final verse that chilled me to the bone because it applied to me now and would be my instructions for this new life.

"And ye shall be hated of all men for my name's sake: but he that shall endure unto the end, the same shall be saved."
—Mark 13:13

Enduring and being hated sounded so hard and impossible. But there was no other way to get to heaven now but to experience the mess I found myself in. "Oh God," I cried, "I'm going to need Your help!"

Thinking of Carrie and the desperation she was also going through, I quickly picked up my phone and pressed redial, asking God how on earth I could help her, and then I knew immediately. After three rings it went into her voicemail, and my voice was strong as I said to her, "Carrie, this is Annie. Call me back as soon as you can and tell me where you are. I will come get you, and you can stay with me. We'll get through this together." As I set the phone down, I felt good about what He had just told me to do.

I sat quietly a moment as the last couple of minutes ticked away. I recalled my mindset yesterday as I had opened my eyes. Planning on being pampered on Mother's Day with a delicious lunch, and in an odd twist of reality, I hadn't eaten a bite or swallowed a drink since awakening yesterday. I was feeling thirsty and decidedly weary after not a moment's sleep. Physical concerns were a rude jolt to my system, knowing I was forced to live in this life, with normal every day needs and issues, despite the more important, even dire spiritual situation going on. I wondered if I was really going to be able to do this.

I glanced over at my Mom's digital clock on her nightstand. Tears sprang to my eyes when I saw it was 10:27. What had they been thinking seconds before they disappeared? Had they felt a sudden deep yearning for Him, or had they lived in that constant state of emotion I hadn't been participating in? Had they anticipated it? *Expected* it? What a wonderful experience it must have been. I had missed the once in a lifetime, breathtaking opportunity, and only with God's strength would I be able to endure to the end.

While I stared at the clock, watching the seconds speed by, the most terrifying of thoughts entered my mind. What if, when things settled down, whether it was a few days or weeks or months from now, what if my old attitude struck again? I knew myself far too well! What if I became hardened, tired, or, God-forbid, "lukewarm" again? What if, after all I'd gone through, I eternally lost my last chance to ever reconcile with God? I knew the old deceiver well, and he would still be after me. I didn't have a good feeling about it, because I knew my heart was fickle! I wasn't strong, and obviously not used to fully serving Him.

And then, like a wisp of fresh air, an idea flitted through my mind. I remembered God telling the children of Israel what to do as they made their trek through the wilderness, fighting for their victory. He warned them never to forget their triumphs *or* devastating losses. He instructed them to make a memorial, something that would force them to *remember* what they'd gone through, and to spread the word and tell others their story. At this moment I *never* wanted to remember the past twenty-four hours, but I was afraid if I didn't, then the end would be worse than this day had ever been.

Should I do something that foolish? Make some type of memorial? I glanced at the clock, knowing any moment the next minute would tick by, and like a light bulb going off, I knew what my memorial would be.

I looked at Mom's old-fashioned clock as if it were a treasure. It was one of the first types of "digital" clocks that annoyingly made a noise each time the number flipped over to the next minute. Many times I had threatened to buy her a new clock, but now I was glad I hadn't because at that exact moment I reached behind the nightstand and unplugged it. When I turned the clock back around I saw that I'd stopped it in time, and I spent a moment staring at my own private memorial. It would be 10:27 forever.

Because I couldn't dare forget.

EPILOGUE

IF *YOU* HAVE never dared to think the unthinkable, I hope you have considered and revisited where you honestly stand with our "perfectly just and rigidly righteous" God.

Whether a brand new or seasoned Christian, someone comfortably sitting on the fence, or if you've firmly decided life is too short to stifle it by serving God, I pray you've been convinced to not let that day catch you off guard, but take a second look at your relationship with your Creator. If your heart is truly right with God, I pray your desire to ensure that those you love follow in your steps becomes stronger as you remember that we will all individually face Him one day.

The most wondrous gift of all is that there is still forgiveness, grace, and mercy available. But in a moment, in less time than it takes to blink and without warning, our window of opportunity will close and those left behind will be living their own story, perhaps chillingly similar to the one in this book.

"The time for repentance is speeding by like chaff whirled before the wind! Therefore consider, before God's decree brings forth the curse upon you, before the time to repent is gone like the drifting chaff, before the fierce anger of the Lord comes upon you—yes, before the day of the wrath of the Lord comes! Seek the Lord, inquire for Him, of Him, and require Him as the foremost necessity of your life. It may be you will be hidden in the day of the Lord's anger."

—Zephaniah 2:2-3

"For in a moment, in the twinkling of an eye, at the sound of the last trumpet call. For a trumpet will sound, and the dead in Christ will be raised imperishable (free and immune from decay), and we shall be changed (transformed)."

—1 Corinthians 15:52

ENDNOTES

Chapter Three

1. 1 Peter 5:7—Casting the whole of your care [all your anxieties, all your worries, all your concerns, once and for all] on Him, for He cares for you affectionately and cares about you watchfully.

Chapter Eight

1. 1 Timothy 4:2—Such teachings come through hypocritical liars, whose consciences have been seared as with a hot iron. (NIV)
2. Isaiah 44:20—…a deceived heart hath turned him aside, that he cannot deliver his soul, nor say, is there not a lie in my right hand? (KJV)
3. Matthew 7:14—For the gate is small and the way is narrow that leads to life, and there are few who find it. (NASB)
4. 1 Corinthians 15:52—…in a flash, in the twinkling of an eye, at the last trumpet. For the trumpet will sound, the dead will be raised imperishable, and we will be changed.

Chapter Nine

1. Ezekiel 36:26—A new heart also will I give you, and a new spirit will I put within you: and I will take away the stony heart out of your flesh, and I will give you a heart of flesh. (KJV)

2. Matthew 18:3—Truly I say to you, unless you repent (change, turn about) and become like little children (trusting, lowly, loving, forgiving), you can never enter the kingdom of heaven at all.

Chapter Eleven

1. 2 Corinthians 5:8—We are confident, I say, and willing rather to be absent from the body, and to be present with the Lord. (KJV)

Chapter Twelve

1. Revelation 21:4—He will wipe every tear from their eyes. There will be no more death or mourning or crying or pain, for the old order of things has passed away. (NIV)
2. Isaiah 34:16—Seek out of the book of the Lord and read: not one of these details of prophecy shall fail…

Chapter Thirteen

1. 2 Peter 3:9—The Lord is not slow in keeping his promise, as some understand slowness. He is patient with you, not wanting anyone to perish, but everyone to come to repentance. (NIV)
2. Proverbs 1:23-25—Suppose you had paid attention to my warning. Then I would have poured out my heart to you. I would have told you what I was thinking. But you turned away from me when I called out to you. None of you paid attention when I reached out my hand. You turned away from all my advice, you wouldn't accept my warning. (NIRV)
3. "No One Ever Cared for Me Like Jesus" By Charles Frederick Weigle.
4. "What a Day That Will Be." Words and Music by Jim Hill.
5. 2 Chronicles 32:31—…God left him to himself to try him, that He might know all that was in his heart.
6. Job 36:5—Behold! God is mighty, and yet despises no one nor regards anything as trivial; He is mighty in power of understanding and heart.

Chapter Fourteen

1. Matthew 25:32-34—All nations will be gathered before Him, and He will separate the people from one another as a shepherd separates his sheep from the goats; And He will cause the sheep to stand at His right hand, but the goats at His left. Then the King will say to those at His right hand, Come, you blessed of My Father, favored of God and appointed to eternal salvation, inherit (receive as your own) the kingdom prepared for you from the foundation of the world.
2. Proverbs 16:2—All the ways of a man are pure in his own eyes, but the Lord weighs the spirits (the thoughts and intents of the heart).

Chapter Fifteen

1. Matthew 25:7—Then all the virgins woke up and trimmed their lamps. The foolish ones said to the wise, 'Give us some of your oil; our lamps are going out. 'No,' they replied, 'there may not be enough for both us and you. Instead, go to those who sell oil and buy some for yourselves.' But while they were on their way to buy the oil, the bridegroom arrived. The virgins who were ready went in with him to the wedding banquet. And the door was shut. Later the others also came. 'Sir! Sir!' they said. 'Open the door for us!' But he replied, 'I tell you the truth, I don't know you.' Therefore keep watch, because you do not know the day or the hour. (NIV)
2. Mark 4:19—Then the cares and anxieties of the world and distractions of the age, and the pleasure and delight and false glamour and deceitfulness of riches, and the craving and passionate desire for other things creep in and choke and suffocate the Word, and it becomes fruitless.
3. Luke 21:34-35—But take heed to yourselves and be on your guard, lest your hearts be overburdened and depressed (weighed down) with the giddiness and headache and nausea of self-indulgence, drunkenness, and worldly worries and cares pertaining to the business of this life, and lest that day come upon you suddenly like a trap or a noose; For it will come upon all who live upon the face of the entire earth.

4. Matthew 7:13-14—Enter through the narrow gate; for wide is the gate and spacious and broad is the way that leads away to destruction, and many are those who are entering through it. But the gate is narrow (contracted by pressure) and the way is straitened and compressed that leads away to life, and few are those who find it.

5. Revelation 2:25, 26—Only hold fast to what you have until I come. And he who overcomes (is victorious) and who obeys My commands to the very end doing the works that please Me, I will give him authority and power over the nations.

6. Isaiah 48:5, 6: Therefore I have declared things to come to you from of old; before they came to pass I announced them to you, so that you could not say, my idol has done them, and my graven image and my molten image have commanded them. You have heard [these things foretold], now you see this fulfillment. And will you not bear witness to it? I show you specified new things from this time forth, even hidden things kept in reserve which you have not known.

Chapter Sixteen

1. 1 Thessalonians 4:17—Then we, the living ones who remain on the earth, shall simultaneously be *caught up* along with the resurrected dead in the clouds to meet the Lord in the air; and so always (through the eternity of the eternities) we shall be with the Lord!

Chapter Seventeen

1. Isaiah 66:4—So I also will choose their delusions and mockings, their calamities and afflictions, and I will bring their fears upon them—because when I called, no one answered; when I spoke, they did not listen or obey. But they did what was evil in My sight and chose that in which I did not delight.

Chapter Nineteen

1. Luke 12:34—For where your treasure is, there your heart will be also.
2. Proverbs 16:9 (NLT)

3. Deuteronomy 32:4—He is the Rock, his works are perfect, and all his ways are just. A faithful God who does no wrong, upright and just is he. (NIV)

Chapter Twenty

1. 2 Timothy 3:16—*Every* Scripture is God-breathed (given by His inspiration) and profitable for instruction, for reproof and conviction of sin, for correction of error and discipline in obedience, and for training in righteousness (in holy living, in conformity to God's will in thought, purpose, and action).

2. 1 Corinthians 4:5—So do not make any hasty or premature judgments before the time when the Lord comes again, for He will both bring to light the secret things that are now hidden in darkness and disclose and expose secret aims (motives and purposes) of hearts. Then every man will receive his due commendation from God.

3. Luke 15:7—Thus, I tell you, there will be more joy in heaven over one *especially wicked person* who repents (changes his mind, abhorring his errors and misdeeds, and determines to enter upon a better course of life) than over ninety-nine righteous persons who have no need of repentance.

4. Isaiah 5:16—But the Lord of hosts is exalted in justice, and God, the Holy One, shows Himself holy in righteousness and through righteous judgments.

5. John 3:16—For God so loved the world that he gave his one and only Son, that whoever believes in him shall not perish but have eternal life. (NIV)
   1 John 4:10—This is real love—not that we loved God, but that he loved us and sent his Son as a sacrifice to take away our sins. (NLT)

6. 2 Peter 3:9—The Lord is not slack concerning his promise, as some men count slackness; but is longsuffering to us-ward, not willing that any should perish, but that all should come to repentance. (KJV)

7. 1 Chronicles 28:9—...for the LORD searches every heart and understands every motive behind the thoughts. If you seek him, he will be found by you; but if you forsake him, he will reject you forever. (NIV)

8. Deuteronomy 31:8—The LORD himself goes before you and will be with you; he will never leave you nor forsake you. Do not be afraid; do not be discouraged. (NIV)
9. 2 Peter 3:9—The Lord does not delay and is not tardy or slow about what He promises, according to some people's conception of slowness, but He is long-suffering (extraordinarily patient) toward you, not desiring that any should perish, but that all should turn to repentance.

Chapter Twenty-One

1. 1 Thessalonians 4:16-17—For the Lord Himself will descend from heaven with a loud cry of summons, with the shout of an archangel, and with the blast of the trumpet of God. And those who have departed this life in Christ will rise first. Then we, the living ones who remain on the earth, shall simultaneously be caught up along with the resurrected dead in the clouds to meet the Lord in the air; and so always (through the eternity of the eternities) we shall be with the Lord!

Chapter Twenty-Two

1. Mark 13:12—Now the brother shall betray the brother to death, and the father the son; and children shall rise up against their parents, and shall cause them to be put to death. (KJV)

Chapter Twenty-Three

1. Revelation 9:6.
2. 2 Peter 2:1—There arose false prophets subtly and stealthily introducing heretical doctrines (destructive heresies), even denying and disowning the Master Who bought them, bringing upon themselves swift destruction; Jeremiah 23:32—Indeed, I am against those who prophesy false dreams, declares the Lord. They tell them and lead my people astray with their reckless lies, yet I did not send or appoint them. They do not benefit these people in the least; 2 Timothy 3:13—But wicked men and imposters will go on from bad to worse, deceiving and leading astray others and being

deceived and led astray themselves; Isaiah 3:12—...O my people, your guides lead you astray; they turn you from the path.

3. Isaiah 46:9, 10—Earnestly remember the former things, which I did of old; for I am God, and there is no one else; I am God, and there is none like Me, declaring the end and the result from the beginning, and from ancient times the things that are not yet done, saying, My counsel shall stand, and I will do all My pleasure and purpose.

Chapter Twenty-Four

1. Psalm 56:8—You number and record my wanderings; put my tears into Your bottle—are they not in Your book?

2. Matthew 25:34—The King will say "Come, you blessed of My Father you favored of God and appointed to eternal salvation, inherit (receive as your own) the kingdom prepared for you from the foundation of the world."

3. 1 Thessalonians 4:16-18—The Master himself will give the command. Archangel thunder! God's trumpet blast! He'll come down from heaven and the dead in Christ will rise—they'll go first. Then the rest of us who are still alive at the time will be caught up with them into the clouds to meet the Master. We'll be walking on air! **And there will be one huge family reunion with the Master.** So reassure one another with these words. (The Message)

4. Proverbs 15:29—The LORD is far from the wicked but he hears the prayer of the righteous.
Psalm 66:19—But God has surely listened and heard my voice in prayer. (NIV)

5. Malachi 3:16—Then those who feared the Lord talked often one to another; and the Lord listened and heard it, and a book of remembrance was written before Him of those who reverenced and worshipfully feared the Lord and who thought on His name.

6. Deuteronomy 11:16—Take heed to yourselves, lest your minds and hearts be deceived and you turn aside...
Obadiah 1:3—The pride of thine heart hath deceived thee...

7. Psalm 90:8—Our iniquities, our secret heart and its sins which we would so like to conceal even from ourselves, You have set in the revealing light of Your countenance.

Psalm 81:12—So I gave them up to their own hearts' lust and let them go after their own stubborn will, that they might follow their own counsels.

8. Proverbs 14:33—Wisdom rests silently in the mind and heart of him who has understanding, but that which is in the inward part of self-confident fools is made known.

Proverbs 11:20—They who are willfully contrary in heart are extremely disgusting and shamefully vile in the eyes of the Lord, but such as are blameless and wholehearted in their ways are His delight!

9. Isaiah 57:1—The righteous man perishes, and no one lays it to heart; and merciful and devout men are taken away, with no one considering that the uncompromisingly upright and godly person is taken away from the calamity and evil to come [even through wickedness].

10. Proverbs 16:2—All the ways of a man are pure in his own eyes, but the Lord weighs the spirits (the thoughts and intents of the heart).

Chapter Twenty-Five

1. Psalm 121:3—He will not let your foot slip— he who watches over you will not slumber; Psalm 66:7—He rules by His might forever. His eyes observe and keep watch over the nations...; Proverbs 15:3—The eyes of the Lord are in every place, keeping watch upon the evil and the good.

Jeremiah 1:12—Then said the Lord to me, You have seen well, for I am alert and active, watching over My word to perform it.

2. Luke 8:11—...The seed is the Word of God.

3. Deuteronomy 30:14—But the word is very near you, in your mout' and in your mind and in your heart, so that you can do it.

4. Matthew 13:23—The one who received the seed that fell on goo soil is the man who hears the word and understands it. He produc a crop, yielding a hundred, sixty or thirty times what was sown (NIV)

Luke 8:15—But as for that seed in the good soil, these are the peopi who, hearing the Word, hold it fast in a just (noble, virtuous) anc worthy heart, and steadily bring forth fruit with patience.

5. Isaiah 55:11—So shall My word be that goes forth out of My mouth: it shall not return to Me void [without producing any effect, useless], but it shall accomplish that which I please and purpose, and it shall prosper in the thing for which I sent it.
6. Psalm 34:17—When the righteous cry for help, the Lord hears, and delivers them out of all their distress and troubles.
7. Psalm 119:11—Your Word have I laid up in my heart that I might not sin against You.
8. James 1:6, 7—Only it must be in faith that he asks with no wavering (no hesitating, no doubting). For the one who wavers (hesitates, doubts) is like the billowing surge out at sea that is blown hither and thither and tossed by the wind. For truly, let not such a person imagine that he will receive anything [he asks for] from the Lord.
9. Psalm 51:6—Behold, You desire truth in the inner being; make me therefore to know wisdom in my inmost heart.
10. Proverbs 20: 22—Do not say, I will repay evil; wait expectantly for the Lord, and He will rescue you.
Proverbs 24:17, 18—Rejoice not when your enemy falls, and let not your heart be glad when he stumbles or is overthrown, lest the Lord see it and it be evil in His eyes and displease Him, and He turn away His wrath from him to expend it upon you, the worse offender.

Chapter Twenty-Six

1. Zephaniah 1:17a—And I will bring distress upon men, so that they shall walk like blind men, because they have sinned against the Lord.
2. Revelation 21:27—But nothing that defiles or profanes or is unwashed shall ever enter it, nor anyone who commits abominations (unclean, detestable, morally repugnant things) or practices falsehood, but only those whose names are recorded in the Lamb's Book of Life.
3. Matthew 6:33—But seek (aim at and strive after) first of all His kingdom and His righteousness (*His way of doing and being right*), and then all these things taken together will be given you besides.
4. Romans 12:2—Do not conform any longer to the pattern of this world, but be transformed by the renewing of your mind. Then

you will be able to test and approve what God's will is—his good, pleasing and perfect will.

5. 1 Thessalonians 4:7—For God did not call us to be impure, but to live a holy life.

6. 2 Thessalonians 2:13—...because from the beginning God chose you to be saved through the sanctifying work of the Spirit and through belief in the truth.

7. Jentezen Franklin.

8. Revelation 2:4, 5—But I have this one charge to make against you: that you have left (abandoned) the love that you had at first [you have deserted Me, your first love]. Remember then from what heights you have fallen. Repent (change the inner man to meet God's will) and do the works you did previously [when first you knew the Lord], or else I will visit you and remove your lampstand from its place, unless you change your mind and repent.

9. 2 Chronicles 32:31b—...God left him to himself to try him that He might know all that was in his heart.

Chapter Twenty-Seven

1. 2 Corinthians 3:18—But we all, with open face beholding as in a glass the glory of the Lord, are changed into the same image from glory to glory, even as by the Spirit of the Lord.

2. Revelation 16:15—Behold, I am going to come like a thief! Blessed (happy, to be envied) is he who stays awake (alert) and who guards his clothes, so that he may not be naked and [have the shame of being] seen exposed!

3. John 10:26-30—Jesus answered, "I told you, but you don't believe. Everything I have done has been authorized by my Father, actions that speak louder than words. You don't believe because you're not my sheep. My sheep recognize my voice. I know them, and they follow me. I give them real and eternal life. They are protected from the Destroyer for good. *No one can steal them from out of my hand.* The Father who put them under my care is so much greater than the Destroyer and Thief. No one could ever get them away from him. (The Message)

Hebrews 12:25: So see to it that you do not reject Him or refuse to listen to and heed Him Who is speaking [to you now]. For if the Israelites did not escape when they refused to listen and heed Him Who warned and divinely instructed them, *how much less shall we escape if we reject and turn our backs on Him Who cautions and admonishes [us] from heaven?*

4. 2 Peter 2:21—For never to have obtained a [full, personal] knowledge of the way of righteousness would have been better for them than, having obtained [such knowledge], to turn back from the holy commandment which was [verbally] delivered to them.

5. Luke 15:7—I tell you that in the same way there will be more rejoicing in heaven over one sinner who repents than over ninety-nine righteous persons who do not need to repent. (NIV)

6. Revelation 3:5—He that overcometh, the same shall be clothed in white raiment; and I will not *blot out his name out of the book of life*, but I will confess his name before my Father, and before his angels.
   Revelation 3:5—He who overcomes will, like them, be dressed in white. I will never *blot out his name from the book of life*, but will acknowledge his name before my Father and his angels.

7. Ecclesiastes 8:11—Because the sentence against an evil work *is not executed speedily*, the hearts of the sons of men are fully set to do evil.
   Psalm 50:19-21—You give your mouth to evil, and your tongue frames deceit. You sit and speak against your brother; you slander your own mother's son. These things you have done and I kept silent; you thought I was once entirely like you. But now I will reprove you and put [the charge] in order before your eyes.

8. Hebrews 13:5—Let your character or moral disposition be free from love of money [including greed, avarice, lust, and craving for earthly possessions] and be satisfied with your present circumstances and with what you have; for God Himself has said, *I will not in any way fail you nor give you up nor leave you without support. I will not, I will not, I will not in any degree leave you helpless nor forsake nor let you down (relax My hold on you)! Assuredly not!*

CPSIA information can be obtained at www.ICGtesting.com
Printed in the USA
LVOW091450181111

255559LV00002B/5/P